WINTERSTEEL

CRADLE : VOLUME EIGHT

WILL WIGHT

HIDDEN GNOME PUBLISHING

HIDDEN
GNOME
PUBLISHING

PROLOGUE

INFORMATION REQUESTED: DEATH OF THE SAGE OF THE ENDLESS SWORD.

[INFORMATION FOUND. SYNCHRONIZATION POSSIBLE. SYNCHRONIZE?]

[SYNCHRONIZATION SET AT 80%.]

BEGINNING REPORT...

Timaias Adama had been a guest of the Heaven's Glory School for almost three months.

They were a collection of backwards savages who had forgotten nearly everything about the sacred arts. It was astonishing, really, how ignorant they were.

But they let him inside the labyrinth.

He marched over scripted tiled floors, past endless rows of polished wooden cabinets. This had once been a storage hall for the belongings of lesser researchers and staff, but every one of the cabinets was empty.

Not because the people of Sacred Valley had looted the place; one step into this place would strike a Jade dead sure as the sun rose in the east. The sacred instruments that had filled this hall had been destroyed by time and by this valley's "curse."

The curse that had drawn him here in the first place.

He breathed heavily as he walked. Not only was his madra down to a bare silver trickle inside him, but even his soul-fire-infused flesh had been drained of power. His pool of soulfire had run entirely dry, and his willpower was so weak that he could exert almost none of his authority as a Sage.

He hadn't been out of breath in years.

His chest heaved and sweat rolled down his face, but he savored the novel sensation. It was a reminder of what his life had been like when he was pushing for Sage. What Yerin felt like now.

He longed for that feeling again, sometimes. The thrill of running from wolves and knowing that if he flagged for a second, they'd tear him to pieces.

For decades, wolves had run from him.

His spirit was so exhausted that he didn't sense danger until the hostile techniques were almost on him.

He turned to fight, his wintersteel blade already bare and ringing like a bell.

Two skeletal spirits of gray-white hunger madra pulled themselves up out of the floor. They gaped at him with unnaturally wide jaws and eye sockets lit by dull fire.

They weren't true spirits, but techniques launched by this prison's lone inhabitant.

Sword aura slashed at the two ghouls, weak as a kitten's claws. The madra forming their bodies shook like he'd waved a stick through fog, but they didn't dissolve.

The Sword Sage's eye twitched.

Ruler techniques weren't ideal against spiritual opponents, but suitability mattered very little in the face of over-whelming power. He should have been able to disperse these two with the twitch of his big toe.

He was glad Yerin wasn't around to see this. She'd lose all faith in him as a master.

The hunger techniques had clawed their way completely

to the surface now. They were gaunt, transparent figures of gray-white madra with spindly feet and bony arms that dangled down all the way to the tiles. Their jaws hung down to their ribs, and they gave off such an impression of inexhaustible, ravaging *need* that it made Adama hungry.

He'd faced a lot of that while exploring this labyrinth.

The techniques moved quickly...by the standards of Sacred Valley. A Heaven's Glory elder who somehow made it into the labyrinth would have been struck down before he sensed danger.

Adama slashed his sword and returned it to its sheath in one smooth motion. A Rippling Sword technique flashed out, the silver crescent slicing through both skeletons.

The madra tore the spiritual entities in half where the aura had failed, and they collapsed into rising motes of essence in an instant. His Rippling Sword was pathetically weak after his time in the labyrinth, perhaps weaker even than Yerin's.

He extended his spiritual perception, though doing so in here was like pushing through thick mud.

More techniques were on the way.

He picked up his step, jogging down the hall. How long had it been since he felt the physical toll of simply *running?*

Sages should vacation here. It might remind them what it was like to be mortal.

By the time he reached the doorway, a dozen of the ghoulish techniques rushed down the hallway after him. For no reason in particular, he turned to give them a wave. "Half a shade too slow," he told them.

He didn't know if Subject One was watching, but if it was, it deserved a little taunting for putting him through this.

With an effort of will, he opened the door.

Or he tried to.

The huge stone panel, carved with the images of the four Dreadgods, failed to move. He hadn't focused enough, his thoughts not coming together, so he couldn't invoke his authority.

Sweat ran faster down his face, and he pushed on the door

with both hands, sharpening his mind to a point.

This would be *far* too embarrassing a place to die.

"Open," the Sage of the Endless Sword commanded, and the door obeyed.

It swung open on soundless hinges, leaving him leaning on nothing and stumbling out. With trembling arms, he slammed the heavy door shut behind him.

Some fingers of hunger madra had come so close that they were crushed by the scripted door.

Adama heaved a breath, slumping back against the carving. All thoughts of vacationing in Sacred Valley vanished. This had been too close of a cut. Bleed and bury the people who made this maze.

Now he was more exhausted than it was normally possible for him to be, and he still had to deal with a bunch of Jades.

The two Heaven's Glory Jades peeked in at him from the entrance of the mausoleum-like structure they called the Ancestor's Tomb. When they saw the door was shut, they scurried inside to attend to him.

He had warned them early on not to be close to him when he opened the door, lest they be struck dead by the hunger madra within. They couldn't open the door themselves, so they had only his word to go on, but they'd trusted him. So far.

He almost looked forward to the day when they tested him, because he'd told them the absolute truth.

From the inside pocket of his outer robe, he pulled his badge. The locals grew uncomfortable when they saw him without one.

The badge hung on a shadesilk ribbon, like most of those worn in Sacred Valley. His badge was plated in white metal the exact color of his blade, though its border and the sword symbol in the center remained bronze.

Wintersteel was too expensive to make into an entire badge, but it was also the symbol of a true Sage.

As long as the people of Sacred Valley respected these ancient traditions, so would he.

The two elders, one a gray-haired woman wearing a Jade scepter badge and another a man with a hammer badge and a mutilated arm, saluted with fists pressed together as they reached him.

"I regret that your expedition was no more productive this time, honored Sage," Elder Anses said.

Adama had a hard time keeping his contempt hidden from these inept children. They had no idea what a Sage was, only a few vague stories passed down about the title. They thought he was a Gold, and they worshiped him for it.

He stopped leaning against the door and straightened his back, controlling his breathing. He still had command over his body, and he wasn't willing to show any lapse of control to Heaven's Glory.

"Empty hands for me, I'm afraid," the Sword Sage said.

There were other labyrinth entrances in the Valley, and some of them were safe for Jades. At least in the outer rooms.

Therefore, everyone who lived here knew that valuable treasures could be found inside. He had been forced to promise a share of anything he recovered to Heaven's Glory in exchange for access.

So, of course, he hid everything he found in the labyrinth inside his private void space.

Anses and the other elder eyed him as though they suspected him of tucking constructs into his robes, but they respected his power even now.

He had shown them only the smallest glimpse of his abilities, and that had been enough for them to treat him like a warrior descended from the heavens.

His pity for them matched his contempt. If not for that, and for the fact that he was too lazy to wash his own clothes and prepare his own meals, he would have punished them long ago for trying to poison him.

Right on cue, the woman produced a stoppered clay bottle from her robes. "Apologies, honored guest, but we have used our lacking skills to prepare a recovery elixir for you. Please taste it yourself and share some small measure of your wisdom with us."

Wordlessly, Adama took the bottle from her. He didn't remember her name. Frankly, he had made it a point to forget the names of every Heaven's Glory elder. Anses had only stuck in his mind because of the man's mangled arm.

Oh, and he remembered Whitehall, the old man trapped in a boy's body. That was a bizarre case Adama wouldn't have minded researching further, had he not been in Sacred Valley for a more important purpose.

Moving his gaze from one elder's eyes to the other's, he gulped the "medicine" down. He never looked away from them as he finished, tossed the bottle back, and wiped his mouth with the back of his hand.

"Like a cool drink of spring water," he said. "My thanks."

Elder Anses shifted in place and his partner struggled not to move her gaze, but they both thanked him and asked for pointers in refining a new version of the elixir. He told them to add mint.

The elixir was poisoned.

They had been slipping him poison almost since his first day here. Sleeping drafts mostly, but there had been some meant to inhibit his spirit, some to paralyze him, some to meddle with his memories, a handful of others.

They were always mixed cleverly, he had to admit. Almost undetectable to the tongue or to the spiritual sense, when combined with his medicine or his meals.

Every time, they watched his reaction. At first, they could have blamed a mistake. *"Oh no, we added too much Nimblethorn."* But when he never said a word, they grew bolder.

They knew he had treasures, and the longer he stayed with them, the better they understood that he wasn't going to share. If he brought up nothing from the labyrinth, they knew his sword was valuable, and they knew he was carrying herbs and seeds and elixirs they had never seen before.

They wanted to rob him, but the joke was on them.

Nothing they brewed here could seriously affect a body thrice reborn in soulfire. If the heavens shone on them and one of their concoctions worked, he carried no void key. As a Sage skilled in spatial manipulation, he stored everything but his sword in a pocket accessible only by his authority.

If they put him to sleep and rifled through his robes, they might take his sword, but they could never bring out its power. And realistically, they couldn't do him any harm no matter how weakened he was.

There was only one being inside a thousand miles capable of being his opponent, and that was a Dreadgod.

The two Jades flattered him for a while as they led him through the snow that surrounded the Ancestor's Tomb and back to the Heaven's Glory School. It was late at night, so the bright ring of light madra condensed around their mountain shone like a pale sun, and their rainstone buildings gleamed as though wet.

Once again, his pity grew to balance his irritation about the poison. They thought this pathetic collection of stone huts was a school of the sacred arts.

How would they react if he showed them his memory of the Frozen Blade School?

People like this didn't deserve his contempt. He reminded himself of that for the ten thousandth time. They were just... ignorant. Isolated. When he and Yerin left, the natives would live out their short lives in relative contentment.

Their condition wasn't their fault, but it was hard to remain charitable when they kept trying to rob him.

The house that Heaven's Glory had given him was close to the Ancestor's Tomb, and at least they hadn't skimped on space. It was a wide three-storied construction of rainstone with its own network of constructs to regulate light and water. The basement had been reinforced into a decent training room, though of course it was only appropriate for Yerin.

The elders walked him up to the doorstep, and the woman cleared her throat.

"It was an honor to serve you today, Sage of Swords."

That wasn't exactly his title, but Adama had never cared much for titles anyway.

"If we could learn from you tomorrow morning, it would

be our good fortune."

He choked down a groan. Every time he came out of the labyrinth, it took him longer to recover. All he wanted to do tomorrow was sleep.

But he had to show strength.

He gave them a single nod. "Not a hair after dawn," he said. "Don't be late."

Only a few hours away. That should be enough to make them think he didn't care about his rest. He could always catch up on his sleep afterwards.

Anses looked relieved, bowing to him again. "Thank you, honored Sage."

Adama gestured them away and opened his front door.

Before he stepped inside, he waved two fingers down the entry.

Yerin's Forger technique, the invisible blade that she'd left hanging in the doorframe, crumbled like half-melted ice at his touch.

The Hidden Sword wasn't a major part of his Path, but it was invaluable for practicing Forging and sword resonance. She had been slacking on her Forger training.

Although it was rare as stars at midday for her to slack on anything. She just didn't see the point of the Forger technique, which he understood. He could let it go for the moment.

When he walked inside and down to the basement, he found Yerin sparring against the training dummy he'd left for her.

She glared out from under her straight-cut hair, holding her sword in both hands. She waited with utter stillness, letting the puppet make the first move.

Her opponent was made entirely of dead matter, looking like a stitched-together Remnant of silver, gray, black, and rusty red. Adama didn't consider himself much of a Soulsmith, so it had been a headache to assemble the puppet from the meager Remnants of sword, earth, or force madra he could find in the Valley.

The scripts etched into its body of solidified madra kept the dummy from moving except when activated, and then only in the few patterns he had allowed. Though his limbs felt like dishrags wrung dry, Adama folded his arms and watched.

A few breaths later, the puppet moved.

It drew a training sword at its side and struck at Yerin, who deflected it with a blade that shone with the Flowing Sword technique. They traded a few moves, both emanating the spiritual pressure of Jades.

He had no complaints with her movements. She had clearly mastered these basic forms, and her madra control had improved in leaps and bounds. It wasn't so long ago that her techniques destabilized the second her mental state did, but her Flowing Sword was steady as the moon.

He did detect some impatience, though. One strike was a little too firm, another step a shade too eager. She didn't like being cooped up in the basement.

Since they'd come to Heaven's Glory, he had allowed her to interact with the Valley natives only at his side, and only while veiled as an Iron. He was thinking of relaxing that restriction soon.

For one thing, the spiritual perception of the Jades here was pathetic. He could barely call them Jades at all. They would never be able to see through her veil, so she could hide easily.

More importantly, while he had initially expected the elders to try to get to him through Yerin, none had. Not one had attempted anything.

They knew his apprentice was here in the house, and that he took her out sometimes to fight Remnants or train against Irons, but they had shown no interest in her. They hadn't asked her so much as her name. It was bizarre.

Over these last weeks, he had come to figure out that it came down to the strange, twisted view they had of honor. None of them wanted the Sword Sage to think they were interested in a lowly apprentice for any reason, because that would...lower their standards in his eyes, for some reason?

He didn't understand it, but he wasn't here for cultural research. If the Jades thought Yerin was beneath them, so much the better. No one would discover their reason for being here and Yerin would be that much safer.

Not that any of these half-baked Jades could touch Yerin's shadow. Every cut on her skin and the edges of her robe was from her own Endless Sword; the only threats to Yerin in Sacred Valley were contained in her own body.

At the thought, he focused his perception on her uninvited guest.

The Blood Shadow was bound into a rope and tied around her waist like a belt, making a wide bow behind her. Ordinarily it should be stirring, restless, trying to tempt her into relying on its power or waiting for a gap in her control to feed on blood essence.

He felt almost nothing from it now. It was sleeping to conserve power, held down by the same curse as the rest of the Valley. As long as she stayed here, she wouldn't be bothered by the parasite sleeping in her soul.

For that reason, this was the safest place in the world for Yerin.

The puppet-construct's motions jumbled for a second as the wills of its various Remnant parts clashed, and Yerin took advantage.

Two motions, and she separated its head from its neck and one arm from its shoulder.

Silver sparks sprayed into the air like blood, and the nested scripts at the center of the puppet registered the damage as a defeat. The construct powered down, curling in on itself like a dying spider, preserving energy so that the Sword Sage wouldn't have to spend so much effort rebuilding it later.

Yerin shone like a lamp uncovered. She turned to him, beaming but trying to hide it.

"Cleanest win so far," she said, staying casual. "Smoother than butter." She dispersed the Flowing Sword and slid her weapon back into its sheath.

Adama gave her some lazy applause. "Cheers and celebration for you." He *was* proud of how far she'd come, but flowery praise wasn't his way.

Still, Yerin drew herself up like he'd handed her a crown. She thumbed a line of blood running down her cheek. "Seems to me like I can walk around by myself now."

He started to brush her off as he had before, but he cut himself off and turned the idea over in his mind. What would the right lesson be?

She didn't know anything about Sacred Valley's nature, or its history, or the years of research he'd done to find his way here.

She certainly didn't know why they'd really come.

The "curse" of Sacred Valley wasn't any kind of curse at all. It was perhaps the largest and most elaborate script formation ever created by mankind, spanning hundreds of miles and buried deep within the earth.

That formation generated a suppression field that weakened everything that crossed its boundaries. At first, he had believed it was a security measure to keep Monarchs out.

Now, he was growing certain that it was primarily intended to keep the labyrinth's lone inhabitant starving.

The father of the Dreadgods.

Subject One.

He was here to find a cure for Yerin...but not just a cure. He wanted a way to separate the Blood Shadow from her with no spiritual damage at all.

That was a degree of magnitude more difficult than just removing it, but he couldn't risk any damage to his apprentice.

This was the birthplace of the Bleeding Phoenix, and he had filled his void space with enough ancient research notes and experimental materials that he was sure he was closing in on an answer.

He was becoming certain that he could do it. There was a way to pull the Blood Shadow out of her without taking a chunk of her soul with it. He only needed a few more weeks. With the suppression field working on her parasite, they had plenty of time.

However, he couldn't keep her sealed in a jar. If he stifled her growth, that would defeat the entire point of this project.

"You've got me," he said at last. "Your chains are off."

She gave him a fierce grin. "You going to burn my ear if I draw swords on some Jade?"

"All right, then, not *all* your chains."

Her face fell.

"Keep your Iron veil on tight and your perception to yourself. Don't tell them anything but your name. And don't eat anything they give you."

Instantly she turned suspicious. "Master, did they try to poison you?"

"Did more than try," he said, patting his stomach.

Yerin's knuckles whitened on the hilt of her sword.

"Whoa there, rein it in. Do I look shaky to you?"

She looked him up and down and her grip tightened. Her eyebrows drew together, and his spirit shivered slightly as she moved her perception through him.

"You look like you've been dragged over ten miles of rocky road," she replied.

He waved his hand through the air. "Bad question. That's my own training, not them."

She still didn't look convinced, so he sighed and reached into his outer robe.

He withdrew a gold badge that he'd commissioned. Like his own, this one was carved with the emblem of a sword.

The tradition of wearing badges was old, its meaning shifting with time and culture. This may have been the only place in the world that still respected it, though they had the significance all wrong.

Yerin gave a half-step forward as she saw the badge, as though ready to take it, but he pulled it back.

"Keep your eyes on your Path," he said gently. "You're almost there."

They'd have to leave Sacred Valley to find a sword Remnant worthy of her. He could push her to Lowgold with his own scales, but that missed the valuable opportunity to learn from the experiences of another sword artist.

Not to mention that separating her from the Blood Shadow would only become harder and harder as she advanced. As long as she stayed Jade, he was confident he could find the answer.

"Only a few more weeks," he promised, and she relaxed.

"I'll hang on," she muttered.

"Good work." He ruffled her hair, which she tolerated. Then he gave an exaggerated yawn.

Halfway through, he realized it wasn't so exaggerated after all. He was more exhausted than he'd thought.

"Gonna go cultivate dream aura until dawn. You should rest up too."

She gave him an absent nod, but she was looking over the training puppet as though hoping it would come back to life on its own.

He'd repair it in the morning. For the time, he left her with nothing to do but sleep, which was often the only way he could get her to rest.

Adama himself didn't need the encouragement tonight. He felt the effort of climbing the stairs.

When he found the bed, he didn't bother taking off his robes. He collapsed in a heap.

He would rest, eat, and examine the research he'd taken from the labyrinth for a few days, until he was recovered enough to be called a Sage again. Then it was back underground for him.

Sleep found him in seconds.

It felt like only seconds more when he was woken by searing pain all over his body.

He screamed and shot up, lashing out blindly with his power. Despite the suppression of Sacred Valley, his madra should have shredded everything in the room. Without the Valley's curse, a single panicked outburst like this one might have endangered the entire Heaven's Glory School.

With his spirit and will so drained by the hunger madra,

his attackers survived.

Half a dozen Jades staggered back, blood on their daggers. The locals had attacked him. A bunch of Jades had *stabbed* him. *Successfully.*

How?

The light of Samara's ring leaked in from the shuttered windows, and between that and his well-honed spiritual sense, he put together a clear picture of the scene. Their blades glittered with points of brighter silver like stars, and they felt like shards of chaos.

Halfsilver blades.

Those would disrupt anyone's madra, which explained the searing pain in his body and spirit, and halfsilver *was* unusually common here. Normally, they wouldn't have penetrated his skin. He hadn't considered the full implications of the strength being leeched from his Archlord body; it had been too long since any mundane attack was a threat.

But...they had *stabbed* him.

Though he was bleeding and surrounded by enemies, he still wondered if this could possibly be real. It was like a bunch of rabbits had taken up spears in their teeth and charged him.

It was humiliating.

The blades had been dipped in poison, which stained their edges dark and leaked venom aura into the air, but such was barely worth a thought. He would never notice the weak poisons here.

And halfsilver knives still gathered sword aura.

The Sword Sage threw out a hand, and though he didn't have a blade in his hands, he activated the Endless Sword.

Every edged weapon in the room exploded with silver light.

The Jade holding onto his wintersteel sword—the weapon Min Shuei had gifted him before their parting—fell to bloody chunks immediately and landed in a pile of gore.

Adama caught the sheathed blade before it hit the ground.

Everyone else survived.

Which was enough to tell him how bad of a shape he was in, even if he discounted the pain in his neck, chest, shoulder, thighs, and stomach. His madra channels were now wounded from putting such effort into the Endless Sword with halfsilver still affecting his spirit, and most of the Jades still lived.

When he survived this, he was going to come down on the Heaven's Glory School like a Monarch's fist.

He drew his sword like a child drawing his father's weapon for the first time. Clumsily, he lurched forward, shoving his sword into a shield of Forged golden madra.

The shield shattered and the Heaven's Glory man flew backwards, leaving a crater in the wood and plaster of the wall.

Though he was weaker than he'd ever thought possible, Adama's Steelborn Iron body still functioned. If he had enough strength to wave a hand, he had enough to hurl a Jade from the room.

But the wounded Jade still breathed. Though he had no doubt suffered terrible internal injuries, his survival was another blow to Adama's pride.

Blood gummed up his eyes, and he focused on healing his body as he engaged the other five in combat.

They couldn't use Striker techniques without hitting each other, and their Ruler and Forger techniques were so clumsy that he could always disrupt them before they fully formed. Which left them hand-to-hand combat.

Every pathetic swipe of his sword took a Jade off their feet.

One Heaven's Glory elder crashed into the ceiling. Another shattered the bed. A third flew through the shuttered window, letting in a wash of light. But they were all armored by iron, goldsteel plates, or scripted devices that kept them alive.

The Sword Sage couldn't clear his thoughts enough for a single working of will. His body and spirit were falling apart, and only his extraordinary Archlord constitution kept him on his feet.

Reinforcements flooded in from downstairs. Irons. They were flinging *Irons* at him.

When he was through killing everyone in the building, he was going to be disgusted with himself.

A new voice shouted from downstairs, a flare of Endless Sword madra sent the Irons on the stairs bowling over, and for the first time since waking he felt real fear.

Yerin was here.

Two of the Jades turned to look down, beginning their techniques, and Adama's fear turned to rage. He took an Enforced hit to the back—his opponents had abandoned their blades almost immediately, so it was just a punch—to dash at those Jades threatening Yerin.

He tackled them down the stairs.

The Jades might be trying to kill him, but they would inevitably fail. He was an Archlord. Yerin was still on their level.

He would pit her against any of them one-on-one, but this was hardly a duel.

As he landed in a pile of bodies on the first floor, he looked up and met Yerin's eyes. In them, he saw the same fear for him that he felt for her. They were wide, her face pale.

He had to drag this fight away.

He shouted and pulled himself to his feet, squeezing madra out of lacerated channels...and swiped a Rippling Sword at Yerin.

She blocked, of course. The technique was weaker than what she would have produced.

But it knocked her back into the basement.

Adama limped out of the house, casting his perception behind him to make sure the remaining elders would follow him. Sure enough, only the Irons stayed behind.

Though there were more Jades coming from all around him.

His every hobbling one-legged leap covered many yards and left a trail of blood in the snow behind him. The only Jades that kept up with him were those who wore shields on their badges: those best trained in their Enforcer technique.

Adama defended himself with his swordplay and his superior Iron body, as well as the fact that his enemies couldn't use proper weapons. They had all armed themselves with makeshift clubs.

He took a few bruises, but nothing to worry about. Nothing he couldn't heal in the morning.

He had to make it to the Ancestor's Tomb.

When he tried to open his void space, just the effort of focusing made his head throb, and he couldn't focus his working enough to reach through the Way. His other weapons, his elixirs, his constructs, his pills, were all sealed off to him.

He had grown too complacent. The lesson here was to never show vulnerability, to never rely on others, to treat all strangers as enemies. Clearly, he had let himself grow soft.

In the future, after he razed Heaven's Glory, he wouldn't forget.

He just had to make sure Yerin survived to remember this lesson too.

He staggered up the mountain, fending off attacks until the light of the dawning sun spilled over the Ancestor's Tomb. The Tomb was one of the most ancient structures in Sacred Valley, a blocky behemoth looming on titanic pillars.

Once he made it inside, he could open the door to the labyrinth.

The hunger madra would spill out, devouring everyone present. The Jades wouldn't be able to handle the power, and he had to hope he could survive Subject One's weakened techniques.

When the crowd was thinned out, he would shut the door again and wait until he had recovered his willpower, then he would retrieve an elixir to heal the rest of him.

In the morning, the rest of Heaven's Glory would find out what made him a Sage.

When he reached the stairs, he cast his perception behind him again to see who had managed to follow him.

Not just the Enforcers this time.

Yerin had caught up.

She emerged from the trees screaming, her tattered robes

rippling in the wind, and she sent a thousand invisible blades slashing at the nearest elder with her Endless Sword.

She would have been better off using a Striker technique, as the man wasn't carrying a weapon. He took a few superficial cuts, but he seemed surprised that she'd wounded him at all. The Jade turned, readying a technique of his own.

Adama was surrounded by a half-circle of other Jades, all of them either beating him with their clubs or readying their own techniques, but all his attention was focused on Yerin.

When he fought his way through and went up the stairs, she'd follow him.

"Go!" he screamed, but of course she didn't listen.

Her expression firmed, and she took a two-handed grip on her sword.

It was the resolve, the determination, the focus that had made her stand out to him as a disciple candidate in the first place.

That was a will worthy of the future Sage of the Endless Sword.

He scraped together everything he had left. Every ounce of thought, emotion, and madra drew together to a point.

"Go," he said again, and this time it was a command written on the world itself.

Behind Yerin, space tore like a cut. Spatial cracks slid out from around the rift, but they would soon heal. The destination of this transportation was beyond his control. It would be close; he didn't have the skill or power at the moment to send her far.

Nor to send her quickly, it seemed. The portal sliced open in slow motion, and she was pulled back as though by invisible hands.

It should have happened in an instant, but she had time to fight, struggling toward him. The Jades near Yerin backed away from her, unsure what was happening, but the ones around him redoubled their assault.

Adama took a club on the jaw and another on the back of his head. A line of madra seared into his back, and his sight started to fade.

With Jades and Irons piled on top of him, he turned from Yerin and took a step up the stairs of the Ancestor's Tomb.

More attacks landed, and he took another step.

Another.

His entire being fixed on the door, and his existence narrowed down to a singular purpose. He was going to that door, and these people would not stop Yerin from advancing. She would succeed him.

Those were the two most prominent thoughts his Remnant inherited when it rose from his body.

The door.

And Yerin.

[SYNCHRONIZATION TERMINATED.]

SUGGESTED TOPIC: YERIN AND THE SWORD ICON.

DENIED, REPORT COMPLETE.

第一章

CHAPTER ONE

"Who's Dross?"

Northstrider clutched Lindon's throat in one black-scaled hand, but his grip relaxed slightly to allow Lindon to respond. Lindon's spirit trembled under the weight of a spiritual scan, and he shook before the Monarch's golden eyes.

Lindon's entire body urged him to cooperate with Northstrider, but he was still afraid. If Dross was peeled forcibly away from his soul, what would happen?

He needed more information. He needed time.

"Apologies, Monarch," Lindon choked out. "I don't understand—"

Northstrider's patience ended immediately.

Invisible weight forced Lindon to his knees. The Monarch's hand left his neck, but Lindon still choked. It felt like the air squeezed every inch of his skin. He tried to cycle madra, but his spirit was just as restricted as his body.

"Manifest yourself," Northstrider commanded.

Don't do it, Lindon urged Dross. *I'll talk to him.*

As soon as he had enough breath to speak.

Dross didn't respond. Instead, he spun into existence over Lindon's left shoulder.

The spiritual pressure released Lindon, who sagged to the

ground but caught himself with one hand and a knee.

Dross manifested as a purple-skinned ball with a single eye and two stubby, boneless arms. His eye was wide, and he coughed once as he addressed Northstrider. [It is an honor to meet you, Master. I am called Dross.]

"You are the mind-spirit born from Ghostwater in its last days," Northstrider said.

Lindon pushed back to his feet; he needed to remind the Monarch he was there. "He is, and I am in your debt for the benefits I gained inside."

Dross bobbed up and down in agreement, but Northstrider did not spare a glance for Lindon.

[Ah yes, Master, you've met Lindon, haven't you? Sorry, I know you have, I'm just nervous. Anyway, Lindon has taken *very* good care of me after I became complete, and I'd say he has earned a reward. Maybe some kind of mind elixir, or a source of powerful dream aura, or perhaps a few delicious Dreamseeds. What do you say?]

A shiny black orb appeared over Northstrider's shoulder, mirroring Dross on Lindon's.

"Do you recognize this?" Northstrider asked Dross.

Dross squinted his eye. [*That* is the temperature construct from the Ghostwater storage room. I'm one hundred percent confident. Unless, of course, I'm wrong.]

Script flashed in various colors all over the reflective surface of Northstrider's orb, so quickly that it was meaningless to Lindon.

"Look beyond its appearance," the Monarch instructed.

Lindon couldn't decide if Northstrider seemed patient or impatient. He observed Dross' performance with no expression, but Lindon could imagine him erupting into violence at any second. Or simply disappearing.

Dross drifted closer to the black orb, peering into its surface.

[Hmmm, let me see...yes, that's...oh. *Oh.* It's the oracle tree! It's so small now.]

Lindon remembered the oracle tree. He had pulled Dross from inside it in Ghostwater. It had been a web of knowledge and memory constructs that had ultimately led to Dross' evolution.

Dross regularly regretted not being connected to that ocean of information longer.

Northstrider's eyes flashed with an emotion Lindon couldn't name. "This is the latest version of that project, which I call the oracle codex."

[You were right to change the name; it doesn't look anything like a tree anymore.]

"It is more than capable of teaching you the next step in your advancement." Northstrider spread one black-scaled hand, gesturing to the orb. "Read it for yourself, if you can."

That set off every alarm in Lindon's mind.

Northstrider was Lindon's benefactor, he was a great enemy of the gold dragons, and he was capable of upgrading Dross. Lindon would have traded his remaining arm for that kind of support.

But this was no act of charity. Northstrider was testing Dross in some way, and Lindon didn't know what passing looked like.

Or what the penalty for failure was.

Dross gasped as though he'd been offered a glorious present, but Lindon held him back with a thought.

"Gratitude, Monarch, but surely we are not worthy of such generosity."

[Yes, we are!] Dross said. In spite of Lindon's alarm, he pushed forward. One of his stubby, flexible arms touched the surface of the orb.

Light rippled on Northstrider's construct, but otherwise nothing happened.

[Just...just a moment, this is...hmmm. This is tougher than it looks.] Dross furrowed his purple brow and pushed harder, until Lindon could feel the strain himself.

More colors echoed out from the point of contact around Dross' arm, and light rippled faster and faster.

Until, as though he'd broken through a barrier, Dross finally pushed through.

The spirit took in a deep breath. [Ooohhh, it's amazing! So much space! And it's so organized in here, like a library run by clocks. *Here's* an interesting memory...not about me. And this one...also not me.]

Dross' arm was finally ejected, and he flew back to Lindon's shoulder as though kicked. [Sorry! So sorry! Just give me *one* more try.]

This time, there was the smallest hint of satisfaction on Northstrider's face. "No. You passed. You're coming with me."

Dross brightened. [Ha-HA! You see, I knew I had passed. I just wanted to pass *harder*. Did you hear that, Lindon? *He* appreciates me.]

Lindon's heart was beating faster, and he was beginning to sweat. He cycled his pure madra to calm himself down.

What was Northstrider about to do?

[Ew, you're all messy. Calm down. Would you tell him he has nothing to worry about, Master?]

Northstrider looked up to the ceiling as several spiritual perceptions locked onto him at once.

Lindon's spirit shook like water in an earthquake.

This was the attention of Monarchs; he was certain of it. More than one. They had found Northstrider, and now some kind of communication was passing between them.

The very air of the hallway warped, and Lindon's madra trembled as it was affected by a will not his own.

Then the sensation passed, and Northstrider scooped Dross up in his hand. "Come."

He turned to the side, waving a hand. There was a brief flash of blue and a hole tore open in the air.

On the other side, Lindon saw a massive, elaborate hall decorated with jewels and shining chandeliers. A room he recognized.

He had seen it in Suriel's vision, years before. This was the room where Sha Miara had been crowned.

Northstrider stepped into the portal...and Dross' presence in Lindon's mind immediately thinned.

It felt as though Dross was being pulled away, like

Northstrider was stretching and stretching the connection between them. Soon, it would reach its limit and break.

Lindon seized that thread, focusing his entire being on it.

Not only was he not sure what would happen to his spirit or his mind, but...this was *Dross.*

Dross noticed what was going on as soon as they crossed the portal, spinning in Northstrider's palm and turning back to Lindon.

[Hurry up, Lindon!]

Lindon dashed for the portal...but Northstrider glanced at him.

Invisible force pushed Lindon back, and the portal winked shut, cutting off Dross' horrified shout.

The connection between them thinned further, fraying more with every passing second. He wasn't going to be able to hold on. The thread melted in his grip.

When it broke, Dross would be gone.

Would he ever come back?

In the center of a hallway in the Ninecloud Court, Lindon set his feet. He clenched his jaw and cycled his spirit.

And he concentrated every ounce of his attention on the link between him and Dross.

Snatches of the spirit's thoughts came through in pieces.

[Master...]

[...why...]

[...gone?]

Only recently, Lindon had struggled against Naian Blackflame for control of a Ruler technique, which had strained his mind and spirit. This felt much the same: like he was trying to hold back an avalanche.

And it was all just to hang on. How long would he have to keep this up?

Dross' voice flickered in and out of his thoughts, an incomprehensible jumble.

Then the force pulling against him redoubled.

The connection almost snapped...but just as he was about to lose it, he *saw it.*

In his mind's eye, he could see the link between himself and Dross as a silver thread stretching into the distance. It was the same way he visualized his madra, and it felt equally real.

Now that he could see the connection, he focused on it even more intently.

He squeezed his eyes shut so the thread became all he could see. He leveraged all the power of his spirit, his madra surging.

Excess pure madra gushed out of him, filling the hallway. Lighting scripts brightened to unusual levels, constructs in the walls overloading or activating in a squeal of sounds.

His spirit strained. He might suffer permanent spiritual injury from this, or from having Dross torn away from him. In the worst-case scenario, this might be the end of his life as a sacred artist.

He might lose.

But it wouldn't be because he gave up.

Lindon's full power trembled. Just as he resolved to die before he let go, Dross' presence filled his mind again. The hair-thin connection between them flexed to a thick, braided cord.

His eyes snapped open to see that the portal had opened again. He now stood, panting and weak and red-faced, in front of Northstrider.

Lindon sagged in place, but thanks to his Underlord body, his knees didn't buckle. "Gratitude," he said to the Monarch. "Please allow me to accompany you."

Dross gave a glad cry and floated over to Lindon, merging once again with his spirit. [You see? I knew he'd change his mind and bring you along. I never...ah, never doubted for an instant.]

Dross' voice was shaky and unsure, and Lindon could feel his fear.

It was nothing next to Lindon's.

While trying to keep Dross, he had intentionally ignored the reality of his situation. He had just openly defied a Monarch.

He glanced up to Northstrider's eyes, terrified to see anger there.

Instead, he saw surprise. Perhaps consideration.

"Come, boy," Northstrider said, and Lindon gladly followed.

[I'm telling you, I didn't think he was going to open the portal again!] Dross babbled as Lindon walked through the gateway. [It didn't look like he would. He had his back to it and everything. But he changed his mind, you see, and I *told* you he wasn't an enemy. He's a generous and brilliant person, he's just a little...scary.]

The audience hall of the Ninecloud Court was just as Lindon remembered it, filled with brilliantly colored tiles and pillars scattered here and there around the room. A forest of jeweled chandeliers hung down from high, arched ceilings.

Each chandelier was a unique work of art, many spinning or flashing with living spirits, and other, equally colorful decorations hung on the walls.

But Lindon had very little time to consider the room when he realized the significance of where he was.

Every person in the room besides him was a Monarch.

He huddled behind Northstrider against one wall, but the other Monarchs of the Uncrowned King tournament were also in attendance.

Reigan Shen stood on an elaborate golden pedestal that held him high above the others, so that he looked down on the rest with hands crossed behind his back. Like Northstrider, he was a powerfully built man, and his fine hair and beard blended into a white-gold mane. The sacred lion paced on his platform, wearing a look of obvious discontent.

Lindon had only seen Emriss Silentborn in the form of a giant tree, but he recognized her immediately. Her skin was dark, like most of her competitors in the tournament, but hers had the consistency of bark. Her hair was made of luminous blue-green vines braided together, and she carried a staff with a blooming diamond flower at the tip.

She wore a look of great sadness, and Lindon couldn't tell if something had happened or if this was how she always appeared.

Three members of the Eight-Man Empire muttered to

one another, and Lindon reminded himself that he *technically* wasn't the only one who hadn't reached Monarch. The gold-armored figures were considered a Monarch collectively, but independently they were only Sages or Heralds.

Only.

The three spoke to one another, but they were focused on Northstrider and didn't look happy.

Seshethkunaaz, King of Dragons, was in the form of a boy perhaps thirteen years old. He had sandy hair and bright gold eyes, and he sat on the floor, most of his body covered in a filthy brown cape.

He glared at Akura Malice, who wasn't watching him in return. She lounged on a Forged throne of shadows, purple eyes locked on Lindon.

Mercy's mother was a beauty out of paintings and legends. Her hair flowed out behind her like liquid shadow, reminding him of her son Fury, and she wore a silken dress of purple and silver. A network of silver chains hung in her hair, dangling a fat amethyst over her forehead. Her eyes were a deeper, richer shade of purple than her descendants, and they rippled with subtle light.

Full, black-painted lips tilted up in a smirk, and she winked at him.

He wasn't sure if he was meant to be honored or entranced, but he broke into a cold sweat. Further attention from Monarchs brought indescribable risk.

Then again, he *had* just represented her in the Uncrowned King tournament. If he made a good impression, she might be inclined to reward him.

He bowed respectfully to her, pressing his fists together.

Her smile grew a fraction.

The room's final occupant was a presence of multicolored light. It was shaped vaguely like a woman, but the rainbow was too bright to make out any features.

The Luminous Queen of the Ninecloud Court. Supposedly Sha Leiala.

For a long moment after Lindon arrived, no one spoke,

which gave him plenty of time to survey the room. He wondered what they were waiting for and hoped that his abrupt entrance wasn't what had delayed them.

Finally, one of the Eight-Man Empire spoke up. "What have you done, Northstrider?" the man demanded.

"Did you promise the Abidan your service?" the Dragon King asked. He was still watching Malice, but he clearly addressed Northstrider. "Is that how you summoned them? Will they restore your champion to his full power?"

Emriss Silentborn gave a great sigh. "The arrowhead will bring only pain and discord, so close to the Wandering Titan's awakening. For the good of all, we should make a pact between us to use Penance to remove a Dreadgod."

"Why destroy such a valuable weapon?" Reigan said, watching Northstrider. "I am more interested in the fortuitous timing of heaven's intervention. It *so happens* that sixteen competitors remained, allowing Northstrider to select a single-elimination round. Then an Abidan messenger descends upon us when one, and only one, competitor has been eliminated. The very young man that Northstrider has chosen to bring along to this meeting."

Lindon shivered, but he felt no spiritual weight settle on him.

[Northstrider is shielding you from the spiritual power in the room, I'm sure,] Dross said. Lindon noticed that he didn't call the Monarch "Master" this time.

Reigan Shen ran a hand across his white-gold beard. "Now, I humbly admit that I do not understand the plan at work here, but to blame coincidence is to strain credulity. Did you calculate all this when you stepped in as judge, Northstrider? Have you deceived us all?"

Northstrider did not step back from anyone. His shaggy head turned slowly from one Monarch to the next until he had met the eyes of all his peers.

"Did I not receive your permission for the arrangement of the fourth round?" Northstrider asked. "*Each* of you agreed. *Each* of you bickered and jockeyed for position like children, and each of you gave your word that you were satisfied with the place you had earned."

"Our lives are at stake," a woman from the Eight-Man Empire shouted. "We would never have settled for a certain loss if we had known that victory would come with power over life and death."

Northstrider turned to her and spoke quietly. "*Your* lives? You think a weapon of the Abidan is cheap enough to waste on one replaceable piece out of eight?"

She bristled with anger, but Northstrider had looked away from her already. "Which of you is so weak-willed that you would doubt a decision you made yourself?"

"If everyone honors their given word, then I have no doubts," Seshethkunaaz said. "If the tournament proceeds with your rules in place, I will be the victor."

He looked over to the figure shrouded in rainbow light, who had thus far not spoken.

Sha "Leiala" raised a light-shrouded fist to her mouth and coughed. "We have no problem with continuing the tournament as planned. Quite the opposite. Because of our prior agreement, we were prepared to forfeit all prizes, but now the heavens have prepared one especially for us."

Her voice was disguised, but anyone could tell how pleased she was.

Which reinforced Lindon's belief. If Sha Miara was the one he remembered, then she was a veiled Monarch. Though her power was restricted to Underlord, he couldn't imagine her losing.

"I am satisfied with the matches as agreed," Malice said, and her voice was as rich as Lindon had imagined.

"We don't doubt ourselves, Northstrider," Reigan Shen said. "We doubt *you.*"

Northstrider took one step forward, and the tower beneath Lindon's feet quaked. Alarm tightened his throat, though none of the other Monarchs reacted.

"I have given my word to administrate this competition," Northstrider said quietly. "Do any of you believe I would violate my oath, even if a son of mine was competing? Do you believe that your panel of judges would have been less susceptible to influence than I am? Do you believe that I have outwitted the rest of you and manipulated matters to my own advantage beneath your very eyes?"

Reigan Shen stroked his beard and Seshethkunaaz glared, but no one accused Northstrider of anything. Still, he continued.

"Allow me to set your doubts at ease." Once again, the tower trembled, but this time it was the resonance of the Monarch's words that shook the ground. "I swear in the sight of heaven and on the name of Northstrider that I have arbitrated the Uncrowned King tournament without bias and to the best of my ability, and that I will continue to do so."

Everyone else in the room except Lindon dipped their heads together, and Lindon sensed a great power pass by him and land on Northstrider.

The whole discussion settled one question for Lindon. Malice had allowed the fight between him and Yerin.

Why?

He quickly answered his own question. With two members of her faction fighting, Malice was guaranteed one spot among the Uncrowned. One of her fighters was certain to be eliminated as well, but that would still be a better arrangement for her than rolling the dice twice.

So what about her other champions? She would want Mercy to have an easy match, but the other Monarchs would try to stop that if they could.

"You have always been willing to set aside your personal ambitions when necessary, Northstrider," Emriss said heavily. "But I am concerned about the goals of the Abidan. Which of us are they here to recruit?"

A look of anger slowly clouded Northstrider's face. "They play with us like toys in their box, and I am as powerless as the rest of you. The messenger was clear. The competition will continue as planned next week. I could not restart the fourth round if I wanted to, nor even withdraw competitors who are grossly overqualified."

He made an obvious gesture to Sha Leiala—or Miara, or whoever was under that light—and the woman gave a tinkling laugh.

Reigan Shen gave a slow, thoughtful purr. "Quite aside from the Abidan's intentions, the arrowhead will certainly resolve disputes among us, don't you agree? Who would dare to deny a proposal from one with the power of absolute execution?"

He spoke casually, but the attention of the room shifted to Malice. The dragon Monarch, leaning against the wall, gave her a cold smile.

The Queen of Shadows lowered one hand to the arm of her throne, no longer looking as content as she had before. "Whatever weapons you have, if you take one step onto my land, you will be forced to use them."

Charity's words drifted through Lindon's mind, from before his training in the Akura family: *"They want the Blackflame Empire."*

And Fury's, from not so long ago: *"The cat has a key to crack open the western labyrinth."*

Blood drained from Lindon's face.

The Monarchs wouldn't think of it in these terms, but they were deciding the fate of Sacred Valley. Right here, right now.

"Demonstrating our strength to earn support is no longer necessary," Shen continued. "Whoever wins will decide."

Seshethkunaaz smiled like a serpent. "The will of the victor be done."

A cold vice settled around Lindon's heart. The winner of the Uncrowned King tournament would decide what happened to the Blackflame Empire...and Lindon had been eliminated.

In fact, he was the only one of the top sixteen to have been removed so far.

Had Northstrider intended that? Or was it the heavens? Had Suriel sent Kiuran to remove her resurrected mortal from contention?

He reached into his pocket and held the warm glass marble, letting it calm him.

Shadows boiled behind Malice, but Northstrider didn't react. He was supposed to be the greatest enemy of the dragons, and Lindon had been told that it was only his support of Malice that had prevented Reigan Shen from invading as he wished.

Was Northstrider just that outwardly calm, or was he really not worried?

Emriss Silentborn extended her diamond-flower staff, which exuded a peaceful blue-and-pink light. It suffused everything, and Lindon found his thoughts and his madra growing calm as she began to speak.

"Our cooperation was already strained, and now with this...I do not see any peaceful resolution. Whatever restrictions the Abidan put on us, I see no outcome to this competition but war."

At the end of her sentence, her light was drowned out by a brighter, more powerful blue coming from the ceiling.

For the second time that night, a white-armored man drifted down from above.

None of the Monarchs expressed any surprise at seeing the Abidan descending here, as though they'd sensed him coming, but Lindon certainly hadn't. Neither had Dross, judging by the shock Lindon felt from him.

The Hound, Kiuran, was a rat-like man with a thin beard and dark, beady eyes. Lindon could picture him as a petty thief more than a heavenly messenger, except for his attire.

He wore the smooth eggshell armor of the Abidan, and a purple eye the size of his head drifted on his shoulder.

[Doesn't that look like me?] Dross asked. [I think so.]

"Do you think the eyes of heaven are blind?" Kiuran asked, and though he spoke at normal volume, Lindon had no trouble hearing him. "Any outcome you see, we saw long ago. Do not worry over the future, for that is my province."

He steepled white-armored hands together. "In that capacity, I have come to give you further instructions. Before I do, let me remind you once again to play your game fairly. Any coercion or intimidation or violence or bending of the rules to influence the tournament will be resolved immediately. By me."

He said it with the smug tone of someone who had complete confidence in his ability to handle a roomful of Monarchs, but none of them reacted in fear. Northstrider glowered, Reigan Shen rolled his eyes, and Malice sneered.

"We no longer need to waste time on your festivities," Kiuran continued. "Events have outpaced you. The next fight of the fourth round will take place tomorrow, with one fight per day until the fourth round is concluded. That is all the time I will allow you."

Lindon was grateful for Northstrider's protection, because the Monarchs did not take the Abidan's words well.

The very world twisted and rippled under their sudden anger, the walls and floor cracking, spirits fleeing and chandeliers melting like wax.

"Ludicrous," Malice spat. "This will ruin everything. The news will have no time to spread."

Though Northstrider's expression was no different from usual, Lindon imagined he was an inch from trying to tear the Abidan apart. "If I had known the timeline would be altered, I would have changed the structure of the entire round. Am I the arbiter of this tournament, or are you?"

The rainbow-shrouded Ninecloud Monarch shifted uncomfortably. "We can't prepare the arena so quickly. The effort and expense..."

"Have we run out of time so soon?" Emriss asked softly.

Kiuran tilted his head to her. "At least one of you understands. *You* are the ones who have no time for a lengthy tournament. If you still wish for time between rounds to train your students, then the length of the rounds themselves must be condensed. Unless you would prefer your competition to be interrupted by a Dreadgod."

Lightning shot through Lindon's spine.

Malice waved a hand dismissively. "We are prepared for the Titan's awakening."

The Abidan gave an ugly laugh. "You are so proud of your

dim sight. I tell you now, you have less than three months before the Wandering Titan rises. If the tournament is not resolved by that time, your squabbling will bring on this world a disaster worse than the Dreadgod. I have saved you from yourselves."

None of the Monarchs looked pleased, but none protested either. They looked worried, pensive, each deep in their thoughts.

Lindon couldn't begin to guess what changes would come from this information, but great wheels had begun to turn in the machinery of the world.

What would this mean for him?

"Now that I have removed your distractions, you can focus on the tournament," Kiuran continued. "If you want to win, then push your children to improve. Of course, if you can persuade your opponents to throw a match without using intimidation or threats, I will accept that result as well."

Lindon's mind whirled. Yerin was still in the competition, but she was unlikely to be able to beat Sophara or Sha Miara, even discounting the other fighters.

If persuasion was allowed, that meant bribery. Maybe she could walk away from this with treasures worth more than the prizes.

But if she *did* accept a bribe to bow out, that was one defender of the Blackflame Empire gone.

"All prior rules and restrictions stand, and the competition will continue. If it turns out that your greatest enemy defeats you and obtains Penance...well, you can stay and face the headsman, or you can join us."

He turned a sneer on them all, but another piece had just clicked into place for Lindon.

The Abidan hadn't come to recruit promising young Underlords, despite what Kiuran himself had implied only minutes before. They were recruiting Monarchs.

By pressuring them to ascend.

The rainbow-shrouded Monarch of the Ninecloud Court stepped forward and bowed at the waist. "Son of Heaven, would you stay and share your wisdom with us? We have many questions for you."

Kiuran sighed and passed a gauntlet over his face. "I don't see how anything I said requires further explanation. Very well, Luminous Queen, I will make an exception and explain myself to you. As for the rest of you...you have work to do."

None of the Monarchs looked satisfied with that, but one by one they all took the dismissal for what it was and left the room.

The Eight-Man Empire walked out a door, Malice melted into shadows, Reigan Shen and his entire pedestal sank into the floor, and Emriss disappeared in a rustle of spectral leaves. Lindon didn't see the Dragon King leave.

Northstrider waved a hand, opening a portal again, but instead of leading back into the hallway, it led onto a steeply sloped roof tiled in rose-tinted crystal. Cold wind howled across the tiles, sweeping through the portal, and Lindon could see the glistening collection of jewels that was Ninecloud City spread out beneath him.

When the Monarch stepped onto the roof, Lindon had no choice but to follow.

Only when Lindon had passed through did Northstrider allow the portal to close. A rainbow halo encircling the tower shone down on them, bright as daylight. The wind was so strong and the tiles so steep and slick that Lindon would have feared for his balance if he hadn't been an Underlord.

As it was, the footing was only a mild inconvenience.

Dross popped up onto Lindon again. [Ah, thank you for bringing Lindon along. I am rather attached to him, you know? And I didn't mean those things I said about you. Please don't unmake me.]

"Now you have glimpsed a Monarch's responsibilities," Northstrider said to Lindon. "Remember it. This experience can be of great value to you later." His arms were crossed, but he wasn't focused on Dross this time.

Lindon wasn't sure if that was an improvement or not.

"I cannot express my gratitude enough, but I admit that

I'm terrified. I fear what the other Monarchs will do to those who remain in the competition."

He didn't want to voice his full concern aloud, in case Kiuran or one of the Monarchs was listening, but he was even more afraid for his friends' lives now than he had been before. The Hound was pushing the Monarchs, and whatever protection he promised, Lindon was afraid Seshethkunaaz or Reigan Shen would find a way around it.

Northstrider nodded once. "It is wise not to rely on the intervention of the Abidan. Whatever they say, they act only for their own benefit. Not ours."

Lindon tried his best not to reach for Suriel's marble. Had she left him with his memories intact for his sake, or her own?

"But you may put your fears to rest," the Monarch continued. "The competitors are under my protection. At least for the duration of the tournament, they will be safe."

He spoke with such absolute certainty that Lindon's concerns eased, though he *did* wonder what would happen after the tournament ended.

"Thank you for the instruction, honored Monarch," Lindon said. "If you'll pardon one more question...why did you bring me along?"

Northstrider examined him for a long moment.

"I will study Dross again." He seemed to have ignored Lindon's question. "For now, I will leave him within you. I would have returned him before either of you were permanently harmed by the separation, but I will allow you to stay together from now on. Clearly you have formed a... symbiosis."

Relief was more likely to take Lindon off his feet than the wind was. Since he had first seen Northstrider, Lindon had always been haunted by the fear that the Monarch would punish him or dissect him to reclaim Dross.

Lindon bowed. "Gratitude."

"Now, until I call for you, do not neglect your training. Sopharanatoth is one of the two most favored to win this competition, and she will use Penance on Akura Malice or myself without hesitation. If you wish to influence the situation, you must be stronger."

Lindon hesitated. "If you will enlighten me, how could I possibly stop Sophara if she wins?"

Northstrider's eyes gleamed gold. "Training will never let you down."

"Then...pardon, but...can we win?"

He was afraid to ask too many questions of a Monarch, but he had to know.

And Northstrider didn't seem annoyed. "The most certain path to victory is to have a fighter representing myself or Malice win the tournament. If we cannot accomplish that, victory becomes more costly or difficult. But not impossible. The only true defeat is death."

Those words resonated with Lindon, as though Northstrider had given voice to something inside *him*.

He strode over to the edge of the roof and turned to look back over his shoulder. "I will see you soon, Dross. And Lindon."

Then he stepped out over the edge and fell.

Leaving Lindon wondering: why had the Monarch changed his mind about Lindon? He had gone from treating Lindon like a patch of mud to answering his questions and addressing him directly. Was he so impressed by Lindon's determination?

[I told you, didn't I? He's a very generous man. And he has a good eye for talent. My talent, anyway.]

He didn't care about me at all, Lindon thought. *Then he came back for me. Was it something you said?*

Dross straightened himself up proudly. [That's what it was. He does value my opinion, you know.]

It was a simple explanation, and maybe it was the correct one. There was no point in making wild guesses.

Lindon looked around at the sloped diamond rooftop. "Now...where are we?"

第二章

CHAPTER TWO

It took Lindon over two hours to climb down from the tower, then find his way back to the Akura building amidst the glistening structures of Ninecloud City.

Dross remembered the city's layout, but every route they tried was blocked. The streets were in chaos. People poured out of doorways from interrupted parties, cloudships reversed course in midair against the flow of air traffic, and every inn was choked by lines that stretched around the block.

Over it all, the Ninecloud Soul repeated announcements at a deafening volume: the tournament schedule had changed. The second fight in the fourth round of the Uncrowned King tournament was scheduled to take place three hours past dawn in the morning.

That change had shifted the lives of more people than Lindon could comprehend, and the city bustled like an anthill.

He had to consult a shining map projected by light madra on the air, repeatedly use his Thousand-Mile Cloud to get a peek over the crowds, and eventually talk to city security.

The Ninecloud peacekeepers, Underlords all, recognized him immediately.

The Uncrowned King tournament was shared with the entire city. Though this would likely be their busiest night of the year, the peacekeepers took the time to commiserate with Lindon on his loss as they directed him back to the tower assigned to the Akura clan.

"What can you do when they set you up against your own teammate?" one gruff man in a stiff peacekeeper's uniform said. "Not your fault. If anyone's to blame, it's No—" He coughed. "Nobody."

Lindon bowed and thanked them for their assistance, but his heart throbbed. That wound was still fresh, and a reminder that everyone in Ninecloud City had seen him lose only increased his shame.

[Not just Ninecloud City!] Dross added brightly. [Memories, recordings, and written accounts of the Uncrowned King tournament are being distributed all over the world.]

Lindon had viewed some memories from previous years, stored in the records of the Ninecloud Court.

Still, he didn't appreciate the reminder.

When he didn't respond, Dross tried again.

[Ah...I *do* feel the need to apologize one more time about things with Master. Northstrider, I mean. Master Northstrider. He did say that he wouldn't have let you suffer permanent damage, so no harm done! Right?]

I'm just relieved we don't have to be afraid of him.

That much was true, but he couldn't rid himself of a small grain of resentment. He had *warned* Dross. Over and over.

But there was nothing Dross could have done when the moment came. The spirit couldn't have resisted Northstrider.

[Relieved! Same. Exactly the same for me. Well, good. That's good! We're both relieved, so that's a relief.]

Lindon pushed his irritation down. Clinging to bitterness was childish.

He finally made his way to the amethyst spire that hosted the Akura family. One of the rainbow-robed staff led him to a cloud, which lifted him up the side of the building and to a dock outside his floor.

It was late at night by the time he returned, but the entire city was awake.

Yerin and the others would be too.

Lindon made his way to the suite of rooms that had been set aside for the Akura prime team. Spiritual perception was muddled in here—not so much that he couldn't push through it, but the restriction was a privacy feature, so it would have been rude to do so. As a result, he couldn't check to see if any of his friends were nearby while remaining polite.

But Lindon knew Eithan.

He activated a scripted card, which resonated with the door to Lindon's room and caused it to slide open.

Eithan lounged in a padded chair within view of the door. He brushed yellow hair behind him and gave Lindon a beaming grin. "Did the walk clear your head?"

Lindon's room was the size of any reasonable person's entire house, and it was like the decorators couldn't decide between opulent wealth and a natural garden. A river trickled through the center of the room between multicolored tiles, birds chirped from the artfully carved beams across the ceiling overhead, and a living tree in the corner held glowing fruits.

As he stepped through the door, he saw Mercy in the section of the room that functioned as a kitchen. She was putting a bowl down and wiping her mouth with the back of one black-gloved hand.

At least Mercy's presence solved the mystery of how they'd gotten in. Her room connected to his and Pride's.

Mercy no longer wore the elaborate costume and makeup that represented the Akura faction, instead settling for a simple set of black-and-white robes. She melted in clear sympathy when he walked through the door, but her eyes moved to the other person in the room.

Yerin stood against the opposite wall, stiff as a board.

She had been fiddling with a gem-like dream tablet before he had come in, and her fingers froze around it. Her other hand gripped the hilt of her master's sword at her waist, and she stared at him with eyes wide.

Lindon had spent much of the last two hours figuring out what to say to Yerin, but he knew what the first thing had to be. He gave her the most genuine smile he could muster.

"Congratulations, Uncrowned."

She started to answer his smile, but her expression became complicated, and her mouth worked as she struggled with her words.

Which was all right with him, because he had more. He bowed to her.

"And please accept my apologies. I made you wait too long. I am honored to have felt your full power." He tapped his ribs and added, "Right through the chest."

Finally, her smile broke through like the sun breaking through clouds. She tossed the dream tablet behind her, accidentally launching it so hard it cracked one of the overhead beams.

She had crossed the room in an instant and was gripping his arms in both her hands. "It was *amazing,* true? I'm down to one thin scale and shakier than a drunken sailor, but I had one more move in me. And you! Making up your own techniques without me!"

She sounded delighted, not offended, which relieved him.

"You didn't tell me about your master's sword," he pointed out.

Yerin ran a hand across the hilt of her weapon. "I thought my heart would pop when I used it. Was *sure* you'd thought of it."

She tightened her grip on his arm. "And *you,* you're scarier than a tiger at midnight, aren't you? Blocking dragon's breath is a chore and a half, when if I slip one inch I'm cored like an apple."

"She has been talking like this," Eithan said, "for the last two hours."

Mercy threw a spoon at him, which he snatched out of the air without looking. "Give them a minute!" she insisted.

Yerin glared at Eithan. "You too stingy to lend me five seconds to celebrate?"

"On the contrary. I thought Lindon might enjoy himself

more if he knew you were this excited while he was gone."

Eithan was right. He wasn't sure he'd ever seen Yerin so clearly happy.

It went a long way toward easing the pain of losing. He'd kept that disappointment at bay by focusing on immediate problems, like Northstrider.

Which reminded him of the reasons he'd been trying to find his friends in the first place.

"Wait! Apologies, but I need a moment of your time."

He hadn't yet told them about Sha Miara.

At first, he hadn't been sure that she was really a Monarch. Could Monarchs restrict themselves down as far as Underlord? Maybe she was just someone with the same name.

But little things had kept adding up.

The Monarch meeting tonight had finally convinced him, but that brought him to the second reason why he had said nothing: he didn't want to offend a Monarch.

He had heard repeatedly about the Monarch ability to hear their name spoken. He still didn't fully understand it—Monarchs were figures of myths and legends, so surely there were too many people talking about them all over the world to pay attention to everyone—but he still didn't want to refer to Sha Miara as anything other than a competitor.

What if the Ninecloud Court forced him to tell how he had seen through their Monarch's disguise?

As the other three looked at him curiously, Lindon spoke aloud for their benefit. "Dross. Show them."

[Right! I'll show them. I'll show them *right* now. Tell me again which—]

Suriel's visit, Dross, Lindon added silently.

It was painfully awkward facing down Eithan and Yerin and Mercy's inquisitive stares while he waited for Dross to project the right memory, and he couldn't help but think how much more impressive it would have been if Dross had done as ordered immediately.

It wasn't as though he hadn't warned Dross about this. They should have practiced.

[Got it!] Dross said triumphantly, and Lindon's room melted away to show the Ninecloud audience hall. Just as he remembered it from Suriel's vision, it was packed with richly dressed people of every description.

It wasn't a perfect depiction of reality. Many of the details were vague, as they had faded in Lindon's mind, and most of the faces were blurred as though they were seen through smudged glass.

He could see Yerin, Eithan, and Mercy clearly. Dross had left them where they were, changing the image of the rest of the room to match the memory. None of them expressed much surprise at being taken inside a projection—they all had enough experience with dream tablets and similar constructs.

Lindon looked eagerly to one side. Suriel would be clear, he knew. He remembered every detail of her perfectly.

"Luminous Queen Sha Leiala," a woman's voice said. "Path of Celestial Radiance."

In the center of the hall, a rainbow cloud descended and a bright light shone, but he was staring in confusion at the woman who had spoken.

It wasn't Suriel.

She resembled the heavenly messenger in many ways. She wore white, but instead of the smooth, almost liquid armor of the Abidan, she was dressed in a white-and-silver coat, shirt, and long skirt.

Her hair was more brown than dark green, and it hung naturally behind her. Her purple eyes made her look like a member of the Akura clan, and she spoke while stretching her neck and wincing. There was a bend to her nose as though she'd broken it at one point.

And *she* hadn't really been the one who introduced Sha Miara and her Path. It had been the gray ghost on her shoulder, which was now missing.

"Tomorrow, an enemy nation is predicted to attack her city," the Suriel imitator went on. "Sha Leiala will strike down their cloudships with one sweep of her sword."

"Stop it, Dross," Lindon said, and he couldn't keep some heat from his voice.

The vision froze.

[You know, it's hard enough projecting to three people, and holding it all in place doesn't make it any easier.]

Lindon waved a hand around them. "I don't need you to change things. Show them my memory."

Color bled from the Ninecloud audience hall, then the vision vanished completely. They were back in his room, and Dross appeared in front of Lindon.

[Um...you're not shouting at me, but it feels like you *want* to shout at me, and I don't understand why.]

Dross often misunderstood Lindon or toyed with him, but this felt different. He sounded honestly baffled.

"I wanted you to show them the memory as it is. Why are you changing things?"

Dross' mouth hung open for a second. [I *didn't* change anything. That's exactly how you remember it.]

For a long moment, those words made no sense to Lindon.

[If you're worried about the blurring, that's how memory works. The best way to get a pristine memory is to use a construct to record it as it's happening. I could sharpen the faces of the crowd, but I'd be making it up myself, so they'd probably all end up looking like Eithan.]

"Good choice!" Eithan called.

Lindon stepped away, holding Dross in his Remnant hand. It was easier to grip him with that than with his left hand.

"Dross...that was how you see my memory?"

[Reproduced exactly!] Dross said proudly.

So you don't see Sha Miara? Lindon thought, still wary of speaking her name out loud.

[I told you I'd never heard of her.]

And Northstrider?

Dross sighed and brought Lindon into another memory. Just Lindon, this time.

He and the imitation Suriel drifted above an endless ocean,

only instead of floating on nothing, they stood together on a blue Thousand-Mile Cloud.

"Northstrider," Suriel said. "Path of the Hungry Deep."

She spread her hands and a viewing construct appeared beneath them. Showing him deeper into the water, where a man plunged with his arms crossed. Northstrider.

"He consumed sacred beasts in the deepest places in the world. Used to take their powers with him when he fought on the surface."

Lindon took an involuntary step back as Dross canceled the vision.

[Lindon, are you okay?]

Lindon's head spun.

He could remember Suriel's visit clearly. So clearly. They had plunged down together into the water. She had taken him to *real* places in the world, not making up visions. And all the details were different.

His left hand plunged into his pocket, feeling the warm marble there.

The glass ball still comforted him, its blue candle-flame burning steadily. He focused his spiritual perception on it, basking in the familiar feel of order and restoration. It made him think that everything was right with the world.

[Lindon?]

Lindon took a breath and faced Dross, calmer than he had been a moment before. He didn't doubt his own memory. Too many things would make no sense if the visit from Suriel hadn't occurred as he saw it.

"Apologies, Dross," he said. "I was confused."

Yerin and Mercy now looked concerned, and they were whispering to one another.

He turned to them. "Is there a way to protect memories?"

"If she was a messenger from the heavens," Eithan said, "then you would think she could do anything. But yes, it is common practice to alter or conceal memories to prevent them from being stolen or recorded."

"But I've never heard of a technique to alter a memory

for everyone except you," Mercy said. "If the memory was changed, *you* should remember the altered version too."

She seemed contemplative, not doubtful.

Eithan raised a hand. "I, for one, need no further proof. I trust you completely, my student."

Lindon was touched for a moment, but he could feel a second statement on its way.

"Also, I had figured it out myself."

Yerin turned to him with doubt clear on her face.

"Many Heralds and Monarchs have made strange comments about the Ninecloud team or one of the competitors. Sha Leiala hasn't shown herself openly in years, the Celestial Radiance ability to transfer power to an heir is something of an open secret, the Luminous Queen has made several *interesting* addresses in recent months that suggest immaturity..."

Eithan paused and glanced around to make sure their eyes were on him. "...and you mentioned her name to us about two years ago. I value you so highly that I remember every word you have ever spoken."

Lindon hoped that wasn't true, but he took a deep breath. "Gratitude. Thank you, Eithan."

Mercy spoke as though each word was being pulled from her. "I'm...really sorry, Lindon, *really* sorry, but...I can't...it's hard to take that on faith. I believe you that your memory was altered! But you were Copper at that point, weren't you? You didn't know what a Monarch was, so...how could you tell you weren't just seeing an Underlady?"

He hadn't even had a dream of Copper at that point, but otherwise he understood her point. He was about to argue for himself when she continued.

"*Please* don't be offended when I check for myself."

Mercy closed her eyes, and suddenly the room grew darker as shadow aura surged. Madra licked out of her, black and unformed, and the ghost of a violet book loomed over her. It was made of bright, Forged madra, and it had an intricate layer of script-circles on its cover.

"Uncle Fury!" she called.

There was a long pause as no one responded.

Unveiling herself and spewing madra while trying to attract Fury's spiritual attention was similar to screaming and waving her arms in the middle of a silent theater audience. Everyone around her would be bothered, including most likely Fury himself.

Lindon slid up to Yerin's side. "Pardon," he muttered, "I'm sure she knows best, but isn't there a more...polite...way to contact a Herald?"

"Bleed me if I know."

"Uncle Fury!" Mercy shouted again. "Please! We have a—"

A gust of wind blew in from the suddenly open window. The tree's leaves whipped, an empty chair tumbled across the floor, and Yerin's hair was blown into Lindon's eyes.

Akura Fury stood in the center of the room.

He was tall and broad-shouldered, muscled like a heroic statue, and his black robe hung open to reveal several inches of bare chest. His liquid-shadow hair drifted up as though caught by a current, and his red eyes shone from the shadows.

He raised one hand. "Hey, Mercy! Sorry, but this isn't a great time. We're pretty busy right now."

"Is Sha Miara a Monarch in disguise?"

Red eyes crawled away from Mercy.

Fury shifted his weight from one foot to the other. He licked his lips. He looked up to the ceiling as though hoping heaven would give him the answer. Finally, he raised a hand to scratch at the back of his head.

"Noooo...?"

It was the least convincing cover-up Lindon had ever heard.

The Herald could tell, because he made a frustrated sound. "I guess that secret is coming out already. No one's going to keep quiet now that Monarch lives are on the line. Still don't...talk about it too much, okay?"

Yerin threw up her hands. "How are we supposed to fight a Monarch?"

"She's limited to Underlord," Fury explained. "The rest of you have the possibility of advancing, but she can't. She had to give up her prizes, all the other Ninecloud competitors on her team were weaker than usual, and the Court paid a fortune in compensation to the rest of us. Plus, it was *supposed* to be a way to avoid paying out on the grand prize, but now..."

He ran both hands through his hair as though he was about to pull it out. "Listen, I *really* don't have time for this. I'm leaving in the morning, and I'm taking most of the family fighters with me."

Mercy's face fell, and she leaned more heavily on her staff. "We haven't even gotten to the Uncrowned yet."

"I *know*." Fury looked more disappointed than Mercy. "Our timeline's been moved up, and we want to get in position before the dragons or anybody else. But hey!" He perked up. "At least it should be fun. There's a Dreadgod!"

Mercy and Yerin exclaimed at that, but Fury was already dangling out the window. He poked his head back in and looked from Lindon to Yerin. "Oh, right! Great fight, kids! *Great* fight! We should spar sometime!"

He smiled brightly and vanished in another mighty gust of wind.

"Don't fight him," Mercy advised. "He doesn't hold back as well as he thinks he does."

"What's he saying about the Dreadgods?" Yerin asked, and Mercy shrugged.

Eithan sighed, and Lindon realized he hadn't said a word while Fury was around. "There's been buzz for quite a while now about the Wandering Titan stirring. But I think I may not be the most informed on the subject. Lindon?"

Lindon had gone so far astray from the message he had originally intended to relay that it took him a few seconds to reorganize his thoughts.

"The *judge of the Uncrowned King tournament* took me aside tonight." He waited to make sure they understood who he was talking about, and Mercy and Yerin both looked at him in obvious shock. Eithan leaned forward, toying with a pair of scissors.

Lindon recounted the evening, trying to avoid naming as many Monarchs as possible. He didn't know that was necessary—he hadn't been instructed not to tell anyone—but it was better to be safe.

When he finished, Eithan looked off into the distance, uncharacteristically serious.

Sword madra flashed around Yerin's fingertips as she thought. Lindon felt blood madra surge within her spirit, so her Blood Shadow was mulling it over too.

"Mother won't want too much out of you," Mercy assured him. "You've done our family proud. I'm afraid it might be my fault that you two had to fight each other; she would have made whatever deal necessary to get me an easy match."

She bobbed her head in apology, but Yerin waved her off. "If she paved you an easy road, then that's one sure win. Two, if you count me and Lindon. She had to give something up."

As one, they all turned to Eithan.

He was still staring off into the distance and fiddling with his scissors. "Yes, it would seem that I have been thrown to the proverbial wolves. Our situation has grown overly complicated. You two might have to fight for the fate of the Empire on your own."

"I'm so sorry, Eithan," Mercy said. "When are you fighting?"

"I have been instructed to prepare to fight tomorrow morning," Eithan said, "but I'm certain you have as well."

She nodded.

"Most of us remaining in the fourth round have, I would suspect, though regrettably I haven't been able to check *everyone*. They wish to keep us unsure about our opponents. But now that we can be sure it isn't randomly chosen..."

He snapped his scissors open and closed.

Lindon took over his line of thought. "Who is a guaranteed loss for you?"

"I just want to see somebody mess up your hair," Yerin put in.

Eithan slipped his scissors away and pressed his fingertips together. "There are six people remaining in the competition who I would prefer not to fight. But there are only three, I believe, that the Monarchs would consider a definite loss for me."

"Sophara," Yerin suggested.

"She is the first. The second is in this very room with us."

Mercy winced.

"And the third is the young woman we were just discussing."

They were talking about Sha Miara as a competitor in the tournament, not as a Monarch, so surely this wouldn't attract her attention. Also, she was restricted down to Underlord. But Lindon didn't want to be the one to say her name.

"You tossing your sword away?" Yerin asked.

Eithan had spent much of his life in the Blackflame Empire, as Lindon understood it. Surely he would feel enough attachment to it to try to defend the Empire when its safety was on the line.

"To tell you the truth, I had intended to withdraw myself from this competition before taking an Uncrowned title. Too much notoriety would tie my hands. However, now...now I believe we might have an *opportunity*."

Hours after returning to his room, Lindon was snapped awake by Dross' voice.

[Hey. Lindon, hey. You should stop being asleep.]

Lindon shot up and conjured Blackflame before he realized he was in his own bed. His spirit was calm, and he sensed no threat. Little Blue mumbled sleepily from the flowerpot where she slept.

Lindon groaned. "What can I do for you, Dross?"

[I know you don't like me waking you up, but you are *really* going to want to hear this. I may or may not have stolen some memories from Northstrider.]

The idea that Dross may have *stolen* something from a

Monarch had Lindon in a sweat, but his interest was certainly piqued. "What memories?"

[You see, that's the thing. I've spent the last few hours putting together some pieces, because I couldn't take everything. A full memory from Northstrider would make me burst, I think. Just *pop,* and there I go. There were memories from lots of people in there, but I was most interested in the ones from Northstrider himself.]

Lindon forced himself to wait patiently. Dross would get around to answering his question eventually.

[I *think* I can show you his ascension to Monarch.]

Lindon instantly forgave Dross for waking him. And for everything he had ever done, would ever do, or might think about doing.

"Dross, I have never been as grateful for you as I am now."

[What about all those times I saved your life?]

"Even then. If you could show me that memory now, I would be in your debt."

[Oh, and you don't even know the best part! We were right! Northstrider uses...well, that would spoil the surprise. Now, remember that this is more like a painting of a memory than a real memory. I couldn't understand the true depths or powers involved, so I can't pass those on to you.]

Lindon sat cross-legged in a cycling position. "Anything you can show me is appreciated." Even a glimpse of ascension to Monarch could guide him for the rest of his life.

[All right, then, here we go. And pay attention to his madra, remember! His *madra.*]

INFORMATION REQUESTED: NORTHSTRIDER'S ASCENSION TO MONARCH.

BEGINNING REPORT...

The Sage of the Hungry Deep tracks a rogue black dragon to the Everwood continent.

He normally wouldn't get involved here, but the Monarch

Emriss is abroad. She spreads peace and education all over the globe, so every decent person respects the sanctity of her homeland.

Only the vilest criminal would bring violence while her back was turned.

The dragon has been careful enough to move under a veil, but sloppy enough to leave a trail of devastated forests and villages in its wake. Northstrider follows it easily, promising justice to the survivors.

Wading through the destruction, too late to save the innocents, is enough to break his heart.

The closer he comes to his quarry, the more careful he has to be. Eyewitness reports can't agree on the dragon's size or gender, only its color, so he is wary about finding more than one.

He deduces that the black dragon must be equivalent to an Archlord, so while he has confidence in hunting one, he will have to flee from more than that.

He finds the serpentine black dragon coiling around a stone tower in the center of a burning town. Ash drizzles from the air as the serpent cycles fire and destruction aura.

It's a disgusting creature in Northstrider's eyes, a scavenger that feeds on corpses. He wants to kill it immediately, but there's one problem.

This beast isn't an Archlord at all. It's a Herald.

None of the witnesses had the experience or the perception to know the difference, and Northstrider never expected a dragon to have the self-restraint to hold itself back to Archlord techniques.

He has walked into a trap.

As soon as Northstrider feels the dragon's power in his spiritual sense, its black-and-red eyes snap open.

Fear shoots through Northstrider like lightning through his spine, and he stretches out to the Way. His only thought is to run somewhere, anywhere.

No sooner has the portal begun to form than the dragon's willpower overwhelms his own. Blue light is snuffed out, space sealed shut.

And the Sage Northstrider swallows his fear, clenches red-scaled fists, and turns to do battle.

Dross' voice interrupts the vision.

I'm sorry about this, but this is exactly where my understanding breaks down. They're both using principles in their techniques that I can't sense.

Lindon is no longer inside the vision, but a spectator of it. His sense of himself returns, and he watches the battle as though a passenger behind Northstrider's eyes.

Though he can see only brief images, the battle is still full of useful information. One of Northstrider's Enforced punches takes a chunk out of the dragon's side, but black-and-red fire madra rushes to fill in the gap in the dragon's body.

And then that Blackflame madra *becomes* flesh. It Forges into something resembling a Remnant at first, slowly hardening into an indistinguishable patch of black scales.

Can all Heralds rebuild their body with madra, or is this a special property of some Path? Northstrider would know, but Lindon is too distant from the memory at the moment to read his thoughts.

Northstrider fights by tearing at the dragon with blood aura, summoning living techniques shaped like red dragons that hurl themselves at the enemy, and by unleashing blows that slam the dragon into the ground hard enough to cause earthquakes for miles around.

The dragon sprays dragon's breath all over Northstrider, calls columns of fiery destruction from the sky, and blackens the terrain. It even *becomes* fiery madra for a moment, to move in a rush of flame.

There are a treasure trove of insights here, but Lindon focuses on Northstrider's techniques.

When he gets an opening, he sinks his hands—which are scaled in red, not black—into the dragon's side.

And he pulls with the full force of his spirit.

A hunger madra technique.

Lindon has to choke off his excitement before the strong emotion disrupts the vision. He and Dross guessed that

Northstrider incorporated hunger madra into his techniques, but they've never known for sure.

Now they know.

Northstrider is beaten and bloody and exhausted when he finally tears off the dragon's head. Only the power he stole with his hunger madra kept his spirit moving.

He drains even more, trying to stop the Remnant from rising, and this time Lindon can feel a little more of the technique. It's pulling not just madra, but *everything*. Life, physical strength, even some of the dragon's thoughts and personality.

Northstrider has to struggle to control it all, and Lindon desperately wished he could feel more of that process.

Unfortunately, the Sage isn't in time. The Remnant rises.

It's nothing like any other Remnant birth that Lindon has ever seen.

The corpse *becomes* Blackflame, transforming into black fire, twisting and evolving until it is a spirit of black-and-red madra that only vaguely resembles a dragon. It looks almost as physical as before, so that Lindon almost can't identify it as a Remnant.

It launches dragon's breath from its mouth and both arms, and Northstrider calls a barrier.

Of this battle, Lindon could see virtually nothing. It's a gray blur with half-felt spiritual sensations.

Sorry, sorry, Dross says. *Fights, like I said. Let's move to the next part.*

Northstrider drags himself across the ground, victorious but gravely wounded.

He can heal himself with blood aura easily, but he needs a safe place to stop and do so. He senses distant enemies.

There were more dragons after all.

These are *actually* Archlords, but Northstrider doesn't feel equal to even a Gold at the moment. If they arrive before he restores himself, he will surely die. But he has stolen power from a Herald; he can try to advance.

He isn't sure if it will work. Isn't certain his spirit is stable or complete enough.

Here, he will become a Monarch or die trying.

In a nearby cave, he carves a script into the stone with one finger. This should hide him long enough.

Then he sinks into meditation.

It takes him hours to manifest his Remnant in front of him, a clawed and scaled monstrous version of himself. It is made mostly of blood madra, with red curling horns on its head, and it looks almost as real as he does himself.

His own Remnant glares at him with the vertically slitted eyes of a gold dragon.

Northstrider draws his Remnant into his flesh, and his Remnant resists. Their wills clash, the spirit trying to consume him even as he does the same.

Though it involves no sacred techniques, only a straightforward competition of focus and resolve, it is the deadliest fight of his life.

Being a Sage makes this harder. His Remnant has power and authority beyond what an ordinary Archlord's spirit should. If he fails, he can't simply try again.

There's a real possibility that his very existence will be erased.

But his will is steel. He weaves his own Remnant into his body, spirit becoming flesh and flesh fusing with spirit.

For the final time in his life, his body is remade.

Reality itself quakes at the birth of a Monarch. There is no Icon in the sky, as there was on his ascension to Sage, but the ground shakes and aura trembles for dozens of miles around. His enemies will find him soon, if they haven't already.

He takes control of the changes.

The scales on his arms transform, turning black, but they want to spread all over his body. He restricts them to the arms, though they still take up more of his skin. Horns begin to grow on his head, and he puts a stop to that. No horns.

Finally, his eyes transform to resemble a dragon's.

That he cannot stop.

His transformation reaches its final stages, and he stretches out with the sense of a Monarch—

INFORMATION LOST.

REPORT COMPLETE.

Lindon returned to himself, still sitting cross-legged on his bed, and Dross manifested in front of him. His huge purple eye was downcast.

[I'm sorry, Lindon, I was sure I could hold it at the end there. If I get to see Northstrider again, I might be able to get more information. I'm sure I can! But I...well, I'm not sure I can read it. That's just about the limit of my understanding.]

Lindon grabbed Dross in both hands.

It would be too strange to give Dross a hug. For one thing, Dross wasn't completely material, and Lindon was worried about pushing the spirit through his rib cage.

So Lindon met his gaze and projected complete sincerity, hoping Dross would feel it.

"Gratitude. Everything we just learned, I can't...I can only thank you."

Dross perked up. [Right? Right! And we were right about the hunger madra, weren't we? Well, I was.]

"You were."

Northstrider's hunger madra was almost the least of the secrets they'd learned. The nature of Heralds, Sages, and Monarchs...these things were considered secrets for anyone below Archlord.

Now Lindon had hints about all of them.

He was far too excited to go back to sleep.

第三章

CHAPTER THREE

Lindon and Yerin stayed with Eithan in the waiting room, anxious for the door to open.

Eithan sat on a bench between them with his eyes closed, cycling. For once, he was really dressed for a fight.

His hair was tied into a tail behind him, and he wore a practical set of gray fighting robes. Instead of the Akura or Blackflame symbols, the Arelius family symbol was displayed on his back in white: a crescent moon next to a pair of symbols in the old language that indicated power.

He had stayed so focused, unsmiling and sharp, that Lindon was starting to worry.

Little Blue gave a sad peep from her seat beside Lindon's ear.

[He looks like he's walking to his death,] Dross said.

"Two scales says he's faking it," Yerin said, but she kept her voice low to avoid disrupting him.

"I was hoping we could help somehow," Lindon responded, but he felt foolish saying it. Eithan never needed moral support.

Yerin sighed. "I'm the same kind of fool as you, I guess. Thought we could do some good, but his own mother's funeral couldn't crack his mask."

"I was quite upset when my mother died," Eithan said. He cracked one eye. "I do have a heart, you know."

"Prove it."

He lifted his scissors—the black Archlord scissors that had been his reward from the second round—and drummed them on his thigh. He still didn't smile, but he didn't seem upset. Only pensive. Like he was chewing on a problem.

That was disturbing. And it reminded Lindon of Eithan's expression upon seeing Penance.

"I was watching you last night, when the Abidan took out the arrowhead," Lindon said.

Eithan nodded. "Yes, that was a...surprise. I had intended to spend several more years helping you grow, but now I'm afraid our time grows short. Which leaves me in a dilemma. I don't know which way to go."

Lindon leaned forward, hungry for more information.

"I will be unusually candid with you both: I had plans for losing this tournament. For helping one of you win. For Sophara winning. I try to make sure that no matter what happens, *we* benefit."

Lindon appreciated being included in that statement.

"I am not certain that winning Penance is the most desirable outcome for us."

Yerin and Lindon both stared at him, confused. Lindon felt almost betrayed.

He held up a hand. "It would be preferable for one of us to win, of course. But preventing the invasion of the Blackflame Empire is a *temporary* solution. It restores the status quo."

Eithan stared off into the distance, still tapping his scissors on his thigh, speaking almost to himself. "We have to break what is normal. Rewrite the rules. And to do that, we must be strong."

"Eithan," Lindon said hesitantly, "what are you talking about?"

"Sorry! Sorry. I'm saying that the only true solution is for us to improve as quickly as we can. For me, winning the tournament might not be the best way to do that. Then again, maybe it is. So is it better to win or to lose?"

Eithan took a deep breath. "And what if I decide to win, but I lose anyway? That would be beyond embarrassing, wouldn't it? But it is possible. Even likely, in some cases. What if I go all-out and win, only to find that I have revealed too much and regret it after the tournament?"

He took in the looks on their faces and winced. "I'm sorry. I habitually cultivate an air of omnipotence, mystery, and sheer charisma, but I have as many worries as the rest of you. No need to burden yourselves with them, I just wanted to assure you for once that indeed, I *am* human."

For several breaths, neither Yerin nor Lindon knew what to say.

Little Blue gave an encouraging chime.

"You should drop that mask more often," Yerin said at last.

Like Eithan, she was unusually sincere. She faced him seriously, arms crossed. "I'm not polishing you up when I say you've done a lot for us, and we're grateful. You called us your family and stuck your name on us. But until you trust us, you're no family of mine."

That rocked him in place. Or at least, he acted as though it did.

Which was exactly the problem. Lindon couldn't tell how much of Eithan was real.

"Apologies," Lindon said, "but it's true." He had never trusted Eithan as much as he did Yerin. Despite knowing him almost as long, Lindon knew next to nothing about Eithan.

Eithan closed his eyes again and took a long breath. His madra stirred and smoothed itself out.

"This is...an area in which I regularly fail. I suppose I should take steps to work against that mistake, shouldn't I?" He cleared his throat and opened his eyes.

"Please help me."

It sounded so unlike Eithan that he might as well have spoken a different language. Lindon felt lost, and Yerin's eyes were wide.

"Now," Eithan said, "I suppose you need to understand me in order to offer me your advice. I do not know the identity of my opponent. I can stretch my bloodline perception outside, but not to the point of penetrating the other room, and of course I have had no time to investigate the other competitors since last night."

"Can you win?" Yerin asked.

"I don't know who's out there, do I?"

"Still asking."

One side of his mouth quirked up. "Yes. It is possible for me to defeat anyone in the Uncrowned King tournament. But any of the three young women I might face right now are also capable of defeating me."

"Then draw swords," she said simply. "It's a tournament. Play to win."

Lindon considered his own response. He thought over what he knew of Eithan, and what Eithan had expressed only moments before.

"It has to be hard," Lindon said at last. "Hiding what you can do, I mean. Keeping people unsure."

"Sometimes it is. It can be fun. Sometimes it's both."

Lindon reached into his pocket and felt Suriel's marble. "Then let fate decide. I want to see what you can *really* do."

Eithan reached into his own pocket for something that Lindon couldn't sense. His own Abidan marble.

Constructs in the doorframe activated, and the stone door started to slide upward. The roars of the crowd filled the waiting room.

So did power from Eithan's spirit. "You are both in agreement?" he asked.

"You need to ask? Whoever it is, cut them in half."

[This is a good plan,] Dross whispered. [Now we'll be able to train against a model of him. Our uprising will be swift.]

Eithan loosened his shoulders. He hopped in place, rolling his neck. "Well then, who am I to deny the request of my two adorable subordinates?"

The door slid upward, and Eithan tilted his head as though listening to something. Then he slipped his scissors back into his pocket.

"I won't be needing those. Lindon, since we're not keeping secrets any longer, you should pay close attention."

The door slid up enough so that Lindon could see the arena floor was covered in white sand, unlike the dark domain that had sealed off Lindon and Yerin.

"This," Eithan said, "is the Path of the Hollow King."

The Ninecloud Soul's voice boomed out across the stadium. "Sacred artists, I present Eithan Arelius, chosen of Akura Malice!

And his opponent, the champion of our very own Ninecloud Court: Sha Miara!"

As Eithan marched out onto the sand, he narrowed his perspective.

He could see Lindon and Yerin taking a cloud up from the waiting room to the shadow-shrouded Akura viewing tower, but he pulled his attention back from them. And away from the other crowds surrounding him, though he would have been interested to hear more of House Arelius gossiping about him.

He withdrew his awareness from House Shen's tower, where the average audience members mocked him as though they had been personally involved in bringing down the Arelius Monarch. It had been Reigan Shen alone, and Eithan could sense nothing from the floating palace where the lion watched.

Eithan rolled up the spiderweb strands of his awareness and concentrated himself entirely on the arena.

Northstrider stood in the center, shaggy and unkempt as usual. He radiated power with his spirit completely restrained, his golden glare and massive frame doing the talking for him.

Across from him, Sha Miara waited.

The girl was maybe fifteen or sixteen, with bright bloody

red hair and nine-colored eyes that she had inherited from a long line of Celestial Radiance Monarchs. She wore a bright red set of sparring robes that matched her hair, and she managed to look down on him despite being head and shoulders shorter.

Long-honed instinct and his own sense of mischief urged him to give her a beaming smile and sweep her a bow, to flatter her as a princess before they did battle.

But that wasn't needed now. He needed to focus.

He spread his bloodline legacy out, but only to the bounds of the arena. As far as the sand stretched, he could see and hear everything.

With a sharp blade, he cut off his good humor, his sympathy, and his plans for the future.

Miara was under Northstrider's protection. It was time to kill.

As the Ninecloud Soul continued their introduction overhead, Northstrider spoke to them both. "The eyes of heaven are on us. *All* of us." That was clearly directed to Sha Miara, and she gave him a condescending look. "Conduct yourselves accordingly."

Eithan watched his opponent.

Though Eithan didn't tend to show others his preparations, he *did* prepare. He had done his research on the Path of Celestial Radiance, with its various techniques to control the madra of others. He had abandoned his scissors because the power inside them would only be another point of vulnerability.

Besides, *she* wouldn't be using a weapon. She hadn't at any point in the competition. He suspected it was one of the terms that allowed her to compete.

Sha Miara had inherited her powers from a Monarch. Though they were sealed down to the Underlord level, she would be in every way an ideal Underlady. Her physical and spiritual abilities would have reached the limit of what her body and soul were capable of handling.

Her madra capacity might be no less than his, her control

would almost certainly be better, her regeneration faster, and she had inherited some measure of her mother's long experience. She was *almost* an impossible opponent to defeat one-on-one.

She knew he was an Arelius. Still wearing that expression of icy royal detachment, she took over the surrounding space with her rainbow madra.

Eithan's bloodline powers went dark as the lines of madra he typically spread all around him left his control. He could still feel, see, and hear everything in *most* of the arena, but a chunk around Sha Miara was a void.

He would have to do this with his normal senses.

The invisible wall separating the two contestants vanished as Northstrider's command echoed: "Begin."

Eithan kicked off, Enforcing his body.

As he dashed into action, he used a whisper of madra to activate a simple device in his pocket. It was not a weapon, and was in fact useless in combat, so the Ninecloud Soul had allowed it.

But thinking about that device was a distraction, so he put it out of his mind and gave himself entirely to the fight.

While the Monarch's voice still echoed, Eithan launched a punch at Miara's face.

Nine-colored eyes tracked him easily, and her hand pushed his aside. In the same motion, she spun into a technique with her other hand.

The heel of Eithan's left hand caught her in the chin, sending a pulse of pure madra through her head.

She was lifted off her feet in a blow that would have rattled anyone else, but her technique was not interrupted.

The Moonheart Iron body. Developed in a country neighboring Ninecloud, it had been co-opted by the royal family to make up for some of their weaknesses.

Not only did it toughen the body and allow for impressive physical feats, its main feature was that trauma to the body did not affect mental or spiritual control whatsoever. It was more than just resisting pain; a high-grade Moonheart Iron body separated the consciousness from the flesh. She could fight as though controlling herself at a distance.

Eithan knew that, so he gave her no space.

Before her body flew away from the force of his first blow, he grabbed the collar of her robe and prepared the Hollow Armor.

Her technique, a net of rainbow light, landed on him. Her Absolute Decree was meant to sink through his skin and restrict his spirit, subjecting him to her control, but it landed on a layer of pure madra around him instead.

He dropped his own technique the instant hers landed, instead of wasting madra to leave it up. The Absolute Decree was disrupted but not broken, but it had been weakened enough that his inherent spiritual defenses destroyed it.

That created an opening as Miara tried and failed to control him. In that second, he swept her legs out from under her. He tried to slam her into the ground, but she spun out of his grip, using the aura control of her soulfire to push against the air and gain unnatural leverage.

He had already begun Forging stars of madra over her head.

The Crown of the Hollow King.

She raised one hand to take them over, and that was the mistake that gave him the victory.

There was one reliable way to defeat an opponent with superior raw abilities: skill.

Sha Miara was *too* focused on her power to take over his techniques. There had been an instant in which she could have seized the lead in the fight instead of staying on the defensive.

She'd missed it. He wouldn't give her another chance.

Now he was one move ahead.

While she was taking over his floating crown of blue-white stars, he used his Striker technique: the Hollow Spear.

At higher levels of advancement, this technique would show its true power. As it was, it was just a hyper-compressed beam of pure madra designed to stab a hole through madra-based defenses.

But he knew what she would do against the Spear, so he started another technique. The Hollow King's Mantle.

Madra swirled around his body in a vortex.

She conjured the Nine-Light Mirror, a circle of royal madra bigger than her body. His spear sunk into it and was reflected, blasting back at him with an added rainbow light that showed her power had been added to his.

The Nine-Light Mirror caught techniques and returned them stronger...but he had a similar power of his own.

The whirlpool of madra around him, the Hollow King's Mantle, caught his returned spear. It whipped the Striker technique around his body in an orbit and flung it at Sha Miara.

To avoid wasting madra and cutting off her own view, Miara dropped the Mirror as soon as she could. Once she did, there was a delay before she could activate it again.

He had expected that. Before the fight had even started.

And he'd timed his Mantle accordingly.

The Hollow Spear pierced her chest the instant the Nine-Light Mirror vanished.

The Spear might inflict some spiritual damage, but at this level it was better at breaking techniques than enemies. At best, it would disrupt any Enforcer techniques she had forming.

Now he was two moves ahead.

He closed the gap an instant behind the Spear, Forging more stars for the Hollow King's Crown overhead. This time, he infused soulfire into the technique, so the stars formed larger and brighter.

The next move he used wasn't technically part of the Path of the Hollow King, but he thought it was appropriate under the circumstances.

He lowered himself to slam an Empty Palm into Sha Miara's core.

The restricted Monarch might as well have been a training dummy. She was so far on the defensive that she reacted only along straight, predictable lines. She leaped back to try to create distance while moving to block his palm strike and hurling rainbow madra up into the sky.

Too easy to read. He had already aimed for where she was going.

His makeshift Empty Palm landed. Her royal madra dispersed, and the Crown of the Hollow King finished Forging.

Even with the Moonheart Iron body, her eyes went wide. She could still read and react to the battle with perfect clarity, but her spirit had fallen briefly out of her control. Her Iron body could do nothing to protect her from emotional shock.

Now that Eithan was three moves ahead, he had a decision to make.

End it immediately, or draw it out to show off more? Which would have more impact?

In his usual state of mind, he would have continued to show off. But he had told his students he wouldn't hold back.

Five stars from the Crown speared down, driving through her madra channels and severing her spirit.

It was the most savage spiritual attack of which he was capable, and ninety-nine out of one hundred sacred artists would be killed or permanently disabled. But he had to assume Celestial Radiance sacred artists had superior spiritual defenses.

Which was where his remaining two attacks came into play.

A Hollow Spear suffused with soulfire pierced her lower abdomen as black scissors flashed into his hand. He couldn't safely activate the Archlord binding within, but he didn't need to. The weapon was a perfect conductor for madra and soulfire.

He Enforced the weapon and drove it through her temple.

No sooner had he pierced the skin than she dissolved into white light.

Eithan sent one more pulse of pure madra into the device in his pocket: a stopwatch.

Nine seconds.

Longer than he'd thought. Maybe he'd wasted too much time after all.

Lindon and Yerin watched the fight from the Akura audience platform. A haze of shadow hid them from the outside, though from this side it was like watching through a thin gray mist.

Mercy was with Fury, Pride, Charity, and the other core members of her family somewhere on the floating mountain over their heads, and Lindon found himself wishing he could see their reactions.

The surrounding crowd cheered enthusiastically but with restraint, as though they wished to go wild but considered themselves too refined.

Only Lindon and Yerin were silent.

"V-victory," the Ninecloud Soul announced. She sounded either hesitant or horrified. Probably both.

"Bleed me dry," Yerin whispered.

In addition to knowing Sha Miara's true identity, they had seen recordings of Sha Miara's previous performance. She was supposed to have been guaranteed a spot among the Uncrowned.

Was this what pure madra could do?

Lindon's mind was already itching to dissect the fight one moment at a time.

[That was a little slow, don't you think?] Dross asked him.

"Slow?"

[We could have done it faster.]

A puzzle piece clicked into place for Lindon. Eithan had fought like Lindon did with one of Dross' combat solutions: as though he could see moves before they happened.

But, for Lindon, sometimes that wasn't enough. Sometimes moving perfectly couldn't erase the sheer difference in strength, or speed, or spiritual power.

So what could?

He chewed on that problem as the crowds in most of the

other viewing platforms roared, excited to have seen a one-sided beatdown, but their cheers didn't matter. They didn't know who Sha Miara really was.

The only opinions that mattered were those in the Monarch platforms overhead.

Charity applauded a handful of times, mindful of her dignity, as she watched on the viewing tablet. A few of the other members of the Akura head family expressed more excitement than she could show, given her position, though she was quite pleased herself.

Her first selection from the vassal factions had always been Eithan Arelius, the Underlord that had once caught even Malice's eye. He had reached the peak of Underlord at a young age, ready to advance to Overlord as soon as he discovered the revelation that would trigger his transformation.

On top of which, he had the legendary Arelius bloodline legacy and a great deal of personal skill. If only he didn't have that personality, he would be a perfect sacred artist.

She glanced over to her father, to see how he'd taken the results.

He was sitting on the edge of his chair, holding his own viewing tablet an inch from his red eyes. "Mercy," he asked, "we can't let this guy go back to House Arelius. I can't *believe* I almost missed this match."

They were supposed to have departed that morning, but Fury had delayed their departure at the last minute in order to watch the day's fight. Pride had given up his chance to spectate to help prepare the Akura family cloudship.

Mercy didn't look as excited as Charity had expected. She seemed disturbed. "Is the Ninecloud Court going to...do something to Eithan?"

"They can't admit who he beat. And they can't provoke the Abidan either."

"What are you concerned about?" Charity asked. Clearly, there was something going on here that she had not been privy to.

Perhaps they were referring to Sha Miara's identity as a direct descendant of Sha Leiala, but Charity had worked that one out on her own.

Fury waved a hand. "Oh right, I forgot to tell you. Sha Miara is their Monarch."

Charity gave that a moment to sink in.

Her father had known this the entire time.

And he hadn't told her.

With a wave of her hand and an exercise of will, she dropped him into a portal of absolute darkness.

It came out five thousand feet in the air, somewhere over the Ninecloud countryside. She hadn't been precise with her coordinates, and working without a spoken command tended to be more difficult.

He would fly back easily enough, but at least now he might remember her irritation and consider her feelings next time.

Mercy raised a hand as though waiting for permission to speak. "Um...Aunt Charity...what does this mean?"

The cool spirit of the Heart Sage had already returned. "It means that we may have better chances in this contest than we feared."

Veris Arelius clutched the railing of her viewing platform and stared out at Eithan.

"We have to bring him home!"

Her cousin, Altavian, grunted. "You think we can offer him more than the Akura Monarch?"

"If he can beat the Ninecloud champion so easily, then

he's a peak Underlord. With talent like that, he might reach Archlord inside twenty years. He could be our next Sage!"

She was already dreaming of everything they could do with an Arelius Uncrowned. The notoriety alone would improve their relationships with other factions, and as a powerful Lord, he could help them secure more of their old territory.

With him, they soon wouldn't have to bow to anyone under Sage. Even if he lost his next match, House Arelius couldn't afford to throw away anyone with such talent in their bloodline legacy.

But with his talents *combined* with his bloodline skills...

Altavian sighed. "He says he'll help us. We have no choice but to trust him."

Veris ground her teeth.

When Naru Saeya picked up her jaw, she started crafting a message to her brother.

Two of the eight Uncrowned were going to be Blackflame Underlords.

If Huan didn't know how to leverage that into an advantage, he wouldn't be the Emperor. Besides that, she wished she could see his face when he viewed the dream tablet and saw what Eithan had done to the best young Underlord in the Ninecloud Court.

Then again...maybe he wouldn't be too surprised.

Reigan Shen swirled wine in his goblet and thought.

He was the only one in this room of his private platform. The platform itself was a miniature marble palace, and the other chambers were filled with servants and revelers, but he watched the fights alone.

Especially this one.

Eithan probably didn't know it, but Reigan remembered him. Eithan had been an advisor of Tiberian's, in the last days. One of those who had pointed Tiberian toward the Dreadgods, and who had allowed Reigan to strike the fatal blow.

One might say that, in some twisted way, Reigan owed Eithan a debt.

And now he had proven himself an obstacle. Someone capable of defeating Sha Miara could potentially beat Sopharanatoth or Yan Shoumei.

He might claim Penance.

A wide wall of gold curved behind Reigan Shen, displaying his treasured weapons. Priceless works of art, and most could be considered the peak of Soulsmith craftsmanship.

Not as devastating as the ones he kept in his King's Key, but deadly and beautiful, every one of them.

Penance was destined to be the crown jewel of Shen's collection, and he didn't intend to *use* it at all. There was usually far more value in the threat of a weapon than in the weapon itself.

Besides, if Eithan got his hands on the arrowhead, he would use it on Reigan Shen.

Eithan was under Malice's protection, not to mention Northstrider's, so Reigan couldn't threaten him directly. He would have held the remainder of House Arelius hostage to ensure Eithan's withdrawal from the competition, but the heavens had removed that option.

Still, he had others.

Every man had his price.

Sha Miara materialized—not in her waiting room, but in her Monarch platform. She was surrounded by opulent decorations: stained glass, gorgeous furniture, ornamental spirits, and light of every color.

She trembled with rage.

Royal madra blazed up around her as space warped and cracked. Her veil faded, the restrictions on her falling away as her oaths were completed.

Sha Relliar tackled her.

Her Herald was a big man, and he tackled her more than just physically, pitting the full might of his spirit and will against hers. In her weakened state, it was enough to disperse her power.

The impact didn't rattle her, though she stared up at the ceiling several hundred yards from where she'd started.

But the extra seconds she'd been given to consider her actions cooled her off.

Her ancestors—her mother—lent her their wisdom. They couldn't speak to her, though she sometimes wished they would, but she could borrow their instincts. She felt their collective reaction to her behavior.

They disapproved.

She shouldn't show her anger in front of the other Monarchs. Not only could they shut down anything she tried, but she would look like a petulant child. And not just to the Monarchs, but to a heavenly messenger as well.

Just like in the arena. She'd let herself be knocked around like a helpless child.

Embarrassment fueled rage, but the sense of her ancestors brought her back to herself. The Luminous Queen wouldn't lose control.

Dignity came from maturity, and maturity meant accepting reality. Her mother had taught her that.

Sha Miara repeated those words like a mantra as she pushed Sha Relliar away. "Thank you, Relliar," she said, unwilling to look him in the eye. She levitated to her feet. "I apologize, that was unbecoming of me."

Though she wasn't watching him, she knew he was looking at her in suspicion. "I apologize, Your Highness, but I believe you may wish to veil yourself again."

"Nonsense," she said. "A gracious queen would not let something like this rattle her."

Even if she *had* been beaten by an Underlord for all the world to see, she wasn't an idiot. She had put herself in a scenario where it was possible. Forced herself into that scenario, really. Seeking vengeance, even petty revenge, would be unbecoming and dishonorable.

"Your...pardon, Monarch, but a *truly* gracious queen would send the winner a congratulatory gift."

With a brief flex of soulfire-controlled aura, she hurled a piano at him.

Sophara coiled herself in the center of a circle of eight natural treasures. A stone head wept tears of diamond, radiating earth aura, opposite an old weathervane that spun in the wind it generated. Water opposite fire, life opposite death, light opposite shadow.

There were many ways to balance aura, but this was a classic. The aura was strong and stable. Perfect for advancement.

The Gate of Heaven elixir spun through her madra channels, a living ball of liquid silver energy.

Sophara was in her serpentine dragon form, which had taken her most of the day to achieve. She had to make herself more human when she advanced, and it was easier to start in a body that was further from her ideal.

Her grandmother Xorrus, a Herald, watched in her perfect

human body. Her golden hair shimmered like the sun, and her limbs were in flawless proportion. Even her eyes were human circles instead of draconic slits.

Sophara hoped to be so beautiful soon.

"This is only an attempt," Xorrus said. "Be cautious. If it feels like advancement will be too much of a burden, then do not begin."

To win this tournament, Sophara's family had stuffed her with powers, elixirs, Divine Treasures, and enhancements of every description. They had pushed her beyond the maximum capacity of an Underlady.

And she had performed flawlessly.

Anyone with less skill and willpower would have collapsed, unable to bear the weight, their spirit ruined. The fact that Sophara could use the sacred arts at such a level was testament to her greatness.

But even for her, there were side effects.

Supposedly.

Sophara had seen none. She trusted her grandmother and was cautious, but she had felt no pain in her spirit. Whoever decided where the limits of the Underlord stage were, they had never met her.

She could handle even more.

"You don't need to worry about me, Grandmother." If Xorrus had a flaw, it was that she cared too deeply about her family.

The Herald frowned. "It's not wrong to have limits. Only to show them to the enemy."

Sophara knew she must have limits, she was just certain they hadn't reached hers yet.

Advancing while bound to more power than she could control would only worsen the imbalance, causing permanent spiritual damage. If this advancement went wrong, then she would—at best—find herself unable to ever advance to Archlord.

The longer she stayed at the Underlord stage, the more stable her spirit would be. If she were cautious, she would wait to advance.

But no other Underlord could handle the amount of power she *already* had.

She had the will to do this.

"I'm ready to begin," Sophara said, settling her chin onto the floor and tapping into her soulfire.

Xorrus' disapproval was silent.

The Gate of Heaven elixir seeped out of her spirit and into her body, and the pressure of the surrounding aura felt ten times stronger. She could feel it so clearly, the power of the world cradling her, resonating with her spirit.

Her madra channels fractured immediately.

Before she could even scream, Xorrus had wrapped her will around Sophara and pulled the Gate of Heaven elixir back, the advancement canceled before it began.

Sophara's screams lasted for several minutes before they died down, and then she hurriedly inspected her channels.

She visualized them as a network of bright orange lines running throughout her spirit, and now *tiny* hairline fractures—so small she could barely see them—ran up and down the length of those channels.

The pain subsided quickly, but the fear was worse.

She hadn't even come close to successfully advancing. The pain was *instant.*

Xorrus sighed. "Do you know what would have happened if you had been here alone?"

"I would have failed," Sophara said. Her words shivered.

"Not quite. You would have successfully advanced to Overlord, but your Path would have ended there." Xorrus put a hand on the side of Sophara's snout—in this form, Sophara's head was practically bigger than the Herald's entire body. "Do not be afraid. Let this *encourage* you."

Sophara didn't see how this could possibly be encouraging.

"If you are so damaged, then only the collective attention of the Monarchs can restore you. Which is the prize of the victor." Xorrus gave her a comforting smile.

"You have a way to defeat any opponent for certain.

But if you use it, you have to win. Win or die. Isn't that comforting?"

In a strange way, it was.

第四章

CHAPTER FOUR

The Akura cloudship was so sleek that it looked smaller than it really was, though it had carried Lindon along with hundreds of Akura tournament visitors and their servants.

Now, it hovered at the end of the dock as people boarded it again. Many were members of the Akura family, but Lindon had also seen members of the Frozen Blade School and others he didn't recognize.

Mercy's brother Pride directed most of the traffic. The short Underlord shouted orders constantly while lifting luggage or leaping around to attend to a task himself.

Lindon had tried to get his attention several times, but it seemed Pride was deliberately ignoring him.

Then Mercy ran out onto the dock, waving. "Good-bye, everybody! Sorry I'm late!" She came to a halt by Lindon, grinding her staff on the stone of the dock.

Immediately, Pride landed in a crouch next to Lindon.

He straightened and addressed his sister. "Mercy. Thank you for coming to see us off." He sounded painfully stiff.

Mercy threw her arms around him. "Try to be safe. Don't poke any Dreadgods."

"I'm not a fool." He pushed her away and glared at Lindon. "Is there something I can help you with, Lindon?"

[At least he's calling you by name!] Dross pointed out.

Lindon looked over the ship. "Apologies, I only wondered where everyone was going. Are you traveling to the Dreadgod?"

"The Wandering Titan has made his way to the edge of Akura territory. We go to protect the people and to drive away the vultures."

That was a relief. He had worried that the Akura family might leave the Titan to its own devices. He had to assume that the "vultures" Pride mentioned were the Dreadgod cultists. "You mean Abyssal Palace?"

"Of course, Abyssal Palace." Pride sounded like he was speaking to an idiot. "But there are always scavengers around a Dreadgod. Not just the cults."

Naru Saeya passed them, a huge trunk floating on wind aura behind her. She bowed to the two Akura, who both commended her on her performance in the tournament.

As soon as she could manage, she escaped the conversation and pulled Lindon over to the side. "When you make it back to the Empire," she said, "present yourself to the Emperor. You have done us proud."

"Gratitude. If you don't mind me asking, why aren't you coming home?"

She rubbed her thumb and fingers together. "The Akura family is paying a dragon's ransom for Lords and Ladies who can fight over the Titan. If you can slip away from Eithan, you should join me. And so should he, if he ever gets the chance."

Lindon thanked her as she waved him off and joined the rest of the passengers. She was half a head taller than almost everyone else, and the peacock feathers over her ear made her stand out further.

Most of the eliminated Uncrowned competitors seemed to be aboard, so Lindon had a new question when he rejoined Mercy and Pride. "Why do they need Underlords?"

Pride made a dismissive sound. "We need Lords more than anything. Controlling the populace, defending our claim, herding refugees, clearing the land of natural treasures before the Dreadgod razes it...honestly, you can't afford to be this badly informed."

Lindon's usual annoyance with Pride swelled to anger, but he kept a façade of polite behavior. He pressed both fists together. "My apologies that I was not born into a Monarch family."

"It doesn't matter if you were *born* into one or not. If you want to join our—"

Mercy pushed both of her madra-gloved hands over Pride's mouth. "Ha!" she shouted. "Ha ha! Good one!" It sounded nothing like real laughter, and she shoved Pride so that he stumbled back a step.

He looked genuinely confused.

"Well, we don't want to keep you from your work anymore," Mercy continued. "Stay safe, tell Uncle Fury I'll see him soon, and I'll join you as soon as I can, okay?"

Pride straightened his outer robe. "See me after you *win*."

Then he strode away again, already barking orders.

[Maybe he'll be eaten by a Dreadgod,] Dross mused.

Lindon didn't want to spend any more time than necessary around the man, but he didn't wish Pride any harm. Just some humility.

Mercy put her hand on Lindon's shoulder and spun him around, so they were walking through the wind and back toward their amethyst tower. "So did you know Eithan could fight like that?" she asked, and Lindon got the distinct impression she was trying to take the subject away from Pride.

"You've seen as much of his ability as I have. He might still be holding back."

She looked doubtful, but shrugged. "Could be! I don't see him performing much better without advancing to Overlord, but if he has anything else in his pocket, he'll be a tough one. I'll need practice."

"Apologies if this seems rude, but I've never seen everything *you* can do either."

Any opponents Lindon had seen Mercy face had either grossly outclassed her or hadn't pushed her to her limit. He still didn't know what her Book of Eternal Night was capable of.

"You will soon!" she said cheerfully. "I wish I could invite you to watch me train, but a lot of it happens inside my Book, so it's pretty boring to watch. But if they match me against Sophara, you'll get to see every card I have to play."

"What about Yerin?" he asked.

He had been curious about this ever since Northstrider had announced that Yerin and Mercy were going to fight each other. That had ended up being a lie, but he had still wanted to ask Mercy how she rated her matchup against Yerin.

Her face fell, and she dragged Suu along the ground for a second. "Yeah...I'm hoping I don't meet Yerin until the finals. It's hard to enjoy the competition when my mother's life is on the line, you know? But at least we have three allies in the top eight!"

She hadn't fought her fourth round yet, but Lindon noticed she had no doubts about winning her way into the Uncrowned.

She also hadn't answered his question.

"Six fights left," Mercy said. "Six days. After that, the Uncrowned will be taken away for a month of Sage training."

Lindon gave a heavy sigh. He'd heard about that already. The reason Eithan and Yerin weren't here with him was because of their status in the top eight. They were having their souls measured for the Broken Crown construct and being interviewed for written accounts of their experience.

The interview was new. Eithan had tracked down scribes of his own volition.

Mercy was waiting for him to respond, but when he didn't, she pressed on.

"So you have the rest of the week with Yerin. What are you going to do?"

They had reached the door of the tower, but Mercy turned to watch the cloudship, which was still loading.

"I'm not sure," Lindon said, watching the people bustle around the deck. "We need to spar a few rounds. There are a few ideas I have to work out after our match, and I know she could be more comfortable with the Final Sword—"

Mercy's staff cracked against the top of his skull.

He flinched back, and the violet gemstone eyes of the dragon-headed staff hissed at him.

"What are you going to do *with Yerin?*"

Lindon took a slow step away from the staff. "Of course, I'm going to train with her every day. She doesn't have a minute to waste, and Dross and I can help."

Mercy closed her eyes and took a deep breath.

[She's trying to say—] Dross began, but Lindon cut him off by speaking.

"I know what you're trying to say. But I'm telling you the truth. *That* is what I'm going to do with Yerin for the rest of the week."

He wanted to work out his feelings for Yerin, and he wanted to do so *with* her. Her month of training with a Sage felt like a punishment looming over him.

It wasn't so long ago that he had been dragged off to the Akura family for training, and he hadn't enjoyed being separated from her then. Now he would be completely alone.

At least he had plenty of training to occupy his time.

In light of broader events, Yerin leaving was the right thing to do. They needed every advantage they could get to win the tournament.

Mercy's purple eyes slowly opened. "I hear you. Now, pretend there *wasn't* so much at stake. What would you do if everything was calm, and you had plenty of time?"

He examined his own mind. It was embarrassing having all this pulled out of him in public, but Mercy was a friend. And she was only trying to help.

"I would want to try doing something together. With her."

It felt like a shameful admission, but it was clearly the right answer, because Mercy shone. It looked like she was about to start hopping up and down.

"There it is! I thought you never did anything fun."

"I don't usually," he said defensively. "I don't waste—"

"I know, I know, shut up. Listen. You had the right instinct. This week, invite her out to do something. Just the two of you."

She leaned uncomfortably close, looking up at him to make sure she had his full attention. *"Not. Training.* Nothing that could *conceivably* lead to advancement in the sacred arts. Do you understand?"

Lindon's face was hot. This whole conversation was an exercise in agony, but he could easily imagine hearing the same thing from his sister. Or his mother.

His father would tell him that anything other than working was a waste of time...but even *he* had ended up married.

"I will invite her," he said. "But her time is so short as it is."

"Lindon, I promise you—I *promise* you—that a few hours off will not do Yerin any harm at all."

Therian Nills was an ordinary man.

He had started as a farmer and the son of farmers, and he still boggled at the twist of fate that had brought him all the way to the Uncrowned King tournament.

He had been born on the Rosegold continent, but far enough away from everything that the great Houses were nothing but distant rumors to him.

Then the Weeping Dragon had brought down the sky.

Therian had lost everything before the Stormcallers found him. They followed the Dreadgod around, capturing its unique madra in themselves and using its divine techniques to steal the madra of others. They sheltered him, taught him, and trained him.

It turned out he had a knack for it, although you wouldn't know it from looking at him. His Underlord transformation hadn't changed him much; he still looked like the son of a farmer, tall and gangly with sun-baked skin and hair the color of mud.

His combat training had built an entirely new set of muscles on him, but his appearance still couldn't be compared to these beautifully carved men and women he was competing against. Most of his competitors looked like they had been sculpted by the heavens themselves.

But over the course of the tournament, his confidence had grown. Thanks to the power of the Weeping Dragon, he had been made as good as they were. He could keep up with any of them.

Most of them.

He sat in his waiting room, unable to control his nerves, bouncing one leg and squeezing his fingers together, as he stared at the stone door as though he could keep it from opening with the force of his gaze.

"I'm just glad it won't be the Dawnwing," Therian said for what might have been the fifteenth time.

His sect brother and team member, Calan Archer, darkened. "I don't know how someone like him is allowed to fight Underlords."

Therian had been too young and too newly inducted into the Stormcallers to be sent to fight against the Dawnwing Sect, but Calan had been there.

He was older than Therian by almost ten years, and *he* looked like he belonged in the tournament. He was thick with muscle, his Goldsigns crackling around thick biceps. The scripted rings of blue-gold lightning looked like they were about to burst off. His hair was blond so pale that it was almost white, and he had a scar across one eye socket.

He had seen battle. *He* belonged in places like this.

So do you, Therian reminded himself.

Calan smacked him on the back of the head. "Focus. Sharpen yourself. You carry the power of the Weeping

Dragon with you. The power of the Sage of Calling Storms. If you go no further, you are already in the top *sixteen* of all Underlords in our generation."

The encouragement worked. He breathed deeper, his madra cycling more easily, his leg going still.

"And you *will* go further," Calan continued. "You were meant to fight Ziel, but they're changing the matchups, so it won't be him. Whoever else is out there, our battle plan remains the same. You will leave them in the sand, and you and I will meet again as Uncrowned."

Calan Archer thought Therian could fight alongside him.

Therian held that golden thought as the door slid open. He called his weapons—a pair of long spears that crawled with smooth yellow light—and focused his madra. The rings around his own arms crackled as the noise from the crowd reached him.

The arena was covered in irregular stone, uneven footing, with fist-sized rocks lying here and there. Lightning swam like snakes overhead, but didn't dive to the ground.

Across the stadium, he faced a man who appeared to be in his early twenties, with dark and messy hair falling around a pair of short green horns that glowed faintly even in the light.

He wore the expression of a man who had walked a thousand miles and might collapse at any second, only dust and apathy in his eyes. A gray cloak fluttered on his shoulders, and he dragged a massive two-handed warhammer behind him as though he could barely support its weight.

Therian and his opponent saw each other at the same time.

The enemy's eyes went from utterly dead to alight with rage. The warhammer gradually rose, inch by inch, lifted in one hand until it was propped against his shoulder.

Calan clapped Therian on the back. "No shame in top sixteen."

"Ziel of the Dawnwing Sect, chosen of Northstrider, you face Therian Nills of the Stormcallers, chosen of Reigan Shen!"

Therian had heard the heavenly messenger's command. He knew he couldn't give up.

But he wondered: if he stood still and let Ziel kill him, would his death be painless?

One more look at the burning fury in Ziel's face, and Therian shuddered.

Probably not.

Therian hefted his spears and prepared to fight for a quick death.

Lindon sat next to Yerin and watched Ziel batter a Dreadgod cultist all the way around the arena.

His techniques on the Path of the Dawn Oath were honestly fascinating. Ziel's Path was a variation of one that Eithan had offered Lindon long ago, and though he had chosen Blackflame, he had never forgotten his interest in this Path.

It was supposed to be a flexible force Path for Soulsmiths and skilled scriptors, and Lindon could see why. Rings of script appeared in midair, Forged by Ziel in an instant. Glowing green symbols circled his wrists and his ankles, and more green rings appeared beneath him when he jumped and where his hammer landed.

The runes he Forged crackled, jumped, and faded in and out as they lost stability. The damage to Ziel's spirit was so extensive that Lindon found it incredible the man could practice the sacred arts at all.

He still gave off spiritual pressure more like a Truegold than an Underlord, but Lindon's research implied he had once been an Archlord. His skills and experience had been enough to carry him this far.

Though watching him toy with his opponent, it was easy to think the power gap ran the other way. Every swing of Ziel's hammer launched Therian Nills into one of the arena walls or slammed him into the ground.

Sometimes, a green script encircled one of the rocks on the ground and hurled it with great force at Therian, stopping a Stormcaller technique or simply drawing blood.

As a survivor of round two, Ziel must have earned an Archlord weapon, but Lindon didn't see him use anything but the same hammer he'd used back in Ghostwater.

[Maybe it only *looks* like the same hammer,] Dross proposed. [It could be a fancy new Archlord weapon made to catch people off-guard.]

Do you think so?

[No.]

Little Blue stood on Lindon's head to watch. She was surprisingly excited, cheering every time Ziel scored a hit. He would have expected her to be scared, and he wondered what the fight looked like through her eyes.

Yerin nudged him. "Give you two diamonds and a pile of gold if you can tell me how that blood bag made it this far."

As far as I did, Lindon realized, and he pretended the thought didn't hurt.

Therian Nills did resemble a bag full of bloody meat more than a human being, and Lindon felt a wince of sympathy for him. At least he would be healed completely whenever Ziel decided to end the match.

"His Striker techniques are powerful," Lindon said. They were alive, like Jai Long's had been. "Last round, he didn't let his opponent close to him."

"I'd bet my soul against a rat's tail that either of us could tear him apart with both hands and both feet tied."

Lindon knew that she was as frustrated by his elimination as he was. Maybe more so, in a different way. She had enjoyed fighting him all-out, but she'd wanted to meet him as Uncrowned.

Even so, he didn't want to keep thinking about it.

[Not that I can hear your thoughts or anything, but it seems like you're trying not to think about something else.]

Little Blue stuck her head down to stare into his eye.

I'm waiting until the match is over, Lindon told Dross.

There was too much on the line for him to interrupt the match. It seemed clear that Ziel was going to win, but you never knew what sorts of life-saving trump cards an enemy might have in store. If Ziel won, that would mean one more ally in the top eight, and his loss would mean that Reigan Shen had another chance at Penance.

Lindon focused on his Heaven and Earth Purification Wheel, pushing a burning circle uphill as slowly as possible.

Though he'd practiced the cycling technique for years, it was still uncomfortable. As always, it felt like he was breathing through a damp cloth, his lungs and spirit straining with every cycle of his madra. But that made the technique a better distraction.

For a few seconds.

Then Ziel's hammer crushed Therian's head, and his body dissolved into white light. So did the blood he'd left all over the arena.

There was a surprising amount.

"Victory!" the Ninecloud Soul announced, and the projection of light overhead showed an image of a dull-eyed Ziel dragging his hammer away.

[Oh, would you look at that!] Dross observed. [It seems the match is over.]

Little Blue gave an encouraging chime.

Yerin stood up and stretched, extending her steel madra sword-arms as well. "Guess you could call that a fight. Let's grab some food while they finish up the tablets."

They had examined the records of every fight together, analyzing Yerin's future opponents.

Though Lindon couldn't get a full breath, he spoke. "Apologies, but tomorrow night, would you like to go with me to—"

"Yes."

She looked like she might say more, but after considering for a moment she only nodded once. "Yes" apparently said it all.

But she had answered too easily. He worried she thought

he was just inviting her to eat together while training, as they often did.

"I mean, I was thinking something different than normal. We can reserve—"

Her reply was even faster this time: "Yes."

That was clear enough.

"...okay. I will...do that, then." And then, because he wanted her to see that he hadn't been forced into this, he gave her a shaky smile. "Gratitude. I'm looking forward to it."

"Same on my side."

He still couldn't read her face. Sometimes she turned bright red, but now she seemed normal to him.

As they ordered lunch from a Ninecloud servant and ate while discussing Ziel's performance, she was unusually quiet. In one lull in the conversation, he noticed her breath coming at odd intervals.

She was breathing according to her cycling technique. Keeping her madra and feelings under control.

Just like he was.

"You've reserved the *best* table?" Mercy asked, looking from Lindon to Yerin.

"Yes. Gratitude." Lindon had been more than willing to book an ordinary table at the restaurant Mercy had recommended, but she had informed him that the Akura family was paying the tab and *insisted* he order the best.

Since she was funding it, she had every right to ask, but Lindon wasn't sure this was the best time.

"Is this really what you want to be talking about *now?*"

Mercy was in her full Akura uniform, purple and black and white, with Suu in one hand and a violet lens over her left eye. Her hair had been tied back, and she limbered up as she spoke.

Her waiting room door was set to open at any moment.

"We cleaned out every tablet on record," Yerin said. "The worst left in the tournament is still no training dummy."

Ulrok Crag-Strider was the one Ghost-Blade remaining in the competition, and Lindon agreed with Dross and Yerin that he was most likely Mercy's opponent. It was either him or the girl from the Silent Servants whose name Lindon had difficulty pronouncing, but Mercy believed it would be Ulrok.

Her mother considered brute-force fighters weaker than clever ones, and Ghost-Blades were not subtle. They practiced a Path of sword and death madra, so their fights tended to be brief.

There were other, lesser aspects of their Path that tended to make them difficult to read with spiritual perception, but those were negligible.

"You'll need to dress up tonight," Mercy warned them, stretching out one arm and then the other. "Yerin, come to my room when you're getting ready. Lindon, wear whatever Eithan tells you."

She thought about that for a second, then added, "Within reason."

Lindon appreciated the addition, because he could easily imagine Eithan telling him to go to the restaurant in some kind of costume. Or a wig.

But he was still concerned about Mercy's attitude. The safety of the entire Blackflame Empire was on the line, not to mention her own mother's life, but she was acting as carefree as usual.

"We can talk about this later," he said. "Are you ready for this? You have a strategy?"

The door started to grind up, and Mercy gave them a sheepish smile. "Sorry. You two had one guaranteed loss and one guaranteed win, and Eithan's match was *supposed* to be a loss for him. Which means the weakest opponent was left for me."

The Ninecloud Soul called her name and Ulrok Crag-Strider. As expected.

The Ghost-Blade was a hulking brute of a man in dark gray robes, with lines of black paint covering his face and a swirling green-tinged spirit over his head. He held a rough saber like an oversized cleaver in both hands.

As the Ninecloud Soul called the names of both competitors, Mercy turned over her shoulder and waved cheerily. "See you in a minute!" she called.

Mercy walked through a darkened arena, which had been sealed off by a massive stretch of shadow madra like a tent's roof. Sharpened bones rose from the ground, giving off death and sword aura in equal measure.

The arena favored neither of them, though Ulrok was trying to gain a psychological advantage by pushing against the invisible wall separating them, snarling like a beast and brandishing his rough saber.

He should have saved his breath. Mercy had done her research.

Back in his homeland, Ulrok was a famous poet and philosopher known for his musings on the nature of the soul. Pretending to be an animalistic brute would only work on someone who didn't know him.

Besides, Mercy was already scared. Just not of him.

She was frightened for her family.

Impassive as always, Northstrider stood between the two competitors. The Ninecloud Soul was probably continuing their introduction, but the thick layer of shadow madra blocked out the sound.

"Do not make light of your opponent," Northstrider said. "Either of you."

He was looking at her when he said that, and Mercy nodded earnestly. The violet lens of the Moon's Eye hung over her left eye, like a layer of stained glass.

It had been her Archlord reward for surviving the second round, selected especially for her. Though it had no binding, it was cleverly made from layers of transparent Remnant eyes.

The device had all sorts of vision-related applications, and she was grateful for it. She examined Ulrok, noticing that he was already spiraling his gray-green madra to his sword. The signature Forger technique of his Path, she was sure.

Mercy smiled and dipped her head to him.

Northstrider waited a moment longer, then raised a hand. "Begin!"

Ulrok's blade whipped in a slash in front of him, Forged madra surrounding it in a ghostly echo. The gray light passed over her.

Mercy covered herself in crystalline armor.

The Ghost Blade technique crashed against the amethyst plates and broke, while Mercy raised Suu. The staff was already in its bow form, its draconic head glaring from the center of the staff, a string of sticky black madra connecting the two ends.

She raised it in gauntleted hands, Forging her String of Shadow into a rigid arrow. The technique was normally a flexible rope of darkness and force, but with practice, she could use it to make arrows.

A Striker technique howled at her like a phantom, and she let it splash against her armor again.

The Akura bloodline armor was well-known and had well-documented weaknesses. It put great pressure on the spirit of the user, it was difficult to control, and repeated attacks could force her to use madra to reinforce it.

Unhurried, she layered another technique onto her arrow, The Enforcer technique from her second page: Dark Tide Incantation.

The light dimmed further and a shadow clung to her arrow, though it was barely visible. This technique carried both spiritual and physical weight.

Ulrok dashed in, closing the gap, slashing with his saber. Not only that, but he had begun gathering the sword and death aura in the air to a point beneath her.

Mercy leaped up and back, spinning away from his

weapon, keeping her concentration on the arrow.

This was all textbook for fighting an Akura. Rapid, agile movements were difficult in the armor, and executing them took extra madra. Keeping the armor up at all was a burden, and it became more so as her defense took a beating.

The plan was to keep up a barrage of weak attacks to force her to exhaust herself with her own defense.

But since those weaknesses were so widely known, any Akura at the Lord stage regularly trained to overcome them.

Her Puppeteer's Iron body made controlling her body effortless as she twisted again in the air, avoiding more Striker techniques. Long practice and training kept her spirit composed as she layered on her third page technique: the Nightworm Venom.

The tip of her arrow took on a dull green cast.

A screaming geyser of green-and-gray madra pierced up from the ground where she was about to land, but she'd seen the Ruler technique through her lens before it formed.

She landed with the geyser an inch away from her face, pulling back her bowstring and taking aim.

As Ulrok dashed in, she layered a final technique onto the arrow: the Shadow's Edge. Harmony's favored technique.

More techniques formed inside Ulrok's spirit, and he charged her like a bull. He was only three feet away, swinging his saber, when she released her arrow.

He gave her a feral, painted grin and unleashed his own prize from the tournament.

A network of bright orange spots bloomed around him, connecting with fiery lines. A matrix of protective madra.

Mercy knew about it already.

Though it was an Archlord instrument, it was gentle enough to be handled easily by Underlords. However, its output scaled down to the power of the user's spirit.

The arrow, seething with four shades of darkness, punched through.

As expected of an Uncrowned King fighter, he reacted in time, moving his saber back to catch the arrow.

The impact punched his weapon back into his own chest, throwing him back twenty feet.

The arrow melted into him.

Mercy let her armor fade away into essence as her combination of techniques squirmed inside him, making him scream, disabling his spirit and eating away at his madra channels.

She winced at the sound and wanted to apologize. It was a competition, so she had to try her best, but she knew from experience how painful that was. She would have preferred to win in a gentler way.

Her bow shifted back to a staff, and she held herself with poise as she waited for him to die. Constructs would be watching her right now, and she had to do her mother proud.

Mercy had to defeat Sophara, and it would help the family if she *looked* like someone who could do it.

The gold dragons had gone overboard in preparing Sophara for the tournament. Too far. It was as though they'd crammed every enhancement they could think of into one body.

Mercy didn't know how Sophara could possibly control so much power. There had to be drawbacks.

And if the dragon won Penance, she would use it on Akura Malice immediately. Her great-grandfather would make sure of it.

Mercy worried for her mother, of course, but not *too* much. Even knowing the danger, she found it hard to bite her nails and fret about the safety of a woman who could literally scoop up mountains in her hand.

She was far more frightened for the rest of her family.

Malice would choose to die rather than leave the world, Mercy was sure. And with her dead, Fury and Charity would take over, but Fury was uncontrollable and Charity unknowable. They would *have* to allow the Dreadgods to invade the Blackflame Empire as Reigan Shen wished, and though they would evacuate as much of the populace as they could, thousands of miles of territory would be destroyed.

And without a Monarch of their own, the family would become easy prey for the others.

Just like House Arelius.

She calmed herself, steeling her nerves against the screaming that had faded to whimpering. Mercy wasn't like her mother, born to the battlefield. But she was good at competitions.

And she would do her duty.

The roof of shadow madra split enough to allow her to hear the Ninecloud Soul declare, "Victory!"

Mercy raised her hand and smiled to the crowd.

第五章

CHAPTER FIVE

The nighttime streets of Ninecloud City didn't differ much from the daytime. The surrounding towers and buildings were all brightly colored and many of them glowed, so the rainbow radiance didn't dim so much as it softened.

Lindon stood in front of the Sundown Pavilion, a wide four-story restaurant lit by shining red-and-orange constructs. Hanging gardens spilled out the front of every window, dotted with burning flowers that gave off strong fire aura.

[You know, showing up early just means you have to wait,] Dross observed.

Lindon would have traveled from the Akura guest tower with Yerin, but Eithan had insisted they meet *at* the restaurant. He still wasn't sure why.

At least Eithan had provided reasonable clothes. They were elaborate multi-layered robes in a style Eithan liked to wear, more suitable for greeting a respected visitor than for fighting, but they weren't in the bright colors Eithan preferred.

They were primarily black, highlighted with decorative red scripts that glowed scarlet. On the back, where Lindon had expected the symbol of the Akura family, was a snarling dragon-turtle that also glowed red and orange.

They had clearly been designed for Lindon, and he hadn't questioned why Eithan had them. Or why they fit perfectly.

Sometimes he just didn't want to know.

Lindon's hair had been brushed and oiled, and a team of Akura servants had applied some kind of cream to his face. He *felt* like he had layers of paint caked on his cheeks, but he only *looked* impossibly clean.

He was keeping his spiritual perception tightly restrained, trying to avoid sensations from everyone and everything on the street, so he didn't notice Yerin had arrived until he heard her low whistle.

"Look at you, all polished and shiny! Have to pay my thanks to Eithan. Thought he might send you here wearing six peacocks."

Yerin wore something like what Mercy had when she had been presented to the entire Akura family: formal layers of black, violet, and silver, but sleeker and slimmer than Lindon's outfit.

Her hair was pinned up by silver sticks, though they left enough free to fall down past her shoulders. Her skin was bright, her lips red, and her eyes bigger than usual. And she wasn't wearing a sword.

Lindon had prepared for this.

He had thought of a number of compliments as he waited, but he was unprepared for the impact of actually seeing her. It was such a contrast to her normal appearance, ready for battle at any second, that the sight of her clubbed him over the head.

She spread her arms, gripping her wide sleeves as she did. "How about Mercy's work? Do we let her live?"

Lindon chose his favorite of the compliments he'd readied in advance.

"You look wonderful," he said, "but I knew you would."

She flushed slightly and dropped her sleeves, brushing at something on the front of her robes. "Yeah, well, she... Mercy's sharp enough, when it comes to this."

[I don't think he was talking about Mercy, I think he was talking about *you*. Unless I'm wrong! I'm not wrong.]

"Dross," Lindon muttered, "apologies, but can you act like you're not here for a while?"

[Oh, I see. Yes. I will pretend I'm not watching you both at every second.]

The streets were packed, thanks to the tournament, and there was a line to get into the restaurant. They chatted as they waited; about Mercy's fight from earlier in the day, about the matches to come, and about who was likely to fill in the remaining spots of the Uncrowned.

When they finally reached a gray-haired man behind a podium wearing what seemed to be one intricate wrap, Lindon bowed and handed over a scripted plate with the Akura symbol on it.

The man checked it, handed it back, and was about to speak when he looked from Lindon to Yerin. His eyes grew wide.

"My sincerest apologies, young miss, young sir, but we... were not aware that *you* were our Akura guests tonight."

Lindon became uncomfortably aware of other people in line and in the restaurant turning and looking at them. He caught snatches of their names and tried to pull his white hand further into his sleeve.

The man looked like he wanted to run inside and attend to something, but he stopped only an inch away as though tethered to the table. "We have made an embarrassing error, and I apologize on behalf of the entire Sundown Pavilion. You see, Sha Siris—the son of our establishment's owner—arrived only minutes ago and demanded the Twilight Room that you requested.

"If he had known that it was *you* who reserved the table, I'm certain that he would never have done so. If you wouldn't mind waiting, I will go and tell him to finish his meal in another—"

A voice bellowed down from upstairs, cutting through the noise of the crowd. "I heard my name!"

The man behind the podium winced and looked around as though for rescue before shouting back. "Master Sha, may I speak to you private—"

"Tell them to come on up!" Sha Siris shouted, and there came a round of raucous laughter.

Lindon acutely felt every eye on them, and he wanted nothing more than to leave. It wasn't entirely fair, but he felt a moment of irritation toward Mercy.

This was why he hadn't wanted too expensive of a restaurant. He didn't know how things worked in Ninecloud City. He didn't know how to handle this.

"If you'll excuse me a moment," the man behind the podium said to Lindon and Yerin, "I will go and speak to our young master."

"What for?" Yerin asked, giving him a feral smile. "He asked us up."

"Send them up here!" Sha Siris shouted again. "I need to be entertained!"

"Not going to be as fun as he thinks," Yerin muttered to Lindon.

A server led them through a maze of packed tables and up some stairs, never meeting their eyes. Everyone else stared at them.

Lindon wondered if there was a polite way to escape.

Sha Siris sat in a dimly lit open room with stars of Forged madra floating a few feet overhead. A sign over the entrance displayed the word "Twilight."

Siris was only a few years into his twenties, with blood-red hair that reminded Lindon of Sha Miara, and his face was filled with so much color that it almost matched his hair. He sat at the lone table in the room, a massive circle groaning under the weight of a feast.

There were eleven other people at the table, all shouting or laughing, most of them visibly drunk. Siris took a swig from a clay mug and cheered as he saw them.

Lindon took a quick sweep with his spiritual perception. Siris himself was an Underlord, and not a weak one, though from the feel of his spirit, Lindon doubted he practiced the Path of Celestial Radiance. Most of those around the table were Underlords too, though some were Truegold and one might have been Highgold.

Upon seeing Lindon and Yerin, one young woman to Siris' left immediately shut her mouth and paled. She straightened her clothes and patted Siris on the shoulder, but he didn't notice.

A couple of the other guests looked confused, but no one commented on their arrival.

Except Siris himself. "Good, you made it! Underlords, the both of you! Perfect!" He gestured to the door with his cup. "There's a dueling room in the back. You show us what you've got, and if you do well enough, you can join our party! What do you say?"

Lindon's discomfort at the situation was easily transferred to Sha Siris.

He surveyed the table. "Would you like to test us yourself, Master Sha, or would you prefer us to face your friends first?"

Yerin snorted a laugh, and a few of Siris' friends snickered. But not all of them.

The girl to his left patted him more urgently, and two or three of the others went pale as something dawned on them.

Sha Siris looked like he was considering a difficult puzzle. "There are two of you, aren't there? Why don't you fight each other?"

The girl to his left had finally had enough. She grabbed him by the collar and pulled his ear close to her mouth, whispering something.

"I have? No, I haven't. They just got here, I haven't seen them..."

Siris' mouth hung open for a long moment before he swallowed visibly. "Good sir, if it's not too much trouble, could you show me your right hand?"

Lindon had kept most of his hand hidden as best he could, to avoid attracting attention. Now, he raised it, wiggling the five white fingers on his Remnant hand.

Most of the table quieted and turned their eyes to Yerin. She gave them another grin.

Lindon caught the word *"Uncrowned"* whispered from several directions.

"Ah, it's as I suspected!" Siris said with forced cheer. "I

recognized you immediately, of course, that was just a little humor. I wanted to welcome you to your table myself, and I took the liberty of ordering your first course."

There was enough food on the table to stuff twelve people, and some of it had already been eaten, but Sha Siris stood and began shoving his friends out of their chairs.

"Get out," he muttered to the table, and most of his guests jumped up as though they couldn't wait another second to leave. They dashed out of the room one at a time, stopping to bob their heads to both Lindon and Yerin as they left.

Siris went from one of his remaining friends to the next, urging them up. He was clearly unwilling to leave before everyone had been cleared out. Some still looked confused. One man held a half-eaten chicken leg.

Yerin tilted her head and looked to him. "You looking to exercise?"

Sha Siris choked out a laugh that sounded like he had swallowed a mouthful of chalk. "He's not, I'm sorry, he's tired out from his training today."

"Didn't train today," said the man with the chicken leg. "And I wouldn't mind putting you back in your—"

Sha Siris grabbed a fistful of the man's hair and hauled him to his feet. "I told you, you're *tired.*"

Amazingly, the man still looked baffled. "What about our food?"

"*Leave it.*"

When he had finally pushed his guests away, Sha Siris ordered the servants to bring whatever the Uncrowned wanted, insisted that the room would be available whenever Lindon and Yerin decided to return, and used a movement technique to disappear down the stairs.

Lindon was impressed with his speed.

"Sobered up fast, didn't he?" Yerin noted as she sat down and started helping herself to the leftovers.

The servers were already replacing the partially eaten dishes with new ones, but Lindon grabbed one of the remaining dumplings. The Iron Heart had increased his appetite, and at the moment he felt like he could finish off everything on the table.

"Apologies. I was unprepared."

Yerin stabbed some meat and raised it to her mouth. "You didn't plan for a baby Sha to throw himself on our swords?" She bit off a chunk and chewed. "Shame his friends had eyes. I think we could have gotten him in the ring ourselves."

He pictured the drunken Sha Underlord facing them in a dueling arena only to recognize them when the fight began, and he laughed.

Yerin joined him, and the conversation flowed smoothly from there.

There was only one thorn stuck in Lindon's thoughts.

They had recognized Lindon, but it was Yerin they had really respected. Siris' guests had spoken of the Uncrowned in hushed tones, and he had invited the Uncrowned back whenever she wanted.

Lindon had fought well, but in the end, he wasn't Uncrowned.

He focused on the story Yerin was telling. She was getting into it, tracing lines of Forged sword madra in the air by way of illustration, and Lindon kept his mind in the present.

He wasn't here to moan over what he'd lost.

But to enjoy what he had.

Lindon, Yerin, and Mercy sat together to watch the next fight of the Uncrowned tournament: Yan Shoumei of Redmoon Hall against Blacksword of Redmoon Hall.

No matter who won, Reigan Shen was getting a representative among the Uncrowned.

Now that most of the core Akura members were gone, Mercy could join the ordinary audience of the Akura faction.

Everyone else with purple eyes had surreptitiously slipped out of their seats in a circle surrounding Mercy, but she didn't seem to notice.

In a red arena filled with stalagmites that oozed blood, the two members of Redmoon Hall flitted around each other.

Yan Shoumei, the ghostly girl that Lindon had faced in Ghostwater, looked like a pale specter with long black hair that hung down into her face. When the match began, she had audibly complained to Northstrider when she saw that he had pitted her against someone from her own sect.

Lindon understood how she felt.

The Monarch had paid her no more attention than a boulder.

Her opponent, Blacksword, was a strapping man wielding a huge, two-handed blade. Unlike what Lindon had expected from his name, his sword was bright red, sheathed in his Blood Shadow. When he attacked, the Shadow whipped out and added reach and force.

He chased after Yan Shoumei, a lash of blood smashing through a stalagmite.

With every step, ripples of light appeared beneath Blacksword's feet, allowing him to run in midair. His shoes had been gifted to him as one of his prizes, allowing him maneuverability that Shoumei couldn't match.

Lindon had researched him, as he had all the remaining competitors, and had expected this to be a short match. Yan Shoumei had always been one of the fighters expected to reach the top eight, but not Blacksword.

"I owe him an apology," Lindon said, as they watched him carve a canyon into the floor with an attack that Shoumei barely escaped.

"That's true and a half. Juggling a Blood Shadow and two bindings and your own techniques isn't simple as I make it look."

Lindon had heard it said that Blood Shadows counted as a second sacred artist in battle, but he had never seen that to be true. Yerin came the closest, and her Blood Shadow still didn't quite match up to her.

But when Blacksword swung his blade, his Blood Shadow lashed out, his own Striker technique followed in a beam, and a rain of jagged Forged madra fell like daggers. All the while, he kept dancing on points of light.

Little Blue gave a gasp like a whispering breeze and leaned forward on Lindon's shoulder.

Yan Shoumei's breathing was rough, and her spirit was growing disordered. Her Blood Shadow hung around her like a cloak, as he'd seen it in Ghostwater, but it now surged and boiled as she moved. It looked as though something within it was trying to escape.

Mercy cupped her chin in one hand. "She can't get close enough to take a bite out of him. I've watched all her records, and she's terrifying up close, but he figured out a way around her. Good for him!"

[I have a model ready for Blacksword whenever you would like to take a look,] Dross said. [We had information on him from the previous rounds, but we didn't really see what he was capable of until now, so *now* I have a solid model. Pretty solid.]

What is pretty *solid?*

[It's an absolute work of art that should be studied by future generations as the apex of all predictive models.]

He must have been sending that into Mercy and Yerin's minds as well, because they both looked to Lindon with varying degrees of amusement.

So he decided to respond out loud. Northstrider already knew about Dross, so overt secrecy was unnecessary. "How would Yerin do against him?"

[You know, they have very similar powers, I don't know if you noticed. It would be close, but Yerin would win. Unless she showed the extra spike of power she showed at the end of *your* fight, and then it would be easy.]

Yerin frowned. "I'd beat him without it, though."

[Oh yes, of course.]

"Then I don't need it, true?"

[I can't speak to *that*. I can't comprehend the nature of

Sage powers yet, but I doubt you would have beaten Lindon without them. You remember, when you tapped into that power to kill Lindon. I mean beat him.]

She mulled over that.

They hadn't talked about Yerin's burgeoning Sage senses since their match. Yerin stewed in silence for a while, and he couldn't tell if she was upset or just trying to recall the sensation.

"I don't even know much about Sages yet," Mercy said. "You're supposed to focus on traditional advancement until Archlord. But they say Lords can do miraculous things when under stress. Sages are the ones who learn to control those miracles."

Lindon had done some research of his own into that topic. There were plenty of works in the Ninecloud records *speculating* about a Sage's power, but all the ones written or recorded by Sages themselves did not discuss the nature of their abilities.

The dream tablets that depicted Sages using these "miraculous abilities" were beyond his ability to read. That, or they recorded only gaps where that power should go, as had been the case in his stolen memory of Northstrider.

But he was certain he and Dross would figure it out, given time.

Yerin grunted, but she didn't say anything.

Down in the arena, the match was almost over. Yan Shoumei had thrown out Ruler techniques to get Blacksword to come down, had stretched her Blood Shadow as far as it would apparently go, and had tried hitting him with Striker techniques.

Every time, he had thoroughly crushed her with a barrage of his own power, but he was clearly running low on madra. After using so many techniques in a row, Lindon would still have madra left, but his channels would be strained to their limits.

How would I do against him? Lindon silently asked Dross.

[That, ah, depends on a few factors,] Dross responded, and Lindon hoped the spirit was keeping their conversation quiet. [He's very strong, and he has a more effective range than you, so you would have to take it in close. *But,* if he doesn't have any more tricks hidden, you would certainly win.]

Dross' presence swelled in Lindon's spirit, and Lindon got the impression that the spirit's chest was puffed out in pride. [You have *me.*]

Which was a relief, but it also chafed a bit.

Dross was implying that, without him, Lindon couldn't beat Blacksword in a straight-up fight. At least, not for certain.

Then again, what was wrong with that? At this point, the man from Redmoon Hall was virtually guaranteed a spot among the Uncrowned. There was no shame in being slightly worse in combat than one of the eight most combat-capable Underlords of their generation.

Or so Lindon repeated to himself over and over again.

Blacksword's strain showed on his face and in his spirit. He had gathered all his madra for a final volley, and this really would be his last. After this, Lindon doubted the man's soul would be in good enough shape for a simple Enforcer technique.

Yan Shoumei looked worse. She nursed grievous wounds all over her body, though it was difficult to see most of them beneath the Blood Shadow she wore as a cloak. Her face was bruised and bloody, one eye swollen shut, and she stared up at Blacksword as though at her executioner.

He raised his sword.

She screamed.

Lindon heard it in his spirit as well as his ears. He flinched, and so did almost everyone in the crowd. Somehow, her scream sounded like a chorus of Remnants, and it drowned out the entire audience.

Misty red madra filled the arena.

And the projection of the match disappeared.

Lindon, Yerin, and Mercy all sat up at once. As far as Lindon understood the constructs involved, this *couldn't hap-*

pen. The recording and projection constructs were made of Archlord madra and were almost undetectable, not to mention resilient.

But that was nothing to his astonishment when he felt the Akura tower tremble beneath him.

Not just the tower.

The entire arena.

"Northstrider, you think?" Yerin asked softly.

The arena was supposed to be able to handle a contest between Heralds, much less Underlords. One of the Monarchs must have gotten upset about their view being interrupted.

Only two or three seconds after the projection ended, the view returned. The red haze over the battlefield began to thin.

Yan Shoumei stood there, wounded and panting, her red robes exposed but her Blood Shadow no longer visible.

It was eating Blacksword.

Little Blue squeaked and covered her eyes.

The Shadow had swollen into a monstrous form, fifteen feet tall and built like a cross between a heavily muscled man and a bear. Its fingers were unnaturally long, with sharp claws on the end, and it had the ears of a rabbit and the maw of a wolf. It was covered in the suggestion of fur, but spines rose in a row from along its back.

Every inch of it was blood-red.

It dug into Blacksword's chest with its muzzle, feasting. In the center of a bowl-shaped crater that covered two-thirds of the arena floor.

They had only a second to take in the sight before Blacksword and his gear faded to white light. The monstrous Blood Shadow roared at having its meal interrupted.

"Victory," the Ninecloud Soul announced, "to Yan Shoumei of Redmoon Hall, chosen of Reigan Shen."

The audience didn't cheer. Lindon caught mostly confused murmurs.

[Do you want to know how you stack up against *that?*] Dross asked.

Lindon did, actually.

Later, he said.

He was about to go comb the records for any information he might have missed on Yan Shoumei.

Seven matches into the fourth round, and seven of the Uncrowned had been selected.

Among those selected so far, only three Monarchs were represented: Ziel for Northstrider, three from the Dreadgod cults for Reigan Shen, and three for Akura Malice.

So four on their side, who would avoid releasing the Dreadgods on the Blackflame Empire if they won. Four allies, and three enemies.

But really it was four against four.

There was one match left, but there was no suspense in it. Yerin, Mercy, and Lindon had gathered to watch, and Lindon had a moment to wonder where Eithan was. He hadn't seen the man at any of the matches, and had barely seen Eithan at all this week.

Then again, there was no need for him to stay in the stands. He could watch from anywhere.

The Ninecloud Soul announced the names of the fighters as they strode out to see each other, though there was no surprise at the matchup since only two competitors remained.

"Kenvata Nasuma Juvari of the Silent Servants, chosen of Reigan Shen, you face Sopharanatoth of the gold dragons, chosen of the Dragon King!"

Kenvata—or Juvari, Lindon wasn't sure which was her family name and which her personal one—was a short woman in a plain white robe. A shawl covered her head, and between that and the cloth wrapping her mouth, the only visible parts of her were her dark eyes.

Sophara strode out, dressed in elaborate jewelry. Gems gleamed in every color. The fine strands of scales that ran from her scalp like hair glistened in the sunlight.

The projection overhead showed that her vertical-slitted gold eyes were calm, her face impassive. Her tail drifted slowly behind her as she paced up to her opponent.

Anger bubbled up in Lindon as he remembered her spraying Naian Blackflame's blood across the floor. Just to send a message.

Yerin's fist tightened on her armrest. "I'll give this Juvari my own sword and a wagonload of scales if she knocks the dragon out here."

"Wouldn't that be nice," Mercy said wistfully.

But there *was* a chance, Lindon knew, and Dross agreed.

[Her dream techniques might be the perfect weapons to use against Sophara. Superior strength and madra would never come into play.]

After reviewing records of previous rounds, Lindon had trained against a simulation of Juvari. Once.

Her entire Path was based around mimicking the dream Ruler techniques of the Silent King, the most subtle and insidious of the Dreadgods, so Lindon had thought she might pose a challenge for Dross.

She didn't. Dross could always hold her influence off long enough for Lindon to cut her in half with dragon's breath.

But throughout the entire tournament, Sophara had struggled the most during the first round when she had been trapped in an illusion. Clearly, she had no way of quickly or easily breaking free from dream techniques.

The two Underladies faced each other, both outwardly calm.

The arena was plain sand again, but this time clouds of purple fire drifted randomly around the battlefield. Strange shapes and images played within the flames. They reminded Lindon of his own family's foxfire, but these were made of dream and fire aura rather than dreams and light.

An even playing field for the two competitors.

Juvari clearly meant to take advantage. A white ring hovered over her head, like Samara's ring back home, and he could see dream aura gathering around her. She was preparing her Ruler technique.

He expected Sophara to do the same, but she stood with hands at her sides, waiting.

Juvari's technique was complete before the barrier separating the two of them fell. In fact, Lindon and Dross discussed with Yerin and Mercy, and they suspected she might have *two* Ruler techniques prepared and ready to launch.

Lindon's hopes rose as he saw that Sophara still had prepared nothing. She only cycled her madra to be ready when the fight began.

Overconfidence. That could be her undoing.

Northstrider dropped the wall between them, and the aura rippled purple as Juvari's dream techniques formed.

Both of Sophara's hands rose in front of her, and a *flood* of liquid golden dragon's breath obliterated one side of the arena.

It was like half of the sun had been born in an instant. Sophara was only a silhouette, dwarfed by a wall of her own madra.

The thunder was deafening. Scripted wards all around the stands stopped the heat from reaching them in the stands, but Lindon felt the spiritual force of the attack.

"Overlord," he said aloud.

Mercy slowly shook her head, and her mouth was set in a grim line. "She's not. She hasn't advanced."

"I know." That only made it more frightening.

She had filled the attack with soulfire, but even accounting for that, the scope and force of the technique were clearly on the level of an Overlord. Though Sophara herself was still an Underlady.

What kind of madra channels did she have to be able to force out an attack like that? And so quickly? Juvari's dream techniques didn't have a chance to touch her.

"Victory," the Ninecloud Soul declared, and only then did the Flowing Flame madra from Sophara taper off.

There was no sign of Juvari. A channel had been scooped

out of the arena floor between Sophara and the far wall, the sand melted into streaks of red-hot glass.

Sophara turned and walked calmly back to her waiting room.

Lindon looked over to Yerin, who met his eyes with a bleak look. She shook her head.

He turned to Mercy, who rubbed her temple with mad-ra-clad fingers. "I don't know," she said, in answer to his silent question. "We have to win. I just don't know if we can."

第六章

CHAPTER SIX

Min Shuei, the Winter Sage, had petitioned Northstrider ceaselessly all week. Every time she could track him down, she requested to be allowed to train Yerin.

He didn't turn her down. He just ignored her.

She had quickly suspected that he was waiting for all the Uncrowned to be selected before he allowed any Sages to select students, but by that time her stubbornness had set in. If he wouldn't allow her to persuade him with words, he would have to at least respect her persistence.

So she had followed the Monarch day and night.

When Sophara's match concluded, finally settling the roster of the eight Uncrowned, then Min Shuei knew Northstrider could have no further excuses.

Indeed, she sensed him in his own guest tower in Ninecloud City, waiting on the highest floor. He had set no barriers to keep her out, and while he hadn't answered his door yet, he would eventually.

She sat in the guest room outside his study. Since he had moved into the room, he had redecorated in his own style.

The guest room was a plain box painted dark gray. No decorations. By way of furniture, he allowed only three chairs for those he had summoned.

That was all.

She found it suited her image of Northstrider: plain and functional. She tried to imagine him picking out curtains or painting walls and chuckled to herself.

There was one window, but it was so high in the wall that it provided no view from the chairs. She paced the room in laps when Northstrider didn't call for her immediately, glancing down whenever she passed the window, but the window didn't take much of her attention.

Until she felt someone approaching.

She knew who it was even without a glimpse. She had expected him; in fact, she had thought he would interfere earlier.

When the window slid open and a man slid up the side of the building, she greeted him with her back to him and a hand on her sword.

"Red Faith," she said.

He said nothing, so she turned.

The Blood Sage, founder of the Bleeding Phoenix's cult, looked as though he had no blood in him at all. His skin was as pure white as his hair, which was so long that it reached down to his bare feet.

His black-and-red clothes were tight enough to reveal his skeletal frame, and lines of red paint ran down his cheeks from both eyes like tears. He perched on the windowsill, hunched like a monkey, chewing on his thumbnail and staring at her with unnerving intensity.

She felt nothing but disgust for this creature. At some point in the past, he was supposed to have been an accomplished researcher, pioneering investigation into dreadbeasts and the nature of spirits.

She couldn't be sure how much of his intellect had survived his Blood Shadow separating from him, but now he was...the kindest word she could think of was "unstable."

He had given up everything in his pursuits. Even his name.

"What brings you here?" she asked. There was no doubt that his reason was the same as hers.

He chewed more viciously on his nail until he drew blood.

Many Sages without significant family backing went by their title rather than their name. It was the same for her; almost everyone referred to her as the Winter Sage or the Sage of Frozen Blade.

But the Blood Sage had lost his name entirely. She wondered if he had forgotten it himself.

When a slow red rivulet ran down the edge of his thumb, Red Faith hurled a glob of blood madra at her.

The Striker technique took on the aspect of a bird, shrieking and diving at her, imbued with the will of the Bleeding Phoenix.

Her white sword split it in two.

The halves began to re-form, gathering into two smaller birds that would continue to attack, but they froze into half-shaped lumps and shattered, fuzzing away to essence.

The righteous anger she'd felt at being attacked faded as the attack did, turning to amusement. She gave him a contemptuous smile. "You almost stained the carpet."

He returned to chewing on his thumb, but this time he was more agitated.

And while she could never know what was going through his head, this time she was prepared when his hand made a claw. All the blood aura in the room clenched, and a pain shot through her body.

Ready or not, she had little time to defend herself. He was still among the oldest of the Sages.

"Break," he commanded, adding authority to his Ruler technique.

But she spoke at the same time. **"Stop!"**

Pressure came from inside and outside her body as his technique tried to crumple her into a ball. Meanwhile, he was frozen in place. A droplet of blood from his thumb hung suspended in the air.

He struggled as she did, each pushing against the other in a silent struggle. The air trembled between them.

Even vital aura was frozen by her will, so his Ruler technique couldn't progress any further, but she still had to pit her will against his command. Otherwise reality itself would break her.

At the same time, he was having his own struggle. His whole body, including his heart and lungs, had been stopped at her word.

This wouldn't finish either of them. They would break out of this stalemate, complete their next techniques, and then—

Their authority was overwhelmed in an instant, and they were both released.

Min Shuei glared at the Blood Sage, furious that he would attack her, but she sheathed her sword. There would be no further combat.

Red Faith evidently didn't agree, because he threw himself at her like a wolf, an Enforcer technique already blazing on his hand and drowning the room in red light.

She spat on his forehead.

Her spittle landed, but his technique didn't. He was locked in place by the same working she had used earlier, only this time it was backed up by greater authority than hers and greater command over blood aura than his.

Northstrider's door slid open and he walked out, a huge muscular man in mismatched rags. Golden eyes glared at the Blood Sage. "You know better than this."

Red Faith's technique died out, and so did Northstrider's restriction. The pale man fell, but he landed easily on all fours.

"People think Sages can't be defeated by sudden attacks," the Sage of Red Faith said quietly, "but of course they can. Was it likely? No. But no one wins a bet without taking a chance. Perhaps the Winter Sage thought she was safe in your waiting room. Perhaps she was simply slow today. If I had been successful, you would have had no other option but to allow me to tutor Yerin Arelius."

Min Shuei had heard him speak before, but it was always a shock to hear him say anything other than guttural snarling. She wasn't sure if he was as intelligent as he sounded, or if he was only imitating his former self.

"There was your reprisal to consider, but you cannot

afford to throw away a Sage before the Uncrowned are trained, you would face consequences yourself from my Herald, and I now have the backing of a Monarch whom even you cannot offend. Especially when he may win a heavenly weapon of execution. So I was safe."

Northstrider waited for the entire monologue to come to an end without any expression on his unshaven face.

The Blood Sage ended with, "I have the right to train Yerin Arelius. She has cultivated her Blood Shadow with a technique I created myself. She is, in a sense, my disciple."

Min Shuei could take it no longer. "She is the *Sword Sage's* disciple, so a sword Sage should train her!"

Technically there were three Sages of their generation who had manifested the Sword Icon: the Sage of the Endless Sword, the Sage of Fallen Blades, and herself. Among them, the only one that used the title of the Sword Sage was Adama, the Endless Sword, though it could apply to any of the three.

"You have your own competitor in the Uncrowned, with her own Blood Shadow," Northstrider said to Red Faith.

"Yan Shoumei needs no more of my guidance. She walks a different road than I, and I have taught her all she needs to know." He took one step closer to Northstrider, hopping from one foot to the other like a bird.

"Yerin Arelius has laid the foundation for something *extraordinary*. This could be a breakthrough, not just in our understanding of the Phoenix and Blood Shadow advancement, but in how we all reach Monarch. We have an opportunity here to revolutionize the sacred arts, and I know you are not the sort of fool to let politics blind you to that chance."

Northstrider nodded once.

Then he punched the Blood Sage.

His fist struck the man in the chest, and the air ignited with the force. The room exploded, the walls cracking, the window shattering and the chairs blasting to splinters. The building shook, and Min Shuei's ears rang. She had flown through quieter thunderstorms.

The Blood Sage was launched through the empty window in a blur, fading to a speck in the distance.

Northstrider had literally punched him out of the city.

Delighted, Min Shuei laughed and applauded. "That was even more satisfying than I imagined."

"He thinks only in terms of life and death. He knew I would not kill him, so he thought he was safe. Fool."

Northstrider gestured, and order reasserted itself. Shards of glass in the window flew back together, the damaged floor and ceiling repaired with visible speed, and the splintered chairs rebuilt themselves.

"I have consulted with the Akura family," Northstrider said, standing in the center of the whirlpool of debris. "They have given their consent. You are to train Yerin Arelius."

Min Shuei bowed at the waist. "Thank you, Monarch."

The ceremony introducing the Uncrowned was held in the arena as usual, but it had a very different atmosphere than normal. It reminded Lindon of Sacred Valley's Seven-Year Festival, or of the celebrations that filled Ninecloud City while the tournament was in progress.

The eight towers that held the audiences of the various Monarch factions remained in place, but the arena floor had been replaced with a pool of shimmering light that slowly shifted from one set of colors to another.

Eight Underlords hovered on rainbow Thousand-Mile Clouds above that surface. The chosen Uncrowned each drifted in front of their faction's tower, which made for a lopsided distribution.

Two men and a woman drifted in front of Reigan Shen's tower: his three fighters.

Each layer of the Shen faction's audience tower was decorated for a different Dreadgod, and of the four, only the Silent King had no representative remaining.

Brother Aekin of Abyssal Palace wore a dark stone mask, roughly carved with thin slits for eyes and a suggestion of a snarling mouth. He was unremarkable otherwise, wearing hooded sacred artist's robes of the same slate gray.

Next to him was Calan Archer, a muscular man whose sleeves were cut short to show the scripted rings around his biceps, which crackled with blue-and-gold lightning. He was a sandy-haired man with a square jaw and a scar across one eye, and he gave off a serious air. He represented the Stormcallers, the cult of the Weeping Dragon.

Finally, there was Yan Shoumei of Redmoon Hall. The girl still stood like a specter in her red robes, black hair falling over her face in a veil.

[Don't you think it's funny that the Dreadgod cults managed to get three spots?] Dross noted. [They've never even competed before! Was it Reigan Shen who made them that much better?]

Lindon wondered about that often. Had the Dreadgod followers always been so strong, or had Reigan Shen's support given them wings?

These three of Reigan Shen's representatives had performed well throughout the tournament, and until the last round, Lindon would have said that Yan Shoumei was the weakest of them.

Lindon wouldn't have been certain of his odds against either of the men, but Dross had suggested that he would win three out of four matches. He should have been able to beat Shoumei every time...except for her new, enhanced Blood Shadow. Now even Dross couldn't tell.

Were the other two hiding their strength as well, just like Yan Shoumei?

That was enough to worry about on its own, but they still had an ally. Drifting alone in front of the dragon tower, Sophara wore gold and jewels and loose cloth that left her midriff bare. Lindon thought she looked more and more human every time he saw her.

She tilted her chin up as she stood on her Thousand-Mile Cloud, surveying the audience as though she stood above all Lords.

[Is it still arrogance if you can back it up?] Dross wondered.

Across from her, she faced another team of three side-by-side.

Mercy was dressed in her finest Akura uniform again, though she didn't carry Suu. No one carried any visible weapons during the ceremony. Eithan's fancy dress was back, and his robes were bright ocean shades that didn't seem to represent Arelius, Akura, or the Blackflame Empire.

Lindon wondered what that meant. Knowing Eithan, it could have been a subtle coded message. Or it could have been that Eithan felt like wearing blue and green.

Yerin wore her standard black uniform, her dark hair flowing behind her in a gentle breeze. She didn't wear her master's sword, but her six silver sword-arms stretched out.

Her eyes stayed on her enemies.

Lindon felt another stab of regret. There they were, the three of them, standing shoulder-to-shoulder. He should be up there with them.

And as soon as this ceremony ended, they would leave. Taken away by Sages to train.

Leaving him alone.

Off to the side, Ziel stood in front of Northstrider's audience, slouched as though he would fall over without something to prop him up.

Eight people fighting for Penance, the heavenly weapon. Four who would support sending the Dreadgods home, and four who would oppose it.

What could Lindon do to influence the outcome?

[I don't want to say there's nothing you can do,] Dross said. [I really don't. I'm focusing *so* hard on not saying that.]

The Ninecloud Soul introduced each candidate one by one, and only when she finished did she start the ceremony proper: the addition of the Broken Crowns.

"The Broken Crown," the Soul explained, "has been the symbol of the Uncrowned King tournament from the beginning. This Divine Treasure, implanted in the souls of these eight young warriors, will immortalize them and symbolize their strength. It will let others recognize them as agents of their Monarch. It will serve as eternal proof of the glory they have earned on this battlefield."

There were wild cheers around the audience as the Ninecloud Soul continued, and the first rainbow cloud drifted to the center of the arena. It was the first to have earned her position among the Uncrowned: Yerin.

Lindon had done his research, and the Broken Crown conferred no additional power. The constructs were colored based on the madra of the representative's Monarch, and they couldn't be faked. Or removed, except from a Remnant.

They were essentially a signature unique to the Uncrowned.

As Yerin closed her eyes and nine-colored light swirled around her, black madra Forged itself over her. The actual Divine Treasure was inside her spirit, but it projected a dark crown—larger than her head—with a crack running down the center.

Black represented Akura Malice's shadow madra, so Eithan's and Mercy's would look the same. As Northstrider's representative, Ziel would receive a Broken Crown the red of blood madra, Sophara's would be gold, and the three Dreadgod cultists would each have the white of Reigan Shen.

[You know, it's a shame no Silent Servant made the top eight. Juvari would have had *two* white haloes. I wonder what that would have looked like.]

The ceremony continued in order, with the Ninecloud Soul reintroducing and celebrating Eithan's accomplishments—though Lindon noticed she skated over the name of his fourth-round opponent.

While the ceremony went on, Lindon stewed in worry.

If you averaged both sides, four against four, then the two teams were roughly equal.

But the enemy had Sophara, who seemed unbeatable in a duel, while Yan Shoumei's monstrous Blood Shadow was too much of a mystery.

It pained him not to be able to help. He wanted to *do* something, but the only thing he could think of was his old standby: pushing for advancement.

At least he had a good idea of what it took to reach Overlord.

He and Dross had worked steadily to analyze many accounts of Overlords regarding advancement, as well as testimony from Mercy and Eithan, among others. There was another revelation required, just as there had been for Underlord, but Lindon would cross that bridge later.

For now, he only had to accumulate power.

Underlords could only advance when they had condensed their soulfire, filled themselves with it, and pushed their madra to the peak of power that their souls could contain. That meant steadily refining and training themselves, usually for years.

One had to be at the peak of Underlord to trigger the advancement to Overlord, at least if you ever wanted to advance again, and peak Underlords were almost always older. That was one reason the age limit for the Uncrowned King tournament had been set to thirty-five.

Which had made Lindon wonder more than once how incredible Ziel had to have been, to reach Archlord at such a young age.

Among these Uncrowned, there was only one even close to the limit of the Underlord stage: Sophara.

And maybe Eithan.

[It's still hard to read that guy. Do you think he revealed some secrets to us as a way of hiding more secrets?]

Lindon didn't think so, but he couldn't prove it.

In order to reach the height of Underlord himself, Lindon needed resources. Over the next month, while Yerin was gone, he wanted to focus entirely on advancement.

And he had one idea that wouldn't leave him alone.

[Northstrider's hunger techniques! Sure, that might get you to advance in a month. But I don't know how to use them. Did you figure them out while I wasn't looking?]

Of course he hadn't, but he was becoming convinced that together they could. If he could drain all the power from others, then all he would need to advance was an endless supply of enemies.

Like, for instance, the enemies that might be found on a Dreadgod battlefield.

[I fully support that, except that Fury and the rest won't even arrive for several weeks.] Dross projected a rough map that only Lindon could see, although the important parts were vague and a lot of territory was covered in fog that represented Dross' uncertainty.

[They can take a more direct route this time, because the west coast of the Blackflame Continent is closer to us than Moongrave was, but we're still waaaaaaaaaay over here.] The map spun across an astonishing distance. [It will take them at least three more weeks to get there, assuming about the same speed they used the first time. So you won't have time to arrive and come back if you don't want to miss the Uncrowned fights. *Do* you want to miss the Uncrowned fights?]

Of course Lindon didn't. Not only should he be there to support his friends, he wouldn't pass up an opportunity to learn.

But there had to be a solution. He had been pulled through space by Northstrider before. Why couldn't he join the Akura troops, come back here to watch the fights, and then return to the battlefield? Then again, Fury himself wasn't doing that. If a Herald couldn't do it—

Blue light consumed him, and there came a nauseating sense of disorientation.

A second later, he stood in an all-gray waiting room. A projection of light in the center of the room showed the same ceremony he had just been watching.

[Wow, that was amazing! Did you cast us through space

just by thinking about it?]

Lindon already had a dragon's breath in his palm and ready, but he hurriedly canceled it when he noticed the man standing in the room.

Northstrider, his black-scaled hands folded across his chest.

"It's time, Dross," he said, and Dross materialized.

[Yes, of course sir! Would you like me to search through some more information today, or would you prefer just to chat? We could discuss the...conditions of the...air. In here. Or out there, it's up to you.]

Northstrider waited for Dross to finish, then held out an empty hand, which was abruptly filled with the gleaming black orb he had shown before. "I would like you to enter my oracle codex completely. It will examine you. When that process is complete, it will attempt to restrain you, while you try to escape. In ten minutes, I will release you myself, but I hope you will have escaped before then."

Dross' one eye widened. [I will not fail you, sir! But just to help me not fail, how about an upgrade?]

"Begin."

Dross shoved his way into the orb, and its surface rippled with light.

The surface resisted for a moment, and Lindon couldn't help but worry about Dross' condition. Northstrider had said that he would release Dross, but what if he didn't?

There would be no need to trick them, Lindon knew. The Monarch could take anything he wanted without trickery. Even so, he was nervous.

Dross passed through the surface like a man pushing through a screen, and he vanished.

Northstrider's dragon eyes flicked to Lindon's face, and Lindon wondered if his thoughts were being read.

"You may sit and wait."

Lindon took one of the chairs and tried to watch the ceremony, but it couldn't hold his attention. He knew who the Uncrowned were, and there was little chance of him learning anything else.

There was a much more valuable opportunity in this room.

He needed to get the Monarch talking. Even a stray comment about hunger madra might be the key to Lindon's entire future advancement.

After a minute or two, Lindon said, "I'm pleased to see that Ziel made it to the current round."

Northstrider was standing with his arms folded, looking into the wall. Lindon couldn't tell if the Monarch was casting his perception around the world, deliberating great thoughts, or sleeping with his eyes open.

He tried again. "Is there anything I can do to assist you? Or Dross?"

Silence.

It was probably too bold to try again, but he'd already made two attempts. The Monarch wouldn't obliterate him for a third.

"If you don't mind telling me, what are you testing Dross for?"

"I'm examining him to see if his initiative and ability to propose solutions are tied to his personality and self-awareness," Northstrider responded. Lindon couldn't tell if he had been annoyed into answering or if he was rewarding academic curiosity.

"I am also testing his capacity and resolve, as well as his spiritual structure. I would like to see if replication is possible without waiting fifty years."

"Ah, I see. Thank you for enlightening me."

Though Lindon was curious about the Soulsmithing principles involved, he didn't want to take the conversation in the wrong direction. Instead, he crept closer to what he really wanted to know.

"I have been training diligently, as you instructed." Lindon didn't need anyone's encouragement to train, but if Northstrider thought he was doing it out of obedience, that could be helpful.

"Watching Eithan fight has given me some thoughts about the direction I could take my own pure madra, so Dross and

I have been testing some of those. My Dragon Descends technique—the one I used at the end of my fourth-round match—is still unstable and takes too long to form, so I practice that regularly."

He flexed his white fingers. "But I've begun to believe that I'm not leveraging every weapon I have to its fullest potential."

When the only response he received was silence, Lindon wondered whether he was being too subtle or too bold.

The gap in the conversation stretched endlessly before Northstrider said, "Four minutes remaining. Did Dross show you the memory he took from me?"

Lindon's alarm raised several levels, but he extended a cautious answer. "He only showed me the pieces he could put together."

"What aspects does my madra have?"

Lindon began to sweat. Maybe all the Sages and Heralds knew exactly how Northstrider's techniques works, but to the average person, Northstrider was a total mystery.

But in front of the stone expression and piercing golden eyes, Lindon was more frightened of lying than of telling the truth.

It was best to pull a dagger out quickly. "Blood and hunger."

Then he clenched his fists, bracing himself for a Monarch's punishment.

Northstrider returned his attention to the shimmering orb. "Hunger madra is perhaps the most dangerous aspect to its user. But danger, properly harnessed, is opportunity."

Lindon eagerly waited for more, but Northstrider glanced at the projection of the Uncrowned ceremony.

The Uncrowned were joined by Sages, each standing behind their chosen pupil. Charity floated behind Mercy, of course, while the Winter Sage chose Yerin.

Unsurprising. Yerin had told him about the connection between her and Yerin's master. The tan, white-haired woman glared at the Dreadgod cultists as though she meant to draw swords right there.

Behind Eithan appeared a woman that Lindon had never

seen before. Her hair was equally yellow and gray, and there were wrinkles on her face, which would make her unique among the Sages that Lindon had seen.

She wore the deep blue of the Arelius family, and a smile that reminded Lindon strongly of Eithan.

Lindon was very curious about this woman's identity, but Dross emerged from the oracle codex, panting and swiping an arm across his forehead.

"Well done," the Monarch said.

Dross raised a shaky limb, the end curled as though into a fist. [I...am...the greatest! My power is endless. Now please let me sleep.]

Northstrider nodded once. Then, finally, he spoke to Lindon again.

"Observe." He waved a hand.

A void key—or something like it—opened in the center of the room. An instant later, the corpse of a giant pig fell out.

Its hide looked like dull metal, and it filled up the entire room, stinking of musk and filth. With a start, Lindon realized he could feel the spiritual pressure of an Overlord from this sacred beast. And its chest was rising and falling.

It was *asleep.*

Northstrider extended one hand, cycling madra in a slow, exaggerated motion that Lindon had no problem following. He could sense only blood madra.

Although...

Now that he was searching for it, and Northstrider was allowing him such a thorough look, he realized that there was a similar *feel* to Northstrider's madra and that in his own arm. As though they shared a personality. An endless, hollow greed that could never be satisfied.

"Open your aura sight," Northstrider commanded.

Lindon did, overwhelmed by the blood aura in the air. It drowned out everything else, reducing the other colors to dull smears.

Then the Monarch put his palm onto the pig's swelling side and...*pulled.*

His hand itself didn't move, but the madra in his body cycled rapidly, creating a suction as though the technique was taking a deep breath.

Northstrider inhaled the blood aura through his hand, but not *just* the aura. Sparks of bright green light joined it, and when Lindon concentrated, he could see that the beast's lifeline had dimmed. He was draining its *life*.

And...everything else.

Witnessing the process himself had far more impact than watching a cobbled-together memory.

More colors joined the maelstrom, including gold and yellow that Lindon took to be its madra. Surely those aspects couldn't be compatible with Northstrider's Path, but he took them in anyway. There were even brighter sparks of red: blood essence, the power in the creature's body, and hazy purple specks that Lindon took to be the dream aura of the creature's mind.

That was dim, as this sacred beast had never gained awareness, but it was still there. And there was something else, gaps where Lindon could sense nothing, but he was *certain* there was something there.

When Northstrider finished, the pig went on snoring. He had taken only a portion of the creature's vitality, and he banished it back to storage with a wave of his hand. A few fleas hopped over the carpet, but were incinerated in midair.

Lindon was grateful for that.

He was about to thank the Monarch for the demonstration, which had given him much to think about in terms of his hunger madra, but Northstrider wasn't finished.

He stood still, eyes closed, cycling the powers. Processing them. Sending them where they were needed.

Though he did not veil himself and allowed Lindon to observe, Lindon couldn't follow all of it. But Northstrider was using his madra, inwardly focused. A spirit Enforcer technique.

When the Monarch opened his eyes a second later, *then* Lindon bowed.

"Eternal gratitude," Lindon said. "I will go to work on this technique immediately."

"This is called the Consume technique. If you can master it, you will no longer need advancement resources. Only enemies."

It would have been embarrassing to show delight in front of a Monarch, so Lindon held himself back.

"I have never had trouble finding enemies," Lindon said. "But I would find plenty if I joined the Akura operation around the Wandering Titan. Of course, if you needed me to stay close for the sake of Dross, I could give up that opportunity and remain here."

The black orb over Northstrider's shoulder shimmered and vanished. "You would be wise to go and train yourself. I will come to you when I require Dross, wherever you are."

"Then...pardon if I overstep myself, since you have already done so much for me, but would you mind sending me there directly?"

"I will not," Northstrider said.

That was as flat a refusal as Lindon had ever received.

"It will be one more week before the Akura expedition arrives in Sky's Edge. You should find a Sage to ferry you there. Or persuade Malice's daughter to petition her mother. My time is too valuable."

"Apologies, but I thought they would have arrived already."

Lindon had seen Sages and Monarchs travel great distances at a thought. They had even transported most of the sacred artists in the Blackflame Empire to the Night Wheel Valley all at once. He had expected Fury's cloudship to pass through a portal and then simply...arrive.

Then again, he knew there was *some* kind of restriction on spatial travel. Otherwise he wouldn't have had to take a cloudship to the Ninecloud Court in the first place.

"Too many people," Northstrider answered. "Transportation requires more power and skill across greater distances. With each additional passenger, the difficulty doubles."

He seemed to be warming up to the subject, as he turned his attention to Lindon. "This can be mitigated by permanent or semi-permanent scripted structures that anchor transportation and create portals that can move any number of people."

Lindon immediately thought of the doorframes that entered Ghostwater and the pillars of darkness that brought him to the Night Wheel Valley.

"However, these portals are expensive to activate. It is usually better to take the time to travel normally. In this case, Malice found the situation important enough to fuel one such pathway. It will shave weeks from their journey."

Lindon bowed over his fists. "Thank you for the lesson, Monarch."

Now he knew a solution existed. And he had a week before Fury and the others even arrived, so he had time to find it.

"When we meet again," Northstrider said, "you will show me what you have learned."

Then Lindon was gone.

At least this time, he was back in the arena. The ceremony was wrapping up, the air alight with fireworks and techniques meant to resemble fireworks.

His mind spun, and his hands itched to record his ideas, but first...

First, he had to bid his friends good-bye.

第七章

CHAPTER SEVEN

INFORMATION REQUESTED: EMRISS SILENTBORN, THE REMNANT MONARCH AND QUEEN OF THE EVERWOOD CONTINENT.

BEGINNING REPORT...

Path: Ten Thousand Dreams. While the Path of Ten Thousand Dreams is not particularly suited to combat, its power is nonetheless undeniable. Sacred artists have shared dreams since antiquity, but Emriss developed the ability to accurately share memories, leading to the development and widespread adoption of dream tablets. This Path involves sharing thoughts widely, coordinating entire armies of sacred arts at once.

Emriss Silentborn was born a tree.

The men'hla tree is famous for its utility in Soulsmithing. Each of its leaves produces a separate Remnant, leading to an almost endless supply of dead matter. It takes extraordinary circumstances for such a tree to attain sentience, and Emriss is the result of such a twist of fate.

When she advanced to Underlord, she took the form of a young woman, using her control over vast networks of dream madra to voraciously learn and spread that knowledge as widely as possible.

She sought to end the tradition of competing over secret knowledge and to make education freely available for all. She spent her lifetime advancing science and civilization across the Everwood continent.

Upon reaching Herald, Emriss crafted the Dreamway, an interconnected library of dream tablets containing endlessly changing fictional worlds. She wanted it to be a place of rest and entertainment to inspire the imaginations of artists the world over.

As she began gathering support for a global portal network, to bring the various continents closer together, three rival Monarchs joined forces and had her assassinated.

Free, unlimited knowledge is a threat to those who hoard secrets.

But death did not stop her. The Remnants that fell from her leaves spread far and wide, defying all attempts to hunt her spirit down.

Over time, they joined together and re-formed, but her memories were fragmented and her sense of identity almost entirely broken.

Fortunately for her, she had spent her life leaving memories all around the world.

With her rebirth came wisdom. While her purpose never changed, her methods did. She is now more subtle, and the other Monarchs consider her both generous and harmless. For she spreads not the sacred arts, but the gift of language, ensuring as best she can that the inhabitants of Cradle all understand one another.

She protects her homeland, but she stays out of competitions for resources elsewhere, so her rivals leave her in peace.

They do not have the depth of understanding she does, and they do not realize how powerful cooperation can be.

SUGGESTED TOPIC: THE SILENT KING AND EMRISS SILENTBORN. CONTINUE?

DENIED, REPORT COMPLETE.

Yerin, Mercy, and Eithan had gathered with their respective Sages at the end of the cloudship dock outside the Akura guest tower.

Lindon couldn't be sure why they had chosen the dock. There was no cloudship at the end, and if the Sages planned to travel directly, then surely they could leave from anywhere.

[Maybe it has to do with the position of the stars,] Dross suggested, drawing Lindon's attention to the night sky overhead. [Or maybe it's just that their students wanted to say goodbye to each other.]

When Lindon arrived, Mercy and Yerin were talking—Yerin laughing and Mercy making animated gestures. Eithan, behind Yerin, dodged her sword-arms.

Once again, Lindon felt the tearing pain and embarrassment of being the only one not to have made it. He should be going with them.

But he mastered himself and focused on the other three people on the platform.

Charity stood behind Mercy, hands folded, an owl on her shoulder. She was calmly waiting to leave, and she looked as though she could wait forever.

The Winter Sage, on the other hand, shifted impatiently from one foot to the other. Her long white hair blew in the wind, and she spoke to Yerin several times, though Lindon caught none of it other than Yerin's name. She radiated a desire to leave as soon as possible.

The Arelius Sage, the woman Lindon had only seen during the Uncrowned ceremony, looked perhaps the most at ease. Her blonde-and-gray hair was tied up in a bun, and she stood with arms crossed and an amused smile on her face as she watched everyone else.

Mercy was the first to react to Lindon's presence. She gave a glad cry and ran up to him, hugging him around the waist.

Charity raised one eyebrow.

"I'm sorry you have to stay," Mercy said. Her eyes were full of sympathy. "I know you're going to work twice as hard while we're gone, but you should remember to relax. Oh, and goodbye Dross! Tell Little Blue I said goodbye, too."

"I can bring her out." Lindon activated his void key, and a closet-sized door opened in midair. A wind treasure tumbled out, but he caught it with his foot and kicked it back inside.

Little Blue ran out, arms upraised as she gave a mournful flute note.

Mercy made a similar sound, scooping up the spirit and promising that she would be back soon.

Lindon wondered when they had gotten so close.

Charity appeared next to his shoulder, startling Dross.

"We will be returning to Moongrave for Mercy's training. Several of my branch's elders remain here, and if you need to contact us, they will know how."

Lindon dipped his head. "Gratitude. Thank you for taking care of me for so long. And Dross thanks you once again for the scales."

[Wait, no I didn't! But I do now. And...if she could spare one more, before her journey...]

Lindon didn't ask why Dross hadn't requested another scale himself, and he didn't relay the message.

Not only did Dross have plenty of advancement resources, if Lindon could master the Consume technique, he could feed Dross himself.

"Taking care of you," Charity repeated. "Hm. Suffice it to say that your performance met or exceeded my expectations. On behalf of the Akura family, I will provide you with an appropriate reward as soon as I am able."

That lifted Lindon's spirits considerably. He bowed deeper this time.

"I would be in your debt if you could provide me with transportation to the Dreadgod battlefield and back."

He had intended to bring up the topic more smoothly, but since she had brought up rewards...

Charity raised one eyebrow. "I will return in a few days. We will talk then."

"Gratitude."

That was as close to a positive response as Lindon could have expected.

Mercy stepped up to Lindon again, Little Blue on her hand. She handed the spirit back. "Goodbye, Lindon! I'll be back before you know it!" She took a deep breath and nodded to Charity, who widened a pool of darkness beneath their feet.

As the shadows crept up, Mercy waved and kept waving. "I'm glad we were on the same team, Lindon! Bye, Yerin! Bye, Little Blue!"

She was still waving when the transportation completed.

[She's friendlier than the rest of you. Why don't you learn from her?]

She's friendlier than you, too, Lindon pointed out.

[Mine is sort of a...dry friendliness.]

The Winter Sage brightened as she saw Mercy leave. "Time to leave, Yerin. See you soon, Thousand Eyes."

The Arelius Sage raised a lazy hand.

"Hold still for a breath and a half," Yerin barked. She pushed her way clear of the Sages, grabbing Lindon by the edge of his robe and pulling him several steps away.

Lindon had practiced what to say here. He needed to stay positive and encouraging, focusing on the important job that Yerin was doing.

"Good luck, Yerin! I won't let you get too far ahead."

He couldn't have her worrying about him while she was gone.

She gave him a frustrated look. "Don't polish me up. I'm not—"

"Yerin!" the Winter Sage called. "Why don't you introduce me?"

Lindon straightened to introduce himself, but Yerin blocked out his view of the Sage with one of her sword-arms. "Don't listen to howling dogs. I've been trained by a Sage before. No cause to think she can change anything for me in a month. Tried to get her to bring you with us, but she's stubborn as a boulder hitched to a donkey."

"I hear you!" the Sage shouted.

Yerin moved another half-dozen paces down the dock, and Lindon walked along with her. "Bleed her. Look, I'll be working my hardest. Don't want Dreadgods trampling Blackflame City any more than you do. But if you asked me to bet on the odds that a Sage can help me beat Sophara in a month's time, I just...well, maybe Mercy can bury her."

She visibly struggled with herself for a moment before leaning into him, both fists resting against his chest.

Lindon's heart pounded in his ears, and he slowly moved his arms around her.

On his shoulder, Little Blue made a questioning noise.

"Yerin," Lindon tried again, "I'm going to miss you. I want you to go...but I wish we could go together."

"You know what's going to be a gem? When the fortress is finished, and we can just leave. Head home, you and me, and we can take our time. Everybody else can go rot."

If Lindon's heart had been pounding before, now it felt like he was in battle. He tightened his embrace, and she looked up.

It would be the perfect time to kiss her.

He knew it. He could feel it.

But he felt someone else's gaze on him.

Even knowing it was a mistake, he looked up, and the Winter Sage's eyes were narrowed and locked on him.

And behind her, Eithan and the Arelius Sage both watched while wearing the same smile.

Yerin shot a glance behind her and reddened, though this time Lindon suspected he was redder than she was. She backed up, and he released her. "Next round in a month," she said. "Don't drag your feet. See you then. Same for you, Dross. Blue."

Little Blue backed up on Lindon's shoulder, then took a running leap and flung herself toward Yerin.

The spirit wasn't strong enough to make it all the way, so Lindon and Yerin both moved to catch her at the same time, but Yerin was faster.

The spirit landed on Yerin's palm, then scurried up her arm and threw two sapphire arms out to embrace Yerin's cheek.

Yerin's eyes welled up.

Eithan stepped up smoothly then, gesturing Lindon aside. "I'm sorry, I wasn't thinking. I should have distracted the Sages so that you two could have a moment."

"So only *you* could watch us?"

"I beg your pardon! I choose not to watch people quite often. Constantly, in fact. Also, the Sage of a Thousand Eyes can see you anywhere I can."

So Lindon *had* heard correctly earlier. He looked back at the woman who looked like she might have been Eithan's mother. The Oracle Sage, or the Sage of a Thousand Eyes, hadn't been active since the death of her Monarch. Lindon had heard speculation that she was dead.

She nodded, and Lindon gathered she was confirming what Eithan said.

Eithan drew Lindon's attention back by growing serious. "Listen, we don't have much time. The Sages have already waited longer than they would prefer. I've spent the last week putting this together for you."

He handed Lindon a scripted river stone the size of a child's fist. It shimmered slightly with the light of dream madra.

A dream tablet.

"This includes the basics of the Path of the Hollow King," Eithan explained, and Lindon shifted uncomfortably.

"Gratitude, Eithan, but..."

He and Dross had looked over Eithan's records and come up with their own theories about the Path of the Hollow King.

"...I don't think it quite suits me," Lindon finished. "Apologies."

Maybe if Eithan had taught him the Path earlier, then he

would have become used to it, but Eithan had waited too long. Lindon would have to abandon or completely re-work the Soul Cloak in order to adopt Hollow King madra. Even the Empty Palm would require reinvention.

Rather than disappointed, Eithan looked unconcerned. "Oh, I'm sure. I didn't want you to adopt my Path. But my techniques will be inspiration for your own, which will help you. As will this."

Into Lindon's hand, he placed a ball of copper plates.

Dross gasped, and Lindon's mouth almost fell open.

The Arelius technique library.

The Sage of a Thousand Eyes craned her neck as though trying to get a better look, though her eyes had nothing to do with her bloodline ability.

"Yerin!" the Winter Sage called, and Lindon felt a cold tingle run up his arm as Little Blue climbed up to sit on his shoulder.

Yerin glanced back at him one more time as she walked over to her Sage.

Lindon raised a hand to her while the Sage of the Frozen Blade pulled a white-and-silver key out of her pocket. A gatekey, which created a portal to one spot.

[Do you think it's easier for her to use the key, or do you think she can't make a portal herself?] Dross mused.

Lindon was wondering the same thing himself.

As Yerin walked through an icy portal, glancing behind her with every step, the Oracle Sage stretched. "All right, that's time for us too, Eithan. Let's go."

"I've given you temporary access to the technique library," Eithan said, his voice low and urgent. "Use it to develop your Paths."

The Arelius Sage used another gatekey, creating a second portal.

"Do you have any tips for Overlord?" Lindon asked quickly. One of Mercy's tricks had helped him figure out his Underlord revelation, and Lindon had wanted to spend this last week pressing Eithan for anything he knew on the matter. Only Eithan had spent most of the week sneaking around on a project of his own.

A wind from the portal was starting to tug on Eithan's outer robe. "Think about the *will* behind each of your three types of madra. The *significance*. The intentions. What do they have in common? Is there one purpose that unifies everything you can do?"

Lindon paid rapt attention, but the portal was starting to physically pull Eithan in. It looked like he was struggling against a strong wind.

"Also, think of how others see you. What are you to them? This perspective will help you understand your revelation!"

He spoke faster and faster, trying to get the message out as he was physically hauled backwards across the dock.

As he was halfway through the portal, pushing forward as though trying to escape a rushing river, he screamed, "Remember, Lindon! Remember to visit a barber! *A barber, Lindon!* Your hair lacks volume and defin—"

The portal closed.

Little Blue gave a brief, comforting chime and patted Lindon on the shoulder.

Eithan had given him plenty to think about, and Dross immediately began giving his own suggestions about hair, but Lindon stared for a long minute into the swirling wind and the passing cloudships.

He stood on the cold dock, feeling very alone.

Eithan flew out from the portal into a plain underground room of packed dirt reinforced with wooden planks. The Sage of a Thousand Eyes stood waiting for him in the doorway.

Only when the portal closed did she say, "That was dramatic."

Eithan had brushed against the dirt wall, so he swept his outer robe clean. "I regret only that I didn't teach him the importance of proper hair care."

The floor was plain dirt with one exception: a scripted stone sticking up about a foot from the center. That would be the anchor, the target the gatekey used to mark this location as a target.

He looked down the long hallway, which was all dirt and wood, lit by flickering scripts.

"Welcome home, Eithan," the Sage said.

"I see we're not quite back to our former glory."

The Oracle Sage gave a halfhearted laugh and started walking. "We can barely afford to use the gatekey. On the bright side, it costs a lot less to maintain a network of underground bunkers than a mansion."

Gatekeys were difficult, expensive, and time-consuming to *create,* but they were not especially expensive to use. If that strained the budget, then there couldn't be many powerful sacred artists left in House Arelius.

"Still much nicer than last time I saw it," Eithan observed.

"Well, nothing's on fire."

He snuck a glance at her through his bloodline powers. The last time he'd seen her, she had suffered a blow from Reigan Shen that had made her vanish from his senses.

"If I may say, Cladia, you look even more radiant than I expected."

She gave him a wide grin. "Compared to a spray of blood and a Remnant, yeah, I'd say I look pretty good. I'm better at restoration than I am at spatial travel, thank the heavens."

At the end of the dirt hallway was a metal door, past which was another sealed chamber to remove their shoes and a wind construct that blew them clean.

On the other side of that chamber was a room that suited Eithan's tastes much more.

The plush carpet was dark blue, the walls spotless and cream, the furniture finely carved and polished. A construct in the corner played soft harp music, and the runelight was gentle and warm. Plants strong in wind aura decorated the room, giving off fresh breezes.

Everything was made of cheap materials, nothing like the opulence of the Ninecloud Court, but it was all tasteful and the craftsmanship was impeccable. Eithan appreciated anyone who could remain stylish on a budget.

There were other rooms off of this one, and Eithan let his strands of awareness brush into them, taking a quick peek. This was effectively a three-story house that had been buried, and it was surrounded in such shielding that a Dreadgod might walk over them without rattling the walls. And without a chance of sensing anyone hidden inside; even Eithan's bloodline powers couldn't penetrate the scripts.

The staff stayed well out of the way, trying to remain invisible to the Sage's guest, though of course that was impossible. He still appreciated their dedication.

"Spotless," Eithan complimented Cladia.

"My people do their best." She sighed and removed her outer robe, tossing it onto a coatrack nearby. "So why are you still an Underlord?"

Eithan considered his answer for a moment. "Fair play?"

The Sage poured herself a glass of wine using only her control over aura. "You think it's still time for that, do you?" The glass drifted into her hand, and she took a sip.

Another glass landed in his hand, and Eithan looked into the pool of dark red. He had initially stayed at Underlord so long to avoid making Naru Huan feel threatened. Then he was waiting on Lindon and Yerin.

He wasn't worried about his *own* advancement, after all.

But now that the Abidan were descending and Dreadgods were stirring...

He sighed. "Just when they caught up to me. This is going to annoy them."

"Frozen Blade will get Yerin to Overlord," Cladia said, reclining in a plush chair. "I don't know about Lindon."

"He'll be fine. Just annoyed."

She crossed her ankles on a footstool and watched him

over the rim of her wineglass. "Do you not want to win the tournament?"

"That depends," Eithan said, "on the highest bidder."

They both laughed. It was refreshing, conversing with someone who could keep up with him.

She gestured to a side door, beyond which was her collection of natural treasures. When compared to the storehouse Charity kept at the Night Wheel Valley, it was painfully scarce, only two or three dozen treasures rich enough for a Lord.

"You advance, we'll have some dinner, and then...well, you've seen the place. We'll have to spend the next month hunting if we're going to get you to Archlord."

"Archlords aren't eligible for the tournament," Eithan said, opening the door, "but hunting sounds wonderful. Just a moment."

He stepped into the natural treasure storeroom, feeling his soulfire resonate with the surrounding aura. He stretched out to the treasures he needed, striking a balance, and held his attention on them as he focused on his Overlord revelation.

He had discovered it long ago, and it hadn't changed.

"I...*see.*"

It wasn't as simple a statement as it sounded. It described who he was.

Eithan was one who saw.

He happened to know that Cladia's Overlord revelation had been very similar. He thought about that as his chosen treasures evaporated and Overlord soulfire passed through him in a breath, refining and strengthening him.

The advancement to Overlord wasn't as dramatic a leap as the one to Underlord, and he easily controlled the reaction to avoid losing his clothes. A good thing, too. He was fond of this outfit.

Seconds after he entered the storeroom, he stepped back out. "Sorry for the delay. Are you ready to eat?"

Mercy sat cross-legged in a shadow aura cultivation room at the heart of Moongrave. She could feel Charity pacing around the edge of the room.

"The dragon girl has harnessed power beyond her limits for victory in this competition," Charity said. "We cannot do the same for you. Which means we are trusting you to perform."

Mercy gulped down air, swallowing nerves. "Yes, Aunt Charity!"

"Are you afraid?"

"Yes," Mercy admitted freely. If she failed, innocent people would pay the price. Not to mention her own mother.

"Good. That will make the fifth page more difficult."

Mercy swallowed and manifested the Book of Eternal Night.

Her Divine Treasure appeared in front of her, a book of bright violet light with concentric circles of script spinning on the cover.

With a focused effort of will, she gave it a command: "Fifth page."

The thumb-thick pages spun, revealing more and more scripts. When the fifth page opened, the power of an Overlord filled her.

And she was drawn inside a new world.

She didn't enter physically, though it felt like it. Her real body was still seated at the center of the cultivation room.

Each page held a mental and spiritual space created by Malice, and this one was made of nightmares.

It appeared as a vast, dark cavern. Wide openings howled in the wind, and formations of stone blocked her vision in any direction.

A heavy burden hung on her spirit, making her madra slide out of her control and hammer against her channels. Overlord power was too great for her, but she had to keep it under control.

Which made the other effect of this page so much worse.

Dread swelled in her heart as though it had been planted there. She *knew* that there was something behind her, breathing down her neck. Her spiritual sense warned her of danger, imminent, in every direction, growing with every second, there was *something there; it was about to pounce—*

Mercy kept her thoughts ordered and her breathing regular. She had trained on the Phantom Islands, a location outside Moongrave that her mother had originally created for Charity's training. There, she was haunted by nightmares.

She had completed that training, so she was sure she could finish this one. Until the phantoms came.

The first revealed itself one finger at a time, each digit pale and rotten, as it wrapped a hand around a nearby outcropping of stone.

When it pulled itself around, showing its face with its teeth bared in a squirming smile, she lost herself to instinctive terror.

The Overlord power inside her broke free, escaping her control, shooting from her in a geyser of shadows.

And she snapped out of the book. The power faded, the book sliding shut.

Mercy's real body was panting and sweaty, her madra churned, and she felt like she might be sick.

"Fear of the mind can be conquered," Charity said, picking up on her previous lecture as though she had never stopped talking. "The Dream of Darkness technique attacks the heart, mind, and soul as one. You must first endure it in order to control it, and enduring fear is a skill. I will teach you."

Mercy could have forced the technique out on her own, but squeezing it out of her Book in the event of an emergency and really learning to wield it were two different things.

She had finally gotten her breathing under control.

She could see ways to improve her command over her own madra and even push back against the shadow and dream madra that filled her with such fear, but she wasn't sure she could do it while fighting her own terror *and* the phantoms born in that space.

But her mother hadn't chosen this technique because it was easy to learn. She had chosen it because it was the perfect technique for Overlords.

"Dream of Darkness is in the Book of the Silver Heart, isn't it, Aunt Charity?"

"It is my sixth technique," Charity confirmed. "I didn't have to learn it until I was an Archlord. But the Monarch expects great things from you, Mercy."

The Monarch did...and so did Mercy herself. If she didn't earn the ability to defeat Sophara herself, that meant she was leaving the task to Yerin or Eithan, and she couldn't allow that.

She had spent too much time trapped at Lowgold, letting them fight on her behalf.

Not anymore.

As anybody without a chipped head would expect, the headquarters of the Frozen Blade sect was in the snow.

Yerin had never liked it here. Not only was she not especially eager to see the place where she had shivered for hours while blood froze on her skin as she tried to sense sword aura for the first time, it was also just freezing cold.

Why would anyone choose to live here?

...because they were a bunch of ice artists, and she knew that, but that didn't make *her* enjoy it any more.

Jagged blades of razor-sharp ice stuck out at chaotic angles from every snowbank, gathering the power of ice along with a silver edge of sword aura. These blades pressed close even to the network of wooden huts where Yerin stayed, making sure the aura was present for harvesting everywhere.

And ensuring that every inch was as cold as possible.

The Frozen Blade School owned a huge stretch of land, and over time had come to protect an entire nation's worth of people from invaders, the deadly environment, and each other.

This little complex of huts, tucked away at the foot of a mountain, was the Sage's personal home. Each hut was connected by a raised walkway covered by a roof, so you could walk around without trudging through hip-deep snow.

Yerin just didn't understand why the walkways didn't have *walls.*

The icy wind was literally cutting, slicing away the ends of her hair and taking scraps from the edges of her outer robe before she spared enough attention to push away the aura. The Sage's home was no place for most Golds; only Truegolds on the Path of the Frozen Blade were allowed to visit, as anyone below could not protect themselves.

Yerin had been allowed to settle into a hut of her own, though that mostly meant looking at the room, confirming that everything was where it should be, and leaving. She didn't believe in weighing herself down with belongings.

She wandered around the compound, familiarizing herself with it. This was more painful a trip than she'd expected, because the last time she'd been to the Frozen Blade School, she was with her master.

He had pushed her Rippling Sword by challenging her to break a chip off one of these bladed ice formations.

When she had been knocked off her feet by a fever, he had sat with her for a day and a night, feeding her medicinal broth and telling her stories.

She had tried to follow him to this compound one night after being explicitly told not to, only to be shredded by the sword aura in the frozen wind. The Winter Sage had found her and moved her back to the Iron guest housing, shouting and weeping in equal measure.

It had put Yerin off. If the woman cried over a girl she'd just met, her tears came too easily.

She was more comfortable with her master's reaction. When he'd seen her covered in blood, he'd cracked a grin and said, "I bet my soul against a rat's tail that you won't be trying that again."

Now, here she was, staying in a house that she'd been too weak even to touch before.

She liked that feeling, but it wasn't enough.

Not only was she alone, but the Winter Sage was going to act like they were family. Yerin wasn't sure how much of that she could take.

But she'd be a fool to pass up the training of a Sage, especially when the Blackflame Empire could be on the line. Although...even her master hadn't made it past the first match of the top eight.

What chance did she have?

Yerin found that her pacing feet had taken her to a wide training room, where the Sage was giving hasty instructions while cradling what looked like a baby rabbit.

"Yes, you can meet her, but later. I need the room. Can you hand me the...yes, the bottle. Right next to that one. Perfect."

Yerin stopped watching through a window and pushed the door open. The Winter Sage didn't look up at her entry, but the two students bowed.

Both were Underlord, and both looked older than she did.

One was the shaky-looking man who had filled in at the Uncrowned King tournament and had failed in the first round. He clutched a sheathed sword to his chest, staring at the ground as though imagining he was somewhere else.

The Underlady next to him bowed more quickly, but she kept shooting glances at Yerin with wide eyes.

"Go, you two! Go away! You can meet the Uncrowned later!" They scurried away, and the Winter Sage smiled over the rabbit in her arms. "Everyone wants to meet you."

The tiny sacred beast squirmed, and Yerin saw it had a bandage around one of its haunches. It had a sharp horn of frozen ice, so Yerin had no doubt that it was native to the area.

It squirmed as it suckled on the bottle the Winter Sage held.

Yerin kept watching the rabbit as she spoke. "If I had a bent copper chip for everyone that wanted to meet the Sword Sage's disciple, I could buy one of your mountains."

The Winter Sage looked astonished, and it occurred to Yerin that there might be an advantage to dealing with someone who wore her feelings so openly. "What? No! They want to see how someone so young could be stronger than the twins."

Yerin didn't know who the twins were, but she didn't particularly care. "Don't have so much time that I'm looking to make new friends."

The Winter Sage watched her seriously, and for once she wore an expression that Yerin thought befit a woman of her wisdom and accomplishment. She nodded slowly.

"You want to hold the bunny?" Min Shuei suggested.

Yerin took back all her compliments. How could anyone become a Sage without taking the sacred arts seriously?

But the rabbit had finished drinking from the bottle and was burrowing down to sleep in the Sage's elbow.

"...yes," Yerin admitted.

If a Sage could afford the time to hold a baby rabbit, then *she* could.

When the bunny was sleeping peacefully in Yerin's arms—and Yerin was staying very still to avoid jostling it— the Winter Sage got down to business.

"We only have a month, and we won't find out your opponent until the last week, so that will be taken up by combat training. Meaning we have three weeks to help you do what even your master couldn't do at your age."

The Winter Sage reached onto a nearby shelf, filled with junk, and pulled out something that Yerin thought was a large book. It ended up being a wide board with a wooden edge and a black surface.

The Sage started writing on it with chalk. "Your Striker and Enforcer techniques are...fine. Not worth working on. But your Hidden Sword is abysmal. You don't even use it in most fights, do you?"

"If you've got a better suggestion, I've got two ears." Her Forger technique was brittle, weak, and its advantage of being invisible was useless against fighters with highly tuned spiritual senses.

Like any Underlord.

"Your master didn't choose his techniques at random. The Hidden Sword has principles in common with my Path, so I can teach you that personally. Your Endless Sword has reached the stage of 'sword like the wind,' but if we can push that to the whisper stage, you'll have more tactical options."

Her brow was furrowed in concentration as she wrote furiously on the board, but Yerin couldn't understand a word of it.

She watched the tiny sacred rabbit instead.

"Your foundation is adequate, but your master reached this point in the tournament using only the Path of the Endless Sword. *You* have made it so far using your other advantages."

Now she was stabbing the chalk angrily, as though just talking about it made her furious.

But then she paused.

In a forced casual tone, she asked, "Right, it just occurred to me to ask, but...where did you get the idea to fight using only your spiritual sense? That...did that come from Adama's Remnant?"

She had utterly failed to sound as though she didn't care, but Yerin didn't mind answering the question.

"Eithan. Perception training so I could keep up with an Arelius."

The Winter Sage let out a breath that meant either disappointment or relief. "He got lucky, then, and so did you. Improving your perception helped you sense your master's authority as a Sage. Between that and your Blood Shadow, you were able to cling to the tournament by your fingernails."

Yerin bristled at the phrasing, but she remembered Eithan looking into her eyes and shaking his head. *"I don't see it in you yet,"* he'd said.

If he had picked that training out of pure luck, she would eat her sword.

"Just have to push for advancement, true?" Yerin said. Technique training was good and useful, but there was no substitute for getting stronger.

The Winter Sage whirled the board around. "*This* will be your training schedule."

It was a chalky mess of nonsense.

"Ambitious? Of course!" the Sage said proudly. "And you can see we've assigned plenty of time to your advancement."

"Can't read that."

Shock slowly spread over the Winter Sage's face. "He...he never taught you to *read?*"

"Don't see how it hurts me." At worst, it was an occasional inconvenience. Dream tablets were more common in leaving behind techniques than paper was, and signs in major cities used constructs or simple symbols that even she understood. Or sometimes pictures.

"It's a basic skill! I'll have to see if we have any literacy tablets left in the Foundation compound. We might not; even our earliest students can read."

"We've got time for that, do we?" Yerin asked, running two fingers down the back of the sleeping rabbit.

"It will drive me insane if I see you advance to Overlord before you learn to read."

Yerin was glad to hear that advancement was indeed on the menu, but she had her sights set beyond Overlord.

"How do I get to be a Sage?" she asked.

She didn't fully understand what she'd done in the match against Lindon, but she had clearly tapped into the power of a Sage somehow.

That was her key to winning the tournament. And to the goal she'd held since she was a little girl: to succeed her master as the next Sage of the Endless Sword.

The Winter Sage's eyes lit up, but she bit her lip and slumped her shoulders. "No...no, we can't. We have to build you a solid foundation until Archlord. Then we can work on developing your authority."

"Authority?" Yerin asked.

The Winter Sage squirmed in place for five entire seconds before her excitement won out and she gave in. "Okay! To become a Sage, you have to contact a greater power, a symbol of a greater concept of reality. We call that symbol an Icon."

Tears welled up in her eyes and she gave Yerin a fond smile. "You have already touched the Sword Icon, which has guided you in battle."

Yerin nodded along. "Okay. So you sense the Icon, that's the first step. What's the next one?"

The Sage laughed. "First step? That's the *last* step."

That should be encouraging, Yerin knew, but she didn't like being laughed at. The softness of the rabbit's fur helped soothe her irritation.

"The *first* step is you yourself becoming a symbol of swordsmanship. In my case..." She spread her hands wide, snowflakes drifting down from the ceiling above. "...I manifested the Winter Icon first. I became a symbol of ice, of cold, of all things that freeze and are frozen. Only later did I also reflect the Sword Icon."

So you could have more than one Icon. That was good to know.

"And this Icon shows you how to win fights?"

The Winter Sage hefted the bottle she had used to feed the rabbit. She held it up so that Yerin could see it, then she tossed it into the air.

"Freeze," the Sage commanded.

The bottle stopped in midair. It had been tumbling end-over-end as it fell, and now it was locked in place.

Yerin crept up. She sensed no madra or aura holding the bottle in place. She ran one hand over it and below it, but felt nothing. She even tapped the bottle with one finger. It was stone solid.

Min Shuei reached out a hand of her own. The bottle fell into her waiting palm.

"Sages and Monarchs can command reality directly, but as you can imagine, there are limitations. We can only affect the world in certain ways related to our Icons, and we call the scope of that power our authority."

This was what Yerin wanted. She finally had a name for it.

This *authority* seemed like the goal of all the sacred arts:

complete control. It was the power that the Sword Sage had mastered.

And Yerin could too.

"We will make you—" the Sage looked up in the middle of her sentence and walked over to open the door.

The Underlord from before stumbled in, balancing four boxes in his arms. "I got it!" he said triumphantly. "I made it!"

One of the boxes tipped and almost fell until he controlled wind aura to push it back.

Yerin sensed the power of the natural treasures and elixirs in those boxes...

...when her Blood Shadow surged forward, leaping for them.

Yerin smoothly knelt, placing the rabbit on the floor, before she reached out with her will and seized the Shadow.

The parasite was only half-formed, essentially a mass of blood madra with fingers clawing for the boxes. Yerin froze it in midair, locking it in place.

For a long moment, they went back and forth as they had so many times, each shoving against the other for control. The Shadow had become so strong...and so *hungry.*

The Winter Sage spoke, and her one word resonated through the entire room. **"Return,"** she commanded.

The Blood Shadow slithered back into Yerin's spirit like wire on a spool.

It raged inside her, though Yerin reassured it that she would feed it soon. "Sorry," she muttered.

The Winter Sage looked both furious and disgusted. "Starve it. You can't remove it at this point without serious spiritual damage, but you can't keep feeding it."

"Was it me that just said the only reason I made it so far was because of this thing?" Yerin pretended to think as she scooped the sleeping rabbit back up. "No, I'm stone-certain that was *you.*"

"You are the *only* heir to the Endless Sword. You *must* stay focused on your Path."

"You think I'm sweet on this thing? I want it out of me!

But I keep it, maybe I win. *Maybe.* I starve it, I lose."

"Even if it stops you from becoming the next Sword Sage?"

Yerin was quiet. The rabbit in her arms squirmed.

"*Focus* is critical in manifesting an Icon. The Blood Shadow is not a reflection of your swordsmanship. It will not help you achieve the Sword Icon, and will only distract you."

"I don't want to keep it," Yerin said. "But I can't just...lose."

"Eat up," the Sage said, and she sounded exhausted. "And do not give a scrap to that parasite."

第八章

CHAPTER EIGHT

After Eithan, Yerin, and Mercy left with their respective Sages, Lindon returned to his room and summoned the Ninecloud Soul.

In addition to covering the announcement of the Uncrowned King tournament, the spirit also coordinated every construct in the Ninecloud Court.

When the rainbow light shimmered in front of him, Lindon spoke. "Pardon, but I would like access to the hunting grounds."

"The Underlord grounds are closed for maintenance tonight, but we have several Truegold locations available."

They had also received another shipment of hunger madra, which Lindon purchased in the name of the Akura family. The Ninecloud Court had provided him with madra—mostly broken-down bindings taken from dreadbeasts—to maintain his Remnant arm all this time.

As a part of his body, the limb required less maintenance than a normal construct would have. It took most of its sustenance from his pure madra.

But since he didn't generate hunger madra in his spirit, he did need to supplement it every once in a while. Especially when he strained it to its limits.

As he intended to do tonight.

The Truegold hunting ground to which he was taken in a flying carriage was a stony maze filled with Remnants and hostile spirits of every description. Signs and glowing constructs provided guidance and direction to those who were permitted access.

Some were Soulsmiths who preferred to do their own hunting, but most were here to train. Usually, entrants were charged a fee based on the Remnants they hunted down, but Lindon was permitted certain privileges as an Uncrowned competitor.

He passed a few late-training Truegolds, most of whom bowed when he walked by, but he wasn't looking for anything in particular. When he first cornered a Remnant without anyone around, he pounced on it.

It was a pink, fluid storm Remnant in a shape that reminded him of a gecko, and it kept repeating a series of buzzes that sounded like the word "grapefruit."

Lindon didn't know if it was trying to say something else or if its original body had died with citrus on the brain, but a quick spiritual scan made it clear that this wasn't one of the few Remnants that had developed a sense of awareness.

His Empty Palm blasted a chunk out of its center, and the rest of its body trembled like a shifting surface of gravel.

While it dispersed, he held out his Remnant arm and asked Dross for help.

With the spirit's assistance, he replicated the technique Northstrider had used.

The storm gecko exploded.

Lindon wasn't too surprised.

Under the protection of his madra, not even his clothes were singed, and he moved on to the next Remnant.

He had known he would need to make modifications to Northstrider's technique. The binding in his arm had been altered by the addition of the Archstone, but it had changed further as he had used and fed it over the last months. As a part of his body, it grew organically.

So while the principles of the original Consume technique would help him, they could only be guidelines. He had to adapt it himself.

He could have drained the Remnant dry of its madra on his first attempt. He had been doing that for years.

But he was trying to take everything.

Without Dross, he suspected this development process would have taken years. As it was, his first three attempts ended in failure, but the third Remnant gave up specks of blood essence, life essence, and that invisible substance that his arm had consumed before.

This time, the Remnant fell into a lifeless pile of limbs *before* it exploded.

Lindon lost all the power he'd drained. He vented the madra from his arm, and he couldn't capture the blood and life essence before they dissipated. As for the invisible force, he didn't know what happened to that.

But by the time his arm and madra channels were so sore that he was forced to stop, Dross had far more information than he'd started with.

Only then, exhausted and with his mind swirling with theories, did Lindon fall asleep.

While he slept, Dross dove into the Arelius technique library looking for information on hunger madra.

In the morning, Lindon asked the Ninecloud Soul for a copy of *The Seven Principles of Pure Madra,* by the Script Lord.

He had first heard of the book when he read a dream tablet left by its author in Ghostwater. Its ideas had allowed him to create the Soul Cloak, but he had taken only memories and impressions of its contents. He had never read the work itself until he came here and found that the Ninecloud Court had a copy in their library.

After that, he booked time in the tower's Soulsmith foundry.

The next few days fell into a rhythm, as Lindon brushed up on areas of improvement that he had neglected while competing in the tournament. He spent the bulk of his time on the Consume technique, but when he or Dross needed rest or when he had exhausted his possibilities, he worked on other areas.

Lindon would go to the hunting grounds in the morning and practice Consuming Remnants, spend midday studying theory as he and Dross recovered, then practice Soulsmithing in the evenings.

He returned to an old project that he had never fully abandoned: armor. He'd kept his Skysworn armor and samples of armor from the Seishen Kingdom in his soulspace, and he found several interesting dream tablets in the Ninecloud library from Soulsmiths who specialized in armor. They gave him entirely new avenues to explore.

Between all that and his daily cycling and physical training, he spent the next five days in a constant state of activity.

In the end, he gained a better understanding of where he stood.

His hunger arm could absorb the full power of a Remnant now with very little waste, but he had nothing to *do* with that power. He could catch it and release it. He needed a technique to process and control the energy inside his body, rather than trying to grab anything he could directly.

Eithan's Path of the Hollow King emphasized the property of pure madra that the *Seven Principles* called Emptiness. Pure madra diluted other aspects, effectively emptying them out and taking their place.

Lindon could integrate that into his own Path. The Empty Palm already worked that way, and he doubted it would change the Soul Cloak much. More importantly, the principle gave him the idea for a new technique.

He had seen other sacred artists use Ruler techniques to duplicate boundary fields, controlling aura to create certain effects inside a certain radius. Why couldn't he flood an area around himself with pure madra, preventing anyone else from using techniques?

It would take an astronomical amount of madra, and he hadn't been able to figure out a stable structure, but the theory was sound. Dross was able to simulate different versions of the technique, and Lindon had already begun testing several of them.

It was in working on that technique and consulting his Path of Twin Stars manual that he realized the solution to his hunger madra problem.

He needed a technique that worked inside of himself, filtering and separating madra. That would be a spirit Enforcer technique, and he had started looking through the Arelius technique library before an idea occurred to him.

He *had* a technique like that.

The Heart of Twin Stars.

It had been designed to split one core into two, but it *was* a spirit Enforcer technique compatible with pure madra. With a few modifications, he and Dross were sure they could get it to work.

Which left him, on the evening of the fifth day, with three projects: develop the Heart of Twin Stars into a proper filter, continue simulating the pure madra boundary field technique until he found a version he was comfortable practicing, and assemble a set of armor for testing.

Lindon wrote as much into his notes and sat back in his chair, satisfied. He had made great progress, and he had plenty in front of him. To occupy his time.

While he was alone.

His satisfaction waned.

Little Blue rolled a scale across the desk in front of him, and Dross spoke into his mind in an encouraging fashion. [Don't worry, don't worry! This should be *plenty* to keep you busy for three more weeks. Who needs a Sage?]

It wasn't the lack of a Sage that bothered him, and it wasn't entirely loneliness. It was that they were out there fighting for something, while he was only preparing.

Other people were fighting over Dreadgods, or training to stop an invasion of the Blackflame Empire. Meanwhile, he couldn't help.

At least not yet.

"Two more days," he said aloud. Northstrider had borrowed Dross twice in the last five days, but neither time had he given Lindon more useful advice. But he had reiterated that Fury was scheduled to arrive at the Wandering Titan's location in two more days.

Charity was supposed to visit before that, and he could try to convince her to send him along.

He could wait two days. It wasn't as though he didn't enjoy Soulsmithing, research, and practice, but none of that could compare to actually stealing power from enemies.

If he could get the Consume technique working, he could be an Overlord before the next round began. Or at least a peak Underlord.

A knock echoed at the door, startling Little Blue so that she let her pure scale fall off the edge of the table. She pouted a moment before scampering down to go get it.

Lindon stretched his spiritual perception outside, and when he felt the identity of the person at the door, he used a brief burst of the Soul Cloak to leap across the room and open it.

Akura Charity stood there, dressed like a peasant worker. She wore simple brown with a stained smock, her hair frizzy and tied behind her with a rag.

The outfit tugged on something in Lindon's memory, but he didn't chase it down, inviting her in.

She drifted inside after him. "I have come to discuss your reward," she said, but of course Lindon knew what he wanted.

"If it's not too much to ask, could you bring me to help your father around the Dreadgod? If you could send me there and bring me back for the Uncrowned matches, I would be grateful."

Ideally, she would transport him to the Wandering Titan battlefield in between each round, bringing him back for every fight, but that might be pushing his luck.

Charity was silent for a moment as she considered. "I had intended to offer you the inheritance of an Archlord

Soulsmith, but if you would prefer transportation, I can agree to that instead."

Lindon's certainty came crumbling down.

A true inheritance was a dream tablet that a Soulsmith spent years working on, containing their life's knowledge of Soulsmithing. They contained such depth, detail, and complexity that they could only be fully integrated by one person, and so they were created to pass on a Soulsmith's knowledge to an heir.

It could also take years to digest the experience in an inheritance, although with Dross' help, Lindon suspected he could make that process much, much shorter.

With an Archlord inheritance, Lindon could go from a talented Soulsmith with a miraculous dream-spirit to a true expert almost overnight.

"I'm...certain," Lindon said, though the words scraped his heart raw. "As long as I will have more opportunity to earn advancement resources on the battlefield."

"That you will. And I must visit Sky's Edge periodically anyway, but taking you along will cost me more of my time and attention. Given that, this will be your only compensation for the tournament."

"I understand."

"Very well. I will be ready to depart in three hours. Prepare yourself." She turned to leave before adding, "Most of our vassal factions are helping us secure this territory. Including the Seishen Kingdom. They may have already arrived."

Lindon remembered the fury of their Overlord king when he had discovered the death of his eldest son. That pressure still felt like it was choking now.

He remembered Kiro's Remnant rising from the floor of the Akura storehouse. A scythe of green flame that had cut short Yerin's life, and the gray-eyed woman who wielded it.

"Gratitude, but that does not change my answer."

He had known he was stepping into danger as soon as he'd chosen to step into a war zone around a Dreadgod. He could accept a little more risk.

And he had overcome the Seishen Underlords when he was a Truegold. He might not be Uncrowned, but he didn't have to cower before them.

If the Consume technique worked as he hoped it would, *they* might have to cower before *him.*

A vague hint of a smile crossed Charity's lips before she left. "Three hours. Be ready."

It took Lindon that long to finish packing.

When Charity finally ushered Lindon away from the Ninecloud Court, he was swallowed up by shadows.

Unlike some other times he had been transported, he didn't see blue light. He felt only darkness swallowing him whole.

[Don't worry about the dark, I'll light things up for you,] Dross said.

A bright light shone straight into Lindon's eyes. Though he flinched and turned away, he couldn't escape the glare.

[Look at that bright, refreshing light. Doesn't it just lift your spirits?]

This hurts, you know.

[Healing is often painful.]

When the darkness retreated, Dross pulled away the illusion of bright light. Though it had never had anything to do with his eyes, Lindon had to blink rapidly to recover his sight.

Heat and smoke choked the air, and Lindon manipulated wind aura to keep his eyes and mouth clear.

"The Firestone Roads," Charity announced. Glowing rocks that shone with the rippling orange of flame were arranged into paths leading away from them, but half of the paths rose into the air and vanished into dark plumes of smoke.

A crimson deer whose antlers were aflame looked at Lindon and snorted. "Dragons," the stag said distinctly, and then galloped away on hooves that trailed ash.

Beside the roads of ember-bright stones rose a scripted spire like a lighthouse. Fire aura was drawn there, and a blazing signal-fire shone from the top.

"Pardon," Lindon said, "but this isn't our destination, is it?" Were they planning on walking from here?

Charity reached into a shadowy void key and pulled out a chair, on which she sat. Its wooden legs began smoldering until she waved a hand and the smoke vanished. "With you along, I cannot travel as quickly as I would otherwise. It will take us until evening to arrive, though it will be morning in Sky's Edge. While we're here, you may cycle the abundant fire aura or explore, as it suits you."

The fire aura *was* powerful, but there was very little destruction to go along with it, as nothing he could see was being consumed by the flame. He elected to explore, pulling Little Blue out so she could see too.

They found a boiling river filled with white-hot fish, a family of those fiery stags attending what seemed to be a cultural history lecture, and a ten-foot-tall ash creature that recognized Lindon from the Uncrowned King tournament.

Charity appeared in front of Lindon after he'd finished recording his voice into a construct for the ash monster. "Time to leave."

Lindon and his two spirits bid the creature farewell.

Their next stop was a web-city of sacred spiders that found Dross fascinating, and then an ancient forest glade full of Sylvan Riverseeds. Little Blue spent over an hour playing with her kind, though she was the only one with any detail or real intelligence as far as Lindon could tell.

After that, they crossed the ocean, where Charity told them to be careful. The inhabitants of the ocean were largely hostile to the Akura clan, she said.

They first landed in a bustling city where every building was on a separate platform raised high over the ocean's surface. The platforms were connected by bridges that swayed in the wind, as a violent storm tossed waves and threw out forks of lightning.

They spent most of their time sitting in a restaurant, watching massive shapes roll in the water beneath them... and the clouds above them.

While idle, Charity usually pulled out a book and began to read, and Lindon didn't want to interrupt. But now that they were sharing a table, he waited for her to glance up from the page before he asked her a question.

"Pardon if this seems rude, but I have often wondered: are you the only Sage in the Akura family?"

"The only direct descendant." She returned her eyes to the page.

"And your father is the only Herald?"

She nodded, but thus far this was common knowledge about the Akura clan. They had many allies among the Heralds and Sages, but Charity and Fury were the only ones in the family.

"If you don't mind me asking...why?"

If their family could raise a Herald and a Sage as well as a Monarch, why couldn't they do it again?

"There is a balance. It would be...dangerous...to have too many individuals of a certain level at one time. So when an Archlord shows signs of advancement, if we believe it would disrupt that balance, we encourage them to ascend."

She flipped a page, and her tone became dry. "The heavens have never turned us down."

Lindon still felt like he was missing something. "Apologies, but do you mean you're trying to stay in balance with the other Monarch factions?"

"These are not matters for an Underlord. When you reach Archlord, you will discover certain truths for yourself."

And that was the end of that conversation.

Two stops later, Charity told Lindon to prepare for the cold. "While the weather in Sky's Edge is no threat to an Underlord, we are arriving at a location of powerful ice aura, so dress accordingly. If you didn't think to pack for the cold, you'll have to—"

Lindon pulled a heavy coat and winter boots from his void key.

They emerged from darkness into a frigid gale of blowing ice.

Lindon slapped a few chunks from the air before Charity's aura control took over and deflected the hand-sized flying blades.

They stood on a smooth, wide surface, like a polished ball a hundred feet in the air. The sun still hadn't risen over a range of white-capped peaks to the east, so the entire world was painted in shades of gray.

To the west stretched the ocean they'd just crossed, and at their feet was a town made of thick wooden logs.

The town had been destroyed.

Houses were burned, smashed, or torn apart. Pillars of smoke and dust rose into the sky, and the streets seethed with shadowy creatures. If Lindon was to open his aura sight, he was sure that he would see the power of destruction hanging over Sky's Edge like a dark cloud.

But he didn't open it. He knew better.

One massive hand of dark stone rested across the shore of Sky's Edge, palm-down and fingers spread. Several houses were crushed under each finger.

An arm stretched back into the ocean, leading to a bulky shadow beneath the waves and a dome of rough stone that rose from the water like an island.

The shell of the Wandering Titan.

He found himself thinking of Orthos.

In a way, the turtle felt closer now than he had in almost a year. As though Lindon could sense him nearby if he stretched out his spiritual perception.

But that was just Lindon's imagination.

The Titan was often depicted as a turtle that walked like a man, and now Lindon could see why. While its shell had become a hill rising from the water, its hand was five-fingered and clearly shaped like a human's.

The Dreadgod had reached up to the land with one arm. Its palm sank into the ground, cracks spreading from its fingers and stretching throughout the town.

He couldn't wrap his mind around the size. He had seen the Bleeding Phoenix take up an entire horizon, and the Titan was on the same scale, like a piece of the landscape rather than something that could rise to its feet at any moment.

"The Dreadgod still has not fully awakened," Charity told

him. "It crawled slowly across the ocean floor, toward the labyrinth that gave it birth, until it made it to these shores. Our oracles predict that this will be its last stop before it awakens in six to eight weeks, by which time we must have evacuated the surrounding lands."

"No one's going to stop it?" Lindon asked, surprised. Malice had stopped the Bleeding Phoenix by herself the last time. Surely another Monarch could do something similar.

Charity turned to him, purple eyes impassive. "Monarchs, Heralds, and Sages are the only ones capable of doing *anything* to a Dreadgod, and among them only a Monarch could match one for any period of time. They would then be weakened for a rival."

"Apologies, but your mother..."

"Grandmother. Stopping the Bleeding Phoenix cost her. Her holdings around the world were taken or sabotaged while her attention was occupied. We have recovered some of them, but not all. It is very likely she lost more than she saved."

Lindon knew a Monarch's responsibilities were broad, but his mind boggled at the scope.

There had been an important reason to stop the Phoenix, and he thought he knew what it was.

"The labyrinth. The Dreadgods are after it."

"They are, though *why* is another one of those mysteries you'll have to discover for yourself." She didn't seem too concerned, explaining impassively. "Even I don't know what's inside."

"And what happens if they reach it?"

If they wanted it so badly, surely it was important for the Monarchs to stop them from getting there.

"Nothing," Charity said calmly.

Lindon waited for the rest of the explanation, suspicious. It couldn't be that simple.

"The defenses on the labyrinth are legendary. The Dreadgods usually can't locate it at all, as the entrances remain sealed, so they spend their time awake wandering around and satisfying their hunger. During the destruction of the original Blackflame Empire, they converged on the location of the labyrinth. They tore up the ground for miles, but found nothing.

"Yes, the labyrinth is perfectly secure. But the people living around it are not. It is still a mystery how one Underlord opening an outer hatch for a handful of minutes caught the attention of Dreadgods so far away. We discussed executing your Blackflame Emperor for dereliction of his duty, but even throwing all the entrances in the Empire wide open for *years* should not have produced such a result."

She shook her head. "In the end, we can only blame fate."

Lindon looked down at the new "island" resting in the ocean and shivered. Only a few weeks, then the Dreadgod would rise.

"Gratitude," Lindon said. "I can make it from here." He sensed a large collection of sacred artists at the edge of town opposite the Dreadgod's hand, behind a large stone wall.

"I will accompany you," Charity said. "I have to speak with the Overlord in charge."

The Sage seemed to be waiting for him to take the lead, so he hopped over the edge. Only while falling did he notice the nature of the ball they had been standing on.

It was the pommel of a sword. He fell past the hilt, guard, and gleaming white blade, which had been driven into the earth.

Extending his perception, he saw that what looked like metal was actually unbelievably dense madra. This was a Forger technique.

Why had it been Forged with a hilt and guard? Why not just a sharp blade?

It reminded him of Yerin's Final Sword. She and her master had Forged the technique into the shape of the full weapon.

There had to be a reason.

When they landed—Charity lightly, as though she weighed only a feather, and Lindon surrounded by the blue-white Soul Cloak—he asked about the sword.

"This town was once the site of a battle between the

Winter Sage and the Herald of the Tidewalker Sect," she explained. "The final attack that drove him off remains to this day, and is one of the reasons we're here."

At the base of the blade, the locals had raised a stronghold of wood and stone against the flat blade. An iron-banded wooden gate kept the fort shut, but he sensed powerful earth aura inside.

"The introduction of such powerful madra from the Winter Sage had a unique reaction. The sword formed a certain synergy with a strong vein of earth aura, and this became one of the few places in our territory where it is possible to mine wintersteel."

She gestured back to the shore. "It is why we're here, and why *he* is here too. The Wandering Titan feeds on powerful materials, especially minerals. Aside from evacuation and protection, we are also here to remove as much of the mine's product as possible."

Lindon didn't see how anyone could be left to evacuate, because every inch of the town swarmed with dreadbeasts.

The creatures filled the streets of the dead town with a putrid stink, but they stayed far away from Charity as she and Lindon dashed to the fortress wall at the edge of town.

The wall was forty feet high, made of stone that had clearly been pulled from the earth and sealed together by a Ruler technique. Blood and scorch marks stained the bottom third of the wall, and dreadbeast corpses were piled at the bottom.

Even more creatures scrambled over those.

Every animal within miles had to have been warped by hunger madra to form the army of dreadbeasts that Lindon had seen already, and sacred artists at the top of the wall swept the monsters with Striker techniques.

The guards were Golds with the occasional Lord or Lady, almost all of them wearing full armor. Over their heads, flags of the Seishen Kingdom flew proudly.

The creatures beneath them must have been Truegold or lower, but the impression they gave off as a group was far more dangerous. Though Lindon could destroy any number of them from a distance, if he fell into such a group, they would tear him limb from limb.

Dreadbeasts flitted through the skies as well, though fortunately fewer than those on the ground, but they kept largely clear of the Kingdom encampment.

In the skies over the fortress, the Seishen King Dakata did battle.

He was a hulking, broad-shouldered bear of a man, especially in his bulky gray armor, but he faced a creature that dwarfed him.

Lindon would call it a dreadbeast, but it had the figure of a human with long, grotesquely twisted limbs. Its pale skin was broken and rotting, its jaw hung loose, and the beast gave off the impression of a horrific puppet made of corpses rather than any sort of living thing.

It flew on wind madra, sending Striker and Ruler techniques after the King in such a furious barrage that Lindon suspected it would tear its own madra channels apart. King Dakata weathered the assault like a boulder in a stream, but the Thousand-Mile Cloud on which he stood wavered with every hit.

This was a dreadbeast with the power of an Overlord. Fear shivered through Lindon's heart. How powerful could these become?

[Uh, well, the one in the ocean can literally eat Monarchs, so...*that* powerful.]

Charity drew her hand back, then flicked her fingers forward.

Clouds of silver-and-purple madra swept forward like a bank of fog, and Lindon was certain that he was watching the Striker technique of a Sage. Then the madra formed into distinct figures, hundreds of ghostly specters condensing from madra.

The phantoms raised their swords, reaping dreadbeasts like wheat. Each figure struck once and then dispersed, puffing into essence. One specter, larger and more distinct than the others, skewered the Overlord dreadbeast through the back with a spear.

The humanoid creature stiffened and screamed in what sounded like terror before King Dakata's sword took off its head.

Every other dreadbeast that had been struck by Charity's technique died. In seconds, the army besieging the fortress had been reduced by half.

Lindon had seen living techniques before, but now he *had* to know the secret. Was that a Forger technique, or a Striker technique come to life?

As the Seishen soldiers sent up a cheer, Charity glanced over to Lindon. "Striker technique," she said. "Imbuing a living will into techniques is very advanced, but you will learn someday."

Lindon wondered how she had read his mind, but he didn't really care. He wanted that power.

The Seishen King descended before them, going to one knee in front of Charity as he removed his helm. His gray beard and hair were matted with sweat, and he spoke with both exhaustion and respect. "I thank you, Sage. I would have felled that beast sooner or later, but I fear what damage it may have done in the meantime."

"What is the situation?" Charity asked calmly.

"I have no doubt the Sage understands it already. We hastened here, to obey the Akura summons as quickly as possible, and arrived only the day before yesterday. The place was...a slaughterhouse. We gathered everyone we could, but that was only two in ten of the town's residents. We suspect there are as many again still alive and in hiding, but that is entirely a guess. We have barely been able to secure our *own* position."

As he spoke, his eyes flicked to Lindon more than once.

He showed no surprise. He'd noticed Lindon already and remembered him.

[Do you think he knows we killed his son? I say *we* because I want him to know that I deserve half the credit.]

Lindon bowed respectfully, hoping that manners might somehow help.

"I see. Good work, Your Highness." She spread a hand to her side. "I'm certain you remember Wei Shi Lindon Arelius, my selection for the tournament. You may not have heard yet, but he earned his way to the top sixteen."

Dakata's jaw stiffened. "I...see. He must be a valuable asset to the Akura clan, then."

"He is. And he will be joining up with my father's forces when they arrive in a day or two. Until then, I will leave him in your care."

Lindon whipped his head around to stare at the Sage. If she left him under Dakata's supervision, he'd be dead within the hour.

Charity went on, serene and unconcerned with Lindon's panic. "My father is looking forward to meeting with this Underlord. If for whatever reason he cannot, he will be very disappointed. In you."

Dakata bowed his head. "I will protect him as if he were my own *son*." There was gruff anger in the last word.

Lindon knew that the Sage was protecting him, but he still didn't trust the Overlord's restraint. "Apologies, honored Sage, but may I—"

"You will be busy before my father arrives," Charity interrupted. "We will pay a bounty for dreadbeast bindings. And you should be prepared to do battle against enemy Underlords when Abyssal Palace arrives."

"If I may ask, can I stay...elsewhere...today?" He was painfully aware of the king kneeling behind him, listening to every word.

"I have every faith in your ingenuity and resilience. As well as Dakata's self-control. Farewell, both of you. I will see you soon."

Then she vanished into a pool of shadow.

Leaving Lindon alone with King Dakata.

The Overlord straightened up, pulling out his Thousand-Mile Cloud and placing his helm back on. "Stay away from Daji," the King said roughly. "He'll kill you. Now get behind the wall and we'll find you a room."

Lindon had no intention of staying in any room the Seishen Kingdom prepared for him.

第九章

CHAPTER NINE

During his first night in Sky's Edge, Lindon didn't sleep at all.

As an Underlord, he needed less sleep than he ever had before...unless he exerted himself. He still recovered faster while sleeping, so he preferred to get five or six hours of sleep a night to maintain top condition. But a night without sleep wouldn't kill him.

Falling asleep inside the Seishen Kingdom's walls just might.

He had stayed long enough to at least *see* the room they had given him, but on his way he had glimpsed both Meira and Prince Daji.

Daji, younger brother to the Prince Kiro that Lindon had left dead in Charity's treasure vault, was a wolf-like young man with a savage air. He was as tall as his father, but not as broad, and he carried two swords as he prowled the wall, shouting at his men.

The Underlady Meira had almost been chosen to participate in the Uncrowned King tournament as part of the Akura vassal team, and that was the lesser reason why she frightened Lindon.

Her hair and eyes were both gray, though she was a young woman, and a pink flower over one ear seemed to be her Goldsign. She was a life artist and carried a tall scythe with a blade made of green flame. Lindon had seen her fight with armor before, but in the fortress she wore simple sacred artist robes.

The robes were stained in blood, which was especially concerning because her techniques were bloodless.

He saw her as she leaped into the sky, pulled a winged dreadbeast apart with her bare hands, and then fell onto the back of another. Only when she was on the ground and surrounded did she pull out her scythe and swing it around her, cutting through the ranks of the enemy in a furious rage.

She had been the one responsible for almost killing Yerin, and Lindon still felt a tight anger toward her for that.

But in the end, Yerin and Lindon had been the ones to walk away victorious. He was content to leave her alone.

The Seishen Kingdom had plenty of other Underlords after their time in the Night Wheel Valley, such that Lindon felt like he was surrounded by them until he escaped the fortress, but none seemed to notice him through his pure madra veil.

And no one cared when he jumped down from the top of the wall and ran into the rocky wilderness.

Lindon didn't know how seriously the Seishen King would take Charity's warning—would he hunt Lindon down to protect him, in order to avoid punishment from Fury?—but he had made his choice quickly. A dreadbeast-haunted wilderness was safer than a base of the Seishen Kingdom.

Lindon had survived dreadbeasts in the wild before, though those had been far weaker. Still, a script-circle and a network of hastily improvised security constructs kept him safe as he scooped a cave out of a cliff face with dragon's breath.

Of course, he made sure to spend a moment stripping the binding from any dreadbeast he killed.

Any bounty was profit.

Instead of sleeping, he spent the night in the cave developing his techniques. The sooner he could get the Consume technique working, the better.

He sat cross-legged on the dusty stone floor as dreadbeasts

prowled outside. His attention was focused inward as he tried to incorporate the principle of Emptiness into his Heart of Twin Stars.

Eithan's cycling techniques were helpful for inspiration, but he didn't have a spirit Enforcer technique in his Path, so there was nothing directly applicable. Lindon was forced to sit and check off variations as Dross simulated more.

[Oh wait, oh wait, I've got it! That's it, that's the key! Just try the last cycling pattern...*in reverse.*]

Inspired by the enthusiasm in Dross' voice, Lindon reversed the course of his madra, matching it up to his breath.

In about ten seconds, he had to stop. Every inch of his madra channels was in searing pain.

[*Perfect!*] Dross shouted. [I couldn't quite visualize what would happen if you tried that. Now we can absolutely, definitively, cross that off the list.]

Little Blue whizzed around Lindon's head on a tiny Thousand-Mile Cloud, laughing like a silver bell.

Ocean-blue hair streamed behind her, as she had gained detail and substance over time. He could even see little feet kicking at the hem of her sapphire dress.

The cloud he'd made her wouldn't last an entire day, and he had made her promise not to cross the script-circle that kept dreadbeasts out, but she loved flying.

At least one of them was having fun.

Trying new patterns for the Heart of Twin Stars over and over again required his entire attention but had produced no results, so frustration grated on him. He and Dross both agreed that separating madra with it should be theoretically possible—the technique was made to separate part of his soul from itself, after all—but his madra just didn't seem to move like it should.

Their progress on his new boundary technique had stalled for the same reason. Not only could they not hold it stable for more than a breath, but it wouldn't block even a Highgold Striker technique. The pure madra he was pouring into it didn't cleanse foreign elements aggressively enough.

Little Blue stopped her cloud in front of his eyes and piped a question.

She wanted to help.

He smiled, trying not to worry her. "You already help. How could I have made it without you?"

The Path of Black Flame still scorched his madra channels, and without Little Blue's help, he would have to use it much more sparingly. The Dragon Descends would damage his spirit every time he practiced.

She cheeped more insistently, and Lindon gave her proposal more thought.

Then an idea clicked into place.

Little Blue was a naturally formed spirit of pure madra. Her power worked by cleansing and pacifying hostile elements in the spirit. He couldn't be certain, but that *might* be exactly what he needed.

"Dross, what would happen if we added Little Blue's madra to the Heart of Twin Stars."

[Eh, um, ah, that...no, that absolutely wouldn't work. Not with the version you're using now. And even if I came up with a variation that would be compatible, you would need her help every time you used the technique. Not worth trying. Should we try it anyway? Let's try it.]

Dross played the simulation in Lindon's mind, and it worked largely as Lindon had hoped. Blood and life essence from his hunger arm went to feed his body and lifeline respectively, and any drained madra was purified.

The efficiency of the madra was poor, as not all madra could be purified, and it required great concentration on Lindon's part to control.

But it seemed to work.

Hurriedly, Lindon rushed out to the front of the cave. A script-circle blocking the entrance kept slathering beasts of every description at bay; the last time he'd looked, there were five of them, but now that number had doubled.

Lindon saw them as walking stacks of scales.

Three security constructs buzzed around him as they aimed their launchers outward. They would attack anything that broke the circle, and none of them would last any longer than Little Blue's cloud, but they gave him peace of mind.

A ward-key at his belt made him the exception to the script as he reached out with his white arm, seizing a dreadbeast of about Truegold level and draining it.

The others pounced on him, but he pulled his hand back in an instant. He only needed a little power to test.

Hurriedly he dashed back into the cave and began cycling. The blood and life essence were already fading away, but the madra—a muddy brown mess of conflicting aspects—raged up his arm and into his channels. If it had been Lord quality, he might have already suffered damage.

"Little Blue," he asked, "would you mind helping me for a moment?"

She glowed with delight and raced over on her cloud. A second later, she poured her soothing madra into him.

He took it, matching the blue sparks of her power to the rhythm of the modified Heart of Twin Stars. It was difficult splitting his attention so many ways, as he had to incorporate Little Blue's madra, control his own in an unfamiliar pattern, and maintain a grip on the energy he'd drained from the dreadbeast.

It took so much of his concentration that he didn't realize it had worked until all the power was gone.

The blood essence went to his body, the life essence to his lifeline, and a trickle of pure madra back into his core. Even his channels felt slightly healthier.

[Blech!] Dross spat. [Ew, I got some of its thoughts. It's so...hungry. And it's in constant pain. I don't like pain, don't make me feel it again.]

Lindon couldn't contain his excitement. This was the breakthrough he'd been waiting for.

Now the Consume technique was in his reach.

When it was finished, every enemy would be nothing more than a spiritual elixir for him to consume. The dreadbeasts didn't *just* look like piles of walking scales, but like walking miracle pills.

He swept Little Blue up in his hands, holding her over his head. "We did it! You were the key!"

She looked surprised, and she burbled a question.

"You! You were what we were missing!"

She cheered like a chorus of whistles, running around in circles on his hand.

Then she plopped down and said something else, and he hesitated.

"I...we need to come up with a different version before we try it again. We'll need to know if it strains you first."

There were a number of areas that could be improved. The cycling path was less efficient than it could be, and it took him too much concentration to channel three things at once. Dross was simulating new versions already.

More importantly, he didn't want to work Blue too hard. All it would take was one accident, and he might crush her with the power of his spirit.

Impatiently, she patted his hand and whistled a low flute note.

"...there is one more thing we could try," he said reluctantly. "But that's all, okay?"

She cheeped at him to get on with it.

Closing his eyes, Lindon concentrated on the latest version of the Empty Field.

[Hollow Domain,] Dross corrected.

We'll name it later.

They hadn't agreed on a name for their new technique yet. Lindon wanted it to sound like it belonged with his Empty Palm, but Dross thought Hollow Domain sounded better. Lindon thought the name fit Eithan's Path more than his own.

He set up the Highgold launcher construct they'd been using for practice, then triggered it.

And used his new technique.

Madra flooded out of him...and with Little Blue's support,

it was tinged more blue than white. The wave of madra filled the room, cleansing everything except pure madra.

The launcher shot a Striker technique of light and force, a beam that entered the zone of blue light...and fizzled out instantly like a candle dunked in water.

The field of pure madra dispersed, flowing away. It was supposed to stay in place, stable, rather than washing over the room like a wave. And it wasn't supposed to take an entire quarter of his pure core's contents.

It *was* supposed to cancel out enemy techniques. Which it had.

Little Blue gave a cheer, but she swayed and fell over on his hand. She pushed back to her feet in a moment, insisting that they keep going, but he was already placing her onto her cloud.

"Apologies, Little Blue, but I need to take notes."

She seemed to accept that, but she kept her cloud hovering close to his head.

He wrote down his experiences and observations, as well as the problems that still needed ironing out, but all his previous frustrations were wiped away. This was a *real* start, and now he was close to having more weapons in his arsenal.

His Path was almost complete.

The main problem still facing him was Blue's safety. Maybe he could imitate her madra on his own, or get her to Forge scales for him to consume in battle.

She whistled when she grew impatient with his notes, and he gave her a smile of apology. "You know I can't put you in danger. Even if I keep you in my core, one good hit to my spirit and you could die. Apologies."

Little Blue scowled at him, then flew her cloud up to the ceiling to sulk.

Lindon spent an entire night and most of the next day working on his new techniques and pushing through the Heaven and Earth Purification Wheel.

Then the Akura cloudship arrived.

He sensed the ship approach Sky's Edge, as Akura Fury was doing nothing to disguise his presence. Lindon flew on his Skysworn Thousand-Mile Cloud back to the wall of the Seishen encampment, killing flying dreadbeasts and tucking their bindings away as he traveled.

The ship on its dark cloud hung between the fortress and the giant, white sword embedded in the terrain. King Dakata and several Overlords flew out to meet the Akura family as they arrived.

Lindon stayed well back.

Akura Fury drifted up, over his ship, and took a deep breath.

A moment later, his voice boomed out over the entire town.

"Hey everybody! Welcome to Sky's Edge! Let's remember why we're here: we need to protect the survivors, clear out the dreadbeasts, secure the mine, and evacuate the citizens *before* the Titan wakes up." He ticked off every point on his fingers.

"In a few days, we'll be joined by Abyssal Palace, so then we'll get to fight them too! Until then, the bounty system works like we discussed. It's set up on the ship. If you don't know your teams, find..."

The Herald scratched the back of his head. "...Justice? No, Justice is still at home. Well, you can find somebody to tell you. Oh, and don't hurt your allies, okay? You can fight if you really want to, but make it an official duel with rules and everything. Abandoning a mission, fighting over bounties, or permanently injuring someone is a punishment. Kill anybody on our side or betray us, and I'll kill you."

He didn't sound too upset about the idea. Fury crossed his arms and furrowed his brow, thinking for a moment. "Hmmm...I think that's about it. Have fun!"

The tiny cloudship of the Seishen Kingdom stopped halfway as figures burst into flight around the Akura ship like bees fleeing a hive. Clouds, sacred beasts, Remnants, constructs, and techniques shot away from the large cloudship and headed to the ground, all carrying teams of sacred artists.

After enduring the wave of traffic, the Seishen king and his entourage continued toward the Herald.

But Fury vanished in a blur of motion.

Lindon only had time for a spike of alarm to go through his spirit before Akura Fury came to a stop in front of him, grinning, his red eyes bright.

The wind of his passage blew against Lindon in a powerful gust, carrying the stink of dreadbeasts and making the Herald's shadowy hair whip wildly.

"Hey, Lindon! Did Charity bring you?"

Lindon pressed his fists together and bowed. "She did, and she suggested that she would be back to meet with you soon."

"Oh, okay." He didn't sound like he cared whether Charity checked up on him or not. "Glad you could make it! We need to get you a team, let's see...aha!"

There was a small cloudship nearby, designed for about ten people, with a purple cloud that was about to touch down to the ground.

Fury made a grasping motion, and a hand of shadow seized the ship and started dragging it backwards.

As it grew closer, Lindon's heart sank.

At the control panel of the ship, with his head in his hands, was Akura Pride.

Six other Underlords rode the ship with him, and Lindon recognized them all. Akura Grace, like a younger version of Malice herself, stood behind Pride and held a hand on her curving single-edged sword. Two of her relatives waited in the back, the other members of the Akura backup team, as did the two women from the Frozen Blade School.

They both had tan skin, white-streaked black hair, and blue-and-white robes, and he couldn't tell them apart. Their names were Maten Teia and Maten Kei, though Lindon had never really had a conversation with either of them, and he didn't know if they were sisters or distant relatives that happened to look alike.

The final passenger was Naru Saeya, who would have been able to see over the heads of everyone else if she hadn't sat herself on a bench at the very back of the deck. Her wings were retracted, she kept her eyes on the ground, and the peacock feathers over her ear drooped.

These were the participants from the Uncrowned King tournament.

"This is our best Underlord team!" Fury said proudly. "You guys are better than everybody else, but we need you for harder assignments, so it evens out. Lindon, you made it the farthest in the tournament, so you're in charge now. Pride, you're number two. Everybody else, just figure it out."

Pride looked like he was trying to launch a Striker technique with his eyes.

Grace frowned slightly, the other two Akura family members seemed uncomfortable, the Frozen Blades muttered to one another, and Naru Saeya looked up from the deck.

All of them watched him.

[Would you like a reminder of how many times you've fought each person on that ship?] Dross asked.

I haven't fought the Matens or Naru Saeya at all, Lindon responded. He was resolved to look on the positive side.

"Good luck, kids!" Fury said cheerfully. "Work hard!"

He left a miniature hurricane behind him as he leaped away again.

"Apologies," Lindon said as soon as the Herald was gone.

"Get on the ship," Pride snapped. "We're wasting time."

Lindon hopped on, and Pride immediately started piloting away. Lindon didn't even know where they were going. "Pardon, everyone. I would never wish to contradict a Herald, but I don't know that it's appropriate for me to be in charge. I don't even know what's going on."

Though he was very interested in the idea of bounties.

Pride looked to him in disgust. "What attitude is that? Raise your chin. Leading this team is an honor, and you should work to be worthy of it."

He tossed something to Lindon. A viewing tablet with text

written on it in light projected by internal constructs.

Lindon's eyes widened when he read the words "Bounty Board."

"Uncle Fury likes to make it a game," Pride said. "Teams get contribution points for contributing to our cause here. There are no individual points. The team's score is pooled together and the distribution of prizes is decided by the team's *leader*."

The stares from the rest of the team prickled him, but he didn't look up.

The tablet recorded a list of bounties that could be claimed by each team.

Dreadbeast binding below Lord: 1 point
Dreadbeast binding, Lord-rank: 5 points
Assignment completion: 20 points
Natural treasures: 5 points minimum, subject to appraisal
Spoils of war: 10 points minimum, subject to appraisal

That explained the teams all around him, who were already flying around and hunting dreadbeasts. Lindon was even more pleased by the collection of hunger bindings he'd earned over the last day.

Then he saw the list of rewards.

Natural treasures ranged from four points to sixteen, depending on strength, and you could use points to purchase materials like scales, dead matter, simple constructs, and weapons. So far, so expected.

When he reached the end of the list, his heart started to pound.

Limited Stock:
Tears of the Mother Tree: 1500 points
Interior Command elixir: 1000
Gold Lion's Heart pill: 1400
Low-grade void key (two available): 1250
High-grade void key: 1750
Diamond Veins: 2000

Divine Treasure - Thousand Swords of Binding Light: 2250

"...spent the last two weeks training together," Pride was saying. "We saw your performance in the tournament, but whatever my uncle says, that's no basis for command."

Striker techniques were lighting up the rocky ground around Lindon. Every second, dreadbeasts died.

Points were being taken from his pocket. He had dreadbeast bindings in his void key, but not enough.

If he played this right, he could get these prizes.

He could get them *all.*

"Pride. One moment."

The short Akura Underlord bristled, then took a step closer to Lindon. "You seem to have forgotten that I'm the one who—"

Lindon seized him, terror filling his words. "Every second we waste is another point gone. You understand? We're *losing points.*"

This could be the greatest harvest he'd ever reaped in his life, and he had started *late.*

Pride tried to respond, but Lindon released him. "How many of you have Thousand-Mile Clouds?" They didn't respond immediately, and desperate impatience clawed at his chest. "Your hands! Raise them!"

[I wish you could see how crazy you look right now,] Dross said. [I wish *I* could see it.]

Hesitantly, everyone but Naru Saeya and the two Frozen Blade women raised their hands.

Naru Saeya didn't need one, but the other two would need to be able to fly to keep up. Lindon opened his void key, used wind aura to grab the bag of dreadbeast bindings, and tossed the sack to one of the Frozen Blades.

"Turn those in for points. There should be forty-six in there, and the lowest level clouds are twenty. Buy yourselves one each, then go hunting dreadbeasts with everyone else."

Grace spoke up. "We need everyone for our current assignment."

"No, we don't." There had been a memory embedded in the tablet explaining the details of their mission; Lindon was viewing it already. "Separate into teams of two, and...you two, please leave. *Please.* I'm *begging* you."

The Frozen Blades looked at each other, shrugged, and hopped off the cloudship. Not nearly fast enough for Lindon's taste. He wished he could loan them madra.

"Teams of two," Lindon continued. "Pride, take Courage. Grace, take Douji. Go get another assignment each." Akura Courage controlled a formation of six flying swords, so he should cover for Pride, who used only Enforcer techniques. Akura Douji was a lightning artist who had practiced extensively with Grace.

Lindon had fought them both several times apiece. In his head, he'd faced them hundreds of times. He knew exactly what they could do.

"If they won't let you take one until our current mission is finished, then hunt dreadbeasts or Forge scales." Scales couldn't be exchanged for points, but they might be able to buy things that could be. "Naru Saeya and I will handle the assignment."

Pride straightened. "This is a task they would normally assign to an Overlord. Don't let your pride drag us down with you."

Lindon seized him by the shoulders and shook him. "This is about *points.*"

Pride looked furious, but he left.

Lindon had already taken over the control panel, shoving his pure madra into the scripts until the cloudship *blasted* forward. Pride had been taking them closer to their mission, where he had surely intended to land and approach on foot, collecting dreadbeast bindings as they went.

The ship shot over treetops in a blur.

"They won't like that," Saeya predicted sourly. "Pride is well-named."

Lindon's void key had opened again, and he manipulated aura and extended strands of madra to flip open scripted boxes and pull out bindings and dead matter. "I know what they're like. I'm sure they didn't listen to a word you said the entire time you were with them, and that's why you're with me."

Dross was working to supplement his concentration and his pure core was emptying like it had developed a leak as he assembled a construct and piloted the cloudship at the same time, so his attention was barely on his words as he spoke. "You also have the skills I need right now. You're faster than they are, your perception extends farther, and your Path is perfect for rescue."

He was as tightly focused as if his life was on the line, his objective all he could see.

Saeya blinked as she looked from him to the construct assembling itself behind him and back.

"You know, you should act like this more often," she said. "Yerin would love it."

Lindon wasn't listening.

Soulsmith products could be purchased for points, which meant that they had Soulsmiths doing that work who must get paid, so he could take on Soulsmithing jobs as well. How many missions could his team complete per day? Two? How many dreadbeasts could they defeat? How many *were* there?

Saeya pointed him in the right direction, and soon he could see a red flame blazing from the side of another rocky fortress. This one didn't have the hastily built look of the Seishen Kingdom's construction, but was as big as a small town, and rose in layers like a cake. The red fire covered half of the structure without going out.

Over a hundred Gold dreadbeasts tore at the sides of the fortress, opposed by sacred artists inside, but it was another humanoid dreadbeast that provided the real threat.

This fat, rotting, man-like creature opened its jaws and spewed red flames across the fortress wall. They splattered like liquid, some fires extinguishing but others burning on.

This creature gave off the pressure of an Underlord. At least. It was hard to rate dreadbeasts like sacred artists, but

Lindon wouldn't be surprised if someone were to compare this specimen to a weak Overlord.

The mission parameters were to rescue a few key members of the sect who had made this fortress their home. Any further sacred artists rescued would mean bonus points, but the situation was more complicated than it seemed on the surface.

A protective script covered the outer wall of the fortress, which was why the Overlord dreadbeast hadn't killed everyone yet. Neither the fire nor the army of monsters had penetrated the outer wall of the fortress yet, but they would soon.

If he engaged the Overlord in battle, the Golds would make it impossible to win quickly. Already flying dreadbeasts were diving to attack their ship.

Their full team of eight would have surely swept this battlefield clean with minimal risk, but their safest options would have also taken the longest.

Lindon's dead matter was all in place, and he let the cloudship's speed fall, devoting himself to Soulsmithing. Every piece of the construct floated in his pure madra, and he Forged them without tools, shaping them according to the image in his mind.

Each binding shone in his spirit like a star, and Dross' calculations prevented the slightest mistake.

The Spear of the Summer King went opposite the red dragon's breath.

The Storm Lotus opposed the Titan-Slayer Axe, and the Grave's Last Word matched against the Bloodwash Wave.

All six Striker techniques reacted with one another, sending off sparks of many colors, settling into an equilibrium with the other bindings, the dead matter, and his own madra. It was Soulsmithing that should have taken weeks of testing, measuring, and planning.

The launcher construct settled into his hands as the fat dreadbeast turned to face him, roaring. Red flame gathered at the back of its throat.

Lindon leveled his newborn cannon and fired.

A lance of blinding light slammed into the creature's belly, carving out a chunk of flesh. The giant gave a pained roar, and this time its hands glowed red as well. A more complicated technique, easily powerful enough to reduce their cloudship to splinters.

Bat-like dreadbeasts screeched as they dove for him, but he gave them no attention. Naru Saeya met them with wind in one hand and a rainbow sword in the other.

Lindon forced his spirit through the cannon, pushing out another shot before the weapon had been given a chance to recover from the last one.

The giant's head exploded. Burning, rotten flesh sprayed across the stony landscape as the dreadbeast toppled.

Lindon's construct broke apart, and he tossed it aside, trying not to calculate how many points its materials would have been worth.

Saeya had rid herself of two flying dreadbeasts, but was flying circles around two more, harrying them with her weapon and techniques.

Lindon took them out with dragon's breath.

The Naru woman hovered down to him as his cloudship slowly came to a stop over the fortress. She looked shocked as she surveyed the dead Lord-stage beast. Rotten blood had splattered across her outer robe.

But she roused herself quickly. "I'm heading inside."

Lindon tossed her another construct, one that he'd prepared beforehand. "Break this if you need help. I'll clean up out here."

She nodded and shot down, stopping to identify herself to the defenders on the wall and convince them to let her through their protective script.

Lindon dropped to the ground himself, switching to Blackflame as he fell. The Burning Cloak ignited, dragon's breath formed in his hand, and Wavedancer flew from his void key.

The flying sword, beautifully crafted from the blues and greens of wind and waves, responded eagerly to his will.

He landed with a squelch on the ruined dreadbeast and laid waste to the army around him.

The Archlord flying sword sliced Truegold dreadbeasts in half with a single swing, as did the thin bars of Blackflame he sent slashing out.

At the same time, he tapped into his soulfire, using the blood aura in the giant's body to pull apart the flesh in its chest. Meat and tendons tore away from the binding he sensed near its heart.

Hurry, Lindon thought. *I have to hurry.*

If even one prize escaped his grasp, he was going to weep blood.

第十章

CHAPTER TEN

Eithan waded through an ashen maze of jagged walls that were all that remained of his homeland.

He doubted he had ever stood in this particular building before, but even if he had, there would be no way to tell now. The earth had shifted and the sky rained living lightning, until what was left was unrecognizable.

The layer of ash only remained now, eight years later, because of the endless destruction aura that enveloped the whole continent. If he were to open his aura sight, he would see a black shadow clinging to every other color. His outer robes and the tips of his hair would slowly dissolve, if he let them.

He stopped in the shadow of the largest chunk of wall still standing, gazing through an empty window down a row of shattered homes. He tried to use that image, to let it remind him of the consequences of his own bad decisions, but it was too late. That wound was too old and too deep. Nothing he could do today would bring feeling back to that scar.

The people who had died here had belonged to House Arelius. Once, losing family had evoked great passion in him.

Time had dulled that edge. So had knowledge. He didn't need vengeance, he needed the power to change a system that had broken long before he was born.

Though he was oddly pleased to feel an ember of fury stoke to life as he saw the man approaching him from behind.

Reigan Shen's steps crunched in ash that he had made himself. "Eithan Arelius. I expected to find you in Tiberian's palace."

He prowled with great confidence, his white-gold mane glossy, and in Eithan's opinion he would not look out of place with a tufted tail swinging behind him.

The Monarch was thoroughly veiled. Here in secret, then. As expected.

Eithan turned and gave him a blinding smile. "What's left of it, you mean? You expected to see me weeping in the ruined foundation?"

"So you haven't returned. I left it mostly intact, out of respect."

Returned.

"Ah, you remember me." Eithan swept a bow. "I'm honored."

The Lion Emperor nodded. "It is not often that understanding so exceeds age and advancement. If Tiberian had used you more carefully, perhaps it is I who would have fallen."

"Tiberian trusted you to act in your own self-interest," Eithan said. He was pleased that he still sounded unfazed, though he was growing closer and closer to angry every moment. "As, I admit, did I."

"None of you understand my interests, which always surprises me. I feel I have been very consistent."

"You could have ascended like a *king*. Who is Kiuran of the Hounds? You know as well as I do those like him would have licked your boots the moment you ascended with a Dreadgod weapon in your hands. You would have dwarfed Northstrider's most ambitious dream."

Reigan Shen laced his fingers together, and his jeweled rings flashed in the dying sunlight. "My desires have only ever extended to this world, not beyond it."

That was almost enough to start Eithan shouting, but Shen continued in a melancholy tone.

"I have heard your arguments from Tiberian's mouth. Perhaps my people would be safer and happier if we had destroyed the Dreadgods. But they are safe, and they are happy, and I am here to guide them. And the heavens have offered me the means to achieve our goal, *your* goal, without abandoning my people."

Eithan focused on his cycling madra, controlling his emotions. Equilibrium returned soon enough, and his smile was more genuine. "We both know that won't work. If you don't ascend, it will be for nothing."

"It will buy us time to put new systems in place. You are not the only one who understands the nature of things, Arelius."

Shen's words sunk Eithan's spirits. *It will buy us time.* That was all they ever wanted. Stall tactics. No real solutions.

Yes, millions of people will die, but still an acceptable number. It's not as if we're doing *nothing.* Perhaps we *could* reduce that number to zero, but it's too much risk. Too much personal sacrifice.

How could anyone justify leaving the Dreadgods alive, even to themselves? Just because he would have to leave this world behind.

"I do," Eithan said heavily. "I understand. But it seems that soon, I will be in the position to decide." His smile returned. "So why has the lone Monarch of the Rosegold continent deigned to visit me today?"

Reigan Shen gave a wry smile. "I have come to buy you out of the tournament."

"That's impressive, considering that the grand prize is priceless."

"Do you know how many priceless things I own? Penance is not in your hands yet, and even as an Overlord, you are not guaranteed to defeat Shoumei or Sophara. You can return to Blackflame City with all your wishes granted."

Eithan gestured to the ash and ruin all around them. "This is not the most conducive environment to a negotiation."

Reigan Shen waved a hand and the ruins of the shattered house were erased. They simply vanished with no more than a slight puff of wind to mark their passing. Another flick of his fingers, and the Monarch opened a swirling portal.

The space was protected, so Eithan could see only a swirl of color before a golden disc emerged. He had to take a few steps back to give it room; the disc was as large as a barn floor, though only as thick as two hands.

It came to a stop, hovering at waist height. The golden disc was a platform supporting a table and two contoured chairs. Eithan hopped up, as did Reigan Shen, and Eithan noticed the difference immediately as he crossed the scripted barrier.

Inside, the air was cool and sweet rather than choked with ash. Though there were no walls and he could look uninterrupted at the ruined city around him, they were far more comfortable. A ceiling hovered above them, blocking some falling ash, though the script would have done that just as well.

They took their seats, and Eithan plucked a flower from a decorative vase at the center of the table. "Before we begin, I would like a void key to contain the cloudship you gave me. It's inconvenient not being able to carry it around."

"Of course. An oversight on my part."

Eithan doubted that. The ship Reigan Shen had gifted him was stored in one of the Ninecloud City's hangars, but Eithan had been unable to remove it until after the tournament because of city air travel regulations. He was certain that had been part of the plan for his "prize."

Shen casually tossed him an ornately carved and scripted golden ring, which Eithan tucked away.

That set the tone for the negotiation. Shen was willing to throw in a top-grade void key, which many Sages couldn't afford, as an afterthought. Then again, he was perhaps the only one in the world who could treat spatial storage so lightly.

"This need not be a long process," the Monarch said. "Tell me what you want so that I may give it to you."

Eithan stopped himself short of saying *"Your head on a platter."* Not only would it set the wrong tone, it wasn't what he wanted.

If Reigan Shen didn't die to a new generation of Monarchs raised by Eithan, that would be the real tragedy.

"Financial support and protection for House Arelius."

"A wise choice. My grudge was never against House Arelius. They are now under my protection, free to operate independent of my rule, and I will honor their borders. I will give them support equal to any of my vassal states, including a restoration package of a billion scales, and Yushi will be at the service of your Sage for one year beginning tonight."

Yushi was a Herald on a lightning Path, and one of Reigan Shen's closest companions. She was colloquially known as the Thunder Fairy, a name she hated. There were children's rhymes about her.

Eithan had written one himself.

That was generous support for House Arelius—more generous than Eithan had expected. Shen had come prepared, and he had obviously anticipated Eithan's first demand.

Shen leaned on his hand, elbow on the table. "Now, surely you want something for yourself as well."

"Certainly I do, but first I have another request on behalf of my House. Your fairy is wonderful, but the condition of my homeland is as you see it. We require the attention of the Rootfather."

"I do not command the dragons."

"Garrylondryth's full attention and a guarantee of behavior from him. You may keep Yushi while he is here, if you like."

The Herald of the green dragons was the right hand of the Dragon King, and rather than destroying human civilization, he preferred to enhance the power of nature. He practiced a Path of water and life, and he had made it his mission to restore the natural world after a clash of great powers.

Despite his generally peaceful temperament, he nursed centuries-old grudges against Akura Fury and Northstrider. Something about a relentless campaign against his family and the death of his children in battle; Eithan wasn't entirely clear on the details.

Rather than continuing to pretend he had no influence over the Dragon Monarch, Reigan Shen said, "Agreed." He leaned back and twisted one of his rings. "And for yourself?"

"I would like to ensure that the Blackflame Empire is evacuated before the danger of the Dreadgods."

For once, Reigan Shen expressed mild surprise. "You don't trust Malice to handle such a task?"

"She will be fighting against the cults. Who are now gathered under your banner."

The Monarch drummed sharp fingernails on the table. "I can issue a standing order to allow evacuating civilians to continue unmolested, and I can respect whatever shelters Malice creates. I expect any of this to be included in whatever agreement I reach with the other Monarchs. It is not your concern."

"Just being thorough. Now, to finally answer your question: neither House Arelius nor the Blackflame Empire can appropriately subsidize my advancement."

"I will sponsor you all the way to Herald once the tournament ends, assuming you can overcome the other barriers yourself."

That was another truly generous offer. Advancing through Overlord and Archlord could be astronomically expensive, and even Monarch factions did not spend such sums lightly.

There was no guarantee of return on such an investment; most would-be Overlords or Archlords stalled out at one of the other bottlenecks that could not be broken through with advancement resources.

If you could simply spend a fortune to power through the Lord realm, as you could through Gold, then every rich merchant would be Archlord.

Eithan gave a beaming smile. "Let's assume that I can. Now, it also seems to me that I'm giving up the most powerful weapon in the world, so I should end up with some weapons of my own in recompense, don't you think?"

"You're giving up your *chance* at the most powerful weapon in the world," Shen corrected, but a spark of interest had kindled in his eyes. "But if one of my collection has captured your imagination, it's possible we can come to an arrangement."

Once again, Eithan was sorely tempted to demand something unreasonable, like Shen's entire arsenal.

If he waited until the final match, he might have enough leverage to force Shen to agree. Now *that* was a fortune that could reshape the entire situation on the planet.

But there was too much risk involved. What if Sophara and Yan Shoumei were both eliminated early, and Eithan was left in the finals against Mercy? What a missed opportunity that would be.

Of course, he could use Penance to blackmail Reigan Shen into giving him what he wanted anyway.

Eithan was aiming for the best of both worlds.

You didn't make it to Monarch by being easy to fool, so Shen wouldn't give Eithan anything that might affect the tournament. Eithan could funnel any advancement resources to Yerin, Mercy, or Ziel, even if he himself dropped out.

But if Reigan Shen bought him off *and* Yerin or Mercy won, Eithan would profit twice.

And if they didn't...well, it was possible that Eithan would have lost anyway, and at least he had a luxurious consolation prize.

"Why would I break up the world's greatest collection?" Eithan asked, with exaggerated horror. "No, I prefer my weapons made to order. Give me the Soulforge."

He held a flower up to his nose and inhaled while the Monarch's jaw worked. "...you're not even in the top four."

"Oh, would you prefer to have this conversation *after* I've knocked out one of your fighters?"

Even Eithan didn't know the distribution of the next round, but given that it was reached by the agreement of the Monarchs, he could guess. Eithan wouldn't be fighting any allies. Which meant a three out of four chance he was matched against one of Shen's team.

Unless it was Yan Shoumei and she managed to defeat him, his position would only be stronger after this round ended. They both knew it.

There came a growl from deep in Shen's chest that rumbled out and shook the table. Shen was perhaps the only Monarch who could make a replacement for the Soulforge, which was the only reason he was considering Eithan's request at all.

Eithan respected that Shen didn't try anything foolish, like pretending the artifact was irreplaceable. Any false position he took would only make Eithan more determined.

"This is the last concession I will make," Shen warned.

"You agree to this and my other conditions, and I will swear on my soul to throw the next match," Eithan promised. "Except...there is one final thing I do require."

"Speak, but I will bend no further."

"Clothes," Eithan said. "I need new clothes."

INFORMATION REQUESTED: TIBERIAN ARELIUS, THE STORM KING, PATRIARCH OF HOUSE ARELIUS AND THE FALLEN RULER OVER HALF OF THE ROSEGOLD CONTINENT.

BEGINNING REPORT...

Path: Raging Sky. Most "storm" Paths are really only lightning Paths, but the Path of the Raging Sky harvests water, wind, and lightning aura in balance with one another. As an interesting side effect, practitioners can adjust their madra to bring one aspect or another to the forefront, so that it can often feel like facing three different Paths—one of water, one of wind, and one of lightning—rather than a single, unified set of techniques.

When Tiberian Arelius was young, he was often called a "perfect sacred artist."

Not only did he have unsurpassed talent in the sacred arts,

mastering each technique with grace and skill, but he never stopped working. He was honest and straightforward to a fault, keeping his power under control, showing perfect deference to his superiors and gracious mercy to those beneath him.

The previous Arelius Monarch was only a distant relative of his, but she ascended with peace in her heart when she realized she could leave their House in Tiberian's hands.

He brought House Arelius to a new era of prosperity, maintaining a tense balance of peace with their rival and neighbor, House Shen.

Until his youngest advisor, a prodigy of their House, came forward to propose something more than an alliance. This advisor had violated family tradition and protocol to raid the tomb of their founding Patriarch, the original Arelius.

From this tomb, he brought relics of an unknown nature.

[WARNING: INFORMATION INCOMPLETE. CONTINUING REPORT.]

With these relics, the advisor was able to convince Tiberian to embark on an ambitious project: the elimination of the Dreadgods. The same task that resulted in the Dread War and the death of the previous generation of Monarchs.

As a first step, Tiberian approached his neighbor, Reigan Shen and proposed an alliance.

Shen responded with violence.

True battles between Monarchs are rare, and this one destroyed much of the Rosegold continent. In the end, even the Weeping Dragon was drawn in, and Tiberian was struck down.

Leaving House Arelius leaderless and in ashes.

SUGGESTED TOPIC: THE FATE OF HOUSE ARELIUS.

ERROR: TOPIC UNAVAILABLE. REPORT COMPLETE.

In a snowy village protected by the Frozen Blade School, Yerin did battle with a demon.

The spirit was originally the Remnant of a man on a Path that combined sword, blood, and destruction madra. He had caused such havoc a hundred years ago that his Remnant had been sealed. Originally, it was as a sort of posthumous punishment.

But, as the Winter Sage had told her, it had become something else over time. The family in charge of the Remnant had fed the Remnant—which was originally Truegold—scales and spirits, and equipped it with a pair of long, sickle-like curved swords.

Now, it exhibited a power not unlike an Underlord, and they had used it to threaten their business rivals for several years. Under the protection of this creature, dubbed the Demon of Twin Blades, their business had prospered.

The Frozen Blade School hadn't intervened as the spirit hadn't harmed any innocents or even killed very many people. Until recently.

Yerin stood on the edge of a flat rooftop, which had been mostly ravaged under the impact of the Demon's madra. Moonlight gleamed down over its long, silvery scripted blades, each of which contained cold power that weighed on her senses.

The Demon itself resembled a gorilla, painted in a complex color like a deep blue mixed with ashes. Its eyes blazed yellow and hot from within a head like an inhuman skull, and its knuckles scraped the ground. It was as dense as any other Remnant she'd ever seen, so that if she'd been forced to rely only on her bare eyes, she might not have known it was a Remnant at all.

It threw its head back and howled, and the world around it drained of color as it called all the aura from nearby to obey its

Ruler technique. Sharp, jagged blades—like obsidian knives—began to Forge themselves into the air around her, and the two techniques pressed in on Yerin from every direction.

Yerin wasn't really paying attention.

Her spirit screamed danger, and she listened to that instead, pushing her perception deeper. She had fought part of this fight with her eyes closed, trying to hear the elusive tune that had guided her in her fight against Altavian Arelius.

The Winter Sage insisted that she could chase it down through combat, and Yerin was trying, but it was like trying her hardest to remember something she'd forgotten.

She needed to be calm. To stop trying so hard and let it come to her.

When blades of aura and madra surrounded her, pressing in on her as though she were wrapped in razors, the sense of danger grew too much to endure.

And then she felt it.

A spark of madra passed from her hand down to her sheathed sword, and her blade rang like a bell.

The Demon of Twin Blades lost its hands at the wrists. When its swords hit the roof, it looked down as though trying to process what was happening. Its techniques destabilized, and then she lazily swung her blade through the air without looking.

A Rippling Sword slashed like a crescent through the night. A flat shield of madra appeared in front of the demon and it leaped backwards, but Yerin's Striker technique had felt more...right...than her techniques usually did.

His defense might have been enough to deflect one of her normal attacks, but this time it passed through with no resistance and sliced him in half.

The Demon fell to pieces, and Yerin stood with her eyes closed, spiritual perception drilling deeper, trying to remember this sensation even as it drifted off.

This was her way forward. As she advanced, it would become easier and easier to sense.

Her Blood Shadow squirmed inside her, restless, hungry

for both action and power, but Yerin forced it down. Soon, she wouldn't need the Shadow at all.

Noise penetrated Yerin's trance, and for the first time she paid attention to her audience. Down on the snowy streets beneath the building, several dozen people had gathered. They raised torches or rune-lights or techniques against the darkness.

And when the Demon of Twin Blades fell, their voices rose in a shout of excitement. It wasn't quite a cheer, but a wave of cries that broke into chatter and a few individual calls.

Yerin wasn't quite sure how to respond, but she felt like she was supposed to do something. She waved her white blade down to them.

The sound from the crowd redoubled, and this time it was definitely a cheer.

Well, that didn't feel too bad.

The Winter Sage had been sending her out to fight with her sword, insisting that this would help her become a "symbol" of swordsmanship and thus get closer to the Sword Icon.

She wasn't sure if popularity or fame would help with that. Did Icons care how well-known you were?

Yerin picked up the two weapons the Remnant had been carrying—no sense in leaving them for anyone else—and hopped down to the street. The people cheered and shouted out questions, but they also backed away from her. So they liked her, but they didn't want her to get too close.

That was how people had treated her master, so she wasn't too bothered. She used the bubble of space around her to make it to the end of the street, but her good mood faded quickly when she noticed another group that the people of the town were avoiding.

The Sage of Red Faith and his students.

The Blood Sage crouched on the street like a frog, looking up at her from his hunched position. Red paint tracked down from his eyes like bloody tears.

A wave of revulsion ran through her, and even her Blood Shadow surged up in willingness to fight.

Beside him was another figure that looked like they

haunted children every night at midnight: Yan Shoumei. Her black hair hid half her face, and her one visible eye was too wide. Her sacred arts robes hung loose around her.

Their third companion, Calan Archer, was the only one who wasn't likely to frighten anyone away. In fact, he had a fine figure, with broad shoulders, muscular arms, and a handsome face. His Goldsign ruined it all, in Yerin's estimation, because the scripted rings of living lightning marked him as a member of the Stormcallers.

Putting a good-looking man in a Dreadgod cult was putting a dress on a hog. Didn't make it any less a pig.

Just seeing the three of them was enough to ruin Yerin's excitement over her progress. She almost wished they would make a move on her; not only would the Winter Sage not rest until she had her revenge, but if they attacked one of the Uncrowned in Akura territory, they'd have a Monarch *and* a heavenly messenger to contend with.

But she still wasn't looking to die, so she dropped the Remnant's swords and cycled her madra. The crowd took another few steps back.

Yan Shoumei scowled at her and let out a furious whisper. "Didn't your master teach you better than to fight in a town? Someone could have been hurt."

The words threw Yerin's brain into a spin. Was a member of Redmoon Hall lecturing *her* about collateral damage?

Shoumei walked up to a trio of little girls in the crowd nearby, going to her knees and speaking in a soothing tone. "It's going to be okay. The demon is gone, and we won't let anything happen to you."

She still sounded like a witch trying to lure them to their deaths.

The girls stammered something and scurried back, scrambling to put some adults between themselves and the evil-looking Underlady. The adults didn't look any more at ease than the children did.

Yan Shoumei hung her head, and Yerin could see the depression and disappointment radiating from her back.

Yerin reminded herself to stay on her guard. She couldn't feel any sympathy.

"You all found a spine and a half if you're after me here," Yerin said, hoping the crowd would sense an incoming fight and leave. "The Sage won't lie down easy when she finds out you're here to hook me."

Yerin wasn't sure if they were here to hurt her or to persuade her to their side, but either way the Sage of the Frozen Blade would be furious.

The Blood Sage wet his lips. "Min Shuei drove me off when I first arrived, and then she appealed to the Monarchs several times to have me removed. She went to Northstrider, to Akura Malice, and to Reigan Shen. They are all aware that I am here, and they will allow me to remain as long as I behave myself. Your Winter Sage is not so tolerant, but she is distracted at the moment."

He took a little hop closer to her, and that seemed like it was enough for the crowd. They started filtering away, which Yerin thought was unusually perceptive for a bunch of Lowgolds.

"I have tried to speak with you face to face several times, but I was always delayed by the ignorance and stubbornness of others. Clearly, you have good judgment of your own, as you have cultivated your Blood Shadow according to my technique. With my help, you can take it to new heights. Even Monarch is not a dream. I am certain that, under these conditions, we can have a civilized discussion."

Yerin drew her weapon back and began cycling for the Final Sword.

She had contained herself at the sight of the Sage, because after all, there was nothing she could do to him. But every word out of his pale lips made her angrier and angrier.

"I used to have a wish," Yerin told him, as madra and aura and soulfire poured into her sword. "I wished that there was one waste of breath handing out Blood Shadows, and if I killed him, mine would go away. All of them would. And everybody..."

She heaved in a breath to stop herself from saying *"..and everybody the Shadow killed would come back."* She didn't need to share that part of it, because it made her sound like a child. She was finding it hard to speak now anyway.

The Sage blinked, looking confused. His two students were alarmed, distancing themselves from him and beginning defensive techniques.

"I have no influence over what the Bleeding Phoenix does," the Blood Sage said, "and even if you could somehow kill me, it would have no impact on your Blood Shadow."

Yerin knew that better than she knew her own name.

"True," she said.

She unleashed the Final Sword anyway.

The crowd was gone, but this still wasn't a technique she would usually use with homes so close. Silver light lit up the night as a fully detailed sword of madra closed the gap between her and the Blood Sage in a blink. Aura chewed up the ground, nearby walls, and the edges of the rooftops. The air screamed.

The Sage of Red Faith stopped it with one hand. He didn't even stand up, just raised a palm and intercepted the technique.

The force almost bowled him over.

He stumbled back, channeling more power into defending himself. When the technique faded, blood flowed from his palm.

Yerin stood, panting and watching. She had known he would stop it. He was a Sage with his students behind him. Besides, if he had dodged, the technique would only have blasted off into the distance. She wasn't so far gone that she couldn't consider her surroundings.

But she was angry enough that she hadn't been able to think of a better way to express it.

The Blood Sage didn't look put off, though. He looked delighted.

He held up his bloody hand to her as though it proved something. "You see? You *see?* Your will is far more developed than an Underlady should be capable of. It's your Blood

Shadow, all your Blood Shadow, and the more of an independent will it develops—"

He stiffened and looked off into the horizon. A frustrated expression spread across his face.

"Your guardian has found me. I have to go fight pointlessly without killing. What a foolish game. Do not waste your potential, Yerin Arelius. Don't let a childish grudge stand in the way of your making history."

Yerin nodded. "Rot and die."

The Blood Sage made a frustrated noise before loping away, leaping into the distance. She still had never seen him use his Blood Shadow. Maybe he *was* the Blood Shadow.

Her own Shadow began raging, its patience gone. It wanted to be free, to face these opponents, to feed.

Yerin struggled with it, but she didn't back down or put away her sword. "If you two want your match ahead of time, you can take it now."

Calan smiled and raised both his hands in surrender while Yan Shoumei shrugged. "The Sage has his interest in you. If we do not end up in the ring together, we are not enemies."

"We're not your enemies," Calan assured her. "Honestly, I'm an admirer. I hope we don't have to fight."

Yerin would believe that when the sun rose green. "Dreadgod cults are enemies to anybody with eyes."

Calan's expression grew sober, and Shoumei darkened.

"Not everyone has a family to pick up the bill for their training," she said quietly.

If Shoumei was looking for pity, she was running down the wrong trail. "I'd shed a tear for you, but I saw what Redmoon Emissaries did to the Blackflame Empire."

"Redmoon or the Phoenix?" Yan Shoumei countered. "And are you responsible for everything the Akura clan has done? What about the Arelius family?"

Calan spoke calmly. "I think you may have a misunderstanding about us. Dreadgod madra gives you a way to improve without spending a fortune. If you want to advance but you were born in a gutter, you don't have much choice."

Yerin had chosen to advance her Blood Shadow differently, in a way that required either far more time or far more resources, but the normal way to advance was to steal power from others. That was the original purpose of the Shadow.

She had seen the other Dreadgod cults fight, in the records of the Uncrowned fights. They all had a component of hunger madra, which allowed them an unconventional path to advancement. It tended to produce sacred artists that advanced quickly, but didn't go too far. And, at least in the case of the Blood Shadows, there was always an element of risk.

"Dress it up however you want," Yerin said.

"I had a lot of talent, but no money," Calan went on. "Less talented students kept passing me up because they had parents to buy them resources. Meaning they advanced and made even more, so I got left further behind. Now..."

He ignited his madra, and a dragon's head of blue-and-gold lightning emerged from his palm, snarling as it did. "Hunting Remnants gives me everything I need. Thanks to the Weeping Dragon, I'm standing with you two. Disciples of a Sage." He gave a crooked smile. "Imagine that."

"I am *not* his disciple," Yan Shoumei spat, and Yerin felt blood madra rising up inside her.

A lot of blood madra.

Yerin began cycling to defend herself, but Shoumei quickly got her power under control. "Sorry," she muttered. "But I'm not his disciple. When I win, I won't need him anymore. Or Redmoon."

"She protects a city," Calan said. "They call her their guardian spirit."

"Shut up."

Yerin finally accepted that there wasn't going to be a fight, slamming her sword back into its sheath. She scooped up the demon's twin swords, unaccountably irritated.

"So you're both innocent souls who don't want to kill me or recruit me," Yerin said. "Okay. So what are you doing here? Not like the Sage needed your help."

Calan and Shoumei exchanged glances. The Redmoon girl scratched the side of her face and looked down.

"I just wanted to meet you," Calan said.

"Not everything is a plot," Yan Shoumei said, and she sounded strangely sympathetic. "It wasn't too long ago that I saw agents of my enemy everywhere. I thought *you* worked for him, all of you from the Blackflame Empire, back in Ghostwater."

"Do you suspect everyone of trying to kill you?" Calan asked.

"They usually are," Yerin muttered. "And there's a Monarch-killing weapon on the line."

He shrugged. "We're not Monarchs. We can fight to win without being sworn enemies. I see it as a unique opportunity to fight to the death with people you don't hate."

Yerin had said almost the exact same thing to Lindon not long ago, and hearing the same sentiment coming from a Dreadgod cultist gave her a strange, unpleasant feeling.

"Don't have any account against *you,* but your Sage needs somebody to take his head from his shoulders." As she understood it, the Sage of Red Faith was the one who encouraged the spreading of Blood Shadows on the wild.

Yan Shoumei gave her a blank look. "Why would I care?"

"My Sage is even worse," Calan put in.

Yerin thought they might be able to get along after all.

第十一章

CHAPTER ELEVEN

Maten Kei stood on her Thousand-Mile Cloud and watched the procession of survivors below her. Her sister was at the other end of the canyon, keeping an eye out from her own cloud.

Back at the Frozen Blade School, they had often been assigned to protecting civilians from stray Remnants or aura-storms or other threats requiring powerful sacred artists, so guarding a few hundred people as they fled to shelter was nothing new.

This crowd hadn't faced any threat yet, but they had to be evacuated before the Wandering Titan woke. Kei and Teia volunteered for these escort missions whenever their team accepted such assignments. Saving people was more gratifying than slaying dreadbeasts or fighting bandits.

They didn't care about the points, though their team leader certainly did. He scared Kei a little. She wondered if there was anything he *wouldn't* do for points.

A flare of madra from Teia signaled her, and she floated up on her cloud, stretching out her perception. The earth aura was very strong in the land around Sky's Edge, and this canyon was surrounded by clumps of trees that had been petrified by that aura.

Inside those trees, Kei felt someone waiting in ambush. Where there was one, there would certainly be more.

Though they were officially called "bandits," these rogue sacred artists weren't opportunistic thieves so much as they were desperate people who had been displaced by the flood of dreadbeasts. While most had sought shelter with the Akura clan factions, some had been unable or unwilling to for whatever reason. They stole what they could from evacuees and Akura patrols, but they were rarely a threat.

They wouldn't likely have any Lords with them, but Kei couldn't take chances with the lives of the ordinary people under her charge. She signaled a halt, then activated her message construct.

"We've found bandits at my current location," she sent. "We're going to double back and take the alternate route. We expect a delay of no more than eight hours."

A construct fluttered off like a sunlight-colored sparrow. It would dissolve into a packet of madra and move much more quickly before re-forming at another construct that Lindon carried.

He wouldn't like that their mission completion would be delayed, but he would understand.

The column of people had already begun reversing direction. She had expected to hear some complaints at the prolonged march, but the people were largely quiet. Either they were so tired that they couldn't even muster the urge to complain or they knew the dangers of carrying on in their original direction.

No sooner had they all started marching the other way than her messenger construct returned. It burst into Lindon's voice.

"I'm on my way."

No further instructions.

Kei called a halt, and Teia flew over to discuss with her. Kei didn't know what to say. How could Lindon's presence change anything?

The two of them could handle combat with the bandits, but not without killing some of them. Unless it was a trap, and there were multiple Underlords hidden among the stone trees. Marching into unknown forces was a great way to die.

They both agreed that Lindon must be bringing the rest of the team.

Until he flew in on his green Thousand-Mile Cloud alone.

Kei stood on her own cloud, irritated, waiting for him to stop and explain himself. But, although he saluted to them as he passed, he didn't slow down.

He dove straight into the trees.

He was going to kill them all.

Horrified, the sisters followed, pushing their clouds to maximum speed. As spirits flared in battle, Kei only hoped they weren't too late.

Lindon was truly merciless. He was going to butcher these people. He...

Kei's thoughts came to a halt as she landed, only seconds behind Lindon.

There were sixteen bandits, and they were all lying on the ground. Some were bound with simple constructs, others were groaning and helpless on the ground, and still others were in the process of surrendering voluntarily.

Lindon's blue spirit chattered from its perch on his shoulder, and he flexed his hand of flesh as he listened. When he saw Kei and Teia, he ducked his head to them. "Pardon, but can you bring these people back?"

Kei swept her perception over them. Two were Underlords, and the rest were Golds. The Underlords were already bound.

It would have been so much easier to kill them. How had he done everything so *fast?*

Wordlessly, she nodded.

"Gratitude. I have to escort a mining team a few miles south of here. Is there anything else I can do to help?"

As he spoke, he slashed a line of black dragon's breath across a dreadbeast a hundred yards away. It fell to pieces, and she knew he was going to grab its binding as he left.

Kei shook her head.

"Very good. Apologies, but I have to go now. I'll see you tonight."

Bowing slightly to them again, he swept off.

As she'd expected, he picked up the dreadbeast binding on his way out.

Grace dashed through the night, perception locked on her quarry.

She whipped her sword down, launching a Shadow's Edge Striker technique after him, but he slipped aside. He followed some kind of illusion Path, and he was as slippery as those types always tended to be.

But when she finally got her hands on him, she was going to tear him apart.

He wasn't an enemy or a bandit, but a sacred artist from a smaller sect who was supposed to be on her family's side. But he was stealing from the cause.

More specifically, he was stealing from *her.*

He had presented himself as a courier, willing to take her natural treasures and dead matter back and turn them in on her behalf in exchange for a fee. Her void key was tiny, about the size of a picnic basket, so she would be able to earn more points if she emptied it.

Lindon's fever for points was infectious. She found herself dreaming about the more expensive prizes and thinking up ways to save points.

And now this traitor had stolen twenty or thirty points from her team.

She fell from a short cliff, sure that she would land just in front of him, but he slipped away from her perception. As he had several times before.

This time, when she stretched out her spiritual sense, she caught someone else with them. That was a surprise; they were quite a way from Sky's Edge, and most people took a break for the night. And this newcomer's spirit was even harder to detect than the thief's.

Until he removed his veil and she sensed his madra more clearly. It was pure.

Relief flooded her, followed by embarrassment. She had hoped to resolve this before anyone else on the team knew that she had lost some of their precious points.

Lindon's large silhouette separated from the shadows, and he held a squirming sacred artist in his Remnant hand. "Pardon, Grace, but were you chasing her? Or do I owe her an apology?"

"Her?"

Now that Grace looked more closely, it *was* a woman. A girl, really; Grace would put her at sixteen or seventeen. Younger than Grace expected from a Truegold who wasn't from a prominent clan. She was probably considered a genius of her Path.

Her previous appearance had also been an illusion to make her seem more masculine, and Grace hadn't seen through it. If she'd gotten away, Grace would never have caught her.

The thief squirmed in Lindon's grip, but she had a better chance of praying to the heavens for rescue than she did escaping from Lindon under her own power. "Let me go! These are mine!"

Lindon pried the sack from her hand and lifted them toward Grace. "Are they?"

Grace braced herself and decided to tell the truth. "They are not. She...tricked me."

"I see." Lindon tossed the sack back to Grace and looked to the girl in his Remnant arm. "Apologies, but why are you stealing from us?"

"I need points!"

"Understandable."

Gently, he set her down. He lowered himself to look in her eyes, and she was shocked to see sympathy in him.

She would never have expected him to show compassion

to someone who had stolen his beloved points, but he put his flesh-and-blood hand on the girl's shoulder and spoke gently.

"Instead of stealing *from* our team," Lindon suggested, "why don't you steal *for* us?"

Now that was the Lindon she knew.

Lindon bent his every second to earning points.

He split up the team to take on multiple assignments a day, whenever they could. He took assignments on his own, worked as a Soulsmith when he couldn't find a mission, and saved enough energy to Forge two pure scales a day.

Even so, they had only managed to earn about a thousand points in the first week.

Their pace was far ahead of the others, but he wasn't satisfied. At this rate, they would only be able to pick one—maybe two—of the high-value items before he had to return to the tournament.

He would be coming back to Sky's Edge after the next tournament round, so he would get another chance, but what if the other teams caught up while he was gone?

The problem was their expenses. He scavenged or made everything himself wherever possible, but oftentimes they had to buy scales or dead matter or simple constructs using points. Sometimes it felt like he had to spend five points to make six.

Another problem was the size of his team.

They had all agreed to his plan of buying the most expensive items first, before anyone else had a chance to afford them, but in the end they had eight members. Most of the limited items couldn't be split up. When one person got a prize, how should the other seven be compensated?

Lindon was adamant that those questions should be

answered *after* they earned all the points they could, but it was still a contentious topic. Certainly, he wouldn't be able to buy the Diamond Veins for himself while the rest got nothing. That would be an abuse of power as the leader.

Although he still kept trying to come up with some kind of excuse.

Lindon considered his situation as he sat on his Thousand-Mile Cloud, Forging scales as he watched a group of earth artists raise pillars of stone from the ground.

Each artist used a Ruler technique to summon a thin pillar about ten feet high in an instant, and then craftsmen came along behind to etch scripts in its surface. When this boundary formation was complete, it would drive away dreadbeasts and even potentially push the Dreadgod back toward the ocean.

As he was on guard duty, he kept his perception extended, trying to sense a threat. He was the first in his group to feel the intruders.

They carried the impression of a mountain's worth of stones rolling in from the north like storm clouds. He immediately signaled the foreman, who sounded a horn, then Lindon flew his cloud up to take a look.

[Wow, it's like a...I want to call it a cloudship, but it's really the opposite of that, isn't it?]

From the distance, so far it was only a smudge in Lindon's sight, a stone temple flew through the air toward them.

The temple itself was like a pyramid with three points instead of one, as though it had been crowned. Instead of resting on a cloud, it was supported by a collection of thousands of flying boulders. As it loomed closer, Lindon picked up a spiritual sensation similar to the Wandering Titan itself.

Abyssal Palace. The Dreadgod cult had arrived at last.

Lindon's workers had begun to pack up, but he signaled for them to hurry. All around the territory surrounding Sky's Edge, alarms were going up as others sensed the incoming power.

The feeling represented a massive force, which only made sense. Abyssal Palace didn't have a Sage, but it had a Herald and several Archlords, and they knew full well that Akura Fury was here. They would have sent everyone they could.

As Lindon and his charges retreated, he used constructs and Dross to send messages to his teammates. When their missions were complete, they all needed to regroup.

Because, while Lindon could sense the overwhelming power of the approaching sect, he mostly felt excitement.

Fury had posted bounties for Abyssal Palace.

It was chaos as Lindon's workers prepared to leave. There were no attacks—the cult hadn't even come close to arriving yet—but the workmen were mostly Golds. Some dropped their tools and sprinted off, others tried to save as much of their equipment as they could, and every other group had started fleeing at the same time. Which made a messy crowd.

Lindon gathered his group together, making sure they withdrew at a reasonable pace, but even he chafed at the delay. Every minute he spent stopping Highgolds from flee-ing for their lives was a minute further away from turning in the assignment.

Only when everyone was ready did he move them all out. They were almost all older than he was, but fear made them act more like children than adults. Several people tried to convince him why *they* should be allowed to go on ahead of everyone else, or they panicked and stampeded away for no reason at all.

As he was wearily explaining to a grown man why they couldn't all turn around and go back for a hammer he'd for-gotten, Lindon happened to feel powerful life madra flying over his head.

He instantly veiled his pure core.

Meira accompanied a squad of Seishen Kingdom Golds on a small cloudship that flew overhead. Judging by their route, they were just scouting to make sure that no one got left behind. Had she checked the roster? Did she know this was his group?

He didn't see her, only sensed her, but when the cloud-ship flew off he gave a great sigh of relief. The last thing he needed was an unprofitable fight.

He continued the march, pushing through a mile-wide patch of sand that rose and fell like waves on a stormy sea.

One of the Lowgolds had hurt her channels as she tried to keep up her Enforcer technique to push through the patch of sand, and Lindon pulled out Little Blue to treat her.

"Pardon, sister, but why didn't you let me know before you injured yourself?"

They were balanced on Lindon's cloud over the surging surface of sand, and the woman spoke with conviction. "I will not be the one to show weakness. If my spirit can't keep up, then I will crawl home on my fingertips or I will be buried here."

This woman was older than anyone in the Uncrowned King tournament, and this was how she thought.

"You don't need to ignore your own limitations," Lindon said. It felt very strange to be lecturing a woman who might be twice his age, but had half his level of advancement. Like the world had twisted on its head. "Pushing too hard will only hurt you. Apologies."

As Little Blue channeled cleansing madra, she added her own cheeps of disapproval.

"I asked for no pity," the woman said calmly.

[I don't want to tell you how to Underlord, but you may want to try, you know, sounding like you know what you're talking about.]

Lindon forced down his discomfort and spoke more sternly. "I have given you none, but I am in command of this group, and I will not lose a member for any reason. Do you understand?"

She straightened and nodded.

Lindon desperately wanted to apologize.

He returned her to the sand. "Now, I expect you to alert me or one of the Truegolds if you find you can no longer continue. Or if you notice anyone else who begins to flag. Can you do that?"

She pressed her fists together.

"Gratitude. Is there anyone—"

[Aaaahhh!] Dross screamed. [Combat report!]

The moment Lindon felt the spike of danger in his spirit, the world slowed down.

INFORMATION REQUESTED: SURVIVING A SUDDEN AMBUSH.

BEGINNING REPORT...

Lindon stood on his green Thousand-Mile Cloud, Little Blue on his shoulder, as the Lowgold woman in warm yellow sacred artist robes saluted him from below. Some four dozen other workers were in the process of crossing the moving dunes, which hung in the air as they were frozen halfway through crashing down.

I thought I'd just...tell you the situation, although it's nothing to worry about! Nothing...nothing wrong here.

A figure fell from above. Even in Dross' vision, Lindon couldn't see their face, because Dross hadn't seen them. Only sensed them with Lindon's spiritual perception.

But his veil was beginning to come off as he attacked, so Lindon knew exactly who he was. Prince Daji of the Seishen Kingdom had come for him.

So Meira had sensed him after all.

Why hadn't she come herself?

Dross, Lindon asked, *how long before he makes contact?*

Two seconds, maybe less if he has some kind of technique.

Lindon was very conscious of Little Blue on his shoulder. If Daji's attack connected, the Riverseed would be in danger.

Thanks to the frozen world, Lindon had plenty of time to feel anger.

Gratitude, Dross. I'll take it from here.

Report complete.

"Blue!" Lindon called, and she heard his intentions. She slapped the side of his neck, pumping him with deep blue cleansing madra.

Before even looking up, Lindon unleashed the Hollow Domain.

[I just want to say,] Dross said, [I'm very happy we're calling it that.]

Blue light surrounded Lindon in a ball. The madra in his cloud dispersed and he started to fall, but he maintained his balance as he looked up.

Daji was covered in a version of the same armor he'd used back in the Night Wheel Valley: a suit of smooth gray plates with liquid silver or yellow showing through the seams. Yellow light shone within the visor, and he had two swords lifted to slash as he fell toward Lindon. His spirit, fully unveiled, radiated fury and pressure.

Until he landed inside the dome of the Hollow Domain.

The sparks of lightning dancing around his blades disappeared. The madra powering his armor faded, sputtering as Lindon's pure madra washed it out.

The Soul Cloak sprang up around Lindon, and he caught Daji in his Remnant hand.

They both fell as his cloud dispersed, and Daji completed his blow in midair. The sword clubbed the side of his head, but he barely felt it.

He gripped the prince by the neck as they hit the sand, and he activated the hunger binding in his arm.

Without Little Blue empowering the Heart of Twin Stars, he couldn't make much use out of the power he took from the armor, but in only a few seconds it went from hampering Daji's movements to weighing him down completely. He was trapped in the armor, struggling only with his raw strength as an Underlord.

Lindon, meanwhile, had the Soul Cloak. He pushed Daji down against the rolling sand, pulling his helmet off with his left hand.

Daji stared up at him with fury in his dark eyes. His hair was matted with sweat, and he snarled like a wolf. The prince struggled against Lindon physically and spiritually, but made no progress on either front.

The field of pure madra around them had already begun trembling. Lindon hadn't practiced the technique enough to keep it stable for long.

So he drove an Empty Palm into Daji's midsection.

A massive palm-print was imprinted over his own hand as he shoved enough madra into the technique to penetrate the armor. The technique sunk in, erasing Daji's control over his own madra even as the Hollow Domain dissipated.

Lindon's first instinct was to kill him.

"What were you thinking?" he demanded. "You could have killed these Golds!"

"You deserve to die a *thousand* times!" Daji shouted, but Lindon had no time to waste.

"Okay, that's enough." He ran his perception through Daji's armor. Lindon had already examined the pieces of Seishen armor that he had scavenged before, so he was familiar with its construction, and it didn't take long to find the scripts he was looking for.

Running his pure madra through the suit, he triggered the clasp holding on Daji's breastplate and pulled it off. In seconds, he had peeled the armor away.

Fortunately, Daji was wearing a tight gray outfit beneath. He might have to abandon this project if it meant stripping an Underlord naked in front of dozens of allied Golds.

"I'm keeping this," he told Daji. "And if you give me one more reason, you're coming with me."

"I will—"

He shook the prince. "Do you understand that Fury would *execute* you for this?"

Daji still looked furious, which only stoked Lindon's own anger.

What right did *he* have to be angry?

"Do you really think I wanted Kiro to die?" Lindon

demanded. "Why does everyone blame me for defending myself? Would you like it better if I rolled over and died? Should I have let Kiro kill me because he was your brother? He gave me no *choice!*"

[Wow, Lindon, look at that grip! Really impressive, truly, I'm impressed.]

He realized he was squeezing the sides of Daji's arms so hard that a Truegold's bones would have broken, but the prince's glare was uninterrupted.

Lindon didn't know why he was bothering talking at all. He stood up, his anger fading quickly. "I have a choice this time. I'm letting you go, just like I tried to let Kiro go, and just like..."

He became conscious of new presences around him.

His team had arrived. Some of them, at least.

Pride stood not far away, and Grace was coming up behind him. He didn't look up at them, but he felt their spirits, and he knew that purple eyes were watching him.

So he stopped himself before he said Harmony's name.

"Anyway, you're free to go." He drew on Blackflame for the strength to speak the next words, making sure he looked Daji in the eyes. "This will be the only chance you get. Now get out."

Daji shot to his feet, and suddenly the prince's anger seemed hollow. Fragile. He dashed off, and even weakened and disarmed as he was, he still ran across the moving sand with more agility than any of the Golds.

Two swords sat on the ground nearby, and he realized he'd almost left them.

He'd have to make room in his void key.

Pride landed by him as Lindon began opening his void key, shifting things around to make space.

"The bounties have been finalized for Abyssal Palace," Pride said stiffly. He had seen what happened, but he didn't want to talk about it. Lindon could appreciate that.

"Apologies, but would you mind telling me?"

"Seven points for an acolyte mask, twenty-five points for a priest, and one hundred for a high priest."

Lindon nodded. "And when are they projected to get here?"

"Just after sundown."

"Gratitude. If you'll take these workers back, we can prepare tonight and be ready in the morning."

Pride nodded, but didn't leave. After a moment, he said, "It is better to put enemies in your debt than to kill them."

"Tell that to them," Lindon muttered.

Yerin woke in the middle of the night to a strange sensation in her spiritual perception. She couldn't put a name to it, it was just...strange.

When she saw the shape of a person sitting in her room, silhouetted by moonlight against the window, Yerin's body reacted before her mind was fully awake. She had already rolled out of the way, sweeping her sword up in a hand and leveling it at the intruder.

She froze when she realized it wasn't a stranger.

It was the most familiar intruder in her life.

The Blood Shadow sat with its back to her, hunched over something that it held in its hands. Empty bottles, fruit rinds, husks, seeds, and pill wrappers dotted the floor—it had gotten into the advancement resources that the Winter Sage had left for Yerin.

That wasn't what disturbed Yerin. The Sage could afford it.

But the Blood Shadow had escaped on its own. Without even waking her.

It could have done anything it wanted.

The Shadow's back shuddered, so it must not have finished some medicine or spirit-fruit. She moved around to the side to see what it was eating.

A tiny, blood-spotted bandage sat at its feet.

And the Shadow cupped something small and white in its hands.

Yerin's fury boiled up as her madra began to flow through her sword, which glowed silver. She had known the Blood Shadow was a danger, but she hadn't done anything about it. This was *her* fault, and she'd solve it here if it meant cutting off her own arm.

The Shadow looked up, snarling, and Yerin got a clearer look at the baby rabbit in its hands.

The rabbit was...fine. It sniffed the air and looked at Yerin curiously, ice aura playing around the tip of its horn.

Its bandage was fresh and clean, and only then did Yerin notice the roll of new bandages sitting to the Blood Shadow's right.

Yerin's thoughts felt like they crawled as she tried to put the picture together. The Blood Shadow had crept out of her spirit without her noticing, and it had used that time to sneak into another hut, steal an injured baby rabbit, and hold it while eating Yerin's food.

The Shadow hissed and pulled the bunny closer to its chest, as though afraid Yerin was going to steal it.

Yerin's Enforcer technique dissipated, but she felt only confusion. "You fattening that up before you eat it?"

The Blood Shadow responded in its broken voice that still gave Yerin the shivers. "You...got to...hold it."

The Shadow was still a frequent guest of Yerin's nightmares, but this was too bizarre to be frightening.

"The Sage will scrub you out," Yerin warned.

"Why...alone?"

Yerin stared. The Blood Shadow glared at her resentfully. "Why...are we...alone?"

"So you know, we've got less than no chance of winning next time unless we train with the Winter Sage." A second later and Yerin realized what she'd said. "*I*. I'm training with the Winter Sage. You're a wound that won't stop bleeding."

The Shadow ran a pink-tinged finger down the back of the rabbit, who didn't seem to mind. "...no."

"If you're talking anyway, you should use more words than just one."

"No need...to be here. Rather...lose together...than win alone."

That stuck in Yerin like an arrow. She didn't want to be here, where the Winter Sage saw her master instead of her and the other students treated her like she had descended from the heavens.

But she couldn't leave, and she couldn't lose. It would be a betrayal of her master's memory.

And the Sage would have her sensing the Sword Icon well before Archlord. That was an opportunity only a blind fool would pass up.

"It's no account of yours anyway. I'll sink or swim without you."

Her bloody reflection sneered. "Good...luck."

Yerin slammed the door open, marching into the icy wind. She was going to the jagged fields of ice to work on her connection to the Sword Icon.

She wouldn't be getting any more sleep tonight.

第十二章

CHAPTER TWELVE

Abyssal Palace moved over Sky's Edge and the surrounding valley like a plague.

They didn't attack. Their goal wasn't to kill Akura sacred artists, but to prepare for the coming of their Dreadgod.

Teams of cultists swarmed over the land, erecting squat towers. These two-story cylinders of stone, raised with Ruler techniques, were covered with scripts inside and out. They served to hide cultists from outside detection, but Lindon didn't understand their other functions at first.

If the towers were only shelters, why build so many? Abyssal Palace was lifting towers from the earth even when there were five others already in sight.

Only when he and his team forced a group of Truegold cultists away from a tower and Lindon got a look inside did he understand.

The towers were filled with scripts that would capture and store Dreadgod madra.

There were other scripts he didn't understand, like one pointed into the ground that he assumed had some kind of mining application, but only one thing mattered: even the masks of low-level acolytes were worth seven points apiece.

The average Abyssal Palace construction team was made

up of three or four acolytes with one higher-value priest. That meant at least forty-six points per team.

Since acolytes tended to be Highgold or Truegold while priests were usually Underlords, not all the Akura clan's teams could handle them.

But Lindon's most certainly could.

Lindon peeled the mask away from a Truegold acolyte and tossed it back to one of the Maten twins, who were covering their retreat. The eight of them stood in a battlefield of still-smoking holes and wreckage that had been an Abyssal Palace tower and a field of flowers only minutes before.

Pride and Grace were both finishing up acolytes of their own while Lindon walked up to the leader of the cultist squad.

Acolyte stone masks were bare and only lightly detailed, carved with what could barely be called a snarling face. Priest masks were more detailed and clearer, with pronounced jaws and fangs. More noticeably, the right eye of the mask shone yellow.

This priest, an Underlord, gathered madra, aura, and stones between his hands. They swirled together in a chaotic ball of golden light and razor-sharp stones, and as he hurled it out, the attack expanded.

Naru Saeya swept it away with a gust of wind.

The technique screamed as it landed in the ground, the flying rocks chewing up stones, but none of the Akura Underlords batted an eye. These cultists were outmatched.

The priest fell to his knees and pulled his mask from his face. He was visibly older than they were, and his skin was covered in patches of living stone. The Goldsign of his Path, and one of the reasons why they wore masks.

"We surrender."

Pride stepped up behind Lindon and spoke under his breath. "If we're not going to kill him, we need to move."

Lindon nodded. Abyssal Palace fighters had been quick to surrender, and after his first attempt to take them captive, he'd learned why.

As soon as they had tried to fly off with their prisoners,

a squad led by an Overlord had locked onto their position. They had been forced to kill or abandon their captives before they could be caught themselves.

Lindon had dumped them immediately. He already had their masks, and if he let them live, maybe they would get new ones. Like dumping small fish back into the lake.

They were allowed to kill, of course. The Dreadgod cults weren't much of a threat yet, but they would be a danger to any survivors of the Wandering Titan.

But Lindon and the other leaders had been warned not to go too far. His team was powerful, but if they stuck out *too* much, then Abyssal Palace would target them specifically. They had to lay as low as they could.

While scoring points.

Fury didn't mind this sort of combat because their entire objective was to slow Abyssal Palace down, not to eradicate them. In fact, killing too many would invite unwelcome reprisal that could end up drawing the attention of the enemy Herald.

Lindon took the mask from the priest and tucked it away, but this time he had a test. "I will happily let you go, but there's one thing I'd like to try first."

The old man hesitated, but his men were bound and he was surrounded by Underlords.

Lindon put his hunger madra hand on the man's head. From Lindon's pocket, Little Blue channeled madra into him.

He drained power from the man, cycling the Heart of Twin Stars as he did so.

A rush of different energies flowed into Lindon, and he and Dross separated them together, processing them according to the Heart of Twin Stars. But unlike when Lindon had tested this on Remnants and dreadbeasts, this influx hit him like a runaway horse.

The priest convulsed and fell backwards, and Lindon let him go. It was taking all his mind and spirit to control the technique.

Soulfire and pure madra streamed into his spirit, blood essence suffused his body, and yellow-and-brown madra vented from his arm. The earth around him shook in response, but by far the most disturbing were the memories.

For a moment, Lindon's point of view doubled. He was standing over the priest and he was lying on the ground, wondering what the young Underlord had done to him.

He wished his son was safe, dreamed that the treasures unearthed by the Dreadgod would be enough to take him to Overlord, and wondered when he could go home.

Then he realized he was in an unfamiliar body. It was taller, broader, younger, with pure madra flowing powerfully through it and the arm of a Remnant. Pure madra didn't respond to any of his cycling techniques—

[Whoops, hang on. I was supposed to handle the memories, wasn't I? I'll filter them and give you what you need to know, that's my fault.]

Suddenly Lindon remembered who he was again—but he struggled to control his own body. Someone else was moving his madra, trying to move it in a pattern that would never work for the Path of Twin Stars. It was as though he'd pulled the man's Remnant into his body.

But now that he remembered himself, Lindon put an end to that immediately.

He crushed the remaining will with his own, flexing his fingers to prove to himself that he was back in his own body.

His team stared at him with various degrees of horror. Pride had lines of black and gray running down his body as he cycled two different Enforcer techniques at once. Naru Saeya snapped her fingers. "Lindon. What did you do?"

He waved a hand, only then realizing that he was covered in sweat. "Apologies for worrying you. I'm fine. We should leave before they find us."

The Overlord was no doubt on his way, so they all loaded themselves up onto the small Akura cloudship and drifted away.

But the rest of the team didn't stop looking at him strangely.

His team would have preferred that he kill the man rather than drain him, but Lindon needed them to understand his Consume technique if they were to help him. They had all seen him absorb Striker or Forger techniques, but it had to be disturbing to witness him siphon power from another living sacred artist.

They had to wonder if it would happen to them.

He had hoped they would let it go, but they still demanded explanations once they were all aboard the cloudship, so he explained: "I can steal power. It's not a complete technique, though. It still needs work."

Naru Saeya made a fist as though she wanted to grab his neck with it. "And that works? You can just...take someone's advancement?"

"It's more complicated than that, but..." He was too excited to downplay his achievement. "It works! I gained *weeks* worth of advancement in my pure core just from what I did back there. It can replace cycling and then some. I gained a little soulfire too, and my body's stronger, although—"

Saeya cut him off with wind madra across the mouth. "Teach me," she demanded.

"Ah. Well...apologies, but I have pure madra."

"I could still use it on wind artists."

"The hunger binding is part of me now."

"I'll give up an arm."

Dross projected into all of their minds. [That's a wonderful idea! Now, the way we have it worked out, you need a soul Enforcer technique to sort the madra, an advanced Sylvan Riverseed to purify it, and a mind spirit without peer to sort the residual memories. Oh, and your body needs to be sturdy enough to handle an influx of blood essence without tearing itself apart. But I fully encourage you to try! Maybe you'd survive!]

Saeya gave Lindon a look, which he didn't think was fair. It was Dross that had spoken.

"I understand, thank you. You don't have to take that tone."

[What tone?] Dross asked, baffled. [It's a splendid idea! I, for one, am delighted that you would risk your body for research.]

"It can't be *that* unique," Pride said. "You should give your notes to the clan Soulsmiths. We have plenty of dreadbeast bindings; this might be the development that gives us an edge over our enemies."

"Of course!" Lindon said brightly. "I'll trade you for the complete blueprint of your Book."

Pride glared at him.

The Maten twins were quiet, only exchanging a glance, and Grace appeared to be working something out in her head.

Akura Douji and Courage muttered to one another in the back. They were trying to speak too low for him to hear, but he caught enough to figure it out.

They thought he would come for them next.

Lindon watched until they noticed his eyes on them, looking up. Then he bowed over pressed fists.

They looked at his right hand and shivered.

That night, Lindon spread Daji's armor pieces out over a table. He'd built the table, and the entire hut surrounding it, himself.

He didn't want to stay inside the Seishen Kingdom's encampment, but he didn't particularly want to stay with the Akura clan either, so he'd used timber from the many flattened homes in Sky's Edge to build himself a shelter.

He'd included six redundant layers of scripted protection against dreadbeasts, and through sheer luck he'd positioned the hut to the south while Abyssal Palace had appeared from the north, so he wasn't close to the enemy.

His hut was basically a giant box made of logs, but at least it was as secure as he could make it.

Fisher Gesha would be proud of him. She'd always said that if a foundry looked more like a palace than a barn, the Soulsmith was showing off.

He moved his perception over the armor and sketched a

diagram...but his spiritual sense had been stopped for five minutes. As had his pen.

His Remnant hand was trembling.

Dross peered at it through one purple eye. [Hmmm...I'm keeping the memories locked up tight. None of them could be doing this, because I wouldn't let them.]

"His oldest son was born during a thunderstorm," Lindon said.

[Well, they're all locked away except for the ones that aren't, obviously. Once I have them sorted out, I'll slip you the ones that have to do with the sacred arts. But it's not the memories messing with your arm, it's some sort of animating force. It feels like your arm is coming to life.]

Lindon suppressed it. "Can we stop it?"

[Ah, but hear me out: what if we evolved it to the next level? We brought me to life, and look how helpful I am! Imagine how much less lonely I'd be if there was someone else in here!]

Consuming part of the Abyssal priest's sacred arts had been incredible for Lindon's advancement, but he was discovering the cost of pushing himself to the brink.

"How are my channels?"

Little Blue shrugged and gave a ring like a bell.

She didn't know, and neither did he. His channels were sore and stretched from over-use every day, and accepting a new rush of power from the priest had strained him further. On the other hand, they had also been *strengthened* by that power and by repeated treatment by Little Blue.

Sudden growth was hard to control, he used techniques constantly all day, and his wounds—all healed by his Bloodforged Iron body—had still taken strength from him. Integrating new blood essence burdened him now as eating high-quality sacred beast meat always had, and though his Iron body could handle it, the burden was adding up.

But he blinked the fatigue away and turned back to the armor. There were points to earn.

"Northstrider advances like this," Lindon said. "So can we."

[Yeah, where *is* he anyway? Didn't he say he could find us wherever we went? Do you think he'll be mad if he thinks we ran away?]

"He told us we could," Lindon said, but truthfully he was afraid of the same thing.

A construct blared a warning, and he looked up to see who had tripped the perimeter alarm. Akura Grace strode up, holding a ward key that let her push through the security measures. They didn't let her pass the alarm, though. Lindon wanted to know when *anyone* approached, even friends.

He tapped his pen dry and put it down, stretching as Dross shifted back into him. He didn't hide Dross' existence from his team, but he did want to keep the spirit's full capabilities a secret.

Lindon tried not to resent the interruption, but he wanted to keep working on the armor. Still, Grace wouldn't visit without a good reason.

She poked her head in, glanced around, then entered entirely. "We're about to eat, if you'd like to join us."

So much for a good reason.

Lindon forced a smile. "Apologies. I don't have enough time to work on my armor during the day, and I'd like to examine these pieces while they're still fresh."

Instead of bowing out, she brightened and stepped closer to the table. "Oh, I had a project like this when I was a Jade! I tried to put together a version of the family's bloodline armor using Lowgold materials. It didn't work very well, but I won a Soulsmithing contest."

"Really? How did you compress the plates?"

"Scripts. *Way* too many scripts."

Lindon had known that the Akura clan had done very little research into construct armor, since all the members of their main family could generate their own, so he was interested to hear the perspective of someone who had tried to pursue that avenue anyway.

But after only a few more questions, he realized he was wasting time and stopped himself. "...apologies, but let's talk more about that some other time. I need to go find some Remnants, if they haven't all been eaten by dreadbeasts. We can't afford to spend points on dead matter."

Grace crossed her arms and leaned against the table. "What are you looking to buy?"

"All of it," he said immediately. "But we're *so close* to earning the Diamond Veins, and I'd love to end up with those for myself. It's always my channels holding me back."

The talk about the prizes only reminded him that his time to earn points was slipping away—he would have to return to the Uncrowned tournament in only a few days.

But still, it would have been impolite not to ask her the same question. "How about you?"

"The Thousand Swords of Binding Light," she admitted, glancing away. "The same as everyone else. They're too expensive. I know it's just a dream, but I might be able to commission an Akura Soulsmith to make me something similar someday."

Lindon looked over his armor. "If we can pick up our pace, it's not a dream. We could separate and go after different teams, or we could bait out a high priest..."

He trailed off, going over plans in his mind for the thousandth time before Grace spoke up again.

She pulled her long, curved steel sword from her soulspace. "I don't know how I'll do in a fight against a high priest. My sacred instrument is getting weaker, and sometimes it takes a blink or two before it activates."

"You haven't been taking care of it," Lindon said immediately, before wincing. "Pardon, that was rude. I know you've been busy."

"I've been using it all day every day," she said with a sigh. "No time to rest."

Lindon was the one who decided that they should be spending every second of every day on missions, so he heard that as an accusation. "Apologies," he said. "I'll keep our equipment in mind. It's important not to abuse the components."

She laid her fingers on his arm until he looked up, surprised.

Then she pointed out of the wide doors, which she'd never closed.

Pride stood just outside the outer layer of his script, standing over a campfire. The Maten sisters and Naru Saeya were behind him, stripping logs with Ruler techniques to make a table.

They were setting up to eat. Right outside his makeshift foundry.

"Why don't we go do some maintenance?" Grace suggested gently.

[Ouch,] Dross said.

Little Blue peeped eagerly and ran for the edge of the table. She agreed.

And, really, so did Lindon.

"Apologies," he said.

"What for?"

Lindon packed away his armor and tools and joined his team. The wasted time weighed on him...but it wasn't wasted time, he reminded himself. It was maintenance.

With that in mind, he was finally able to relax.

Two days before the next round of the Uncrowned King tournament, Lindon held a shimmering blue-white crystal in his hands. Its energy felt pure and cleansing, almost like a mix of Little Blue's madra and the impression that Suriel's glass marble gave him.

He finally had the Diamond Veins.

It was beautiful. He had been looking at it all day.

Pride cleared his throat. "You can't take it."

"Yes, of course. Of course. But if I *did,* can you imagine how many points we could score in a day? It's an investment, if you think about it."

It had taken more than two weeks to earn enough points

for the Diamond Veins, which was far longer than Lindon had expected. He just couldn't get the expenses down far enough, when he had to subsidize an entire group of eight.

If he could have hunted Remnants, it would have been far cheaper, but dreadbeasts fed on Remnants and left none behind themselves. So both Remnants and natural spirits were rare whenever a Dreadgod was nearby.

The entire team agreed that they should clear an expensive item out of the store before one of their competitors could buy it, but no honorable leader would spend all his team's points on something for himself.

But Lindon couldn't help but imagine. And he would be far more likely to get the other expensive items if he wasn't slowed down by his madra channels.

"We can't give exclusive prizes to anyone until we earn as many as we can," Pride said firmly. "You said that. This was your idea. We could have cashed them all in for scales."

"I know," Lindon muttered. But he couldn't stop staring into the faceted surface of the Diamond Veins.

Pride plucked the Divine Treasure from his hands. "I don't need this, so I'll hold on to it. Mercy wouldn't forgive you if you gave into temptation."

Lindon thought it was strange how much Pride brought up his sister's opinion, especially related to Lindon. But he wasn't wrong; Mercy wouldn't approve of him using resources on himself instead of the team.

"Yes," Lindon said. "Gratitude." His hands itched to take it back, but he cleared his mind and focused on the mission at hand. "You have your gatestone?"

Pride lowered the cloudship, of which he and Lindon were the only two passengers. "Worry about yourself."

"I have mine." It was one of the expenses that Lindon had resented. Gatestones were far cheaper than any other device that allowed for spatial transport, and common enough that the Akura clan would supply them for contribution points, but buying some for the entire team had set them back almost two hundred points.

They were worthwhile as life-saving measures, he knew, but Pride and Maten Teia had both used one and needed to have it replaced. Every time, that was another step further from a *real* prize.

Today, Pride and Lindon were going after a small Abyssal Palace tower erected in a crossroads of two canyons. They had settled into a routine: go in, destroy the tower, take masks from anyone who fought, and leave.

Usually, few of the cultists fought. They just fled.

In fact, it was rare that any of the combat teams reported killing a member of Abyssal Palace, and there had been very few casualties among the Akura as well.

The danger was minimal, and time was short. So Lindon had finally decided to try completing an assignment using the people on his team least likely to be killed in action: Pride and himself.

They set down the cloudship well beyond the reach of anyone's spiritual sense in the canyon, hiking over the land overhead. They walked through clouds of dust, as this stretch of terrain was almost a desert.

Lindon wasn't sure why Abyssal Palace even wanted an intersection of two crossed canyons, besides the heavy earth aura here, but Fury paid in points for destroyed towers and stolen masks.

There was one other reason why he and Pride were perfect for this assignment: their veils were hard to penetrate. Shadow and pure madra were both difficult to detect, so they had the best chance of reaching the tower undetected.

Still, they would have been caught if not for Dross. Lindon's perception was restricted under a veil, but Dross used the little information they had more efficiently.

He spotted a line of script covered by dust, allowing Lindon and Pride to quietly disable it and move on. They dodged a flying construct, and before long they were lying at the edge of a canyon, looking down.

Sure enough, at the crossroads of two ravines was a classic Abyssal Palace tower: a squat brown cylinder of packed dirt and stone, ringed with scripts that blocked intrusion and hid them from spiritual perception. Three acolytes in their simple masks huddled outside, hunched up against the cold wind.

Lindon told Dross to relay the plan to Pride.

[Here's what we—oh look, he knows the plan already!]

Pride had leaped down into the canyon.

Two Gold acolytes went flying into the distance before the third reacted, swinging a massive club into Pride's side.

Pride, of course, caught the weapon easily in one hand, then flipped it around and knocked the cultist onto the roof of the tower.

Lindon jumped down after him, irritated. There was an alarm blaring now, which meant they were on a time limit.

Sure, *this* group wasn't a threat. But they could summon more.

Lindon landed next to Pride as three more Abyssal Palace members emerged from the short, scripted tower. Two acolytes stood on the roof with madra gathering in their hands, and a priestess came out of the doorway. One of the eyes in her mask blazed yellow.

"Your masks or your lives," Lindon said. At first, he had included a short speech about sparing their lives and being unwilling to shed blood, because he felt like a bandit extorting them for their masks.

Now, he just cut to the chase. There was no point in drawing it out. They had never run into an enemy that was a match for him or Pride.

The priestess surveyed them, and Lindon scanned her spirit. She wasn't even an Underlady. Most priests were, so the Truegolds that made it to that rank were considered real monsters, but Lindon wasn't too concerned.

"You're the Monarch's son," she said quietly, and Lindon felt the first tingle of alarm.

Pride drew himself up to his full unimpressive height. "I am Akura Pride."

"Use your gatestone. We would rather not hurt you."

He barked a humorless laugh. "It would be to your credit if you could."

The priestess stepped aside, revealing someone standing in the tower behind her. Both of his eyes glowed yellow.

A high priest.

Lindon's gatestone, like a lump of sparkling blue chalk, was already in his hand, but Pride was too slow.

He shouldn't have been. He was a master of Enforcer techniques; he should have been faster than Lindon.

But he had hesitated to retreat in front of the enemy, so the high priest was already out of the doorway and holding a dagger to his throat.

The two yellow eyes turned to Lindon. "Not you. Drop it, or we will kill him."

[Perfect!] Dross said. [Let's leave him.]

It was Pride's own fault that he was in this situation, and Abyssal Palace likely wouldn't kill him. Both sides of this conflict had been tiptoeing around each other, afraid of drawing too much blood, and knowingly killing the son of a Monarch would surely count as "too much." If Malice intervened, the entire balance would tip.

But leaving would mean abandoning a member of his team to the mercy of Dreadgod cultists.

He extended his spiritual sense delicately, trying to avoid upsetting anyone, and he got a sense of the pressure emanating from the high priest's spirit. When he did, the knot in his stomach loosened slightly.

He wasn't an Overlord. Like the priestess with him, he had earned his rank earlier than his advancement, which spoke greatly to his achievements.

But that meant Lindon faced one experienced Underlord and three Golds.

It wasn't impossible.

Slowly, the Soul Cloak built around him. The dagger pushed into Pride's neck, drawing a trickle of blood.

"Drop the technique!" the high priest snapped. "Gatestone down!"

Dross couldn't give Lindon an accurate prediction of the enemy's movements without a model, but he fueled Lindon's senses so that the world appeared to slow down.

Lindon whipped the blue ball at Pride.

He had hoped the cultist would stay close enough that he would be included in the transportation, but he had no such luck. The high priest pushed his way apart as blue light surrounded Pride and space crackled.

He disappeared, leaving behind a spray of blood.

The cultist had drawn his dagger across Pride's throat on the way out.

Everything had happened suddenly, but Lindon took a moment to think. He could fight to escape, or he could try to truly defeat his opponents.

He was in real danger here...but nothing he hadn't seen before. There were points to be earned. He didn't have Little Blue out to power his new techniques, but he had fought this far without them.

He may not have been one of the Uncrowned, but that didn't mean he was helpless.

Earth aura and madra gathered at his feet, loose stones rising from the earth and sharpening into blades. It was the chaotic field that he'd seen Abyssal Palace cultists use before; a combination Ruler and Striker technique that created a ball of physical and spiritual destruction.

It was too slow.

Let's go, Dross, Lindon thought. *We're playing to win.*

[Were...were you playing to *lose* before?]

Blackflame gushed through him, and he tore away from the Ruler technique with the explosive strength of the Burning Cloak.

Stone exploded behind him as a strange field of light covered the high priest. It resembled a golden Remnant of the Wandering Titan that covered the enemy Underlord's body like armor. Lindon's spiritual sense was overwhelmed by a sense of solidity and furious, ancient hunger.

The dagger in the high priest's hand swept toward Lindon, and Lindon pulled a shield from his soulspace.

This was his sixth version of the impact shield he'd used

in the tournament, and while it was a typical round shield with a force binding in it, he'd made some improvements.

Inspired by the Seishen armor, he'd given it several layers, including a layer of water madra and a layer of wind. It could take quite a blow without buckling, now, and the binding was an Enforcer technique that made it all but indestructible to Underlord attacks.

The dagger slammed into it, chipping the material of the shield and sending Lindon flying backwards.

Dross, how does that Enforcer technique work? Lindon demanded. The members of Abyssal Palace he'd seen *had* full-body Enforcer techniques, but it hadn't covered them in transparent madra that looked like a Dreadgod.

[I don't know, but run! Run from it! And while you're running, try to observe it more, because I'm very curious myself!]

The two Gold acolytes on the roof had formed more Chaos Fields the size of their heads, which they threw at Lindon.

Balls of yellow, filled with writhing storms of razor-sharp stones and crushing earth aura, flew toward him.

That was easily dealt with, but the high priest was dashing at him like a bull, his eyes glowing. At least his overwhelming Enforcer technique didn't help his mobility much.

[Above you!] Dross shouted, and Lindon returned his attention to the Truegold priestess.

She hovered above him, standing on the flat of a flying sword, and the palm of her hand faced downward.

One eye of her mask flashed yellow.

Lindon opened his void key.

It didn't open fast enough to help him, because a rush of earth and force madra slammed him down, shoving him out of the air and into the ground. The two Chaos Fields arrived a second later, crashing into his hastily upraised shield.

Little Blue screamed at him like breaking glass, but he wasn't opening the key for her.

Wavedancer flew out, and Dross took over its control.

The Archlord weapon rushed up at the priestess, entangling her while Lindon focused dragon's breath on the Underlord rushing him.

The high priest had already pulled out a shield of his own. His was smaller, tipped with spikes, and it gave off a venomous aura. Blackflame splashed into him and the shield began to smolder, making the other Underlord falter.

Meanwhile, the Golds on the roof had pulled out bows. A pair of arrows arced through the air. Rather than simple Forger techniques, these arrows were constructs made from Underlord parts.

If this had been a fight in the Uncrowned King tournament, Lindon would have had to run.

But it wasn't a tournament, and it wasn't a game, no matter how it had felt.

There were no rules here.

He pushed Little Blue back when she tried to leave, and he willed his armor to him.

The breastplate rushed into his hand, and he raised it into the air like a second shield, activating the emergency binding within.

The armor wasn't complete. He'd cobbled it together from his Skysworn armor and the scavenged plates he'd taken from the Seishen Kingdom. He didn't even want to call it a first attempt; this was more of a functional prototype.

His Skysworn armor had once contained an emergency binding of Grasping Sky madra that pushed everything back. He had installed that again, but he'd made some upgrades.

A pulse of wind, force, and destruction madra tore out from the breastplate, pushing away everyone but Lindon.

The damage was too much for the high priest's shield, and he tossed it aside, coming to a complete halt. The priestess above Lindon lost control of the technique she was going to use, and the two arrows from the acolytes exploded in midair.

There was venom madra in those too, so Lindon was doubly glad he hadn't been hit. He shoved his head through the breastplate, tucking it onto him in the lull in the battle. The binding was expended for now, but its scripts and layers of madra would still protect him.

Then he let the void key close and dashed away as more techniques tore up the space where he had been standing.

He slashed dragon's breath behind him, leaping up the canyon wall from one outcropping to the next until he reached the top. He reached back into the void key, once again keeping Little Blue inside, and touched the rest of his armor.

But he wasn't far ahead of the priestess. Under Dross' control, Wavedancer kept her occupied, but she managed to follow him on a flying sword of her own. It took three weapons of hers to counter his one, but she was gathering a ball of golden earth-aspect chaos between her palms.

While plates flew onto his body, guided by madra and the aura controlled by his soulfire, Lindon spoke to Dross. *Give me control.*

[Oh good, I was getting tired anyway.]

Lindon let Blackflame drop, taking control over his flying sword with a thread of pure madra.

Then he *poured* power into it.

The three Gold swords shattered before Wavedancer, and the priestess had to drop her half-formed Striker technique and switch to Enforcing herself. Even so, she was thrown to the ground.

He drove Wavedancer down on her, but he couldn't finish her, having to spin and focus on the Underlord coming up behind him.

The high priest used the last of his dissolving shield to block the attack, and from somewhere—Lindon couldn't tell if it was from the man's soulspace or not—he pulled a long stone staff.

It didn't look like anything special, but the pressure it emanated was beyond normal. It was more than an Underlord weapon.

He swung it down with the force of that Dreadgod Enforcer technique, and Lindon brought up his shield on an armored forearm, with the Soul Cloak running through him.

He even activated the Enforcer binding in the shield itself.

The blow from the staff landed like a collapsing castle. The Enforced shield cracked, as did the outer shell of Lindon's armor. Pain flooded through his body, he was forced to one knee, and dust blasted away from him as the ground around his feet splintered.

More than anything else, it reminded him of taking a direct hit from Yerin at her full power. He shouldn't have blocked it.

But finally, his helmet settled around him, and his prototype armor came to life.

[Do you want me on the armor or the sword?] Dross asked. [I would suggest the armor, since it's more complicated, but if you wanted to--]

The sword!

[Right then!]

Lindon's pure core started to drain rapidly. More quickly even than when he used the Hollow Domain. He couldn't use either of his new pure techniques while wearing the armor, as the pure madra empowered by Little Blue would interfere with the armor.

It was that interference that had almost made him discard the idea of the armor entirely, but after a number of experiments, Lindon had finally had an epiphany.

He'd been thinking about the suit of armor all wrong. Like it was a system that unified many constructs with different functions.

That was a dead end. There was a reason why not every sacred artist fought with fifteen constructs at all times, beyond the obvious difficulty and expense. A weapon with the full force of the spirit behind it was always more powerful than one operating independently or with just a trickle of madra.

Lindon's armor wasn't a collection of weapons.

It was *one* weapon.

Madra flowed through every piece of the armor in an uninterrupted network, and when it completed its circuit, six full-body Enforcer techniques activated at once. All compatible with one another. All resonating.

He and Dross had tested hundreds of defensive Enforcer techniques before coming up with this combination.

It would put great strain on his body and spirit, and it would drain his madra dry. But for a few minutes, Lindon would be invincible.

Gold light poured from black armored plates, and Lindon leaped forward.

第十三章

CHAPTER THIRTEEN

Maraan, High Priest of Abyssal Palace, was approaching one hundred years old. He had given up all hope of reaching Overlord decades earlier, thanks to a spiritual injury when he was a young man, and had dedicated his life to training future generations.

Even so, it was a point of pride that he hadn't lost a duel against anyone else at his own stage in twenty years.

When he'd landed a clean blow with his staff on Lindon Arelius, he had enough experience to know it was over. He wouldn't need a second strike. His Staff of Condemnation added great weight to his attacks, and he had complete mastery over his Embrace of the Titan Enforcer technique. New Overlords were often surprised that they couldn't endure one of his swings.

Until the young man *had* blocked it.

Then a black helmet covered his face, and Maraan felt something he never felt from an Underlord: danger.

Maraan had seen to the early parts of Brother Aekin's training. He kept up with news from the Uncrowned King tournament, so he knew who Lindon was. He just hadn't paid the boy any special attention.

That was starting to feel like a mistake.

He swept the Staff of Condemnation in from the side, but an Archlord flying sword deflected him. He hadn't had the time or attention to spare to activate the binding in the staff, so the sword was enough to stop him.

By that time, gold light was rising from the seams of the young Underlord's armor. It felt like half a dozen sacred artists all Enforcing themselves at once.

Maraan's wariness grew to full-blown alarm.

This was obviously a suicidal technique. No Underlord's body, spirit, or mind could afford the burden of so many powerful techniques at once. If most of them were bindings embedded in the armor, that would only make the burden worse.

Era, the Truegold priestess and his second-in-command for this post, brought out a simple construct like a writhing birdcage the size of her two hands. She hurled it down, and he quickly recognized her good judgment.

Just in case, he pulled the same construct from his own soulspace, throwing it down at the Underlord's feet and jumping back out of the way.

Pillars rose from all around the armored Underlord as the Ruler technique in the construct pulled the rocks and loose grit and hardened them into a stone cage. At the same time, bands of earth madra were Forged around the outside, and the pillars themselves were Enforced.

Maraan breathed more easily when he saw that the young Underlord was still standing there, gushing madra from his armor. The power for which he'd damaged his own soul had been too much for him, and now it was all he could do to control it while standing still.

Their Deep-Fathom Prison constructs were quite complex, not to mention expensive and difficult to produce. They were designed to trap Underlords, and with two of them layered on top of one another, the pillars formed an almost solid wall.

"Good work," Maraan called, but Era was doubled over and panting. The Deep-Fathom Prison was an Underlord construct and would be difficult for her to activate.

Maraan circled around so he stood between the prisoner and Era, lazily cycling his next technique. He had intended to kill this young man from the beginning, both to teach the Akura clan a lesson about taking Abyssal Palace lightly and to study his arm, which appeared to be made from pure hunger madra.

Now he could finish Lindon off at his leisure, or just wait until the suicidal techniques took their toll.

"Acolytes retreat!" Era called back down into the canyon.

"No need for that," Maraan said, though he didn't say it loud enough for the acolytes to hear. He couldn't contradict his second in front of them. "He's quite—"

The armored Underlord punched through both prisons with one blow.

Stone and madra blasted forward for hundreds of feet. If Era had been standing in their way, she would have been shredded.

Maraan's years of experience did not go to waste. He spun, activating his Staff of Condemnation and fueling the Embrace of the Titan with soulfire. The butt of his staff slammed into the black breastplate in a blow that would have collapsed a castle wall.

It was like throwing a fistful of straw at a bull.

Lindon crashed into him, but Maraan stood his ground. His soulfire-fueled Enforcer technique blazed around him, the yellow image of the Wandering Titan solidifying as the will of the Dreadgod itself lent him its strength.

He stood with the solidity of mountains as he pushed against this young Underlord.

Pushed...and was shoved back.

His shoes slid across the stone, and as he dug in, drawing on his earth madra to make himself heavier and more solid, he continued to move. Even the stone beneath his feet began to crack.

The boy had given up the nimble movements he'd shown before, and he hadn't launched a single Striker technique.

But he didn't need to. Maraan's muscles strained.

That flying sword of his flashed at Maraan's back, and Era managed to deflect it with a Striker technique, but it only banked around for another attack.

Lindon drew his fist back, and Maraan felt his own death approaching.

At the risk of damaging his own channels, he poured all the madra he could into another Striker technique.

The Eruption Ring technique had been modeled on one of the Dreadgod's powers. It released a wall of madra all around, shoving enemies back, and with great control it could be focused in one direction.

Maraan blasted a solid wall of force and earth madra in front of him to give him some space.

The wave of yellow power splashed over the armored man like water.

He crashed through the Eruption Ring with his fist swinging.

Maraan held up the Staff of Condemnation and focused all his effort on his Enforcer technique, but when the punch landed, his vision whited out for an instant.

His back crashed into the side of a plateau. He made a crater in the rock.

His Embrace of the Titan faded.

His mask cracked in half.

He stared blankly forward, too dazed to feel pain or much of anything. A black visor turned to him, and then Era was there.

Her expression was hidden by her priest's mask, but he could feel the desperation in her spirit as she leaped up and wrapped her body around him.

A black figure loomed over them, shining gold, as Era crushed a blue ball. A gatestone.

An instant later, they were back in the Abyssal Palace itself, the fortress that now hovered over Sky's Edge. He and Era rolled to a halt on the polished floor, and only then did the pain penetrate.

His ribs were fractured, his arms useless, and he couldn't feel his legs. Era struggled to her feet, groaning, and then he saw that her sleeve was a ragged, bloody, empty mess where her left arm used to be.

An acolyte cried their names and ran for help.

Maraan let his pain wash over him. With trembling effort, he turned to look at the Staff of Condemnation, which had snapped into two pieces. An Overlord weapon he had been given along with his position.

His head fell back down to the tile.

This was his own fault for not paying more attention to the Uncrowned King tournament.

He had thought of the competition only as a way to prove their value to Reigan Shen and for his apprentice to gain experience. But Maraan knew Brother Aekin's strength better than anyone; he had practically raised the boy.

Aekin could not handle opponents like this. And this boy hadn't even made it into the top eight.

No...Lindon hadn't beaten him under tournament conditions. In fact, he'd given his life for this temporary power.

If he wasn't dead now, he'd be crippled for life.

Maraan consoled himself with that knowledge as he allowed the acolytes to carry him to medical care.

He spoke with great effort to Era as they were both gathered up. "What...was his name?"

"Lindon Arelius," Era responded grimly.

"We struck...a great blow...killing him. They will...want... revenge."

The fights had been mostly bloodless so far, but this was worthwhile. Maraan may be in recovery for a few weeks, but the Akura had lost one of their rising stars forever.

Lindon peeled himself out of the armor, letting Little Blue berate him as he fed each plate back into the void key.

He deserved her lecture. Not for the *reasons* she was upset, but he deserved it nonetheless.

She was angry that he hadn't accepted her help, and insisted that he could have made quick work of the enemies using her power.

He didn't regret leaving her in storage, but with every piece of armor he loaded back into the void key, he couldn't help calculating how much repairs would cost.

Fifty or sixty points, he suspected. And the fight had earned him zero more.

Well, the twenty from completing the assignment of clearing out an Abyssal Palace tower, but he was always going to get those.

[We have information on how the prototype performed in real, live combat!] Dross said cheerily. [That will cut down on costs in the long run, since instead of performing more tests in the boring world of flesh, we can perform them inside my amazing mind.]

"It's too fragile," Lindon said.

[You were like a rock covered in steel and wrapped in more rocks.]

"Not *me,* I mean the madra layers in the armor. They can't handle the resonance, so the armor tears itself apart. Instead of a sacred instrument, it's like strapping simple constructs all over my body."

[What's so wrong with that? You could be the construct man! That would certainly be memorable!]

"If I want to fight once for five minutes a week. Even if we could solve that, I didn't...like it."

The armor was too bulky. Not just physically, but spiritually, as though he had to lift heavy weights with both his body and his madra.

"I can't help but think there's one technique that would provide the same benefits without being so...complicated."

[Look at it this way: it only cost you points to make an entire team retreat!]

His pure core was still almost half-full, his Blackflame

core virtually untouched. His madra channels were sore, but no more so than after a day of hard exercise, and his body had handled the strain of all those Enforcer techniques unscathed. He could fight another battle immediately, if he had to, thanks to the effects of the Heaven and Earth Purification Wheel.

But the thought only depressed him further, and he gave a heavy sigh. "We still don't know what happened to Pride. If he..."

He trailed off, but if Mercy's brother died under his orders, it would be his fault. And the Akura clan had taken him to task over Harmony. If Fury's nephew was killed, what would his response be?

Charity was supposed to take Lindon back to the tournament in only two days. He couldn't hide from her. What would she do to him?

Lindon had sent messages requesting updates on Pride's condition, but no one so far had responded.

So it was with a heavy heart that he stood on his Thousand-Mile Cloud and began drifting back to the camp.

He was surprised to run into Pride halfway there.

He was standing behind the control panel of the small Akura cloudship, racing across the dusty plains. His collar was still smeared with blood, and there was a scar across the side of his throat that looked like it had been healing for weeks.

When he saw Lindon, he pulled the cloudship up alongside him in an instant. "You got away!" Pride said in evident surprise.

"Apologies." He bowed over fists pressed together.

Pride scowled. "I didn't think I'd have to tell *you* not to waste gatestones. What were you thinking?"

That was not what Lindon had meant to apologize for.

"I was trying to save your life."

Pride gave him a blank look. "Why would my life have been in danger?"

"He had his knife to your neck!"

"And did you see me use my armor?"

"He drew blood!"

Pride stared at him for another moment and then opened a void key. Like some other Akura void keys Lindon had seen before, it was blocked with shadow madra so he couldn't see within.

A moment later, he emerged with a dagger and stabbed it into the side of his own neck, pulling it out as blood gushed onto the console in front of him.

All the while, he wore a reproachful look.

The blood stopped flowing almost immediately, and Pride wiped the knife clean.

He tried to speak, coughed, spat up some blood, and continued. "A dagger to the neck is only threatening blood loss. Between my Iron body and one of my Enforcer techniques, it is almost literally impossible for me to bleed to death."

"Well, I...did not think of that."

Lindon had seen Pride's abilities before. He should have put that together.

If the Underlord had activated a binding in the dagger that might have cut Pride's head off, Pride would certainly have sensed that and used his bloodline armor.

So he had been in no danger at all.

[If it helps at all, *I* remembered all that, but even I didn't know he could brush off a knife to the throat. It's good to remember when we end up killing him.]

Pride's eye twitched. "You don't have to save me. Remember that. Just worry about yourself."

Lindon's own irritation with Pride returned, and he gave an even deeper bow than he had before. "Pardon, but would you mind letting your aunt know? I don't want to owe her another debt if you die."

Pride ground his jaw. "Get on the ship."

⬡

When Charity appeared in front of Lindon to take him back to the Uncrowned King tournament, he felt like she was tearing points away from him.

He wanted to see Yerin again, and of course he needed to witness the rest of the tournament, but how much would his team slow down without him around? What would happen to his *points?*

Charity noticed his hesitation, raising one eyebrow. "Did you enjoy it here that much?"

"Apologies, no, I'm...I'm ready to go."

"When my father was younger, he would have stayed in battle rather than returning home. Sometimes for months."

"It's not battle that concerns me. I just can't afford to stay where I am."

And every day he was gone, the Uncrowned would be growing stronger. He would be left further behind than he was already.

The tournament would only remind him how far he had to go.

"I had to visit for my own reasons in any case. If you would like me to leave you here—"

"No. No, my mind is made up."

If for no other reason, he hadn't seen Yerin in a month.

Charity nodded, giving him an hour to speak with his team and pack. Only when he was certain that they would all dedicate themselves to earning points while he was gone did he feel any sort of comfort about leaving.

Just like their trip to Sky's Edge, their trip back took half a day of transporting through seemingly random locations. This time, Charity was in a more talkative mood, asking both Dross and Lindon about their experiences in Sky's Edge.

"And you haven't seen any hint of the other Dreadgod cults?"

"Only Abyssal Palace, although other teams may have seen what I haven't."

She waved a hand. "No, that lines up with what my father said. It simply concerns me. But how about you? You were placed at the head of a team with no time to prepare."

Lindon wasn't sure what kind of answer she was looking for, so he gave a noncommittal answer. "It has been a valuable learning opportunity for me, and a good chance to earn contribution points."

"I see." Purple eyes watched him, and he couldn't read them. "And your team members? Have you grown to know them better?"

"We often work separately, but I have spent time with each of them."

Less so with the Maten sisters, who seemed not to talk any more than necessary to anyone but each other, or the two lowest-ranking Akura Underlords. Douji and Courage went out of their way to avoid Lindon whenever possible, no doubt worried that he might take revenge for their treatment of him in Moongrave.

Their fear was not improved by Dross, who kept whispering threats into their minds as they tried to sleep.

"Hm." She raised an arm, and an owl of living madra came down to perch on it. She scratched it behind the head as she asked, "What do you think of Grace?"

Lindon sensed danger, but since he still didn't know where the Sage was headed, he continued to answer safely. "She has performed admirably, both in and out of combat. I can trust her judgment more than...others."

He had almost given in to his temptation to insult Pride.

The Sage of the Silver Heart turned and speared him with a gaze that examined him far beyond the point of comfort. "What if we allowed you to marry her?"

They had stopped in a beautiful glade, where Lindon sat on a plush cushion of moss, but suddenly he couldn't find a comfortable position.

"I...would be...flattered by the offer, but certainly she has better prospects than me."

Charity continued examining him as she rested her hand on the owl. The owl, too, stared fixedly at him.

"How many better prospects do you imagine there are?" the Sage asked. "You must know that you caught my grandmother's attention. She instructed us to tie you to the family, and this would be the easiest way."

[Wow, marriage is easy! I had always imagined a lot of nonsense building up to it, but this is nice and fast. You should do it.]

Lindon focused on watching dew bead at the end of a huge leaf so that he didn't have to keep staring into piercing purple eyes. He declined as graciously as he could. "Apologies. I doubt I can live up to your expectations. I have never interacted with Grace as anything other than a teammate."

"You will become a significant power in the future," Charity said. "It is in our best interests to tie you to our name as early as we can. As for Grace's personal feelings, while I intended to propose this issue to her, she brought it up first."

For a moment, Lindon had a hard time believing that. But the Sage would have no reason to lie.

Then he couldn't help but be flattered. More than he would have expected.

He understood the reality of Grace's position: she saw him as a good prospect that her family would accept and that she could get along with. He had no illusions about his own charm.

"I am honored," he said honestly.

"Good. We would also like to avoid the possibility of any... missteps...on your part. We are aware that the only young women you have spent significant time with are Yerin and Mercy, and we would like to act before you develop too much attachment to either of them."

Lindon studiously examined the dew-spotted leaf.

"Mercy cannot afford any distractions until she reaches at least the peak of Archlord, at which point she will make her own decisions. And Yerin is not a member of our family. Yet. But we will be doing what we can to change that."

"I appreciate your honesty," Lindon said automatically.

"Yes." Charity waved a hand, dismissing her owl. "Now, I would appreciate some from you."

While Lindon couldn't detect any clear change in her

expression, somehow she seemed more relatable. Less like the Sage of the Silver Heart, and more like Mercy's aunt.

Or, technically, Mercy's ancient niece.

"I am genuinely flattered by the offer," Lindon said, "but I am interested only in Yerin." That was uncomfortable to say out loud, so he tried to soften the statement. "Presuming she feels the same way. I would like to try, at least."

Charity folded her arms. "I knew we had waited too long when I saw your reservation at the Sundown Pavilion."

He gave an awkward laugh that he didn't feel. "Ah. My apologies."

"None necessary. If you're serious, you should strike sooner rather than later. Yerin has become one of the most eligible young women in the world."

Lindon tried to imagine Yerin's reaction to a stranger asking her for a stroll in the moonlight.

He couldn't picture it going well.

"Pardon if this sounds too proud," Lindon said, "but I don't think that's my greatest concern."

When Charity made the final jump to the Ninecloud Court, she told Lindon to expect that they would emerge at the end of the cloudship dock.

So when he ended up inside a familiar gray, simply decorated room with Northstrider standing in the corner, Lindon was caught off guard.

At first, Lindon thought Charity had brought him to Northstrider as the result of some secret deal, but the Sage spoke in a flat voice. "Monarch. You could have summoned me."

"I did," Northstrider said. "Now I dismiss you." His muscular arms were folded, and he stared into the walls as though watching something far away.

"We are allies. We may as well be cordial to one another."

He slowly turned to regard her with his draconic gaze, but if he meant it to be intimidating, it didn't seem to work. Charity met him evenly, impassively, without any disruption in her madra that Lindon could sense.

"Very well," Northstrider said at last. "Thank you for your assistance. You may go."

That didn't sound too cordial to Lindon, but Charity accepted it, as she bowed. "Of course. Lindon, I will speak with you later. And I will relay your greetings to Mercy, Yerin, and Eithan."

With that, she stepped into shadow and disappeared.

Dross spun out onto Lindon's shoulder. [Sir! It's been too long! I mean, not *too* long, unless you think so.]

The black orb appeared in Northstrider's hand. "This time, I would like you to attempt some simulations, to show me the true extent of your predictive capabilities."

[Of course! Of course, delighted to. I remember exactly—]

"Begin."

Instead of pushing his way in, this time Dross was absorbed straight into the center of the black sphere, leaving Northstrider and Lindon together.

Before Lindon could say a word, Northstrider spoke. "You used my technique."

Lindon immediately worried that the Monarch might disapprove, but pride in his accomplishment won out. "Gratitude for your guidance. It took me great effort to separate the powers from one another."

"Has Dross helped you overcome the effects?"

Lindon quickly realized he must be referring to the burden that absorbing power put on his body and spirit. "Dross has been invaluable in helping me to separate memories, but my madra channels are still not quite as resilient as I would like."

He studied the Monarch, hoping that Northstrider would take the hint and gift him with a set of Diamond Veins. Then Lindon wouldn't have to use the treasure he'd bought from the Sky's Edge battlefield.

"Your madra channels. Good. If you continue to use it on the battlefield, you could reach Overlord in a matter of weeks."

"Gratitude, but I am not certain I have the insight to advance to Overlord. I have much yet to learn."

"But you have investigated the Overlord revelation yourself."

It wasn't really a question, but Lindon nodded anyway. "It seems to be based on seeing yourself clearly, as the Underlord revelation was. I read a theory that Underlord requires meditating on the past, Overlord on the present, and Archlord on the future. But pardon me if I am incorrect."

Northstrider ran his spiritual sense through him, keeping it on him until Lindon found it hard to breathe. "That is the path for you," he said at last, and Lindon took a deep breath when his perception lifted. "Consider yourself as you are now. What is the nature of the will that drives you? What principles guide your madra?"

He tapped the black orb, in which Dross still swam, and then nodded to himself. "Yes. That is the way."

Lindon bowed as he committed the words to memory. "Gratitude, Monarch. I hope to one day repay you for your wisdom."

"You may soon have the chance." Northstrider darkened, scowling but not at Lindon. "The Ninecloud Court has announced their support for Reigan Shen. Leiala would never have allowed it. She hated him almost as much as he deserves."

Lindon thought back to Eithan's fight and wondered if it was appropriate for him to speculate. "Is...is that Eithan's fault?"

"It could be Miara's immaturity, but the Ninecloud Court is far from the Blackflame continent. They have nothing to risk from this experiment, but they will provide little support to Shen either. The more pressing issue is the Eight-Man Empire. They are looking for an excuse to throw their weight behind one side or the other."

"I thank you for sharing your wisdom."

"I'm sharing so that you may understand," Northstrider said sharply. "You will return to the Dreadgod battlefield, so you should know. Right now, a flight of dragons is poised to cross the continent and head to Sky's Edge. They are held back by Heralds in the Wasteland, but those Heralds have no allegiance, even to me. They will bend with the wind. And they look to the Uncrowned King tournament to gauge the direction of the wind."

Lindon thought he understood, and his stomach clenched. Depending on who had the best showing in the tournament, Abyssal Palace could receive reinforcements. The Eight-Man Empire could tip the balance in war zones all over the world.

And depending on who ultimately won, it could shift again.

"I only wish I could still influence the tournament," Lindon said. He still hadn't quite gotten over his disappointment with Northstrider at matching him against Yerin.

"Do not pretend you don't understand that situation. The placements were a game among all eight factions." Northstrider unfolded his arms and stepped over to Lindon, standing so close that Lindon started to sweat.

"The world will not end with this tournament, nor even with the awakening of the Dreadgods. One day, you may become an asset."

This made the second time in quick succession that Lindon had heard something about how influential he would someday be. Evidently Charity, Northstrider, and even Akura Malice had expectations of him in the future.

Rather than honored, he was growing suspicious. What had he done recently to attract their attention? Or did they treat him this way just because he earned top sixteen in the tournament?

Dross emerged, gasping, from the black orb. His purple arms drooped, and he shivered. [You lied to me! That was so much harder than last time!]

When Northstrider turned his gaze to Dross, the spirit coughed. [Ah, you know what, I misinterpreted what you said. Don't blame me. It's *his* dream aura that I run on.]

"Both of you, continue your training," Northstrider said. "You should have new insights to pursue."

Dross and Lindon both thanked him, and the Monarch waved a hand. As usual, he dismissed him the instant he was done with them.

As they appeared in Lindon's room in the Ninecloud Court for the first time in a month, Lindon sent a thought to Dross: *Did you get any more memories*

[Not from *him*,] Dross said dismissively. [He's locked those up now. Most of his "tests" involve sorting facts, and of course I remember them. I was hoping he'd give me some kind of memory erasing technique. But hey! I did get some records from the tournament! Straight from the recording constructs, fresh and delicious.]

Lindon wasn't one to dismiss the value of information—anything the Monarch could give Dross would be as valuable as any technique library—but he did admit a *little* disappointment. He had been hoping for more Monarch sacred arts he could steal.

That disappointment was nothing next to what he felt when he tried to visit Yerin.

"Due to increased security measures, the Uncrowned have been separated for the duration of the fifth round," the Ninecloud Soul said apologetically from outside the empty room that had once belonged to Yerin. "You may apply for a visit when the fights are complete, and in the meantime, you may avail yourself of Ninecloud City's many world-renowned entertainment venues!"

Lindon went back to his room to Forge scales.

INFORMATION REQUESTED: THE EIGHT-MAN EMPIRE, WANDERING CONQUERORS AND COLLECTIVE MONARCH.

BEGINNING REPORT...

Path: the Eightfold Spear. What the Empire calls "the Path of the Eightfold Spear" is not a Path in the traditional sense. It is a complex bond of mind and spirit woven through a network of Divine Treasures that allow the eight members of the Empire to access the powers of the other seven. In reality, each member of the Eight-Man Empire is on a separate Path.

When Sages and Heralds refuse to ascend, it is almost always because they dream of becoming a Monarch and ruling over the world of their birth. Over the course of history, therefore, there have been many attempts to create a reliable way to advance to Monarch.

All those who pursue such research eventually have the same idea: if Monarchs are those who have advanced both to Herald and to Sage, why not link a Sage with a Herald? Surely they would then, together, exert the power of a Monarch.

If this research reaches the stage of experimentation, it almost always ends in tragedy. The strain is too great for both the Herald and the Sage, as neither has the insight required to control the power of the other.

All who tried this technique have been torn apart by their own spirits...with a single exception.

The founding members of the Eight-Man Empire, four Heralds and four Sages, suspected that spreading their power more widely could lessen the burden on any one member. They crafted eight Divine Treasures, suits of golden armor, that linked their wills together.

It is unknown how sacred artists who never ventured beyond Cradle understood such principles so thoroughly, but Abidan intervention is suspected.

The Path of the Eightfold Spear is unique in all the world, and the Eight-Man Empire is always on the lookout for heirs to inherit their positions in the event of death or ascension. Their suits of armor can be passed down and repaired, but not replaced.

Their experiment has never been successfully repeated.

SUGGESTED TOPIC: SQUIRES OF THE EIGHT-MAN EMPIRE. CONTINUE?

DENIED, REPORT COMPLETE.

第十四章

CHAPTER FOURTEEN

Yerin sat in a plush seat in the audience hall of a floating castle covered in shadow: the Akura family Monarch platform. Constructs of light projected the contents of the arena so that she could see everything in perfect detail, and she had a personal servant to cater to her every whim.

If she could have cut her way out, she would have.

"It's for your own security," the Winter Sage reminded her for the tenth time. "The Ninecloud Court couldn't afford it if anything happened to the Uncrowned under their watch, and our political relations are more strained than ever."

Yerin still seethed. "Show me the face of the killer with so much courage that they'll attack while I'm protected by the heavens."

"It's not courage we're concerned about," the Sage snapped. "Who can count on the Abidan?"

Mercy leaned forward and laced her black-gloved fingers together. "It's about to start," she said quietly.

Yerin eyed her. Mercy wasn't acting like her usual self. She was on the edge of her seat, tapping her foot, and she hadn't tried to make Yerin feel better.

Mercy's match was in two days, and it was enough to put anyone on the edge.

Which meant it was Yerin's turn to try cheering someone up.

"Look at it with new eyes," Yerin suggested. "When you win, she won't make it any further."

Mercy let out a long, heavy breath and slumped down further in her chair. "Yeah, but I *have* to win," she muttered. "That takes all the fun out of it."

Well, I tried, Yerin thought.

The Ninecloud Soul introduced Yan Shoumei, and Yerin paid more attention to the projection. After all the dream tablets and recordings Yerin had seen of the Redmoon girl, she recognized the signs of nerves in her fixed expression and the way she let her hair hang over the sides of her face.

Yerin was particularly interested in this match because she had never actually seen Yan Shoumei use her Blood Shadow. She had only summoned it in the match against Blacksword. To Yerin, it seemed like the woman was on a standard blood Path.

And while Yerin knew that she hadn't seen everything Shoumei was capable of, she suspected she hadn't seen everything the other fighter had to offer either.

Yan Shoumei stood in the middle of a field full of obstacles that resembled ancient ruins. Dark stains spattered everything, and since the projection of these high-quality constructs even conveyed spiritual impressions, Yerin could sense that the stains gave off blood aura.

So the aura would allow Shoumei to use the full extent of her Path, but the obstacles would break sight and force both participants to rely on their spiritual senses.

Which would greatly favor Yan Shoumei's opponent.

The Ninecloud Soul was wrapping up her introduction. "...and facing the prodigy of Redmoon Hall, we have a prodigy in his own right: the exile separated from his homeland and fighting for the glory of a new Monarch. Eithan Arelius!"

There came the faint sound of applause, though Yerin could only hear it because of the projection. The Monarch platform blocked all outside sound.

A stone door lifted, and out came...not Eithan.

Two Remnants, like chubby golden phoenixes, soared out of the waiting room. Rainbows streamed behind them, and they cried in a chorus that seemed like it couldn't possibly come from any less than a hundred throats.

Eithan drifted out, floating not on a Thousand-Mile Cloud but on a platform of shimmering light generated from diamond shoes. His robes were five shades of gold, sewn with images of dragons and phoenixes and tigers in even more gold. The robes glowed, too.

He held an ivory pipe encrusted in jewels, and it must have been two entire feet long. When he held the pipe out to the side, the smoke drifting up from the bowl spelled out letters in the air.

"...do I want to know what that says?" Yerin asked.

"It's his name," the Winter Sage said icily.

Mercy choked down a laugh.

A gold-rimmed glass lens sat over one of Eithan's eyes, and a crown of shining crystals hovered over his head. As he came to a stop, shimmering white wings of light spread from behind him.

It was the ugliest, most unnecessary thing Yerin had ever seen.

Northstrider stood with his arms crossed between both fighters, and while Yan Shoumei looked confused, the Monarch gave Eithan a sharp glare.

"I did not call for a clown," he said.

"Really? I could have sworn I heard my name." Eithan took a puff of the pipe and blew out the smoke, which formed the shape of a star in midair. "It's an important occasion, so I thought I'd dress my best."

Northstrider turned to Yan Shoumei. "Will this distract you?"

Shoumei was still examining Eithan the way she would a mysterious creature of unknown origin, but she shook her head.

"Very well," the Monarch said. "Then...begin."

He vanished, and so did the barrier separating them.

Eithan adjusted the lens over his eye. "I say, I hope you're prepared for a real tussle. Yes, a knuckle-scraper. Put up your—"

Shoumei threw one Striker technique, a simple nest of bloody whips that struck Eithan in the chest.

Eithan didn't defend himself at all. The madra tore through him, and Yerin knew what the technique would do. It was easy enough to block or avoid, but blood madra affected bodies directly; undefended, the Striker technique tore his heart in half.

He and all his clothes dissolved into white light.

There was a moment of silence from the crowd, and then jeers that grew louder and louder.

"...victory in fight number one goes to Yan Shoumei," the Ninecloud Soul announced. "Has Eithan Arelius underestimated his opponent, or did he intend to give up the first fight for a more stunning victory later?"

Yerin turned to the Winter Sage for an explanation, but she was grinding her teeth together so hard that it looked like she was chewing strips of invisible leather. Frost had begun growing on her chair, and wild sword aura slowly tore rips into the fabric.

Yerin turned to Mercy instead.

"They bought him off," Mercy said with a sigh. "The Abidan specifically mentioned it as an option. I still don't understand why. Are they hoping the richest faction will win?"

"They're not looking for a recruit with no spine," Yerin said. "If you can be bought, why would they want you?"

That felt right to Yerin, if maybe incomplete. It wasn't as though she knew what motives drove the heavens.

"Well then, we know he'll allow it. But I hope..."

She glanced up to the top of the room, where a mass of darkness and dense spiritual power waited.

That was the seat of Akura Malice, and while none of them could tell if the Monarch was actually inside that cloud of shadow or not, she would certainly be watching from somewhere.

If Eithan had thrown the match while fighting in Malice's name without warning her, the Monarch wouldn't be happy.

The heavenly messenger might personally intervene to stop reprisals, but Malice could still find a thousand ways to make Eithan's life miserable.

To Yerin's own surprise, she found herself hoping that Eithan had gotten permission for this. Normally she would say that Eithan had earned whatever he got by acting like a fool, but this time she was afraid for him.

A few minutes passed before Northstrider announced the rematch.

The fourth round had been single-elimination duels, according to Northstrider's preference, but the fifth round gave each competitor the chance to show more of what they were capable of. The winner of each match would be the first to win two fights out of three, with half an hour in between each fight for the fighter to adjust their strategy.

When that half an hour ended, Yan Shoumei walked out to the center of the arena as before. The battlefield had changed slightly, with the obstacles rearranged. Some of them moved along tracks, while others looked insubstantial or like blobs of shifting liquid.

Eithan rode out of his waiting room on the back of a blazing white Remnant that resembled a skull-headed horse.

He galloped out, leaped off, and flipped in the air as the Remnant trotted back to the room behind him. When he landed, he spread both his hands wide.

"Well, my worthy opponent, you may have caught me off my guard once. But I assure you that this time, you will face my full fury!"

"Begin," Northstrider said.

Yan Shoumei lashed out with a Striker technique again, but this time she didn't go for a quick kill. Whether she was trying to make Eithan suffer or to avoid the potential of falling into a trap, she lashed her blood madra at his legs.

As soon as the technique made contact, Eithan exploded.

Simple constructs strapped beneath his clothes detonated

at the touch of blood madra, annihilating him in an instant.

"Victory to Yan Shoumei," the Ninecloud Soul said with a sigh.

Eithan re-formed in his waiting room laughing.

Reigan Shen would have preferred it if he hadn't flaunted his bribery, but that was all the more reason to do it. Malice wouldn't like it either, but Eithan had pacified her before the match began.

He wasn't *entirely* happy about his deal with Malice. He now owed her a favor, paid at a time of her choosing, which was too much of a potential liability for his liking. What if she held on to that token until he advanced to Monarch?

But some jokes were worth it.

It was at that moment that he realized how cold it was in his waiting room. He had been brought back to life without a stitch of his clothing.

"This doesn't seem fair!" Eithan called. "Northstrider!"

He knew the Monarch could hear him.

Oh, well. The clothes had been expensive, but Reigan Shen had paid for it all. He reached into a cubby for his void key, only to find it missing.

It would be back in his room, he was certain—it was beneath a Monarch to steal from an Overlord. Then again, it was also beneath a Monarch to strip an Overlord naked.

Eithan looked toward the door and sighed. "On the bright side," he said aloud, "at least I look fantastic."

Yan Shoumei marched toward the Akura waiting room, seething.

She had been told to expect that Eithan would throw the match, and she would take any victory she could get. She wasn't here for honorable combat.

Even so, Eithan had been supposed to make it look like a real fight. This brought her no respect at all, and it made her look like he could have destroyed her and had chosen not to. She was certain she could have won the fight even if he had given it his all, and part of her still resented that the Monarch had no faith in her.

Her anger only faded when she thought of the prizes she would soon receive. Respect or not, a win was a win. This was one step closer to overall victory, when neither she nor her homeland could be ignored ever again.

She was debating with herself when she came to the Akura waiting room. The Uncrowned were still allowed to interact with one another outside the matches, which she had thought was strange. Surely the eight of them were the most likely to attack one another.

Who could try anything under the observation of both the Ninecloud Soul and the Monarchs?

The door swung open, and Eithan Arelius emerged.

She wondered if he was deliberately trying to provoke her.

A cloud, which he'd clearly condensed out of aura, wrapped around his waist. Otherwise, he was completely naked. His ostentatious clothes had vanished as though they'd been dissolved with destruction aura.

When he saw her, he smiled brightly and put both hands on his hips.

"Yan Shoumei! Wonderful to see you. Would you mind if we spoke later? I'd love to have a heart-to-heart, but I can't keep this cloud up forever."

Shoumei pulled an outer robe from her void key and tossed it to him.

"Ah! Thank you." He wrapped it around his waist and let the cloud puff apart. "Now, what can I do for you?"

"Why?" Her voice came out more puzzled than angry. "Are you trying to embarrass me? Or make an enemy of the Monarch?"

"I apologize for the lack of respect toward you," Eithan said. "But I apologize not at all for the lack of respect toward your master."

That phrasing grated on her. "He is not my master. And he should have let me beat you myself."

"Ah, that is a disappointment. We'll have to see about that some other time. Until then, enjoy your prizes. And I will repay you for the robe! Unless you would rather I wash it and send it back?"

Yan Shoumei couldn't take him anymore, so she turned and marched away.

On a whim, she reached back with her spiritual perception. It was hard to get a passive sense of his spirit, since pure madra was naturally subtle, but she probed his spirit accurately. It was rude, but not as rude as what he'd done already.

When she felt his spirit, she stopped in her steps.

Overlord.

Yan Shoumei spun around to see him wave lazily to her as he walked away.

The Forest Sage had given up on Ziel halfway through their training, but that was understandable. Ziel had given up on himself long before.

He stood in the center of the Uncrowned King arena, letting the cheers and shouts of the audience wash over him. The arena was an elaborate machine of crashing steel and falling stones, a three-dimensional maze ripe with aura of force and earth.

He would have to navigate it carefully, and he was certain the shape of the arena had been designed to encourage mobility. On its own, this fight was likely to be nothing more than two sacred artists crashing hammers into one another until one fell over, and the Ninecloud Court wanted a more interesting fight. Especially after the last round.

Northstrider was here, and his opponent was on his way. Brother Aekin wore a dark stone mask carved to resemble some kind of snarling monster, the right eye of which glowed with a bright yellow light. His robes were black and brown, representing the Wandering Titan's cult: the Abyssal Palace.

When Ziel had learned they weren't matching him up against the last remaining Stormcaller, that had sapped even more of his motivation.

Even now, he wondered why he bothered. It would take the attention of multiple Monarchs to restore him to his former power, which he would only get if he won the tournament. Not only were the odds too low to bet on, what would he do with the power of an Archlord?

He just wanted his own spirit to stop hurting. Emriss Silentborn's treatment had helped, but it needed a long time to do its work. Rather than fight, he wanted to go home and wait for that elixir to slowly heal him.

Even if it would only ever make him an Underlord.

But he did have one more hope.

He glanced at the Arelius tower, with its blocks of white stone held up by fluted columns. Tiberian Arelius had been known for his spiritual attacks, and in fact the Sage of Calling Storms had abused some of the Arelius Monarch's research to damage Ziel's soul in the first place.

Tiberian had created a spiritual restoration process to undo long-term soul damage: the Pure Storm Baptism. Once, Ziel had hunted for it, until he had learned that the Arelius Monarch was dead.

Only days ago, the Arelius family had contacted him. If he defeated Brother Aekin, they would ensure that their prize in the next round was one of the few remaining Pure Storm Baptism courses.

Without Tiberian alive, they couldn't replace those. Any they used would be gone forever.

And it wouldn't restore his power as an Archlord, but it would allow him to live as a perfectly healthy Underlord far faster than Emriss' elixir.

With the two combined, he might even be able to advance again.

He had already passed his soulfire revelations, so his body would be even stronger than any other Underlord's. And now the revelations couldn't bottleneck his progress if he *did* manage to advance again. It was a great offer.

Too great to pass up. He *knew* that in his head, but his heart wasn't convinced.

He'd been worthless for too long. Nothing could turn that around now. The belief was engraved in his bones.

Cylinders crashed to the ground around him, casting off force aura and kicking up wind that billowed his cloak. He leaned on his hammer, facing Brother Aekin.

Northstrider asked them both if they were prepared, and Ziel wondered if anyone got to this point in the competition and required another minute for preparation.

Finally, the Monarch ordered them to begin.

The Path of the Dawn Oath had only two techniques, and Ziel used them both.

The Stone Anchor, his full-body Enforcer technique, ran through him like iron bars reinforcing his skeleton. It bound him to the ground, so that with stable footing he could stand as though nailed in place.

But the cornerstone of his Path was the Oathsign technique. He Forged eleven green, shining runes in a circle that hung in the air in front of him.

This circle hardened force aura into a solid barrier that stopped physical impacts.

Brother Aekin's hammer crashed into the barrier and cracked it, ruining the Forged symbols, but the blow was stopped.

Ziel's own hammer, driven with the force of his Stone

Anchor, slammed into Aekin an instant later.

The Dreadgod cultist blocked it with one upraised arm, sliding a few feet back instead of flying across the arena. A full-body Enforcer technique flowed through him as well, appearing outwardly as a yellow light covering him like armor.

They each gripped a hammer in both hands.

Aekin's weapon looked like it had been hewn from rough stone, and it gave off the pressure of an Archlord weapon. Ziel's steel hammer had been made for an Archlord as well, but there was no way he could activate its binding. His madra channels were already screaming at him after using only a handful of techniques.

As he expected, he should give up.

But while he was here, he might as well give the fight a token effort.

New scripts encircled his wrists and ankles, stimulating the blood aura in his body and strengthening him briefly. He kicked off from the ground, launching himself into the air and landing on a platform that drifted across the arena on a cushion of force aura.

He expected Aekin to follow him, but the Abyssal Palace priest pulled a second weapon out of his soulspace. It was shaped something like a crossbow made from polished wood, though if he was storing it in his soulspace it had to be very dense madra.

A launcher construct made into a sacred instrument. That was rare, as launcher constructs typically didn't get any stronger when powered directly. A sword produced more power in accordance with its user, but launchers had static output.

Globs of a dark, oily liquid shot out of the construct. Ziel had already dropped the scripts around his limbs and switched back to the Stone Anchor, so it would be a moment before he could dodge again. He had no choice but to block.

A new script-circle appeared in front of him, this one designed to seize madra rather than aura. The globs of oil struck the circle and were sprayed out the sides, away from him.

But a few droplets landed on the ends of his cloak and splattered onto his feet. They began to grow, drawing strength from his blood and sticking him to the flying surface.

He broke them quickly, but Aekin had already leaped onto the platform, and a rush of his yellow madra shoved Ziel backwards.

The duel took another minute or two, but Ziel never recovered.

Aekin kept him on the back foot as Ziel grew more and more exhausted, his own techniques burdening him too much to continue.

Eventually, he couldn't support his own madra and Aekin crushed his head.

Ziel was remade from white madra in his waiting room. Alone.

Shame and disappointment draped over him in a crushing weight.

That had been *pathetic*.

Would the spectators think that was the limit of his abilities? His master would have disowned him if she'd witnessed that sort of behavior. What would the people who saw him think about the Dawnwing Sect?

Ziel rested his head in his hands. His horns were cool against his fingers.

What was wrong with him?

He had gone into this match knowing he was going to lose. Expecting to lose. Fifteen minutes ago, he'd been fine with it.

He couldn't even count on his own heart to be consistent.

No matter how many times he was certain that the Archlord of the Dawnwing Sect was dead, he always found another scrap of that man clinging to life. Ziel should have no pride left to be hurt, and yet here he was.

The truth remained: he didn't want to lose.

Ziel reached out to the shield to his left. It looked like a steel castle wall, with elaborate designs that made it worthy of being carried into battle by an Archlord. The shield had been his prize from the second round, but he couldn't hold it in his damaged soulspace, and carrying it along with his hammer strained his Enforcer technique, so he hadn't bothered using it until now.

Maybe he was a hypocrite to start caring about the fights this late in the tournament, but so what? Let him be hypocritical.

He strode out of his waiting room for the rematch against Brother Aekin, huge hammer propped up on his right shoulder and over-sized shield covering the left side of his body. He had to use the Stone Anchor just to carry them, so his soul already ached, but he set those concerns aside.

It was time to see how much of his former self still remained.

Northstrider looked him up and down. "Welcome to the tournament."

Ziel nodded to the Monarch and faced his opponent. If Brother Aekin was a real enemy, how would Ziel face him?

It was easier to remember than Ziel had expected.

Northstrider waited until Aekin's full-body Enforcer technique covered him in translucent yellow madra like armor. Only then did he command them to begin.

Against Ziel's expectations, Aekin leaped back, conjuring a ball of golden light and stone fragments in his left hand as he held his hammer in his right. A combination Striker and Ruler technique.

Ziel Forged six circles at once.

One wrapped around Aekin, choking off the energy coming from him.

Two hung over Ziel's weapons like haloes, lightening them so they were easier to carry.

Two more appeared around Ziel, strengthening him.

And the final script, the biggest of all, appeared over a pendulum the size of a house swinging nearby. Multiplying its force.

Ziel's spirit felt like it was tearing in half, but he pushed through.

Aekin's technique faltered before he broke the ring of script around him, but the pendulum tore free of the chain holding it up and crashed into him.

The Abyssal Palace cultist stood as firm as a fortress, denting the metal ball as it crashed into him.

Until Ziel arrived, slamming his hammer down onto the pendulum. Aekin was crushed to the ground beneath it, and Ziel Forged another script on the ball to shove it harder into the earth.

A column of yellow light blasted up from beneath it, shoving the ball to the side, but Ziel had already moved. He stood in front of Aekin, shield raised to catch the cultist's wild swing.

Ziel's counterstroke landed with another green circle, multiplying its force.

Aekin crashed into a cylinder that pumped in and out of the ground, denting it so severely that it bent in half.

Several of Ziel's circles had fallen apart—most only tended to last a few seconds—but he re-Forged the ones around himself and added another circle to his feet. It launched him forward as though thrown by the hand of a Monarch, and he slammed into Aekin shield-first, knocking the Palace priest deeper into the metal column.

His body was mangled and bent, but members of Abyssal Palace modeled their Path after the Wandering Titan. They were all but indestructible.

But now he was trapped.

Ziel's spirit was fresh torture, but he felt alive. He felt like himself again.

His next hammer-blow tore the entire cylinder apart.

Its top half crashed to the ground behind him with a sound like a collapsing house, and Brother Aekin's body tumbled across the arena leaking blood.

The crowd's cheers were deafening, and Ziel thought he heard people chanting his name. He remembered this feeling. Life crept back into him, as he hadn't felt in years. The exhilaration didn't cancel out the pain, but it made the agony more bearable.

Aekin's arms and legs were broken, his neck hung at a strange angle, and the light in his mask was flickering, but he hadn't died. His Path emphasized endurance, but Ziel would end it here. He may not have the power of an Archlord anymore, but there was no substitute for skill.

He raised his hammer, Forging a circle around it.

The green runes fuzzed to essence before they were half-complete, and the hammer fell from his numb fingers.

He stared at it for a long moment, uncomprehending, but then the Stone Anchor Enforcer technique dropped. His shield was too heavy for him, tugging him off-balance as he tried to keep it upright with his whole body weight.

His spirit had failed him.

No matter how much he endured the pain, his soul was still shattered. Determination alone didn't let you run on two broken legs.

Aekin's hand raised, and one last technique formed between his fingers.

Ziel closed his eyes.

As a ball of madra and flying rocks tore his head apart, Ziel chastised himself. He knew better than this.

He should never have forgotten who he was.

When Ziel came back to life in his waiting room, he left his hammer and shield sitting where they were.

Northstrider restored him to the condition he'd been in before the match started, so his spirit was no more strained than usual. He could have carried both weapons back, but he couldn't muster the energy to care.

He'd come back for them later. Or the Ninecloud Soul would bring them to his room, or Northstrider would, or maybe no one would and they would sit in that room forever.

The hammer held years of memories for him, but it was hard to remember why he should care.

It took him too long to realize that someone was standing in front of him, smiling broadly and wearing an outer robe of turquoise and thread-of-gold.

Eithan Arelius was competing in an Akura vassal team, but he was still a member of the Arelius family. He may have come here on behalf of House Arelius, or he may have had goals of his own.

Ziel just kept walking.

"I see you found some inspiration during the second match! Good for you."

Ziel didn't respond, but Eithan fell into step beside him.

"It is a shame that you weren't able to receive your prizes for this round, but I may have an alternative offer for you."

It didn't surprise Ziel that House Arelius had something else in mind, but it *did* somewhat surprise him that they still needed him for anything. Now that he was out of the tournament, why would they care what happened to him?

"You know, there are a handful of people left with the knowledge to perform the Pure Storm Baptism, they just don't have the resources. However, thanks to some fortuitous circumstances and a few carefully laid plans, I happen to find myself in possession of both!"

Ziel turned and examined Eithan carefully. His smile was too bright.

"No, you don't," Ziel said at last.

He kept walking.

"Ah, but what if I *did?* I can't restore the original power you lost, of course, but I can turn you into quite an extraordinary Underlord."

"So you're telling me that you have the materials for the elixirs—"

"My private garden is being prepared as we speak."

"—and a refiner skilled enough to make them—"

"That part is still a work in progress."

"—and the skill to perform the procedure—"

"I give great massages, too."

"—and lightning madra of sufficient power. Without Tiberian Arelius, that leaves you scales from the Thunder Fairy, the Storm Sage, or the Weeping Dragon itself."

Eithan's smile was painfully bright. "Which would you prefer?"

"I don't believe you." Ziel turned away and kept moving. "And I don't do favors on faith."

"Ah, but what if you were paid up-front?"

Ziel stopped.

Eithan rolled out a hand-sized scroll. A contract. "I perform the Pure Storm Baptism, and only if it is successful to your expectations, you repay me with your services as an employee for one year. Standard conditions for a Blackflame Empire Arelius family worker, though scaled up to reflect your position as an Underlord."

Ziel tried to parse out whether Eithan was insane, overly idealistic, or trying to scam him.

He was leaning toward the scam.

The conditions were too good. *If* Eithan could successfully perform the procedure, that was worth Ziel's oath to House Arelius for life.

"No," he said at last. He couldn't see the trap here, but he was certain there was one.

Eithan shrugged. "Ah, well. Let me know if you change your mind."

He tossed the scroll and Ziel caught it on reflex.

For a moment, Ziel considered tearing it up to demonstrate his commitment. He was still sure this was a deception of some kind.

In the end, he slipped the scroll into his pocket.

第十五章

CHAPTER FIFTEEN

Mercy's Uncle Fury had left the Dreadgod battlefield to come see her fight.

He had personally killed Sophara's great-aunt, and had lost friends of his own in his personal crusade against the gold dragons. He had spent hundreds of years campaigning against them, and she had been raised on stories of the thousands of human settlements they had annihilated.

He lowered himself to look her in the eyes, smiling easily, his hair drifting like black seaweed. "Loosen up," he said. "You'll be fine. We know all their tricks. Just go kill her."

All the elders in the Akura head family were up next, giving her last-minute advice or cheering her on. Even Yerin gave her a straightforward attempt at encouragement.

When the time came and Mercy was released by the crowd, Aunt Charity took her by the shoulder and transported her to the tunnels beneath the stadium. "Sophara has not advanced yet. We have a solid plan for the first fight. Keep a calm head and a cool heart, and you will do us proud."

Calm head, Mercy reminded herself. *Cool heart.*

As long as she won, the previous few matches wouldn't matter.

Lindon, Ziel, even Eithan—she could make up for their elimination. If she won, the Heralds would know that the Akura clan would continue to be stronger than the gold dragons, and would hold the dragons back from reinforcing Sky's Edge.

If she won, the Eight-Man Empire would throw their support behind her mother.

She wanted to prove Charity's faith in her justified, she wanted to show her pride in the Akura name, and she knew that her victory here would save lives. Possibly including her mother's.

And although it was less important, she just...*wanted* to win.

Sophara had burned her side, scorching her face and her scalp. She had recovered, and Charity had even helped her soothe the mental trauma left behind, but that didn't mean she'd forgotten. It had been agonizing.

She didn't need to get back at Sophara. She had never really seen the point of revenge. But that burn was a reminder of how much stronger Sophara had been than Mercy.

She had been weak for too long. This was her chance to be the strongest again.

Charity reminded her to stay focused and to control the fight, not to get swept up in Sophara's pace, and that they would reevaluate after the battle was over. But when the door to the waiting room opened, Charity didn't enter.

Mercy's mother was already inside.

Mercy couldn't help it; she brightened and rushed up when she saw Malice. Though she still bowed in the presence of the Monarch.

Malice's black lips turned up into a fond smile. "You're not as excited as I thought you might be."

"It's hard to enjoy," Mercy admitted, taking her void key from around her neck and putting it into a cabinet prepared for that purpose. She had Suu in her hand and the Moon's Eye lens in her soulspace.

"You have been tasked with a burden far beyond what an Underlady should be responsible for. The lives of Monarchs are in your hands." Malice leaned forward, and her smile showed teeth. "Isn't that a *rush?*"

Mercy echoed her mother's smile, but less confidently.

She didn't particularly like having dominion over the fates of others, but she knew Malice felt differently.

Malice tapped her on the forehead. "That tells me no. But you understand my meaning."

"I'm sorry, but I don't think that's me."

Malice lifted her eyebrows in exaggerated surprise. "Isn't that up to you? I can tell you this much: it's easier to love ruling than it is to love being ruled."

Mercy limbered up, cycling her madra, tapping her bloodline armor for a moment so that her eyes started turning to amethyst before she released them. She was ready. She was in peak condition, and now she was about to unleash her full power against an opponent who could push her to her limits.

It had been years since she'd *really* let herself loose. At least if you didn't count sparring against opponents like Fury or Charity, who could flatten her if they actually tried.

She didn't know if she could enjoy wielding control over Monarchs, but channeling overwhelming power...that was fun.

Malice patted her on the arm. "That's it. Now, remind them what my daughter can do."

Sophara touched the guardian's helmet and wished her sister good-bye.

They had covered Ekeri's Remnant in plates of golden armor, so that her serpentine dragon form was more beautiful than ever, and had planned to use her as a guardian of her homeland. She could protect her home territory forever, or at least until she was finally destroyed in battle.

Instead, Sophara kept her sister's Remnant in her own void key. The storage was now filled with beneficial natural treasures to create an aura-rich environment, and Sophara fed Ekeri scales whenever possible.

The dragon-spirit nuzzled against Sophara's hand before the void key closed. A Remnant would never become the living person again, but it could eventually develop its own awareness. When it did, Sophara intended to treat the spirit as family.

As the space closed, it revealed that she wasn't alone in her waiting room.

She panicked, dropping to her knees and pressing her forehead to the ground so that she wouldn't look too long on the face of her ancestor.

Seshethkunaaz commanded her to rise, so she did, though she continued to avert her eyes. She was taller than he was, which made her too tall.

"Are you prepared?" the Monarch asked.

"I am."

Sophara's spirit was still cracked, but it hadn't gotten worse. The longer she remained at the Underlord stage, the better.

But she could advance whenever she wished. Even if she ended up stuck as an Overlady, it would be worthwhile if she could eliminate the Akura family heir.

"Fight with the pride of the dragons," the King said, "and I will be satisfied. Win or lose."

Sophara was so shocked that she almost looked at his face. He was merciless toward weakness.

"Malice's daughter is a true opponent, and you have already proved the might of my blood to the world. If you show your full power here, it will be no shame to fall to her. Look into my eyes."

She did, reluctantly, and he met her draconic golden eyes with yellow human eyes of his own. They were so much more beautiful than hers that she lost herself in admiration.

He smiled on her. "I will be proud to care for you as a mighty Overlady and one of the eight Uncrowned of your generation...but I would rather lift you up as the victor of the Uncrowned King tournament and my third Herald."

Strength and pride she'd never known flooded through her, and she drew herself up straight. "It will be my honor."

The Monarch's face darkened, and he turned to the door. "The moment is upon us. Go, and savor the opportunity to tear Fury's sister limb from limb."

Mercy's battlefield against Sophara was an isolated space, sealed off by madra. The arena was as wide as usual, but all noise and spiritual sensation from the stands were cut off, and the audience would have to watch them exclusively through viewing constructs and projections.

The floor and ceiling were knobby and black, so that they resembled Mercy's bow, though she didn't sense any shadow madra from them.

Shadow *aura,* on the other hand, was thick in the air. The arena was dark, the shadows in the corner impenetrable to the naked eye.

Winding through the center of the arena, cutting it in half, was a flowing river with a line of fire dancing on its surface. That would be for Sophara: a plentiful source of water and fire aura.

But the flames did little to push back the darkness, and Mercy faced Sophara over a line of fire.

The dragon had her chin lifted even higher than usual, an arrogant tilt to her lips. Her strands of golden scales hung from her scalp, flickering in the firelight, and her eyes seemed to glow. She wore no sacred artist's robes, but simple pants and a tunic that left her arms bare.

No jewelry either, though all her clothes were lined in golden silk. She had dressed simply, for a gold dragon.

Mercy raised a hand in greeting. She couldn't afford to lose, but Sophara was surely in the same situation she was.

The gold dragon didn't respond, turning to Northstrider.

The Monarch hovered inches over the fire, so that the flames occasionally licked his mismatched sandals. His ragtag clothing didn't burn, and he looked from one of them to the other.

"Prepare yourselves," he said.

He didn't ask if they were ready. He could see they weren't.

Both Underladies cycled their techniques, watching each other. Mercy tapped into the Book of Eternal Night, preparing its power. Suu's head drifted down the length of the staff as it bent into a bow, a string coming down from one tip to the other.

Mercy calmed her heart and mind, as her aunt had suggested. She forgot the potential execution hanging over her mother's head, and the thousands of lives at stake from the deals of Monarchs.

And she allowed herself to look forward to the fight.

"Begin," Northstrider said.

Gold dragon's breath annihilated the space where he stood.

It engulfed Mercy in a violent world of sunset-orange light, overwhelming her senses.

And harming her not at all.

Crystalline purple armor covered Mercy from head to toe. From beneath her amethyst helmet, the Moon's Eye lens continued to show Sophara as a silhouette of madra standing right where she'd begun.

Still inside the Striker technique, Mercy pulled back the string of her bow.

The second the air cleared, she Forged an arrow on the string and released. Then another, this one with an added punch from her Enforcer technique. Then another, and another, and another.

As she loosed her arrows, she let her armor puff back into essence and began cycling her Dark Tide Incantation. Madra of shadow and water strengthened her, from the soles of her feet to the tips of her fingers.

Sophara had her own Archlord weapon in her hands: Quickriver, a whip of liquid steel that stiffened to a saber as she swatted the arrows out of the air.

The first, she slashed apart. The second hit with more force than she had evidently expected, knocking her blade a hair out of line. The third stuck to the blade, the fourth into her shoulder, and the fifth she dodged.

Mercy's arrows were made from solidified Strings of Shadow, so they didn't hurt much. But they stuck, and they interfered with the circulation of madra.

Before Sophara could recover, Mercy drew her hands down as though painting a line. The Shadow's Edge flew out, slicing the flame between them in two.

Harmony's favored technique was notoriously difficult to block, cutting through physical and spiritual material with equal ease, but Sophara had a way to defend.

As expected, she used it.

A golden disc bigger than her head flashed out of her soul-space and intercepted the Striker technique. The Shadow's Edge shattered, its madra dissipating on the script around the edges of the construct.

The disc—her Imperial Aegis—had its full power scaled down for use in the tournament. It was too much like armor. But it was still allowed, as shields were permitted.

Sophara's own full-body Enforcer technique filled her now, and as she leaped over the fiery river, she trailed orange madra behind her.

The Riverflame Dance gave her physical power that Mercy didn't want to meet head-on, so she used her own Dark Tide Incantation to slip aside.

Quickriver melted back into a whip, extending its reach and slashing at Mercy, but Mercy slipped below it and splashed out with another Striker technique: the Nightworm Venom.

The Imperial Aegis intercepted that, moving it into place for Mercy to leap onto it, jumping over Sophara and loosing another arrow straight down onto the dragon's head.

She smashed it with an Enforced fist and returned dragon's breath, but Mercy had extended a String of Shadow and lashed herself to a distant point of land. She pulled herself backwards on the line, firing arrows as she flew.

Sophara took the bait.

She dashed forward, trailing gold madra, her flying Aegis shielding her from Mercy's arrows. Sophara would know from previous matches that Mercy never preferred to close the distance, fighting only from afar until she was forced to use her bloodline armor to defend herself.

Dragons had innately powerful bodies—Sophara kicked up chunks of the ground every time she took a step. And Sophara's spirit had been strengthened beyond its limits. She would *know* that if she closed the distance, she could pull Mercy apart.

That played perfectly into Mercy's hands.

A wall of dragons' breath thundered past her, but Mercy had seen it forming in her Moon's Eye, and she took an extra moment to layer techniques into her arrow.

When she released her bowstring, the arrow flew with speed that tore the air, crashing into Sophara's Aegis.

There was a deafening explosion of shadow, and the Archlord shield construct was blasted away. The detonation destroyed the floor and carved into the river, launching water and fire into the air to fall as rain.

Sophara had followed up her dragon's breath with a leap, hanging in the air over Mercy. Her liquid metal weapon condensed into a short broadsword, and her every movement trailed a shadow of Flowing Flame madra.

With a confident smile, Sophara brought her hands down with all her strength.

Mercy's bloodline armor returned, covering her whole body, and she finally unleashed her Dark Tide Incantation to its fullest.

Though even Mercy herself tended to forget, every one of the techniques in the Book of Eternal Night was one that Malice considered powerful enough for a future Monarch. This technique was the foundation of an entire Path in the

Trackless Sea.

It could be used as an ordinary full-body Enforcement, but only with training and mastery could it reveal its true power.

Mercy caught Sophara's blow in one gauntleted hand.

The strike still forced her down, the impact cracking the ground beneath her feet, but Mercy's armor protected her. For the moment, Mercy could stand up to Sophara's full strength.

Mercy didn't have time to see the shock on her face, but she felt it in the hesitation of the other woman's spirit.

The Akura bloodline armor was notoriously difficult to control. When summoned over the entire body, it made the user clumsy and slow.

On the other hand, Mercy's Puppeteer's Iron body gave her perfect control over her movements. And the Dark Tide Incantation flowed with the flexibility of water and shadow.

Mercy punched Sophara in the gut, launching her backwards, but snagged her with a quick String of Shadow before her body could fly too far. Mercy whirled Suu into a staff strike.

The Imperial Aegis returned, blocking one of the attacks, and Sophara used her tail to brace herself on the ground, launching another dragon's breath.

The other end of Mercy's staff punched through it, catching Sophara in the face. The rest of the Flowing Flame madra washed over her armor.

Sophara's body flew backwards, crashing into the far end of the river, but Mercy was already there to slam her back up to the ceiling. As soon as she hit, the dragon was dragged back down by Strings of Shadow.

Sophara broke every technique she could, but Mercy was always using the next, filling her with arrows of shadow.

When she finally landed an arrow loaded with the Nightworm Venom, that was the end of the battle. Sophara's spirit eroded, her madra losing cohesion, each Striker technique fainter than the one before.

Mercy's armor faded when she ran out of madra to support it, and she was heaving for breath, but she had enough power left for a Shadow's Edge.

She swiped her fingers down, Sophara's flying golden shield blocked it, and as Sophara tried to use another technique, Mercy put an arrow into her eye.

Five more followed.

Only when Sophara's eye socket looked like a vase stuffed with flowers did she dissolve into white light.

"Victory to Akura Mercy!" the Ninecloud Soul announced.

Mercy heard no cheers, so she gave one of her own.

Sophara returned to her waiting room panting like a dog. *What was that?*

How had a human met her fist-to-fist? Mercy had never shown anything like that! Not even in the rumors! Physical strength was her weakness!

In the second round, Sophara had single-handedly outclassed everyone on the Akura and Blackflame teams together. Even if Mercy had learned to unlock more of her Path of Seven Pages, she couldn't have improved her body so much in such a short time.

Unless she had been holding back, even then.

Sophara opened her void key, and the armored serpentine Remnant tilted its head in confusion as she reached in.

This time, she didn't want her sister's comfort. She wanted the natural treasures.

At her beckoning and a quick use of wind aura, she summoned them all. Stones that burned with eternal flame and those that wept spring water, goblets filled with rain clouds, torches that blazed green. And those she didn't use for her usual advancement: feathers that carried a deadly white mist, bells that rang with haunting tunes.

She shoved Ekeri's Remnant back in, hauling all her treasures out and then shutting the door.

The longer she remained at the Underlord stage, the more stable her spirit would be. And the greater her chance of becoming an Archlady before her permanent spiritual injuries slowed her down too much.

If she lost.

But she didn't intend to lose.

She spread the artifacts out in a circle and calmed herself, focusing on the pool of soulfire within her. Humans had to discover truths about themselves in order to trigger their advancement, but sacred beasts were different. They had to choose to change their forms.

Sometimes, these advancements could take weeks, but Sophara had been certain of her primary form since she was a child. Most of the gold dragons spent as little time in their serpent bodies as possible.

Say what you would about humans, but their bodies were elegant.

She connected herself to the unity of aura, focusing on her new form. A dragon's transformation was often slower than a human's advancement, but she still had the Gate of Heaven elixir inside her.

The soulfire from the burning treasures passed through her quickly and easily, transforming her from the inside out.

It was painful, in her state of imbalance. Unbelievably so.

But rage and fear carried her through.

Her madra channels had been strengthened by the Symbiote Veins, which drained her of vitality even as they allowed her to use more powerful techniques quickly. Now, those channels were fortified, but so were her Symbiote Veins.

Her core grew denser, thicker, wider. Her claws shrunk until they were little more than sharp fingernails. Her remaining patches of scales faded into smooth skin, and she finally had glistening golden hair instead of strands of scales.

When she finished advancing, she reached back into her void key to pull out a stand mirror. Ekeri's Remnant watched as she examined herself, twisting in the mirror.

She was smooth. Beautiful. Perfect.

And even more powerful.

The spirit of an Overlady radiated out in her waiting room. This time, she would juggle Akura Mercy. Not only was she stronger in every way, but now she had a better idea of her opponent's capabilities.

Her mental power elixir, the drop of white liquid hovering at the base of her skull, was refreshed and ready to use. It hadn't done her much good in the first fight, but she had fallen into Mercy's trap.

Her Madra Engine churned, processing blood and life essence into madra. She could keep fighting almost forever. And the Crystal Nexus floated over her core, strengthening her madra at the cost of extra strain on her channels.

She was ready now. She knew what to do.

So when she went out to face Mercy, she didn't start by cycling her Enforcer technique. She started one of her two Ruler techniques.

Mercy didn't seem intimidated, though Sophara didn't veil herself. She wanted everyone to know that she had advanced, but Mercy merely nocked an arrow.

Water aura drifted toward Sophara as soon as Northstrider announced the beginning of the duel.

Mercy fired a volley of arrows, but this time Sophara burned her mental elixir immediately. The pale droplet in her spirit vanished, and Sophara slipped between the attacks, using Quickriver in the form of a saber to knock the arrows aside.

Her sword would be a blur to the onlookers, as would the arrows, but to Sophara everything floated along. It was child's play to continue gathering water aura into a globe over her head, reinforcing it with Forged madra.

As the two forces combined, a sphere the size of Sophara's torso began to shine blue. Azure Moon Reigns was one of the most complicated techniques in her arsenal, combining a Forger and Ruler technique. It looked like a softly shining azure cloud inside a clear bubble, but just by existing it turned water aura against Mercy.

The Akura girl loosed Striker techniques at the orb, but

Sophara had formed it in seconds, and the world was still slowed. Sophara batted one technique out of the air, the Imperial Aegis intercepted another, and then Sophara leaped over to Mercy.

She only started her Riverflame Dance in midair. Her Overlord-level body would be enough to carry her through.

As the world returned to normal speed, Mercy summoned her armor, but Sophara had been prepared for that. In the form of a whip, Quickriver slashed at Mercy.

The Akura girl kept launching arrows, but Sophara wove between them. Her limbs moved so much more easily now that she had advanced, it was effortless to dodge, and every scrape on Mercy's armor would put it one step closer to dropping.

Meanwhile, Azure Moon Reigns had begun to work.

It pushed against the water in Mercy's body, slowing her, making her clumsy. The blue orb itself could be used to attack, but their battle was moving away from it, and it was limited in its range.

The second Mercy stumbled, Sophara opened her mouth and breathed gold dragon's breath into her opponent's face.

She didn't like using Striker techniques from her mouth. It looked undignified. But humans tended to forget she could do it.

The word "breath" was even in the name.

Mercy was driven down, but her armor hadn't broken, and Sophara slapped her across the side with her tail. The Akura girl flew away, twisting in midair to launch another arrow.

But Sophara had leaped with the power of her Enforcer technique, catching Mercy mid-flight and spiking her down into the ground.

The floor burst into a crater, sending sharp black madra flying everywhere.

Mercy's armor puffed to essence, and she even coughed up blood.

Sophara's instinct was to follow up, to drive Quickriver through Mercy's bare chest and finish it there. Instead, she leveled her palm and unleashed another gold dragon's breath.

What a laughably easy match.

Her spirit screamed danger as she sensed an Overlord-level spirit join her own.

Mercy, battered and bloody, knelt on the side of the crater. Sophara hadn't seen her move. The human's hair had torn loose, hanging into her face, and she wiped blood from her lip with the back of her hand.

That gesture shook Sophara with fear. Mercy was a devil. A ghost. A spirit of terror. She had come to track Sophara down, to torment her, to torture her with nightmares—

Sophara had to use soulfire to push away the dream aura that was keeping her in fear, but she'd already stumbled back, holding her Imperial Aegis and Quickriver in front of her to defend herself.

The unnatural terror was a Ruler technique, and one she hadn't sensed coming, but she'd had no idea Mercy could do that. That was the Sage of Silver Heart's technique.

Sophara had seen Mercy advance temporarily, but that was back when she was Gold. She hadn't expected Mercy to be able to advance to Overlord as well, but she had known it was possible. That didn't throw her off, but the nightmare-inducing Ruler technique did.

She was so focused on pushing the dream aura away that she almost didn't react to the arrow in time.

The Imperial Aegis threw itself in front of the attack, and Sophara brought up her hand for a Striker technique.

Mercy was already in the air over her, arrow nocked and blazing with an Overlady's power. The Imperial Aegis was out of position, but Sophara's dragon's breath was ready.

She unleashed the flowing golden power just as Mercy released the arrow.

Shadow madra smacked through Sophara's chest and spirit, blinding her with pain. It carried too many techniques to count, and it tore her up from the inside. Spirit and body.

She choked, unable to breathe, unable even to cough as the arrow ravaged her insides. Her madra began to leave her control.

But Mercy was in even worse condition.

The entire left side of her body had been burned off. She was blackened and pitted red, her eye mangled and her ear melted. She fell to the ground and curled up with an agonizing scream.

Sophara didn't have time to gloat or to enjoy the sight.

She used her last trickle of madra to extend Quickriver, whipping it into the side of Mercy's head.

An instant later, Mercy disappeared.

And as the Ninecloud Soul announced victory, Sophara vanished too.

Mercy gasped for air, hand flashing to her ear.

Unspeakable pain had vanished in an instant. She had suspected all along that Northstrider did something to heal their minds as well as their bodies, because she felt much less trauma from this wound than she had from the burns Sophara had given her as a Gold.

Even so, the fight dominated her thoughts. Sophara really had advanced, and had even adapted strategically in a way Mercy had hoped she would overlook.

Sophara could outlast Mercy in any prolonged contest. Mercy's armor would only last so long, as would her temporary advancement to Overlord.

Charity and Mercy had both suspected that Sophara would begin the first fight by leaning on her superior power to crush Mercy, and they'd had a plan for that. Their entire strategy for the second fight had been to surprise Sophara with the Dream of Darkness technique.

Mercy had only one more card to play, and the final duel was the time to go all-out. There was no sense holding anything back now.

Of course, Sophara had more to show as well. Azure Moon Reigns had been completed, but like any persistent Ruler technique, it showed its true power the longer it was allowed to remain. And Sophara's Path had one more technique, not to mention the Archlord binding that was certainly inside her liquid metal sword.

Mercy looked over to Charity, who sat in the corner tapping her foot.

"What do you think, Aunt Charity?"

"Nothing you don't know, I imagine. That was a close fight, even with her advancement. She will be warier of you now, which is not entirely to your advantage. The quicker the fight, the better."

She spoke as usual, but something was wrong. The Sage of the Silver Heart never showed nerves, and here she was tapping her foot and chewing on her lower lip.

"Don't worry," Mercy said. "I can do this."

Charity relaxed and gave a faint smile. "I'm sorry, that was rude of me. I have no doubt in you...but it is not often that I have to sit by the sidelines and watch. I'm not used to being unable to help."

Mercy knew that feeling. "You've helped enough already. Now leave it to me."

This time, as Mercy faced Sophara across the burning river, the dragon didn't look so confident. Her Imperial Aegis drifted around her head, ready to intercept attacks, and Quickriver coiled and uncoiled around her feet.

Mercy limbered up Suu...no, she limbered up Eclipse, Ancient Bow of the Soulseeker.

She needed a quick fight, and she needed to catch Sophara by surprise. That meant she needed the bow.

This was her chance.

Mercy didn't even hear Northstrider announce the beginning of the match, she just felt the barrier fall. Sophara leaped backwards, launching her huge dragon's breath.

Rather than intercepting it with her armor, Mercy slipped to the side. The heat was scalding, but her concentration was locked. The Book of Eternal Night flashed behind her, unleashing the power of the fifth page, and Overlord madra cascaded through her channels.

She Forged an arrow onto the string.

Sophara held out both hands. To her left, water aura and madra gathered into a floating blue light. Azure Moon Reigns.

To her right, fire aura and madra condensed into a matching ball of red. Crimson Sun Rises.

The second technique would control fire aura as the first controlled water. Rather than interfering with the aura in her body, as the Azure Moon did, the Crimson Sun would induce all the fire aura in the area to burn her.

Simple burns weren't much threat to an Underlady's body, but she would have to spend a little power and concentration keeping the aura away. Which would distract her and bring her madra to its end that much sooner.

There were other attacks Sophara could use with the techniques, but Mercy was going to end the fight before she saw any of them.

The Dark Tide Incantation went into the arrow, adding the force of a crashing wave. Then the Nightworm Venom and the Shadow's Edge.

Finally, with great difficulty, she wove the Dream of Darkness into the arrow. Its tip began to warp like a heat haze.

Attaching a technique to an arrow took intricate madra control, and she wasn't familiar enough with the Dream of Darkness to make it easy. So as she did so, Sophara completed her two techniques and released another gold dragon's breath larger than Mercy's entire body.

Mercy could endure it with her armor, but the Striker technique would destroy her arrow—with so many techniques combined, it was unstable. She leaped into the air with the power of the Dark Tide Incantation, flipping over the Striker technique and taking aim.

She sensed a change in Sophara's spirit, focused on her mind. The mental enhancement she'd used before.

Quickriver whipped out, slashing at Mercy in midair and spoiling her aim.

Mercy could have unleashed the arrow there, but it would only have been intercepted by the Imperial Aegis. She kicked the end of the whip, a crystalline boot appearing on her foot as she did, but then Sophara followed up with another dragon's breath.

This one didn't cover a huge chunk of the arena, but it would still be enough to erase half of Mercy. She lashed Strings of Shadow to the ground, pulling herself down and out of the path of the beam.

Sophara's mental enhancement would only last a few seconds, so Mercy just had to dodge until it dropped. That would be her opening.

No sooner had she thought so than Sophara's blade cut her across the back of the ankle.

She tried to stand, but her left leg almost buckled beneath her. Mercy was forced to fire the arrow, but as expected, it detonated against the Imperial Aegis.

Sophara slipped out of the area of the explosion, but she did so with no difficulty, keeping up a barrage of whips and dragon's breath.

Mercy would have no chance to load up such an arrow again.

She released the Shadow's Edge, pulled at Sophara's feet with Strings of Shadow, kept her body upright with the Dark Tide Incantation, pushed against the aura using her soulfire, and blocked attacks wherever she could with her bloodline armor. All the while keeping her temporary advancement to Overlady under control.

It was too much. She was juggling twenty knives at once; sooner or later one of them would slip.

So when she sensed the power fading from Sophara's mind, she dropped everything she was juggling except one. She kept her Overlord-level madra and joined her spirit to the bow.

Quickriver shredded her right arm, and gold dragon's breath had already ruined her left.

Mercy fell backwards, twisting in the air to hold her bow with her right foot and pull the string back with her teeth. The arrow was a plain, unadorned String of Shadow, and as she watched her aim through the Moon's Eye, she knew Sophara's scripted golden shield would block the shot.

Mercy's spirit strained past its limits, her channels screamed in pain, and her core dimmed to almost nothing.

As she activated the technique in her bow.

Arrows of violet light formed in the air all around the weapon, dozens and then hundreds Forged in a blink. Their color matched the blazing eyes of the dragon's head at Eclipse's center, which was currently glaring at Sophara.

Mercy released her black arrow, and two hundred violet arrows followed as the Archlord Forger technique launched at the same time.

The Imperial Aegis intercepted one attack...but only one.

Sophara wrapped liquid dragon's breath around herself, but Suu's arrows twisted in midair, seeking her with the will of the Sage's Remnant that had gone into the bow's creation.

The arrows exploded into violet lights as they landed. Made of shadow and force and destruction, they were an equal threat to the body and the spirit, and the barrage blinded Mercy both physically and spiritually. Tiny chunks of the floor were sent flying into a cloud that completely obscured Sophara.

Even her Moon's Eye couldn't pick out the dragon from the chaos, but Mercy pushed up on Suu to hop on one foot. She couldn't hold the fifth page anymore; her Overlord power faded.

The barrage slowed, but the match hadn't ended. Sophara was still alive.

She let her bow melt back into a staff; her arms were too ruined to draw the bow quickly anyway. Only her burned arm could somewhat move, and then only through agony.

But Sophara was trying to kill her mother.

She focused the Strings of Shadow technique through the tip of her staff, shooting black madra indiscriminately through the hole where the dragon had been. With only a little more effort, she brought up the Nightworm Venom technique, spraying it over everything.

The Imperial Aegis emerged, catching most of the poison. From the web-filled pit, a dragon roared.

Sophara's hair had been seared off, as had most of her clothes and huge patches of her skin. A sacred artist's clothes were not often destroyed in battle; not only were they made of sturdy materials, but a person's inherent spiritual protection extended to their clothes as well. Sleeves and hems were often damaged, but you usually only saw completely ravaged clothing on corpses.

Her left arm was a withered, bloody mess that looked like it had been torn apart by wolves, and blood spread across her middle. Even a chunk of her jaw was missing.

But she gripped Quickriver in her less-mangled hand.

And the liquid metal blade began to glow orange.

Fire aura flowed easily to it, thanks to the Crimson Sun that still shone behind Sophara, but it was the madra that really concerned Mercy. It was Archlord madra.

She had activated her own weapon.

The Enforced whip blazed like the setting sun, whipping at Mercy, and she desperately conjured her bloodline armor. If she could endure this, then surely Sophara could take only one more—

Mercy slipped.

She couldn't afford to push away the subtle Ruler techniques of the Azure Moon and Crimson Sun anymore. Water aura had gathered around her foot and knocked her off-balance.

Her other leg gave out as she landed on it.

And a fiery blade passed through her neck.

第十六章

CHAPTER SIXTEEN

The Akura audience stands were very quiet.

Lindon sat staring into the projection as the Ninecloud Soul replayed moments from Mercy's three fights, spread out and slowed down for the sake of the spectators.

None of the Akura around Lindon seemed to want to watch the images again, but none left either. Lindon himself kept watching Sophara's huge Striker techniques that she could release so easily...and Mercy, who could dodge or weather them with ease.

Layering techniques onto arrows like that was much harder than it looked. He had experience combining compatible techniques while building cannons, and he knew what kind of madra control and how much practice it would take.

And what could he have done against that echo Forger technique from her bow? The barrage of arrows would have destroyed him. His Hollow Domain could have eliminated a weaker version of the technique, but each arrow was too strong and too solid to be erased.

That was when it was being used by an Underlady, who had to struggle to maintain an Overlord's madra at the same time. The technique would only show its true power when used by a real Archlord.

[And that completes my model of both Mercy and Sophara!] Dross said cheerfully. [Yes sir, it's getting easier and easier. Between the Arelius library and Northstrider's codex, I'm more amazing than ever before. Do you want to know how you stack up against them?]

Lindon watched Mercy pull her bow back with her teeth. *I already know.*

So that was what a fight between two Monarch heirs looked like.

He had been proud of his battle with Yerin, but Mercy must have seen them as children playing. She or Sophara could toy with Lindon as they pleased.

[Ah, well, actually, I'm not sure you know what I was going to say.]

Lindon stood up from his seat. *We'll practice against them tonight.*

He couldn't say he was looking forward to it. Just when he had gotten somewhat of a grasp on fighting Sophara, she'd advanced.

[We don't have to, you know. We could do something fun instead, while everyone else you know and love progresses without you.]

It didn't matter how far Mercy outclassed him. His answer was the same as it had always been.

As Suriel had once told him, *"There are a million Paths in this world, Lindon, but any sage will tell you they can all be reduced to one. Improve yourself."*

Though he didn't have time to be concerned about himself at the moment.

Akura Malice's daughter had lost to Sopharanatoth. The power balance between the Monarchs was shifting.

Mercy was at the center of it.

[I could use a vacation too. Working all day, all night. I don't mean to complain, but my working conditions—]

Lindon cut him off. *I need you on something else. What security measures are keeping us separated from the Uncrowned?*

He walked behind the stands and through a sealed passage, where a bare hallway led to a locked and scripted door.

Within was a cloud that led down to the waiting rooms behind the arenas. Now, only the Uncrowned and their sponsors were allowed back there. Lindon no longer had permission to enter.

He pressed a hand against the door and extended his perception.

[Well, let's see...it's all Lord-level security, of course, because a Sage or a Herald will be able to force themselves in anywhere. The Ninecloud Soul is monitoring the outer layer of security, but it's nothing incredible. They're counting on the Monarchs to be watching and protecting their own candidates; this is just to keep out the rabble.]

Lindon reached his pure madra through the script that required a ward key to activate, and he began warming up the hunger binding in his arm.

"Apologies if I'm intruding, Monarch Malice," Lindon said aloud. "But please don't stop me."

Sha Miara sensed the alarm of the Ninecloud Soul as someone broke through the security at the back of the Akura viewing tower.

Her perception covered him immediately. It was the other pure madra Underlord, Wei Shi Lindon Arelius.

She chuckled. He was trying to get to the Uncrowned, but he hadn't earned that right. She stretched out to lend her power to the Ninecloud Soul, to remind him who was in charge in her court.

Her spiritual sense was swallowed in shadow.

Miara sat bolt upright in her seat, from which she'd been watching the fights. "I was doing *you* a favor," she said.

Akura Malice and the entire Akura area remained completely dark.

Miara flipped a hand and fell back. "Fine! You deal with it, then."

Mercy emerged from her waiting room sheepishly rubbing the back of her head in a gesture she'd adopted from Fury.

"Sorry! I messed up."

Fury himself put his hands on his hips and laughed. "What are you worried about? You fought your hardest! I wish I'd had any competition like that!"

He was forcing it.

Mercy and Fury had always shared certain similarities, so she could read him better than most. He was acting carefree for her benefit.

But she appreciated it, so she smiled for him. "I almost had it!"

Ordinarily Fury was the open book and his daughter was an icy riddle, but this time Charity did a worse job hiding her true feelings. She glanced to Fury and then softened as she turned to Mercy. "It was never fair for you to worry about this. You've done your best, and now Sophara is our problem."

"She sure is," Fury said, and there was a soft menace in his voice.

It was tempting to fall for that lie, transparent though it was.

All her life, Mercy had complete faith in Charity and Fury. They were unstoppable, and more present and human than her mother ever had been. They could be counted on to do anything.

Now, not only would the Dragon King do anything to protect his future champion, but the very heavens would intervene to defend her.

Mercy pushed Suu against the ground and stood straight. "It won't be too long before you can lean on me! I'll keep working hard!"

"For now, you should rest," Charity said.

Fury looked to the exit at the end of the hall and perked up. "Oh, hey! It's—"

His daughter elbowed him in the ribs.

He had obviously sensed something, but whatever it was, Charity had stopped him from saying it. She was probably being considerate to Mercy, and she appreciated the thought. She couldn't handle any bad news at the moment.

Shadows deepened on the floor as Charity and Fury began to sink into a spatial transfer. "We'll talk to you tonight, Mercy."

They vanished, leaving Mercy to her thoughts.

She kept replaying moments from the fights in her mind. Little things she could have done differently, moves she could have prepared for.

The competition had been close enough that it could have gone either way. If she had made better decisions, she could have won. If she had advanced to Overlord for real, as Sophara had, she could have won.

It was easier for sacred beasts, but would that matter to the people in Sky's Edge who would have to face dragons on the battlefield? Would that matter for her mother, if the dragons got Penance?

She opened the exit and saw Lindon crouched on a Thousand-Mile Cloud.

He had folded his bulky frame in half to examine a script-circle low on the wall, and his white Remnant fingers were half-sunk into a shimmering construct that he'd pulled halfway out. Dross was manifested on his shoulder, pointing to a specific part of the construct, and as the door opened both of them turned wide eyes on Mercy.

Lindon released the construct and straightened, smoothing his outer robe. "Ah, apologies. I thought I could make it here faster."

Dross disappeared, and Mercy peeked around Lindon's shoulders. There was no one else behind him.

"Did you break in?"

"I thought you...well, I mean, I just wanted to talk to you."

She forced another smile. "Thanks. I guess it's up to Yerin now, huh?"

"I'm sorry," he said simply.

For some reason, she hadn't expected that.

Then again, she hadn't expected him here at all. He had broken through the Ninecloud seals, and her mother must have allowed this, but he had come entirely out of sympathy. It wasn't like Lindon to act on sentiment.

But he knew how she felt, didn't he?

"I know..." he began, but caught himself. "Well, I can't say I know how you feel. But I know how I felt."

Tears welled up in Mercy's eyes.

"I wanted to win," she said at last.

"I know."

"I tried really hard."

"Yeah."

Her tears were coming more freely now, and she leaned into his shoulder. "Just...give me a minute, okay? My family...I can't..."

She couldn't talk to her family like this. How could she? She'd let them down. If anybody had a right to cry or be angry, *they* did.

After a minute or two, she realized she was leaving a mess on Lindon's outer robe and pulled back. She wiped her face with the edge of her sleeve. "Sorry. I'm all right. How's Yerin?"

Yerin was the only one left in the tournament. Whatever happened from then on, it was all on her shoulders.

Lindon looked upward. "Actually, she came to find you right after I got through the door. But the Ninecloud Soul is mad at me, so I'm locked in. I was trying to figure out how to go back for her."

Mercy extended her spiritual perception. It was hard to penetrate the walls in here, but sure enough, there was a mass of familiar sword madra outside the door a few floors up.

"Pardon, but Dross and I should probably get back to work. If we don't open the door before she loses patience, she'll—"

A lance of silver light blasted the door apart, sending debris raining down on Lindon's face.

"...apologies."

In his waiting room, Calan Archer meditated and focused on his cycling.

There was no one in here with him. Therian would have come down here to join him if he'd been allowed, and the other Uncrowned in his faction—Yan Shoumei—had been called away by the Blood Sage.

His own Sage, the leader of his sect, hadn't shown his face once all month.

Calan had taken whatever lessons he could from the Sage of Red Faith, but the Sage had his own student. Students, really, if you counted Yerin.

He'd never met Reigan Shen, of course—people didn't meet Monarchs, even if you represented their interests on a global stage.

Which meant there was no one left who could support him here, as he prepared to face Yerin in battle.

He decided to use the isolation to focus on his task.

Yerin, he knew, had others pressuring her to win. Like the other seven Uncrowned, Yerin was concerned about the broader situation in the world. If she lost here, Penance would go to the Dragon or Lion Monarchs. The political landscape would shift, and great sects would rise and fall.

Calan didn't care about any of that.

He had always been a talented sacred artist, but great schools and sects and clans lived in their own worlds.

He had earned his way up to the top of his generation on his own, and he would win this tournament for his own sake.

A disc-shaped Divine Treasure floated in his soulspace,

and seven jade rings hovered around him. The rings around his biceps crackled, and his madra moved smoothly.

After poring over the records from Yerin's fight against Lindon, Calan had a good idea of her capabilities. She was impressive, certainly, but he could win.

He strode out of his waiting room to the roars of the crowd and examined his arena.

They had plenty of open space, but blades the size of his whole body jutted up from the sand every few yards. Three or four dark clouds made lazy circuits of the space, flashing with lightning.

Calan didn't position himself exactly in the center of the arena, moving as far as he could from the swords. These arenas were supposed to be designed to allow each participant to show the full extent of their Path, but from what he'd seen of Yerin's Endless Sword, he would lose the second he stepped too close to one of these blades.

Or if he brought his own flying blades too close to himself, for that matter. He spread the seven razor-edged jade rings away from them, so they hovered and spun at least thirty feet off the ground.

Yerin nodded when she saw him, but her jaw was clenched. She wore the pressure she felt openly, even closing her eyes and rolling her neck to release tension. She hopped in place, grip tightening and loosening on the hilt of her sheathed sword.

Calan still thought that Northstrider looked nothing like any Monarch he'd ever imagined, with his scruffy unshaven jaw and wild hair, but he certainly carried himself like a king. He looked from one to the other and ordered them to prepare themselves.

Stormcaller madra coiled and writhed, hungry to be unleashed. Calan cycled the beginnings of his Ruler technique, sure that Yerin was doing the same.

Northstrider looked over them both, spread his hands, and ordered them to begin.

Calan released his Harbinger of the Storm. Everywhere

the Weeping Dragon flew, a storm followed, as it agitated the water, wind, and lightning aura for miles around.

This technique had been modeled on that one, and it allowed Stormcallers to slowly dominate a battlefield. Dark clouds gathered overhead, merging with the clouds the arena already contained.

Rain fell, and lightning cracked down to the sand. The storm was self-sustaining, and as time went on, it would grow more violent and powerful until it peaked. There was no stopping it now.

Yerin hadn't moved. Or opened her eyes.

Calan didn't question it. He controlled his seven bladed rings together, directing them so that they would collide with Yerin at a different angle and timing. This wasn't a formal madra technique that created a binding, but a skill that he'd spent years mastering. He could control more constructs and weapons at once than anyone he knew.

Yerin's sheathed sword chimed, and sparks flew out as every one of his flying rings was deflected by invisible blades.

He had expected as much, and he'd prepared two responses.

Simultaneously, he brought his rings back around for another pass, directed the storm aura to target Yerin, and began preparing a Striker technique.

His crackling blue-gold madra formed the head of a roaring dragon in his palm. Stormcaller madra was born when a person took madra from the actual Weeping Dragon inside of themselves. Later they built on it by harvesting the different aspects of storms, but members of their sect forever carried a measure of the Dreadgod's hunger and animating will.

This Dragonblood Thunderbolt technique was not only the most powerful technique in his Path, but it was how the Weeping Dragon fed. It was closer to a Forger technique than a Striker technique, but he'd heard it called both, and its power was undeniable.

Calan hurled the dragon of storm madra, and it twisted through the air, a serpent made from gold-and-blue lightning. At the same time, his Jadeclaw Rings fell on Yerin and lightning flashed from the cloud above.

Yerin's eyes opened.

Blood spurted from Calan's neck.

His Jadeclaw Rings exploded backwards again, the lightning struck the sand, and her madra-clad sword clashed with the dragon. She clearly had to exert herself to destroy his technique, but he was too busy pressuring his artery to throw another one.

How had she done that? He had a good grasp of the range of her Endless Sword technique, and he'd been far from any source of sword aura.

Now he had a time limit.

Before he bled out, he had to win.

The first of his two Divine Treasures activated, and a white eye of Forged madra appeared hovering over his head.

The eye allowed him to map madra flow in his opponents, and he saw what he expected. Her madra was going to her Iron body and to the Enforcer technique making her sword glow as she finally sliced through the dragon.

The second she did, she re-focused on him, building up a Striker technique.

That was the opening he'd been waiting for.

He activated his second Divine Treasure, and a ring of light appeared behind Yerin. She wouldn't see it, and it was difficult to sense. Even if she did feel it, she wouldn't know what it was. Spatial transfer was his ultimate trump card.

Only a breath later, he appeared in that circle a foot from Yerin's back, ready to unleash a Dragonblood Thunderbolt at point-blank range.

As soon as he appeared, a sword swept through his head.

⬡

The Winter Sage threw her head back and laughed proudly. "I told you he would show up behind you! Didn't I tell you?"

"That was a help and a half," Yerin admitted, "but don't polish yourself up too much."

The Sage looked like she'd just won a championship fight herself.

Mercy punched Yerin's arm. "We should have left everything to you all along!"

"A closer shave than it looked. At the start of it, I could feel the Sword Icon. But whenever I have to push myself, it shakes me out."

For the first few seconds of the battle, Yerin had felt perfectly in control. She had known exactly what to do against Calan's first moves.

But she hadn't been able to break his Forged dragon in one slash, so she'd focused her spirit on it and therefore lost her concentration.

She'd only been able to win so quickly because the Winter Sage had scanned Calan Archer, sensing that he had a spatial transfer artifact and predicting that he'd use it to move behind Yerin.

It wasn't one of his prizes from the tournament, and he hadn't used it in previous rounds. It must have been a gift from Reigan Shen.

As soon as Yerin had sensed strange madra gathering behind her, she'd spun and struck without holding back.

It had *still* been close. If she'd been half a second too late and he had shoved one of those dragons into her back, she would have been the one melting into white light.

"It's only natural that you can't hold on to a Sage's mentality," the Winter Sage said. "You're only an Underlady."

"What good is a sword I can't grip too hard?" It was disorienting to get shaken out of a state of concentration in every fight. Eventually, that was going to cost her.

"Using it to any degree of consistency at your level is nothing short of extraordinary. When you reach Archlord, you will be Adama's true successor."

Mercy gave Yerin a look of exaggerated confusion. "What's to complain about? You won. You *won!*"

"Now let's go do it again," Yerin said. She wore her usual attitude like a mask, but her heart was tight.

She was so close to achieving her master's dream. To prizes beyond her imagination. Every step forward meant there were fewer people in the world who could threaten her.

But she was close to defeat, too.

And she didn't feel any closer to becoming a Sage.

Lindon believed she could win, so did Mercy, so did Min Shuei, and she still might let them down. One of the enemy Monarchs could end up with a weapon of heavenly death.

And it all came down to her, right now.

"Not a worry in the world," she muttered.

A door popped open to the waiting room. Not the exit; the entrance.

Lindon stumbled in.

It looked like he'd been leaning on the door and hadn't expected to get it open. Constructs hung from the wall like a deer half-gutted, and the sealing scripts on the door had been scratched up. His Archlord flying sword hung over his shoulder; he must have used that.

To break in and see her.

Yerin's spirits lifted, and she had to hold back laughter as the Ninecloud Soul manifested as a beam of rainbow light. "Contestant Lindon, you cannot keep doing this. We thought the increased security this time would teach you a lesson."

Lindon pressed his fists together. "I did learn quite a bit. Gratitude."

Yerin's laughter escaped, and Mercy joined her. The Winter Sage's face paled.

"Next time, you will be charged for the cost of repairs and punished according to Ninecloud City law," the Ninecloud Soul insisted.

Lindon inclined his head as though he understood, but immediately afterward he turned to Yerin. "They told me I couldn't come see you."

"Are you *insane?*" The Sage demanded. "What if you distract her? Yerin, look, focus on me! Don't lose the trance!"

She tried to grab both sides of Yerin's face, but Yerin pushed her away.

Lindon looked horrified that he might have ruined her chances.

"She sounds the horns at every breeze," Yerin assured him. "This is where you should be."

There were tears in the Winter Sage's eyes, and Yerin couldn't tell if the woman was hurt or worried. Or proud. Yerin found no point in trying to figure out the source of the Sage's tears.

But then the exit door began to slide open, and Yerin really did need to re-focus herself. She spun around, gripped her sword, and took several calming breaths to keep her madra moving easily.

She extended her senses into the aura gathering around her blade, finding that it helped her focus. The aura wanted to move in a certain way, and she had to quiet herself to hear it.

"This can be it," the Winter Sage whispered. "Let the Icon show through you."

Yerin's delicate focus wobbled. Wasn't *she* the one telling everybody to leave Yerin alone? Now why was she whispering in Yerin's ear?

The battlefield was a clash of sword and storm aura, with thunder rolling overhead. Yerin felt like she heard something as she passed the sword blades rising from the ground, like the distant ring of metal.

She kept her eyes closed, using only her perception to guide her to stand opposite Calan.

Northstrider asked if they were both ready, but he would know when she was prepared. She sensed inside herself—the orderly flow of sword madra, the dormant Blood Shadow lurking inside, the flow of power between herself and her master's blade—and she extended that perception outward.

Thoughts tried to crowd in: what if she couldn't touch

the Sword Icon? What if she lost the fight? Everyone was counting on her.

She pushed them all aside and stretched out her perception. She stopped watching herself, sensing everything else. It felt as though she'd moved herself from her body; she couldn't even tell if her madra was cycling correctly.

It was hard to escape her panic. This went against her every instinct, but she stretched out to the world around her as she had when she was advancing to Underlord.

The barrier holding her apart from Calan dropped, and storm madra gathered around him. She fought against all her training and experience, waiting until that silent music moved her.

A Striker technique blasted toward her, and it took all her willpower to stay still.

Someone's sword madra sliced it apart.

Did I make it?

Maybe this was what it felt like to succeed in manifesting the Sword Icon: like she was feeling someone else fight instead of herself.

The moment she had the thought, she knew it wasn't true. That sword madra had a source.

And it radiated the power of blood.

Her concentration vanished, and she opened her eyes and drew her sword at the same time.

The Blood Shadow dashed after Calan Archer. The big, sandy-haired man jumped and landed on a Thousand-Mile Cloud, which he used to speed away, but the spirit raised a black blade and used the Endless Sword.

Aura erupted from each of his seven bladed rings. They weren't knocked back as effectively as if Yerin had deflected them—the Blood Shadow still had to dodge two. But she managed to put a cut on Calan's forearm.

The Shadow's smile gleamed white. She looked more and more like Yerin, except for her ruby eyes and bright red hair. Her teeth had once looked like she'd chugged a tall glass of red paint, but now Yerin couldn't tell the difference between the spirit's smile and any human's.

Her skin was still tinged pink, and she let out wild laughter that never could have come from Yerin.

The Blood Shadow was trying to cheat her out of a chance to advance like a Sage.

Furious, Yerin pulled on her connection to the Shadow. The spirit stumbled, red robes waving in the air like actual cloth, and from its knees it turned and gave her a scarlet glare.

Then it pulled right back.

Yerin stumbled this time, her madra faltering in its cycle as the Shadow regained control and continued pursuing Calan. Rain began to fall as his Ruler technique spread a storm over her.

For a moment, she was frozen in indecision. Should she stay and try to recapture the feeling of the Sword Icon, or should she join the fight and push to win however she could?

The Blood Shadow traded blows with Calan, leaping off one of his jade circles and tossing a red-tinged Rippling Sword at him. A thin line of blue-gold light lanced down from the clouds; Calan's second Striker technique. It drilled a hole through the spirit's hand, and though it growled in pain, the power of blood madra stretched out and flesh knitted back together.

The Shadow was keeping his attention, and though Yerin hated to waste the opportunity to sense the Sword Icon, there were lives at stake.

She had to fight.

Even if it meant giving up this chance to get closer to her master's power.

She lifted her sword, reversing the white blade and gripping the hilt in both hands. Then she bent all her madra and soulfire to the binding within.

With great effort, she could activate the Archlord binding, but there wasn't enough madra in her entire core to fuel it. The technique drew its power from the sword itself, which was dangerous and unstable.

It could damage the blade if she used it too much, although

it was safer with the Winter Sage around to do maintenance. But it was doubly dangerous for her. Without Northstrider's protection, she wouldn't have been willing to risk it.

Archlord madra exploded from her blade, filling most of the arena.

Raindrops froze to ice...and stopped in midair, hanging in place.

A lightning bolt in the clouds overhead stopped, glowing in a cloud like a light trapped in smoky glass. Calan and his blades froze too, but he could fight back against the technique. He *could* move, if he pushed through.

But there was more to this technique than locking the subject in place. Tiny shards of Frozen Blade madra hung in midair, ready to cut. The solid raindrops gleamed silver with sword aura.

Lines of red had already appeared on Calan's skin where the madra and aura had sliced him.

Yerin's spirit trembled and her core drained noticeably. She couldn't move while controlling this technique; without the Diamond Veins, her madra channels would have torn apart, but now they were the most stable part of her.

One of the most difficult parts of the technique was keeping the Blood Shadow as an exception. The spirit could still hurt itself on the floating Frozen Blade madra, but Yerin could keep the aura from restricting it. But doing so took even more concentration and control, and she was strained to her limit already.

The Shadow wove easily through the specks of white power hanging in the air, getting closer to Calan. Yerin hated that she was reliant on the Blood Shadow to win the fight while she was locked in place, but she had to admit it was an effective combination.

Suddenly the aura rushed away from Calan. He must have used all of his soulfire to push away an Archlord's Ruler technique, but he didn't waste the opportunity, shoving his hands up and blasting a thick lightning dragon through the Blood Shadow's middle.

Rather than defending itself, the spirit snarled and swept its blade at Calan's legs.

Half of the Shadow was torn away, and Yerin felt its pain. It was enough of a shock to her mind to shake her concentration, and she lost the Winter Sage's technique.

All around the battlefield, frozen raindrops crashed to the ground.

Calan didn't come off any better than the Shadow. He fell off his cloud, blood spraying into the air.

He landed in one place, his legs in two others. The Shadow had sliced through his knees.

The lightning dragon looped around and returned to him, and from what Yerin knew about the Stormcallers, it would be carrying some of the Blood Shadow's madra back to Calan.

She whipped a Rippling Sword at him. Finishing him off was no more than mercy.

But a brief shower of bright lines fell from overhead. A Striker technique he must have already prepared. The blue-gold madra pierced through her own Rippling Sword, destroying her technique.

The Blood Shadow hadn't re-formed, and the dragon sank into Calan's body as it returned. He clenched his jaw, red madra blasting out behind him as he vented blood madra. Yerin was surprised to see that his technique was so similar to Lindon's arm.

Then his seven jade rings gathered, his Thousand-Mile Cloud swooping down. He hauled himself up with his arms, levering his body onto the cloud. The bleeding from his severed legs had already stopped; either his Iron body healed injuries, or he'd controlled the blood aura in his own body to seal the wounds.

His eyes turned to her, and his gaze was firm as stone. The pain of losing his limbs hadn't shaken him at all.

Yerin couldn't help but be impressed.

Out of respect, she had to match that determination. She drew her sword back, cycling her madra.

Then he vanished as the Blood Shadow re-formed and slashed a sword through the space where he'd been.

He reappeared closer to Yerin, but had to turn to face the spirit, and Yerin used the Endless Sword.

She felt dirty for doing so.

When his Jadeclaw Rings went out of his control, the Blood Shadow dealt with his Striker techniques, and Yerin's follow-up Rippling Sword cut him in the back.

It didn't sever him in two, which was a testament to the power of his spirit. He didn't scream, either.

Until the Blood Shadow pounced on him.

When it gleefully leaped on him, he shouted. Then it began to draw blood aura from his wounds as though inhaling...and the longer it inhaled, the more of his power escaped. And the louder his scream grew.

The entire purpose of the Blood Shadow was to steal power by killing or possessing others and bring that power back to the Bleeding Phoenix, but Yerin hadn't allowed hers to escape.

Not since it had killed her parents.

Yerin launched another Striker technique as fast as she could. Not at Calan. At the Shadow.

The smartest thing would have been to kill him and end the match, but she had reacted out of pure guttural disgust.

No Blood Shadow would have a meal where she could see it.

The Shadow sliced her technique in half with its black blade and winked at her. Uninterrupted.

This time, Yerin used the Endless Sword. The Shadow's black blade was close enough to Calan; she could cut his throat from here and end the duel.

Yerin's sword rang...and so did the Shadow's.

Sword aura was agitated for a moment, but then it died out. The spirit had canceled her technique.

But Yerin had reached the limit of her patience.

She kicked off with all the power of her Steelborn Iron body, a dune's worth of sand spraying up behind her. Bright specks of blood essence were flowing into the Shadow, and it was cycling its own madra to fight Yerin.

Yerin began cycling the Final Sword.

So did the Shadow.

In a frontal contest, Yerin would win. She was still stronger than the Shadow, and sword madra operated on a more spiritual level than blood madra did. But that was only in terms of whose technique would destroy whose.

The Shadow had a strong element of blood madra, which would tear flesh apart. What would happen if Yerin died while it survived? Would the match end? Or would the presence of Yerin's Shadow be enough for Northstrider to continue the fight?

Yerin's sword shone bright silver-white, and the Shadow's was silver tinged with bright red. When Yerin landed, they were both a hair's breadth away from completing the technique.

But Yerin didn't finish it. She swung at Calan.

The Shadow read her intentions and stretched out to defend her meal, but there was one area in which Yerin clearly outmatched her copy: physical strength.

The Blood Shadow gained a measure of the Steelborn Iron body thanks to Yerin's blood essence, but it was nothing compared to having the real thing and a corporeal body to back it up.

Yerin's blow slammed the Shadow's sword aside and split Calan into two pieces.

Instantly, his body blurred into white light. His legs shone as they were taken away as well.

In the moments after the Ninecloud Soul announced Yerin's victory, Yerin stared into her Shadow's eyes.

The Blood Shadow licked its lips and patted its belly.

She didn't need the bond between their spirits to understand its intentions.

It was full.

第十七章

CHAPTER SEVENTEEN

How would I do against Calan Archer? Lindon asked Dross.

[He couldn't even handle Yerin's Blood Shadow. Do you think *you* can handle Yerin's Blood Shadow? You can.]

Lindon sat in Yerin's waiting room, watching the fight conclude on a projection construct. That made two members of the Uncrowned he was certain he could beat.

But only two.

Ziel was a mystery, and Dross agreed. His brief rampage against Brother Aekin had astonished Lindon, before Ziel had succumbed to spiritual injury. Whether Lindon won that battle depended on how much Ziel could express his power and how long he could stay whole.

But the fact remained that Aekin and Calan were the only ones that Lindon was confident against.

[You know, you can train against them some more if you'd like.]

Tonight, Lindon promised.

He wasn't likely to fight Sophara anytime soon, and losing over and over to Dross' illusory version of her was depressing him. If he fought outside of tournament rules, he could win, but he still had no confidence in defeating her in a straight-up fight.

He needed new opponents, and the two Uncrowned that seemed weakest would be perfect. He was growing tired of losing so much, even in practice.

The important thing was that Yerin had won.

She had grown stronger, which he was glad to see, so now she would enjoy the prizes of the top four. And she was the only hope remaining for the Akura clan to win Penance.

Now, they would spare no expense for her.

Lindon clenched his right hand. The Consume technique alone might not be enough to catch him up to Yerin.

His desire for the prizes of Sky's Edge redoubled.

Yerin re-entered the waiting room with her body and spirit repaired. Not that she'd suffered much injury. She gave off the spiritual impression of someone in peak health.

Though she looked miserable.

Mercy screamed and cheered and clapped all at once when Yerin arrived, but Yerin didn't bother to respond. As for the Winter Sage, she looked like she was ready to grind steel between her teeth.

"We *must* seal that parasite," she said, the moment Yerin appeared.

"Are you crazy?" Mercy asked. "It almost beat the Stormcaller on its own!"

"It's out of control!"

"Then we should help her control it!"

While they debated—Mercy not backing down in front of a Sage—Lindon watched Yerin. She looked like she'd just *lost* the fight.

He had to try something.

"I didn't know your master," Lindon said quietly, "but I know he would be proud."

Her face wrinkled until he thought she might cry. "Would have been proud of me if I'd done it. Why would he give one thin hair for a match my Shadow fought?"

Lindon knew he might be stepping into hotter water, but from what he'd learned from Yerin, he thought he'd put together a decent picture of the Sword Sage's personality.

"Apologies, but do you really think he would care *how* you won?"

She looked like she wanted to argue, but the cloud over her face slowly lifted.

"Adama would never have allowed your Blood Shadow to develop to this point," the Winter Sage said with certainty.

Lindon wanted to punch her, Sage or not, as Yerin's shoulders slumped again.

The Sage noticed and backtracked. "But he would have been proud of you, of course. Whatever the...means...you cultivated the Blood Shadow yourself, no different than a weapon you created. He would be very proud. But he would be *more* proud if—"

Maybe it was the look on Lindon's face or maybe she realized what she was about to say, but the Winter Sage cut off her own words.

"Well, at least top four's a treat," Yerin admitted. "When do I get my prizes?"

Lindon had been wondering that already.

"There's a ceremony for the top four tonight, but the prizes won't be ready for a few days. We'll have them sent to us back at the School."

Yerin glanced up to Lindon. "Two weeks until the next round."

That reminder raised complicated feelings in him.

On the one hand, he'd barely gotten to talk to Yerin at all since he'd been back from Sky's Edge. Now that chance was over, and two weeks sounded like forever.

On the other hand, he was confident he could earn two thousand points in two weeks. Maybe a little more, since Abyssal Palace was supposed to receive reinforcements. That was one more prize, maybe two.

From that perspective, two weeks felt too short.

"We have the rest of the day," he responded.

Then Charity swept in, one of her owls perched on her shoulder. "I'm afraid not. You'll be accompanying my father back to Sky's Edge immediately; we need him back in place without delay. Congratulations, Yerin. Your training has now become our family's number one priority."

Lindon was paying attention to Yerin's reaction, so he felt when blood madra surged within her. She grimaced as she suppressed her Shadow.

He expected her to respond lightly, but she pressed her fists together and bowed. "I'll be grateful."

The Winter Sage looked delighted. "You'll see amazing things if we can get her to Overlord, I guarantee it."

The stirring blood madra inside Yerin stilled as she spoke. "Means I could use another training opponent, true?"

Lindon saw where she was going with this, and he brightened.

It would be a shame to give up the opportunity in Sky's Edge, but if the full resources of the Akura clan were focused on Yerin, he could potentially get more from helping her train. Surely they would want her training partner to be as strong as possible.

And, of course, he'd be with Yerin.

"You will no longer have time for that," Charity said, and Lindon's vision was crushed. "Min Shuei and I will be handling your training directly. Sparring against others at your level will have only minimal impact at this point."

The Blood Shadow went from silent to fighting so violently that everyone felt it.

This time, the struggle inside Yerin caused the air around her to glow red. She strained visibly, forcing the parasite down, but both Charity and the Winter Sage had their attention focused on Yerin.

"...and we'll have to seal that *thing*," the Winter Sage spat.

Charity shook her head. "On the contrary, we'll need to improve its state of existence. It's perfect willpower training, and I can't imagine any advantage we could give her in only two weeks that is better than a more complete Blood Shadow."

The Winter Sage staggered back in shock.

When Mercy had learned that Aunt Charity couldn't transport them to Sky's Edge on her own, she had felt a nervous fluttering in her stomach.

When Malice had sent word that she would be the one to cast them on the first leg of their journey, Mercy's nerves had gone from fluttering to churning.

Then her mother had instructed Mercy to arrive early for a private talk.

That was when Mercy really began to feel sick.

The Monarch hadn't spoken with Mercy since her loss, nor made her opinion known to the rest of the family. She had stayed as aloof and apart as ever.

As a result, Mercy didn't know how her mother felt about the fight against Sophara. But she wouldn't be pleased.

Mercy arrived in the floating Monarch viewing platform to find it occupied only by one person. Dozens of comfortable seats remained empty, the corners of the vast room were draped in shadows, and the silence echoed in the empty space.

Her mother lounged in a dark throne, hands folded in her lap, waiting for Mercy to enter.

Mercy had far greater access to Malice than most anyone else, but that still meant that months often passed with no contact between them at all. As she approached, she felt as much as she ever had that she was a stranger in the presence of her Monarch.

She went to one knee, bowing before her mother. "My greetings, Mother." While she didn't enjoy being so formal, she wasn't sure what else to do.

"Rise," Malice commanded.

Mercy did, hoping to see the Monarch soften into a mother. When her smile remained cold and distant, Mercy knew she was in trouble.

"How should I treat someone who let the family down so badly?"

Mercy straightened her back. "I know my weaknesses better now, and I've already started to train my Dream of Darkness again. In the future, I will do my best to represent you better."

"In the future?" Malice asked. "You've failed already."

The Monarch spoke offhandedly, but Mercy's heart tightened.

"I'm so sorry," she whispered.

Malice sighed. "Failure can be a teacher, and of course one can try one's best and still fail. There is no such thing as an undefeated warrior. But you have my Book. You carry my bow. You represent me. Should you be treated as though you were victorious?"

Mercy happened to think defeat was often punishment enough, and there was no point in disciplining someone who had tried their best.

But then...*had* Mercy tried her best? It could be hard to tell. She felt like she had, but what if she hadn't been motivated enough? What if she could have done more?

"There is no physical punishment that could motivate you," Malice went on, "but you must feel the sting of failure if you are ever to appreciate success."

Around the room, shadows opened into windows that looked out onto other locations. Other people.

Purple eyes turned in surprise as miniature portals appeared next to other members of the Akura clan. Whatever was about to happen, Malice was displaying it to dozens of people, and Mercy's cheeks began to burn in shame already.

Aunt Charity appeared, looking faintly disturbed, but she said nothing. When the window appeared next to Fury, he glanced at it and then waved it closed. Pride scowled through his own window.

Then Mercy saw a window opening onto Yerin and forced herself not to squeeze her eyes shut. Malice was spreading her punishment to a wide audience, not just the family.

And she dreaded the window that was going to open next. It would be Lindon, she knew it. Yerin was one thing, but if *he* witnessed Mercy being punished by her mother like a little girl, that would be even more mortifying.

She waited in agony for the next window to open.

It never did, which was one tiny relief.

Malice's eyes shone purple in the darkness. "Mercy. Let the family witness my displeasure. You have dragged the Akura name through the mud. Though you use the Book of Eternal Night, though you carry my own bow into battle, even so you failed. You are a disappointment to me, and to all of my descendants.

"You have let me down, and you have let the family down. You will dedicate your mind and soul to repaying this debt, or you will no longer have the right to call yourself my daughter."

Mercy kept her eyes fixed on the ground.

She said the only words she could possibly say in that moment: "Yes, Mother."

Lindon stepped into a towering pillar of darkness alongside Eithan, Mercy, and Fury.

As he'd experienced back in the Night Wheel Valley, all his senses disappeared. He was blind and deaf to the world, unable to feel even his body. Only he and Dross drifted in endless darkness.

Not only did Charity have to stay and train Yerin, but Fury needed to return to Sky's Edge faster than a Sage could carry him.

Even a Monarch couldn't transport them there directly without a permanent portal, but she could put them on the continent at least. From what Lindon gathered, they would emerge somewhere in the western Blackflame Empire.

[I wonder if we'll fly over your home!] Dross said happily.

With a strange rush, Lindon realized they just might.

Of course, they might not. They were talking about many thousands of square miles and hundreds of possible routes, so there was nothing to guarantee that they would come out anywhere near Sacred Valley.

But the idea of possibly seeing Samara's ring in the distance as they traveled by filled him with a strange excitement.

When the darkness lifted, they were standing on the dune of a strange desert. The corner of a building stuck up from the sand alongside a startled-looking creature bigger than Lindon. It resembled a cross between a mole and a lizard, and when it saw them—or maybe when it sensed Fury—it clawed its way rapidly down into the dune.

Lindon felt power radiating from above him, and he looked up.

Miles across the desert, huge green stalks rose from the sand. They stood higher than Elder Whisper's tower back home, and at the top bloomed massive flowers supporting what looked like cities.

If they hadn't been under such a time limit, Lindon would have wanted a closer look. Mercy shaded her eyes to stare at the flowers and made noises of amazement.

Fury stretched his arms up and yawned. "Okay, let's get on with it. Who's got a cloudship?"

"I have been reliably informed that mine is one of the fastest in the world," Eithan said. He swept his arm in a grandiose gesture, and a gold light manifested over the sand next to him. It looked like the Remnant of a ship for a moment, until it solidified into the real thing.

It was a sleek and opulent ship, made of dark polished wood and outlined in gold, and it looked sized to carry ten or fifteen people. The cloud beneath it was a bright white-gold, and the prow was carved into a snarling lion of white and gold.

"The decorations leave something to be desired," Eithan observed.

Fury gave him a sidelong glance that Lindon would have called disgusted. "At least you're good for something." Then he leaped aboard.

Lindon had never heard Fury speak in a less than friendly tone to anyone but an enemy Herald. Mercy noticed his surprise and sighed.

"He doesn't like anyone who gives up. For any reason."

"I got his mother's permission, but that doesn't mean getting everyone's approval." Eithan shrugged. "Ah, well. I have nothing if not confidence in my likeable demeanor."

Lindon suddenly worried if Eithan would survive all the way to Sky's Edge.

The trip would take almost nine hours, which surprised Lindon. That wasn't much faster than when Charity had taken him to Sky's Edge before.

But, as Dross reminded him, there was a significant difference between transporting two people and four. If Charity had been the one to send them instead of Malice, it might have taken them an entire day to arrive.

For the first few hours, Fury napped as Eithan lurked nearby and made continual comments about how nice the weather was and how it would be a shame to sleep the day away. At one point, Fury tossed him off the side of the ship.

Lindon cycled the Heaven and Earth Purification Wheel until he could stand it no longer. Then he worked on his armor as Little Blue ran around the deck, which ended when she almost pitched over the railing. After that, he kept her in eyesight and chatted with Mercy.

Eventually, the topic turned to their purpose in Sky's Edge.

"I was surprised to see that Fury made it to see your match," Lindon said. "I thought he had to stay and keep the Abyssal Palace Herald in check."

Mercy idly extended a String of Shadow and watched it flutter in the wind. "Everyone is playing by the rules for now because of Penance. If a Herald kills all our Lords, he's made himself a prime target if we end up with the weapon."

She gave a heavy sigh. "But you can't lean on your enemy's restraint for long, so we still need to be back before the dragons get there."

She was more subdued than usual, and Lindon knew she was thinking about her loss.

But he'd been wondering about the dragons' strategy. It was too expensive to transport a whole flight of dragons through space, so they would be making a trip across an entire continent.

And...why? They had nothing to gain from the Dreadgod. They couldn't even kill Fury, in case Yerin won the tournament and decided to get revenge by using it on their Monarch.

So what were they thinking?

When he asked Mercy, she gave a deeper, heavier sigh. "It's like Northstrider told us: dragons would rather burn a field to the ground than give their enemies a bite to eat. Or however he put it. They have nothing to gain, but as long as we'll lose out just as much, they're happy to do it."

That seemed unsustainable to Lindon. They had to gain more than they lost or their faction would never grow.

But Malice and Fury had been fighting the dragons for centuries, so they knew the nature of their opponents. There were more factors at play here than he could know.

Mercy gave a third sigh. The deepest and heaviest of them all.

Dross was concerned. [Do you think she's having breathing problems?]

Even Little Blue scurried up to lay a hand on Mercy's knee and let out a worried cheep.

"It's difficult," Lindon said, "watching and not being able to affect anything."

Mercy patted Little Blue with one blackened finger. "I had my chance. And I just..." She spread her hands and mimed dropping something.

"We still have Yerin."

Truthfully, Lindon understood how she felt. He hated

leaving his fate in the hands of others. But if it had to be someone, at least it was Yerin.

"That shouldn't be her responsibility. It's mine."

Lindon had intended to lighten the mood, but he couldn't help but saying, "You made it further than I did. I think I could have beaten Calan Archer or Brother Aekin, but I don't know if I'd have been any good against anyone else. I could never have beaten you, for instance."

That should encourage her, but it was also honest. She had fought far beyond her level.

She looked at him out of the corner of her eye. "Did losing hurt you that much?"

"Oh, no, apologies, I didn't mean to suggest that."

"Aren't you the one who fought an Underlord prince as a Truegold?"

Lindon hadn't meant to make this about him, and he tried to backtrack, but she kept talking.

"I'm surprised to hear *you* say you could never win against someone, that's all. If I asked you to punch a hole in the sky, I thought you'd say 'Apologies, it might take me a few years.'"

Was that how she saw him?

Eithan and Northstrider had both encouraged him to think about himself from the perspective of others, so he probed a bit deeper. "I don't see it like that. I try to do whatever I can, or whatever I have to, but even I know that sometimes there's no way to win."

Mercy released Little Blue and turned to look him in the eye. "Says who?"

The heavens? Lindon thought. *Reality? Whoever decides what 'truth' is.*

That would have been too rude to Mercy, so he didn't say it aloud.

When he didn't respond immediately, she continued. "You look different when you're fired up to win and when you're not. Did you know that? Usually your face is like *this.*" She scrunched up her eyebrows and firmed her jaw into an intense stare. "And then when you give up, you look like *this.*"

Her head drooped down and she used her fingertips to pull her lips into a frown.

Little Blue fell over laughing. It sounded like bells in a high wind.

Lindon couldn't tell if Mercy was making fun of him or not. "Is that true?"

Dross popped into existence in front of him. [I'd say your face looks more like *this*.]

His mouth gaped open and his one eye grew huge, so that he looked like a shocked and betrayed child. A one-eyed, purple child.

"Do you think I wanted your best impression? Can't you show me?"

[I can indeed! Thanks to Sir Northstrider, I now have the recordings from the Uncrowned King tournament.]

He projected an image onto the deck, though he used no light aspect, so Lindon was sure it was only an image in his mind.

It was a frozen image of Lindon in battle, dragon's breath streaming from his palm, as he fought Naian Blackflame.

"That's it!" Mercy cried, pointing to the projection. "That's the face!"

So Dross sent it to her too. Lindon hadn't asked for that.

The view changed. This time, it was an image of Lindon looking upward as Yerin fell toward him, sword raised. This came from one of the viewing constructs in the arena, so it was somewhat far back, but Lindon could see his own expression.

Dross had shown him this perspective before, and he remembered how weak and conflicted he looked.

Then he saw himself change.

Dross advanced the moment slowly, so Lindon watched as life kindled in his own eyes. There was no specific difference he could point to, but it was like a different person had taken over his body. Like his soul had been brought back from death.

[This next one is a creation of mine, but I think it's even more accurate than a recording.]

Back in a small room in Moongrave, Lindon faced Charity and begged her to let him return home. The details of this one were fuzzier, slightly different than in Lindon's memory, but he could see the weakness in his face. Doubt, hesitation; a slump of the shoulders, a flicker in the eyes as he tried to think his way free.

Nothing like the gaze of the man he'd seen before.

Dross released the projection, panting and leaving Lindon to think.

Was this what Eithan had meant about seeing himself as others saw him? Would this lead to his Overlord revelation?

"Gratitude," Lindon said.

Mercy turned away and leaned both her forearms on the railing. Her hair blew behind her in the wind of their passage. "I can say all that to you, but I've thrown up three times since I lost."

"You have?"

"Three times so far. I start thinking about mistakes I made, and that makes me think about what I should have done, and then it's a spiral all the way down!"

Despite the subject, she still sounded pleasant.

"You've hidden it well," he said. He wasn't sure if she would consider that a compliment.

"Hmm...I don't think I'm really trying to hide it, though. I'm just not letting those feelings decide what I do."

At the front of the ship, Fury shot up. He went from loudly snoring to standing in a motion so fast that Lindon didn't catch it.

His hair drifted up, and spiritual pressure weighed on them all as his veil slipped away. A shadow crept over the entire ship.

"Prepare for battle, kids," Fury said. "They're already here."

At that, he kicked off the deck with such force that it sent the cloudship plummeting a hundred feet before it stabilized.

When they had all caught their balance—with Lindon sheltering a trembling Little Blue in his hand—Lindon turned to Eithan. "How long until we arrive?"

"Still four more hours. If you were wondering, I can't see anything."

The closer they got to Sky's Edge, the more Lindon could see in the distance. And the more of the situation Eithan shared with them.

It always looked worse and worse.

Darkness collided with golden light in an explosion that lit up most of the horizon and pushed back entire banks of clouds. Even dozens of miles away, the spiritual sensations buffeted their cloudship.

This was why Heralds never came to open blows.

"They're both holding back," Mercy said. "If they weren't, everyone below them would be dead."

Eithan shaded his eyes as he peered at the battle. "Ideally, a balanced fight will look like this. The most advanced sacred artists will keep each other in check so that those below them are unaffected. Otherwise, all battles would start with the most advanced fighters annihilating the enemy's entire force of Golds."

Lindon supposed that made sense, but the problem was that the two sides were not balanced.

Fury wasn't exchanging blows with the Abyssal Palace Herald who had been there before, but with Xorrus. The left hand of the Dragon King.

That meant at least two Heralds on one side against Fury, though the leader of Abyssal Palace didn't seem to be taking part in the battle.

Worse, he was starting to see the hundred or so dragons flying circles around the floating Abyssal Palace fortress.

And even that wasn't the end.

A towering red-tinged cloudship painted with a symbol resembling the Bleeding Phoenix obviously belonged to Redmoon Hall. A floating island covered by a giant pure-white tree must belong to the Silent Servants, as a halo of light that resembled their Goldsign crowned its branches. The Stormcallers were carried on a long storm cloud that drizzled a curtain of rain on the mountains surrounding

Sky's Edge. A number of structures had been built on the cloud itself, so that it looked like they traveled with their entire sect.

Lindon didn't sense any more Heralds, but he suspected there was at least one. The Blood Sage had attended the tournament, which left the Herald to continue running Redmoon Hall; he couldn't imagine the man not being here.

But this sight sickened him. Surely no one from Sky's Edge had been left alive.

He turned to Mercy, but she seemed calm.

"Oh, our side is still alive," Eithan explained while keeping his eyes on the horizon. "As Mercy told you, everyone is playing quite strictly by the rules. For now. While the battle below is quite heated, it is strictly between Golds and the weaker Lords. They toy with us."

"For them to have beaten us here, they must have gone to great expense," Lindon said quietly. "Are they positioning for the end of the tournament? If so, why didn't we...pardon, Mercy, but why didn't your mother see this coming?"

"My mother's weakness is not a lack of foresight."

Eithan flipped hair away from his face. "I suspect the situation is thus: they are poised to secure the labyrinth as soon as their champion wins the tournament. They have arrived so...aggressively...merely to express superiority and exert their confidence in Sophara."

"That's it?" Lindon blurted.

When he put it like that, it sounded...petty.

"I'm boiling down a great many factors, and of course this is all speculation on my part...but many Monarchs are such people. Those who enjoy throwing their power around. They would be certain that Fury can't fight them all, and even if Yerin wins the tournament, there are so many together that they can retreat without reprisal."

A hand of dense shadow madra struck a golden spear from the air before it could be fully formed, kicking up a wind that pushed the Redmoon Hall cloudship back.

[I have some idea of what it costs to move this many

Heralds,] Dross said. [As you may remember, some of them were our guests in Ghostwater. They'll have given up fights all over the world to make this demonstration.]

"What happens when Fury loses?" Lindon asked.

"This isn't a fight," Mercy responded. "This is him saying he won't back down. But...I know him. There *will* be a fight."

Lindon noticed they were still heading straight for Sky's Edge.

[I appreciate how fast and fuel-efficient this cloudship is,] Dross said, [but don't you think we should check its turn radius? For instance, we could turn around and go the other way.]

"You can drop me here," Mercy said. She tapped Suu on the deck, and the staff's dragon head hissed. "I'll go the rest of the way myself."

"There's no barrier stopping us from entering?" Lindon asked Eithan.

"None. If I had to bet, they won't mind our arrival at all. But they may take issue if we try to depart."

"And the Lords are fighting on the ground?"

"The strongest participating in the battle are Overlords. They would very much appreciate the arrival of a few more skilled combatants, I suspect."

"No," Mercy said firmly. "I have responsibilities here, but there's no reason for you two to risk your lives."

Lindon continued speaking to Eithan. "If Sophara wins, are we all going to die?"

He would happily put his faith in Yerin, but he didn't want to bet his life on the Uncrowned King tournament if he didn't have to.

Yerin hadn't even made it through the top four yet.

"Malice has certainly prepared for this, which means that Fury has a way to escape. It's probable that we will have an opportunity to survive, even if the worst happens and the Monarch is killed. But..." He shrugged. "We will certainly be safer if Yerin wins. Or if we don't go down there at all."

Lindon thought of his expression in those tournament recordings.

And he thought of what he'd felt when Suriel gave him a second chance.

He looked down into his palm, where Little Blue was hugging Suriel's marble. The tiny blue candle-flame matched her perfectly.

"Apologies, Little Blue," he said. "I need your help."

She dropped the glass ball and gave a whistling cheer.

There was only one step he could take at the moment to improve his power, and Dross had confirmed it would work. He had hesitated only out of fear for Little Blue's safety.

But she was eager to help, and he needed her.

"I swear to open my core to you and share my power," Lindon said, for the second time in his life.

Little Blue regarded him solemnly as she knelt and pressed both hands to his skin.

Then she gave one bright, piping note of agreement and their contract was complete.

Deep blue power slid into him; not an overwhelming amount, certainly not compared to the sea of pure madra he already contained. But more than he'd expected from the Sylvan Riverseed, and more than enough to stain his pure core a deeper blue.

As it did, his own power crashed into the Sylvan Riverseed.

She fell over on his hand, and if Lindon could have interrupted the process, he would have done so out of panic. Her color brightened to a lighter shade, but she became clearer, more solid, more defined. Her eyes gained a new shine, and legs and feet appeared beneath her long skirt.

She doubled in size until she was about a foot tall, and Lindon wondered if she might grow to human size until her form settled.

When she stood on his hand, he felt her weight more than he ever had before.

A new sensation settled in his pure madra as it took on a cleansing, emptying aspect. It wasn't entirely like her original power, but not exactly the madra he was used to using either. A combination of both.

Little Blue lifted both her eyes and gave a loud chime.

He didn't hear words, but now he could vividly understand the emotion behind them.

Victory.

Now, after so long being carried around, she could help carry him.

第十八章

CHAPTER EIGHTEEN

Pride trembled, bruised and panting, on the stony ground. He wanted to sink to his knees, but he would rather die than kneel to these opponents.

Not that they seemed likely to kill him.

Most of the Akura forces were inside the fortress walls that the Seishen king had raised in Sky's Edge, but Pride and his team had been caught on the stony hills outside when the dragons had arrived.

The mine was all but empty, everything of value stripped from the town, and they'd evacuated everyone for miles. The territory was ready for the Dreadgod to arrive, and Pride had only been supervising the return of the Gold workers.

When dragons had swooped in, cutting off their retreat, he hadn't been too alarmed at first. They would receive support, and there was no one in this group of dragons above Overlord. And they clearly weren't thirsty for blood, or their Herald would have annihilated them from a thousand feet up rather than sending her descendants.

Then the other Dreadgod cults had arrived, and his heart had fallen past his knees.

Even when Uncle Fury had begun fighting, it hadn't helped Pride's position at all. A dozen Lords sat on clouds or floating mounts around Pride and the others, watching. Four of them were Overlord. Five times that many Truegolds and Highgolds watched from further back, a mix of cultists and dragons of all colors.

They just kept sending Underlords forward to duel. There was some joke about reenacting the Uncrowned King tournament for themselves, but really they just wanted to see their opponents suffer.

There were no rules. Whenever it looked like one of them would win, an Overlord on the bench would throw in a Striker technique and claim he was swatting a fly.

Every one of the Underlords on Lindon's team was beaten and bloody. Grace had a cloth wrapped around a missing eye that became harder to heal with every passing second, Courage was unconscious with a mangled lower half of his body, and one of the Maten twins was covered in burns.

Pride had just been forced to fight, even with his core almost empty and his flesh battered, and he thought he'd made a good accounting of himself. One of the green dragons, in a humanoid form, was now missing a tail.

She'd have it reattached, but it had felt good to tear it off with his bare hands.

Naru Saeya was fighting now, hammering away at an Abyssal Palace priest with a chipped and broken rainbow sword that was slowly losing light.

The priest weathered the blows, but they were beginning to draw blood. Saeya was spattered in more blood than anyone, most of it belonging to others, but she was running more on anger than on madra by this point. She used no techniques, screaming as she hacked at her opponent.

The enemy Lords and Ladies laughed and shouted bets.

Pride was certain he would already be dead if not for his name. While the enemy at large was hesitant to end too many lives before the tournament concluded, there had been a handful of deaths among their Golds. Courage and the Frozen Blade woman would die if they weren't healed.

This was a game for them. The Akura sacred artists would be humiliated and eventually released.

Pride would have greatly preferred a straightforward fight to the death.

Their side was surrounded, their retreat cut off, and the dragons controlled the air. Archlords were rare, so there were none close, but enough Overlords were here to make reinforcements almost impossible.

Pride had to hope that Uncle Fury would conclude his fight and come to save them. *Without* teaching the other side a lesson and wiping them all out.

As cathartic as that would be for Pride, it would ensure that an enemy Herald would kill an equal group of Lords in retaliation.

Saeya's scream cut off, and Pride's gut tightened as he thought she'd been hit by some weapon he hadn't seen.

She sagged to the ground with an expression of great relief, panting, letting her sword hand drop. "Sure took their time," she muttered.

A few of the Overlords launched Striker techniques into the distance, and Pride followed them.

A gold speck in the distance resolved into a small cloud-ship speeding toward them. The dragons that filled the skies struck at the ship, but they were mostly Truegolds; they were driven away by dark arrows and beams of black dragon's breath.

Instead of relief, Pride filled with anger and despair.

What were they doing here? The second they dropped off Fury, they should have turned and run away!

The first Overlord technique—a crimson bird launched by a member of Redmoon Hall—landed on the cloudship and burst harmlessly against the hull. Pride couldn't tell if the ship itself was protected or if Eithan had extended his pure madra to cover the entire vessel.

A ghostly rain of swords struck next, but they were overwhelmed by a wave of pure madra. *That* was certainly Eithan, unless Lindon had added a new Striker technique to his arsenal.

Then an arrow of light shot toward them, fired by an archer among the Silent Servants.

An Overlord presence bloomed on the deck of the ship, and the shining arrow was overwhelmed by a volley of hundreds of violet arrows heading the other direction.

Mercy's bow.

A dozen other Gold-level techniques crashed against the ship and did nothing, but none of the Archlords made a move. Either they were still strictly adhering to the unspoken rules of honorable combat, as Pride hoped, or they didn't think the passengers of this ship posed a significant threat.

Probably both.

The Overlords all defended their side from Mercy's volley easily enough, but the cloudship made it over Pride's head.

As soon as it did, it vanished in a flash of gold light and the three passengers fell from the sky.

Pure ego and foolishness. The fall would be no threat to any Underlord, but they had made themselves easy targets for every sacred artist on the enemy side.

Sure enough, all the Lords and most of the Truegolds launched attacks at the falling trio. The air shook with the power of so many techniques at once, and the glow actually outshone the Herald battle in the distance.

Mercy would be fine—her armor was perfect for this— and Pride had no idea what the limits were to Eithan's defensive technique. But if Lindon was counting on the healing from his Iron body...

Well, he might survive, but he'd be a useless pile of meat. Maybe one of the others would cover for him.

A blue sphere of pure madra surrounded Lindon, fifteen feet in every direction, covering all three of them. It was deeper blue than the madra Pride had seen from him before, and it carried a different impression. Like it would scrub everything clean.

And while the ball of light surrounded him, his eyes turned solid, oceanic blue, as though they were made from sapphires.

The strongest attacks hit first, and they crossed the bubble and weakened visibly, but they did penetrate. Eithan blasted a few apart and Lindon absorbed one into his hunger arm, but two or three landed.

Pride expected to see wounds.

But it didn't look like they suffered anything worse than ruffled clothes.

Maybe not even that.

Some Underlord techniques were wiped out a few feet into the blue sphere, but the others were destroyed by Eithan or Lindon with little effort. The Truegold attacks vanished the instant they touched the bubble.

Mercy seemed to simply be enjoying the ride down.

The blue field of madra vanished before it touched the ground.

Lindon landed with the subtlety of an ape.

Eithan drifted down next to Naru Saeya on a flow of wind aura so tightly controlled that he kicked up no dust. "Were you winning?" he asked cheerfully.

"I heard you advanced," Saeya said from the ground. "Huan is going to put you to work."

Mercy rode Suu down toward Pride, concern filling her eyes, and she was already rummaging in her pocket for some healing salve or pill.

He stopped her with a raised hand. "Fools. You've trapped yourselves."

She removed the stopper to a white bottle. "This will make you feel better. I've got plenty to go around."

"Take care of them first, if you want to do some good." He knew what his sister was like, but he still couldn't believe they'd come without help. "You should have brought reinforcements."

She looked confused. "We did."

Lindon walked into the open space where Naru Saeya had been fighting. His eyes had faded back to normal. "Pardon, but is this a game?"

Pride would have shouted at him not to be an idiot if he

thought that would help. But then, Lindon gave off a different impression than he had before.

Normally, he felt domineering and aggressive when he held Blackflame, but now he gave off a similar impression with pure madra.

Pride doubted his own spiritual sense.

Some of the enemy camp laughed, but many didn't. A few of the Overlords muttered to one another.

If they hadn't seen the recordings of the Uncrowned King tournament, they had at least heard the reports. Some of them had undoubtedly watched the fights live.

They knew who Lindon was.

An Overlady from Redmoon Hall called out, "A bit of sport to liven things up. Would you like to play?"

"What are the prizes?" Lindon asked.

This time, there was more laughter, and even the Redmoon Hall Lady's lips moved up. "You fight as long as you can. While you're fighting, the rest of your team gets to rest."

"Apologies, but that isn't a prize." Lindon reached around his neck, pulling up a chain that hung inside his robes. The chain was usually hidden beneath the shadesilk ribbon that held his halfsilver hammer badge, but Pride knew what it was even before Lindon held up the bronze key for inspection.

His void key.

"How about the winner gets to keep whatever the loser has on their person when they enter the ring?" Lindon suggested.

The Redmoon Lady's eyes lit up, and she laughed. "*Wonderful.* Now, who among us is brave enough to face someone who was almost one of the Uncrowned?"

Half of the Underlords raised their hands.

Including the priest from Abyssal Palace already in the arena. His yellow eye blazed, and he looked at Lindon hungrily.

The Overlady waved him back. "You've had your turn. What about one of the Servants? Juvari, how about you?"

A woman with dark skin and eyes stepped forward, all her other features obscured by either her robes or the cloth wrapped over the lower half of her face. A ring of light floated over her head.

Pride recognized her, of course. She had been eliminated in the fourth round of the competition.

A dream artist.

Pride began to feel some hope. Lindon's mind-spirit could fight against dream techniques, though Pride didn't know how effective it would be in direct combat against a Silent Servant.

Naturally, she removed a number of artifacts and jewelry and left them on the sidelines before she entered their makeshift arena.

Obviously she would. Lindon's "prizes" were idiotic at best and naïve at worst. The enemy would just leave their valuables behind before entering.

But Lindon didn't protest. He tucked his key back into his robes.

Pride wondered if he was too embarrassed to say anything. While it would be gratifying to see Lindon lose after that arrogant entrance, Pride still held on to some hope that his confidence was justified.

As nice as it would be to see Lindon's opinion of himself taken down a notch or two, Pride wanted the enemy to lose.

An orange barrier appeared in the air in front of Juvari as she began weaving dream aura. There was nothing so formal as a signal to indicate the start of the match.

A bar of Blackflame punched through the barrier, but the Silent Servant had already completed her Ruler technique. She held out her hands, and while it was invisible to Pride's mind, he sensed an overwhelming, tempting dream.

Even on the sidelines, he wanted to give in, to see whatever vision she was going to show him. He blinked his way free.

Lindon's white hand was already around Juvari's throat.

And he was *draining* her.

Power flowed into him, just as Pride had seen before, but this was somehow even more frightening. It was powerful and thorough, and Pride couldn't help but wonder if he himself could escape if he found himself in Lindon's grip.

Spikes of dream madra pierced Lindon's head, but he ignored them completely.

Juvari's spirit became weaker and weaker. Even her lifeline faded in front of the horrified onlookers.

One of the Overlords Forged and threw a spear, but it was knocked aside by a blast of pure madra.

"Did you see that mosquito?" Eithan shouted.

Lindon released the woman in his grip, and she crumpled to the ground. She was still alive. Judging by what Pride saw of her life and spirit, she would live, but it would take expensive treatment to return her to fighting shape.

Pride expected the dream madra to vent out of Lindon's arm, but instead it cycled up to the base of his skull. Where his mind-spirit lived.

Lindon looked to the Overlords and bowed with his fists pressed together. "Gratitude. Who's next?"

Pride's opinion of Lindon went up a level.

They didn't play the game after that, of course. They blasted Lindon until he was forced to retreat, mocking him and shouting names.

The thunder from overhead slowed as the battle from Heralds began to die down, and the enemy grew restless. They lobbed techniques at the Akura Golds, forcing the combat-capable Lords to defend them.

Lindon had ruined their game, which made them angry. And they couldn't send an Overlord into the ring either, with Eithan standing there grinning like he was waiting for a chance.

As the uneasy peace deteriorated further, Pride walked up to Lindon. "Open your void key," he said.

Lindon eyed him. "Why?" he demanded.

Pride couldn't stand his attitude. Why did Lindon treat everyone else with respect except him?

Then again, Pride hated the way he apologized for everything just as much.

"I have something to give you."

That brought a greedy glint to Lindon's eye, which made Pride reconsider what he was doing.

When Lindon opened his closet-sized void key, Pride opened his own...and withdrew the Diamond Veins.

Lindon's brow furrowed. "Pardon. You trust me to carry these now?"

Every word stuck in Pride's throat, but they had to be said. "Is there anyone else on our team who can put them to better use?"

"Gratitude," Lindon said, and Pride had never heard him sound so sincere. He pressed his fists together and bowed.

That improved Pride's mood immensely.

"Is your uncle still paying out contribution points?" Lindon asked, when the icy blue crystalline construct was in his hands.

"He hasn't said anything. But if I know him, the situation getting worse will only make him more generous. He loves it when people do well in a fight."

"Good." He surveyed the forces surrounding them. "It takes three days to process these Veins. Then I'm going hunting."

A gold light shimmered in the open space they'd been using as an arena, and the cloudship appeared again.

The enemies immediately began hammering it with techniques, but Eithan waved them all aboard. "This was one of Reigan Shen's pet projects. It can withstand anything short of a Sage or a Herald, so have no fear and get aboard!"

A hatch opened in the side and a ramp extended down to the cloud bed. No less than three attacks flew across it: a flying sword, a beam of blood madra, and a ball of fire. They would have struck anyone crossing the ramp to board the ship.

"Have no fear, I said!" Eithan announced more loudly.

Pride lifted Grace with one arm and Courage in the other, using wind aura to support them more comfortably. The other able-bodied among them carried them up to the ship.

The surrounding enemies had held back up to this point for fear of killing their quarry, but now that safety was nearby, they let loose. Forger, Ruler, and Striker techniques lit up the air, and weapons rained down.

It was only thanks to the combined defensive techniques

of all their Lords, including Lindon's dome of blue light, that they made it aboard without losing more lives. There were still injuries, but no further deaths.

Lindon was the last one, staring out the hatch and back down, and Pride found himself wondering what he was thinking.

An Overlord spirit flared, and Pride shouted a warning. An arrow, shining with golden light, *blasted* into the open deck.

It hit the edge of Lindon's blue field and weakened, but not enough to stop it. It flew forward, still a deadly attack.

A blue nimbus sprung up around Lindon as he used his full-body Enforcer technique, and with his white hand he snatched the arrow out of the air. The force carried him backwards five feet, but it didn't hit him. It didn't strain his spirit. It didn't tear his arm off.

He landed, examined the arrow, nodded appreciatively, and then tucked it into his void key.

Back in the Frozen Blade school, Yerin sat in front of a pile of presents wondering where to start.

Before she'd been taken in by the Sword Sage, Yerin's parents had celebrated her birthday by hiding a few small toys or trinkets for her around the house and setting her loose to go find them.

She hadn't felt anything like that since. Until now.

After agonizing deliberation, she decided on the package she wanted to open first. It was wrapped in Forged life madra so dense that it looked like a nest of real, living vines, and an accompanying card of polished wood showed the name of the sender. Or so the Winter Sage said.

Yerin tore away the vines around Emriss Silentborn's prize, revealing a shimmering brick the size of her palm.

It carried veins of every dark color, and it pulsed eagerly in her hand.

A quick scan of her spirit told her it was a dream tablet, but more complicated and deeper. It felt almost like a hundred dream tablets all nestled into one.

The Winter Sage ran her own perception over it and gasped. "*That* is a sword codex. It contains the memories of thousands of sword artists of all advancement levels as they practiced or meditated on their techniques. It's invaluable for any sword Path. Can I...could I borrow it when you're not—"

Charity, who was sitting in a chair nearby sipping tea, cut her off. "Any codex provided by Emriss will be of the highest quality, and this will help you develop your connection to the Sword Icon. However, it requires years of practice to show its full value."

"No matter how the tournament turns out, life goes on!" Min Shuei said, then she clapped a hand over her mouth. "Oh, Charity, I'm...I wasn't thinking. Your grandmother will be fine, I'm sure."

Charity didn't seem to care any more than Yerin did. "I suggest you move on, Yerin, so that we can see what we're working with."

It seemed like they were trying to drain all the fun out of this, but Yerin wouldn't let them.

She skimmed across the memories in the sword codex. It contained experiences from swordsmen executing techniques at every stage, from Copper to Archlord. She noted a few that she wanted to dive into later, but ultimately she set it aside. There were more to open.

A rather plain—but intricately carved and decorated—box came from the Arelius family. She didn't have to break it open, though she almost did so by accident while trying to slide out a panel.

This one held an ordinary dream tablet containing a soulfire control art. This time, Min Shuei dismissed it while Charity examined it appreciatively.

Any soulfire art would improve Yerin's control, allowing

her to slip soulfire into techniques more efficiently and control aura more powerfully. The hard part was matching the right art to the individual. The Arelius family had put either a lot of thought or a lot of research into preparing one for Yerin.

The Akura clan had thousands of soulfire arts, so it wasn't the value of the object itself that Charity praised, but the care that had gone into its selection.

She was still going on about it when Yerin reached for the next container.

This was a mechanical box of brass and steel that hissed and vented madra essence every few seconds as pistons worked in and out.

Opening it was as simple as activating a script-circle, which made the whole box fold backwards on its own and reveal a...thing.

Yerin didn't have the words for it.

It was clearly a construct of some kind, because it was made out of madra, but it looked like an ever-shifting and folding network of purple, pink, and violet light. It felt like dream madra, but also like life and some other, subtler minor aspects that Yerin couldn't begin to name.

Yerin looked to the Sages for an explanation, but they had both begun shouting at her immediately.

"Take it! Take it now!"

"Absorb it into your core, as you would aura..."

"Now! Now!"

"...and hurry, because it will dissipate slightly by the second."

"Take it!"

Their words tripped over one another, and when Yerin finally decoded them, she hurried to cycle her madra and reach out for the power she sensed inside the box.

The construct, which now looked like a dozen flowers folding in and out of each other, dissolved into essence and flowed into her spirit.

It nestled near her core, but it didn't seem to want to stay there.

"Cycle it to your head," Charity instructed, with Min Shuei nodding rapidly behind her.

Yerin did so, and the light settled like there was a notch inside her skull where it was specially designed to fit. The room immediately changed.

It wasn't as though Yerin could now see more than she could before, but her spiritual sense felt clearer, her thoughts came more smoothly, and she felt somehow more awake. Like she had just risen from a perfect night of rest.

The Winter Sage took a deep, relieved breath. "They should have warned us!"

"The Eight-Man Empire is not known for its meticulous attention to detail," Charity said. "Still, this is exactly the sort of gift we were hoping for. It will allow your mind to keep up with the speed of your body and spirit. The effects are subtle, but you will begin noticing it in small ways."

"That sounds all shiny and sweet, but I'm not sure how thrilled I am about some construct tinkering with my mind."

"It will do nothing more than help you stay at peak concentration and reach decisions more quickly. It will have no effect on your judgment whatsoever."

"Even when your judgment could use some help," the Winter Sage put in.

Yerin ignored that, moving on to the next gift.

Which Min Shuei opened.

It was from the gold dragons, and it came in a thick wooden box carved heavily with sealing scripts, so she and Charity contained it in power first.

They didn't expect a trap. If the dragons gave an explosive construct disguised as a gift, then who would ever accept a gift from them again? The Dragon Monarch considered such tricks to be beneath his dignity.

Still, there was no telling what he might try with Penance on the line.

The box revealed nothing harmful...and the feeling of power it gave off made Yerin's hopes rise even higher.

The prize within resembled a nest of tubes made out of

crystalline pure madra, like the Diamond Veins she'd used already. But before she could reach for it, Min Shuei showed clear disappointment, and Charity a cold anger.

"It's a Madra Engine," Charity said, before Yerin could ask. "A Divine Treasure of great value, using as it does dead matter of pure madra."

Yerin understood the implications of that, and she felt her own disgust.

They had made this from the Remnants of human children.

Charity wasn't finished. "On top of which, it converts life and blood essence to madra faster, increasing the speed at which your spirit refills your core. Sophara has one of these, and it provides a beneficial effect, so they can claim that it was a gift in good faith. But she has the body of a gold dragon, and it is eating into even her lifespan. For you, it would kill you in ten years."

"And with the Blood Shadow?" the Winter Sage pointed out. "You'd be lucky to survive the year. It's worthless."

Yerin's anger reached new heights. "And they can just do that? If they're allowed to send us garbage, what good are the prizes?"

"As I said, it's technically a very valuable gift. And you didn't see what we sent Sophara." Charity gave a cold smile. "I made it myself."

The Winter Sage was looking into a corner, where another container was veiled in hazy rainbow light. "It's the responsibility of the host to ensure that the prizes aren't lacking."

Naturally, that drew Yerin's attention to the Ninecloud Court's present next.

At the touch of her spirit, the voice of the Ninecloud Soul echoed throughout the room. "Congratulations, Yerin!" the construct said warmly. "Reaching top four in the Uncrowned King tournament is an accomplishment reserved for the elite. We have prepared an appropriate prize for you, taking your other gifts into account, but first it is my pleasure to announce your opponent for the semifinal round!"

Yerin leaned forward, and so did both of the Sages, though

it wouldn't help them hear any more clearly.

They had known they were going to receive a message from the Court containing the identity of Yerin's next opponent, but who would have expected it to come with the prize?

"You face Yan Shoumei of Redmoon Hall, chosen of Reigan Shen," the Soul said, and Yerin felt an odd mix of relief and frustration.

She was glad not to be fighting Sophara, but at the same time, she wanted to get that battle over with.

But her fighting Shoumei meant that Sophara would be fighting Brother Aekin, and unless he was also a Monarch in disguise, Sophara would tear him apart like a pack of wolves on a lamb. So Yerin's match would determine who faced the dragon in the finals.

"...and we hope this rare and valuable treasure will assist you in your victory!" the Soul finished, and the rainbow light fell away.

A fruit sat on an ornate platter. It looked like a fat pear, there was a piece of the branch still attached with a single leaf, and its skin was an artistic swirl of red and green.

Min Shuei laughed aloud, clapping her hands, and even Charity gave a small smile, but this time Yerin didn't need the Sages to tell her how valuable the prize was.

She could feel it. This was a powerful spirit-fruit of blood and life, and even her Blood Shadow stirred at its smell. The interior of their cabin was filled with the complex scent of a dozen rich, ripe fruits.

"The Heart-Piercer Fruit," Charity said, and Yerin imagined that was what the characters written in gold on the platter said. "It comes from one tree that blooms once a year in a single garden in Ninecloud City. This is the last elixir for life or blood essence you will ever need."

The Winter Sage knelt to admire it, as the platter hovered over the floor. "With just this fruit, you would have the lifespan of an Archlord as an Underlord. Or...you could run the Madra Engine with no harm to yourself."

Yerin had thought she couldn't be more excited about the

fruit, but her expectations shot through the roof. "My heart won't stop if I take a bite right now?"

"I might stop your heart if you don't," Min Shuei said.

Yerin devoured it. Its flavor seemed to change from one fruit to another every second, but she didn't take the time to savor it; she wanted its power.

She could feel the essence flooding her, filling her body, but it would take a while to process it all. Maybe weeks.

"It's going to be a wait and a half before it soaks in," Yerin warned.

The two Sages exchanged glances.

"That is one issue facing us," Charity said. "We need you to advance to face Sophara, but we risk destabilizing your spirit by pushing so fast. And you need time to adjust to these gifts, which will put an additional burden on your soul."

"How much time do we need?" Yerin asked.

"By traditional wisdom, even a year is too fast to guarantee your safety and your future advancement. In terms of maturing your power and skill, it would be better to take ten years. Even if we accept a critical instability that will harm your future advancement, then we still need at least a month."

The last gift began to flash and pulse with madra.

Yerin had left it for last because it was the least exciting to look at. It came from Northstrider, and was just a plain ceramic tile with a script on it. It looked like he had pulled it off a roof.

A three-inch projection of Northstrider appeared above the tile. "Use this device as a key to open a separated space."

The Winter Sage reached for the tile, but Charity snatched it up first. "Why don't I handle this, Min Shuei?"

"You think I can't do something so simple?"

Charity stood straight and focused on the empty air in front of her.

"Don't ignore me!"

"Open," Charity said.

A swirling green light appeared in the center of the

room, widening into an emerald plane roughly the size of a doorway.

"There is no gift I can offer you more valuable than time," Northstrider said, and Yerin wondered if this was a recorded message or if he was communicating to them directly.

Either way, it had incredibly good timing.

"The temporary pocket world before you has been untethered from the normal flow of time. It can support three to five people for one day, after which you will be ejected."

Yerin was about to ask what good that was, but the tiny image of Northstrider looked to her as though he could read her mind. "In that time, thirty-six days will pass inside."

The Winter Sage, who had been reaching for the portal, jerked her hand back. "You can't be serious."

Charity dipped her head to Northstrider. "On behalf of my family and my grandmother, I thank you."

"I cannot demonstrate any less than total commitment when my own life is on the line," Northstrider said. "The decay of the world will begin when you enter, and I have prepared a full training course for her within. With two Sages to guide her, she will be as prepared as possible."

He turned back to Yerin. "Work hard. Do not let us down."

Then he vanished.

At least that answered the question of whether it was a recording.

Yerin looked at the portal. "Well, that's an easy fix." At least there was a training course inside; she was looking forward to whatever the Monarch had left for her.

"I'm concerned you don't appreciate how rare this opportunity is," Charity said. "There is nothing more valuable than time. He no doubt intended to use this himself."

The Winter Sage visibly steeled herself. "We *must* be fully prepared before we enter. Which means we need the last prize."

Yerin had wondered about that. There were supposed to be seven prizes, but they'd only opened six. The one from Reigan Shen was missing.

Charity waved the tile and the portal closed. "We can't allow him to see this. Send up the signal."

The Winter Sage removed the veil around her spirit, and the temperature in the room dropped dramatically. She kept her power in check before ice began to form, but Yerin noticed icicles growing quickly outside the windows.

Only seconds later, a powerful presence landed outside with a thump. Snow blew away, and Yerin sensed the disgusting power that she associated with her Blood Shadow.

The Sage of Red Faith didn't knock. He pushed the door in, snapping the lock and causing a script-circle to fuzz out.

His feet were still bare, but he had drawn himself up to his full height, so that now he looked like a lanky skeleton with skin stretched over his bones. His white hair hung down to the backs of his knees, and he looked straight to Yerin. The red tracks down his face made him look like he had been weeping blood.

Yerin had to suppress anger and disgust every time she saw him. This was not only someone who reveled in the power of his Blood Shadow, but someone who encouraged others to do so. A ghoul who fed on carnage.

"It is my right to deliver this prize in person, as it was I who provided it in the name of the Monarch who sponsored me," Red Faith began. He had started lecturing the second the door opened, and he hadn't once glanced at either of the other two Sages in the room.

"You have enough wisdom to use my techniques, but not to seek my guidance. If I cannot force a fool to drink from the deep well of my insight, perhaps I can entice her."

He was calling her a fool right to her face, and he expected her to be grateful for it? She hoped the prize was trash so she could throw it back at him.

The other two Sages looked no happier. Charity had raised one eyebrow, and Min Shuei had a hand on her sword and her madra was cycling faster and faster.

Without a glance to them, Red Faith reached into a small hole in space and pulled a container from his void key. It was a glass cylinder large enough to contain a small dog, and it was covered in sealing scripts. At the center of the mostly empty cylinder floated a single drop of blood.

But it *gushed* blood aura. The building filled with it, so that the sensation of blood outweighed even the power from the Winter Sage's spirit.

"This is a Heart's Gem," the Blood Sage said, "the ultimate source of blood aura. As Heaven's Torch is the pinnacle of fire aura and Titan's Bone is of earth, this is the greatest natural treasure of its type in the world. Furthermore, it is condensed from the blood of the Redmoon Herald, who was once my own Blood Shadow."

Yerin's Shadow stirred at the feeling of the aura in the air, and it began pulling power to itself without Yerin's intervention.

She let it happen. Even Yerin knew the value of this gift, and she was surprised to see it come from Reigan Shen. Or from Yan Shoumei's master.

"You're giving this to me out of the sweetness in your soul, then," Yerin said dryly. "So I can use it to beat your apprentice like a rented drum."

Red Faith loomed over her so suddenly that her hand shot to her sword.

Another white blade was already pointed at his neck, and dream aura danced around his head, but he hadn't even touched his madra. He leaned down close to her, eyes wide.

"What is this tournament? What are the lives and deaths of Monarchs? In my youth, I devised a method to fuse with my Blood Shadow instead of my own Remnant to grant me the power of a Herald. When I became a Sage, as I knew I would, I could then ascend to Monarch as easily as slipping on a new robe."

His face contorted like it was being pulled in three different directions. "But the *treachery* and *selfishness* of my Shadow knew no bounds. It fled from me until it had become a Herald in its own right, so we could no longer become one.

"Hear me, girl: feed your Shadow, but do not trust it. Use

this aura for its nourishment that it may become a potent weapon, but your will must remain dominant. And *do not* fuse with it until you become a Sage. Your will is not developed enough, so the blending will result in an imperfect fusion when your Shadow fights you."

He stuck a finger in her face, and this time Yerin couldn't resist. She shoved it away from herself.

Not that it stopped him from speaking. "No one else other than myself has reached your stage. They were devoured by their Shadows because their wills were weak, or they lacked the insight to become a Sage, or they fell in battle, or they succumbed to their own lack of discipline or talent. It is your *duty* to complete this process. Prove to the world that it can be done, and usher in a new generation of Monarchs born from the Bleeding Phoenix."

A crazed fervor had grown in his eyes, and Yerin had finally had enough.

She snatched the cylinder from his hands. "Your duty can go die and rot. The first chance I get to send my Shadow out on its own, I'm jumping right on it."

"No..." the Blood Sage whispered, "...you won't. The lure of power is too much for you, as it is for all of great ambition. You will soon manifest the Sword Icon, perhaps before Archlord, and you will know that your genius has given you a unique opportunity. You have a path to Monarch that none others have achieved, and you will give in to—"

"Do people dress up like you to scare children?" Yerin interrupted.

His face twitched.

"You look like you sleep under someone else's bed. Do mirrors break when you walk by? I figured why your Shadow left: it couldn't stand looking at its own face every day."

She lifted up the cylinder. "Thanks for the jar. Now take a step back, then keep doing that until you freeze to death in the snow. Or else have mercy and cut my ears off so I don't have to listen to you talk."

Yerin knew it was dangerous to provoke a Sage, but she had two of her own for protection.

And she hadn't been able to stop herself. Every word from his mouth made her sick.

The Winter Sage shoved him back from Yerin with a smug look. "You heard her. You've delivered the prize, now get out of my home."

He didn't look as furious as Yerin had thought he would. He didn't try to strike her down or swear revenge. His face rippled again, like a puppeteer was pulling at his cheeks and couldn't figure out how to make a human expression, and Yerin sensed nothing in his spirit but dead calm.

Then he turned and walked out the door. A moment later, he vanished.

"That was unwise," Charity said, picking up her cup of tea and taking a sip. "And not nearly as harsh as he deserved. Before we begin your training, let me help you work on some better insults for next time."

第十九章
CHAPTER NINETEEN

Sophara held a ball of Forged madra in her palm. It would have been hard for an observer to notice, but the madra trembled ever so slightly.

Now that she had reached Overlord, her spiritual imbalance was becoming more obvious by the day.

It wouldn't slow her in combat, but she could tell. Souls didn't age quite like bodies did, but her channels were starting to feel...worn. Old. As the Symbiote Veins wrung them out, they could only take so much more abuse.

She would last through the end of the tournament, but then she would begin falling apart. After that, she might only live...ten more years? It was hard to say.

She ran a hand over Ekeri's Remnant to drive off her fear, as the glowing dragon-spirit nuzzled her side. This tournament was all she needed.

If she won, the Monarchs could fix her spirit.

And *by* winning, she would be humiliating her enemies. Those who sought to humiliate her.

As her rage burned, she looked over her prizes.

Reigan Shen had given her a doll, seemingly made of clay, that made it easier to shift forms. It resembled a dragon when she was in human form and a human when she wore her dragon body. He appreciated how difficult it was to shift as an Overlord, and he knew that she had already received all the combat gifts she could handle. It was her favorite prize.

The Arelius family, poor and hostile to her cause as they were, had admittedly given her a pleasant gift as well. The Dawn Sky Palace was a tiny pocket world—smaller than some void keys—containing only an opulent home. It had once belonged to Tiberian Arelius' wife, and it was gorgeous.

She lounged in it now, and they had even redecorated for her, lining all the furniture in gold and planting trees that shone with a golden light. She would have to think of a gift to send them as thanks.

The Eight-Man Empire had given her a Tear of the Deep, the highest grade natural treasure that produced water aura, though it would be useless to her without the fire equivalent. Her Monarch should be able to track down a Heaven's Torch, so that was useful enough.

It was the gifts from her two enemies that grated on her.

Northstrider had given her a thumb-sized bottle containing a drop of luminous white liquid, and she had been shocked when she opened it. He must have sensed her mind-enhancing elixir and sent her another dose.

Then she'd read the note accompanying it. *"This is called ghostwater. It is the prize your sister failed to win."*

If it hadn't been such a powerful weapon, she would have shattered the bottle against the wall.

Not only was he mocking her, but the mental elixir she had relied on to make it so far had been a product of Northstrider's.

If she had known that this "ghostwater" came from Northstrider, she would never have taken it.

Her King would say that pleasure could be found in taking the enemy's weapon and turning it against him, but she could only see the shame that she'd needed help from their great enemy to succeed.

Of course, that was nothing next to the Akura clan's gift.

It was a life-size statue of Ekeri made of goldsteel, crafted by the Heart Sage herself.

Sophara tore it apart with her bare hands.

About a week since the dragons had come to pen them inside their own fortress, Seishen Daji lost his patience.

The dragons and cultists outnumbered them at least four to one, and with Fury in the fortress they couldn't attack. According to the reports, they hadn't even attacked the shelters containing the evacuated civilians, which Daji thought was too good to be true.

Dragons had no compassion. Neither did Dreadgods or those who worshiped them. If they were sparing the evacuees now, it was for something worse later.

When they couldn't attack the fortress, they had resorted to taunts. Volleys of insults peppered the fortress at all hours, along with bright lights and loud noises to stop them from sleeping. Corpses of dreadbeasts or of their own dead were hurled over their walls to be incinerated by defensive constructs, leaving a stench that hung in the air everywhere.

They had lost relatively few lives—only a dozen or two between all the Akura loyal factions, hardly worth mentioning—but being sealed up in the fortress had chafed Daji raw. He was restless, and he was sick of being disrespected.

Only a day or two ago, the enemy had started a new tactic: trying to lure them out.

They would slam a valuable weapon onto a hill visible from the fortress walls and dare the Akura sacred artists to come take it. Or they would send out a duelist who would swear to veil himself, or wear a blindfold, or tie one hand behind his back.

No one ever took them up on the offer. Not even when a Highgold Abyssal Palace acolyte challenged any Underlord. Daji himself had picked up his swords and started to leap out, but his father had grabbed him from the air.

What kind of fish knowingly bit a hook?

Daji knew what was wise, but he hated how often what was *wise* and what was *cowardly* looked like the same thing.

Meira reacted to the siege the same way she'd reacted to anything since Kiro's death: quietly. She trained every day, performed tasks as assigned, and tended to a garden that she'd started inside the grounds.

His father had wanted to execute her, when he learned of Kiro's death. He'd held a blade against her neck.

She hadn't even tried to resist.

That had won Dakata's pity. And Daji understood.

Even when he saw her out there by herself, the glowing flower in her hair blending with those she'd planted, she didn't look happy. She looked like she'd given up.

He avoided her as much as possible. His own grief was hot and angry.

The Blackflame Empire had humiliated Kiro before they'd killed him. They had embarrassed him and Meira just as much...and then shamed him *again* only weeks ago.

It had done nothing but stoke his hatred hotter. He had seen the reports from the Uncrowned King tournament, but that opportunity should have been his. Or at least Meira's.

Knowing that Akura Mercy and Lindon Arelius were in this fortress with him made the days of suffering unbearable. He'd even seen Mercy, who had the *audacity* to smile and wave at him when she saw him, but he hadn't sensed the Blackflame.

Still, he had to get out. He would do anything to escape.

That was when he overheard the newest scout report: Abyssal Palace had grown complacent and had placed one of their pointless collection towers just out of sight of the fortress. Fury was looking for a team of volunteer Underlords to wipe it out and return, and had placed a bounty of contribution points.

Points were scarce since the battle had died down, and Daji leaped at the chance to persuade his father.

It was the lowest risk possible, being close enough that King Dakata could rescue them if something went wrong.

And it would give Daji a chance to *do* something.

Daji intended to take the assignment whether his father approved or not, but the king needed little persuading. He wanted to demonstrate the value of the Seishen Kingdom to Fury, and contribution points were valuable to anyone.

So Daji chose his team. Meira came with him almost by default, and he picked the other four youngest Underlords he could find. He wasn't eager to split the prize six ways, but he also wasn't an idiot. He knew he couldn't do this on his own.

As soon as night fell, he and his team snuck out.

The outer wall had been designed with several hidden entrances, so they essentially melted the wall and passed through it before it re-formed. He also carried a construct designed by the Seishen Kingdom Soulsmiths to hide them from observers in the air; it bent the light around them and assisted their spiritual veils, so they would be all but invisible unless someone scanned them directly.

Creeping over the hill in the dead of night went without a hitch. The squat tower, made of packed earth pulled up from the ground with a Ruler technique and scripted in haste, stood there as though to mock them.

The script around the top of the tower prevented his perception from entering, but their scouts had reported no more than two Underlords and a handful of Golds. They could destroy it from here, if the scripts didn't stop them.

But the towers were made to take a beating, so the easiest way to destroy them was from the inside. They would go in, kill the inhabitants, take their masks, and then blow up the tower. Simple, easy, effective.

Although it concerned Daji that there didn't seem to be any guards or lookouts posted around the outside. Their reports were clear that six people had gone into the tower, and there was no other exit. Were they all just huddled up inside?

That ceased to matter when a line of script lit up beneath Daji's feet.

He shouted a warning and drew his swords, but he needn't have bothered. It was an alarm.

Nearby, a flock of dragons unveiled themselves and swooped closer. Underlords.

"Retreat!" Meira shouted, but he cut her off.

"Not yet!" There were four Lords with the dragons and two more in the tower. If they could deal with the group in the tower first, then they could accomplish the mission and still avoid fighting an equal group. The dragons would have to wait for backup, and by then Daji and the others could be back to the fortress.

He dashed for the tower as soon as the thought occurred to him, swords drawn. The others would have to follow him. They couldn't abandon their prince.

This plan required them to obliterate the two Lords inside the tower as soon as possible, so he began rousing the bindings in his swords. Lightning, light, and force crackled down the weapons.

He'd had them made with the same blueprints as his first pair, which had been stolen. By the Blackflame.

He was about to blast through the door when it opened, and he was so astonished at the face on the other side that he came to a stop.

Lindon Arelius filled the doorway, shuffling half a dozen Abyssal Palace masks in his hands. He tossed them into a closet-sized opening to his right, through which Daji caught a glimpse of metal and glowing dead matter. Pieces of his own armor.

His spiritual sense couldn't pass into the tower, but he saw bodies piled behind Lindon, and the interior of the room was scorched. He couldn't tell if they were dead or alive.

Daji remembered the ease with which Lindon had dispatched him before, and glee rose up as he realized that this time he had the advantage. And he had five allies backing him up, while Lindon was alone.

Seishen Daji launched the two Striker attacks with all the force of his spirit, blasting two streams of bright, crackling madra as though he meant to blow up the entire tower.

At the same time, a great force slammed into the back of his head.

He landed face-first in the ground. There was heat nearby, like someone had lit a fire, and panic seized him.

How had Lindon hit him in the *back?*

He scrambled to his feet, preparing a defensive technique, only to see Meira—in full armor—pressing her fists together before Lindon.

Meira. *Meira* had hit him.

He ignited his swords, ready in his fury to turn them on her...and then he saw the deep groove burned into the ground in front of him. A bar of black dragon's breath had passed inches in front of his face.

"I apologize," Meira said quietly. "Please let him go."

Lindon watched them both for a second or two. "I expected you to be the one coming for my head."

Daji couldn't see her expression, but she dipped her head deeper. "We are not all idiots blinded by revenge."

Daji bristled at that, but then Lindon stepped from the doorway. Blackflame raged through him, and the spiritual pressure stopped Daji in his tracks.

When he'd tried to ambush Lindon before, he had sensed only his pure madra. His black dragon madra was far, far more frightening.

It felt like a flame with an endless hunger that would burn without stopping.

Daji's fear was like a bucket of cold water over his anger, and Lindon wasn't even looking at him.

"Gratitude," the Blackflame said to Meira. "Please keep him restrained. If he attacks me again, I will have no choice."

"I'll keep him on a tight leash," Meira promised, and under other circumstances Daji would have resented that.

"If you would allow us to deal with our pursuers, we will leave you alone," Meira continued. "We have dragons coming in."

"Not anymore," Lindon said. He had already begun hiking back up the hill.

Sure enough, the sensation of the dragons was growing more distant in Daji's perception. He didn't understand it. Other enemies had unveiled themselves nearby, even Overlords, but none approached.

Lindon spoke over his shoulder. "Those dragons were in the tournament."

Then he waved behind him, and Daji realized for the first time that a vortex of fire and destruction madra had gathered over the tower. He hadn't sensed it before because it was still within the effect of the sense-dampening script, but he also hadn't seen it as they approached. Lindon had begun the Ruler technique while speaking with them.

A column of dark, spinning fire consumed the tower.

When it dissipated, Daji saw that only the walls had been destroyed by the Ruler technique. The interior of the tower was intact, including the pile of enemies. He'd left their bodies in one piece.

Daji ran his perception over them and realized they were all still alive...but barely. He didn't even know if you could call that living. They felt like husks.

Lindon hopped onto a green Thousand-Mile Cloud and flew away. Daji started to follow, but Meira held out a hand.

"He took our points," Daji muttered, but only once Lindon was out of earshot. "And he made some deal with the dragons so they wouldn't attack him."

Meira pulled off her helmet specifically so she could glare at him with withering fury. "How did you survive to Underlord? How do you survive getting out of bed every morning? If you were the *smallest fraction* of the man your brother was, your father wouldn't have to cry himself to sleep every night."

Her anger built with every word, and Daji's pain gave birth to a sudden ugly rage. He swung his sword, striking blindly. There was no plan behind it, and no Enforcement, just anger.

The end of her scythe was unlit, making it a staff, and she swept his feet out from under him before he could react. He caught himself on his palms, flipping in the air and beginning to cycle his madra.

He was in the right. Meira was a coward. She had given up on avenging Kiro, but he hadn't. He was strong.

"Someone carry him back," Meira ordered, and then her staff clipped him on the chin.

It wasn't the first hit that did it, but somewhere in the ensuing rain of blows, he lost consciousness.

Mirror images of Yerin surrounded her, each showing different perspectives of her taken from her own memories.

She saw herself across the table from Lindon at the Sundown Pavilion, and her face looked unfamiliar to her as she was animated and laughing.

She watched as she knelt in the snow as a girl, shivering and covered in cuts, wanting to give up but terrified that if she did so she would be left alone again.

Yerin saw her own look of serenity from the outside as she opened her eyes facing Calan Archer, calmly crushing all his techniques at once.

She focused on her own connection to the aura around her. *I am the next Sage of the Endless Sword,* she said in her mind.

The aura remained calm.

I am the champion of the Uncrowned King tournament.

No change.

I am about to gouge out my own eyes.

That one produced a change, but not in the aura. It finally made her frustrated enough to stand up, breaking the boundary field in which Charity had trapped her.

Northstrider's pocket world looked like Ghostwater in miniature. She knelt on the sand surrounded by stalks of drifting seaweed as high as trees, and they were covered by a dome of aura that held back an ocean's worth of water.

But Lindon had described the water around him as utterly dark and swimming with creatures, while this was bright blue and clear. There were no monsters here that Yerin had found.

The entire space was only as big as what Yerin would call a large house. It was divided roughly into quarters: the sandy area where she was now, a forest of blades that was thick with sword aura, a cave containing two wells of glowing water, and a fenced-off living area.

She walked away from the boundary field Charity had set up, heading over to the cave.

Lindon had mentioned three wells, but there was no life well here. Not that she needed one anyway; since she'd eaten the Heart-Piercer Fruit, her lifeline had become thicker by the day.

Having almost died of a severed lifeline once before, she felt that as a breath of fresh air.

She dipped a bowl into one sink-sized well, the one that shone purple. This water refreshed her like a night's sleep, sharpening her focus.

She didn't need it so much since she'd absorbed the thought construct from the Eight-Man Empire, and as an Underlady she could go without sleep longer than before, so as a result she'd slept an average of maybe one hour a day since she'd gotten here.

Charity insisted she sleep a *little*. Apparently, no matter how effective an elixir was, there was no total substitute for true rest.

When she felt awake again, she dipped into the blue well. Her veins were cleansed, her core replenished, her spirit refreshed...

But she still wasn't quite at the peak of Underlord.

Even so, Charity and Min Shuei had both directed her to spend an hour or two a day hunting down her Overlord revelation. Any insight she could glean would make it easier once she really needed it.

She finished off the bowl of spirit well water while ignoring the battle thundering behind her.

The Winter Sage was using no techniques, only raw strength and sword skill, and the Blood Shadow was under the same restrictions.

So naturally, the Shadow was getting battered all the way around the sword training area. It was impaled on a thicket of sharp blades, screaming in pain as the Winter Sage danced past and lopped off its hand.

"Wrong!" the Sage shouted, grabbing Yerin's Shadow with one hand and tossing it to the ground so hard that it sounded like thunder. "You have no grace! No thought!"

The spirit panted and shoved its severed hand back onto its stump. It looked so human now; its red hair was matted with sweat and stuck to the back of its neck, and it glared at the Winter Sage in furious frustration.

The Shadow snatched up its black blade and attacked, but the Winter Sage slapped the attack away contemptuously and then clubbed the spirit on the head.

"Mindless beast!" She slapped it with the flat of the sword. "Clumsy ape!"

Yerin retrieved a round circle of bread and began piling grilled meat and vegetables on top. She needed a snack to go with the show.

Charity was making notes nearby, and after a moment she folded them up to join Yerin. Every day in here, she wore an outfit like what Yerin had first seen her in: plain gray clothes and a stained artist's smock, with her hair tied up and out of her way.

"Did you feel any progress?" the Heart Sage asked.

Yerin spoke from around a mouthful of food. "Right in the middle between zero and none."

"Thinking about yourself on a deeper level always brings some benefit," Charity said. "Of those attempting to reach Overlord, most fail because they lack the talent, the foundation, or the resources. You, of course, are in none of those categories. Those who knowingly discovered their

Underlord revelation are almost always capable of discovering their Overlord insight as well."

The Winter Sage kicked the Blood Shadow away, and a red blur crashed into the sandy beach. "As I said, this thing has no sword authority at all. You will *never* touch the Sword Icon with it inside you."

"That seems hasty," Charity observed. "It's rare to have any stable connection to the Sword Icon before Archlord."

Min Shuei slammed her sword back into its sheath. "I'm taking a break," she announced, stalking off and leaving the Blood Shadow to clean itself of sand.

"Is it really going to keep me from the Sword Icon?" Yerin asked, her voice low.

"The only thing stopping you now is that your willpower is unfocused, but your will is refined as you advance through the Lord realm. Bringing you to Overlord accomplishes both goals."

"Didn't think we'd made it that far yet," Yerin said. The Akura clan contribution to her training was an absolute trove of advancement resources; they were going to force her to advance to Overlord if they had to cram her to the gills with elixirs day and night.

But there was only so much she could process at any one time.

Charity reached into the black hole that was her void key and withdrew the blue crystal nest of tubes. The Madra Engine.

The Blood Shadow looked up sharply at the Divine Treasure's power.

"The power of the Heart-Piercer Fruit has matured inside you sufficiently," Charity said. "We need to introduce the Engine now to give your spirit time to adjust, but I must warn you again: I would ordinarily advise you to stay an Underlady for at least another year to integrate all these changes and the sudden growth to your spirit.

"Pushing you to Overlord so quickly and with so many added powers will make it more difficult to reach Archlord.

Then, even if you manage to manifest the Sword Icon, you will never become a full Sage. Unless you win, and the Monarchs reverse the injury."

Undoing the damage she was about to do to her spirit would require not only spiritual surgery, but rewriting the fundamental principles of madra at a level only several Monarchs working together could achieve.

As long as she won the tournament, it would be no problem.

Yerin could easily see a future in which she couldn't keep up with Lindon. Her fear said that he would leave her behind, even if her head knew it wasn't true. He would spend the rest of his days looking for a solution before he abandoned her.

Then there was the fear that they might go to all this trouble and expense and find out that she couldn't handle it. That they were wrong, that the Sword Sage had been wrong all those years ago. That she wasn't good enough to justify their faith.

"No point in stewing on it," Yerin said finally. "There's no backing out now."

The dice had left her hands as soon as she'd beaten Lindon in the fourth round.

Charity swept a spiritual scan through Yerin, checking her condition. "While that's true, the Madra Engine will settle faster if you are at peace with this."

"I'm more at peace than a frozen corpse."

So Charity sank the Madra Engine into Yerin's midsection.

The process didn't feel like much. The construct settled into the center of her madra channels, surrounding and containing her core. While her core was full, it wouldn't do anything.

Charity warned her to use as little madra as possible for at least a day or two, to allow the bond to settle with minimal chance of failure. So Yerin spent the rest of the day bored, cycling sword aura amid a forest of blades.

She usually spent two hours a day harvesting aura, but

that didn't mean it wasn't boring. It just meant she'd gotten used to the boredom.

She didn't know how many hours had passed when she felt a disturbance next to her. Not much, nothing so sharp as danger, but just enough of an annoyance to break her out of the cycling trance.

Finally, she looked over to see her red-haired twin in a cycling pose next to her.

That was startling enough on its own, but the Blood Shadow was also blindfolded, and balanced a dark, shimmering brick in its lap. The sword codex from Emriss Silentborn.

Yerin watched for a few minutes as the Blood Shadow cycled aura under its own power. Then it rose and—still blindfolded—pulled its black sword.

It went through the motions of several sword styles. One would be fast and aggressive, another had wide circular motions, and a third had sweeping patterns that were clearly meant to launch Striker techniques.

Each one was visibly distinct, and the Shadow executed them well. *Too* well. Maybe as cleanly as Yerin could have done herself.

"You seeing if you can beat me to Sage?" Yerin asked.

The Shadow tore off its blindfold to scowl.

"Heaven's luck to you. Maybe you can go off on your own. Then you can eat all the babies you want. Me, I'm going to win a tournament."

She closed her eyes before the Shadow could respond, reaching out for sword aura. Though she still kept her perception extended in case of an attack.

But her madra froze inside her when she heard a perfect echo of her own voice speak.

"Well," it said, "cheers and celebrations for you."

第二十章

CHAPTER TWENTY

Northstrider resented anyone summoning him.

Especially if that "someone" was a low-ranking Abidan who saw everyone still in Cradle as misguided infants.

He stepped through the Way into the audience chamber of the Ninecloud Court, where the Monarchs usually gathered. Shen was already there, for once without his golden stage or other ostentatious prop, though he still swirled wine in a jeweled goblet.

Seshethkunaaz lounged against a pillar, glaring up into the center of the room. In his arrogance, he didn't even spare Northstrider a glance.

He was confident in his own invincibility. But one way or another, he wouldn't be for long.

Northstrider turned his attention to the white-armored, rat-faced Hound looking down on them like they were all his subjects. He longed to punch this sniveling messenger out of reality, but that would only invite someone higher up on the food chain.

One day, Northstrider would join *them.* Not the low ranks of Abidan drones, but the true world-striding champions.

"What is this about?" Northstrider demanded, but Kiuran held up a finger.

"Patience. We're waiting on one more."

That tone brought Northstrider's patience one step closer to its limit, but he had assumed they were waiting on *three* more. If only one more Monarch had been summoned, then it had to be Malice.

Sure enough, the woman herself strode from the shadows a moment later. She had chosen to wear dark blue instead of the usual purple, her hair streaming behind her like cloth woven from the shadows themselves.

He sometimes wondered why the other Monarchs cared so much for their appearance. No one judged them on their dress when they could shatter fortresses with a word.

Even the dragon cared about his physical image, or he wouldn't always run around in the same form.

With Malice's arrival, Kiuran finally began to speak. "It has come to my attention that you are hedging around the borders of my instruction not to interfere with the tournament. Positioning yourselves to take advantage of the outcome, moving your pieces around the board."

Of course they had. It would have been idiotic not to, and the Abidan would certainly have seen that before he made his restrictions, especially as one of those with the power to read and direct the future.

But Northstrider didn't point out this hypocrisy, only waited.

"I've allowed it thus far because nothing has been too flagrant a violation, and because your games amuse me."

Northstrider *could* destroy this man. He could do it. He didn't know if Kiuran would stay dead, but he was willing to put that to the test.

"I'm becoming concerned that the temptation to interfere will be too great, and that you will continue to push my instructions until I am forced to punish you. Since I would rather not be so harsh, I've brought you all here to discuss a mutually beneficial arrangement."

Northstrider sensed a chance.

He had expected the Hound to impose some extra restriction, or just to toy with them for a while, and he was prepared to tolerate it.

But this could be exactly what he and Malice needed. What they had planned to instigate.

Maybe the Abidan could be useful after all.

Malice played her part perfectly, drawing herself up and turning a venomous glare on the Hound. "You forced us to obey you, and now you want to dictate our every action? Do the Abidan wish to move us like puppets?"

They couldn't, Northstrider knew. It was one of their restrictions. They were limited in their ability to interfere somehow, though he hadn't successfully determined their laws yet.

"It can be hard for some of us to keep our impulses in check," Reigan Shen said, sipping his glass of wine.

On cue, Malice widened her eyes in anger. It was nice to have an ally who could play a role well.

Kiuran scoffed. "You should take your own lesson, Shen. You're the one moving your Heralds as though the tournament is already over."

The lion tilted his glass in acknowledgment. "Very well, then, we require an equal restriction on the four of us. By mutual agreement, we can confine ourselves and our powers to this city. Unable to act until the conclusion of the tournament, when we will free each other together."

A smile played on the dragon's childish face, and his eyes shone as he looked to his enemies.

They couldn't have played into Northstrider's hand more perfectly if they had tried.

"No," he said, because that was what was expected of him. In a head-to-head confrontation, the dragon could defeat either of them, while the cat had a thousand weapons and could escape any trap. If it came to a fight between the four of them, Northstrider and Malice were clearly the weaker side.

So it was natural that he would resist.

Malice played along. "You want me to leave my children surrounded by enemies while I lock myself away?"

Reigan Shen turned to Seshethkunaaz. "I believe we can arrange an agreement between our Heralds, can't we? No aggressive action until the conclusion of the tournament."

"That sounds civilized," the dragon agreed. "I can't imagine the humans having any further objections."

"Good enough," the Abidan said impatiently. "Do it now."

Northstrider and Malice both objected again, putting up a token resistance, but with the Abidan in support the issue was closed.

Together, they contacted their Heralds and Sages, limiting their actions until the conclusion of the tournament.

With that settled, they needed the permission of the Ninecloud Monarch to seal themselves in the city, which they received in a matter of seconds. Sha Miara was delighted by their arrangement.

As well she might be. Four of her rivals were locking themselves away from the world for another week.

Finally, the four of them bound their wills together to one purpose.

There was little they could not accomplish with such unity, and the restriction settled in an invisible column surrounding Ninecloud City. The barrier was perceptible only to the four of them and affected them only, but now it was literally impossible for them to touch anyone outside without first removing the restriction.

It was perfect. Northstrider had already done all the work he needed in the world at large, and now his plans were falling into place.

Though he was certain the other Monarchs were all thinking the same thing.

"So go get them," Yerin demanded.

"I *can't*," Charity insisted. "Do you understand? I am not capable. If I could go snatch my family from under the noses of hostile Heralds, I would be on my way right now. A Herald may not be able to travel through space directly, but they can stop *me* from doing so, so if I showed my face I would be trapped."

It was the most agitated Yerin had ever seen the Sage, but that was tough for Charity, because Yerin had plenty of her own agitation to work through.

Charity had received a message from her mother only the day before, when Northstrider's training world had finally collapsed, but it had been sent two days prior. Malice said that Fury and the others were now pinned in Sky's Edge by the gold dragons and all the Dreadgod cults and that she couldn't help because she had somehow agreed to nail herself in place.

Yerin must be a long way from understanding the ways of Monarchs, because that sounded like sheer idiocy.

But the rescue Charity described didn't sound impossible, it sounded very difficult. Which meant they were leaving Lindon, Mercy, and Eithan in a dangerous situation that *could technically* be solved.

"There's two of you," Yerin pointed out. "How many does it take?"

Charity was really wrestling to keep up that icy mask of hers. "How can I make you understand that *you* are not the only one with loved ones in danger?"

"Difference is, you can do something about it."

The only reason the enemy Heralds hadn't attacked Fury already was the threat of Penance. Meaning that if Yerin left, she'd be signing over her friends' lives.

If she left...or if she lost.

For once, Min Shuei was the one to play peacemaker. "We all know that Malice wouldn't have allowed this situation if Fury didn't have a way out. She didn't tell you to go save him, did she? No. So we have a very simple situation."

She clapped her hands together. "Yerin, you just have to win two fights."

That didn't calm Yerin down. Even her Blood Shadow was boiling.

The Sage noticed. "You want to go save them? Perfect! That's what you're doing by fighting Yan Shoumei."

The statement didn't instantly solve all of Yerin's worries, but it *was* true. How often in her life had she wished she could fight her way out of a situation?

Tomorrow, she could.

She dipped her head to Min Shuei, but turned to Charity. The Heart Sage was taking deep breaths, visibly trying to master herself.

She needed something to do just like Yerin did.

"Run me through a course," Yerin demanded.

There was little chance of making any kind of break-through overnight, but a small chance was better than none, and it wasn't as though either of them would be resting.

Charity silently agreed, leading the way to the training facilities inside the Akura guest tower.

The Winter Sage beamed.

Yan Shoumei noticed that they had started putting her in a sealed-off arena for every one of her fights.

She couldn't blame them. Crusher demonstrated power beyond what any Underlord Blood Shadow should be capable of.

The arena this time was like a huge cave with thickets of blood solidified into razor-sharp blades. Sword and blood aura were thicker than air here, which meant there would be no escaping from Yerin's Endless Sword.

Shoumei had a plan for that.

As usual, Northstrider stood in the center of the arena with an invisible wall dividing the space in half. With his shaggy hair and rugged, unshaven look, Shoumei had always thought he was the most handsome Monarch she'd had the privilege of seeing.

Not that she would ever say so out loud. He might hear it.

Powerful golden eyes fixed her. "Are you prepared?"

She nodded once, feeling Crusher's eagerness for battle. He was ready to be unleashed.

Northstrider looked to Yerin, who looked like she hadn't gotten a wink of sleep in days. She paced nervously, her hand clenching and unclenching, her hair was disheveled, and there were bags under her eyes. Even her black sacred arts robes were in disarray.

Yerin had obviously never put much stock in her appearance, but this still struck Shoumei as strange. Had she been fighting already? Had someone threatened her?

Shoumei focused. Every win for her was safety, prosperity, and a bright future for her family.

And while Yerin could beat Shoumei in any one-on-one contest, this was two against two.

Yerin's Blood Shadow flowed out of her, carrying a black sword from Yerin's soulspace, and the spirit's state of existence had clearly improved. It barely had a pink tinge to its skin now, its crimson hair and eyes being the biggest difference from Yerin herself.

The Shadow looked just as unruly as Yerin did, prowling and snarling like a caged beast. Something had Yerin's soul in disarray.

When her Blood Shadow was summoned, Yerin nodded.

Northstrider told them to begin.

As the command still hung in the air, Yan Shoumei unleashed Crusher.

There were three methods for cultivating a Blood Shadow...although since the clone technique always failed, there were really only two. The most common was raising the Shadow as a weapon, a shifting tool, and it was this method that Yan Shoumei had used through Truegold.

But when she'd been given the opportunity to enter the Ghostwater facility, as part of preparing her for this tournament, the Sage of Red Faith gave her special instructions.

In his pocket world, Northstrider kept samples of rare and powerful sacred beasts. Some were the only individuals remaining of their kind, while others were unique in their own right.

When she retrieved blood samples from those ancient and powerful creatures, the Blood Sage showed her how to integrate them into her Shadow, creating a spirit whose power dwarfed her own.

She called him Crusher.

A monstrously muscled humanoid body formed from the blood madra she usually wore as a cloak. The Shadow inherited its body from a Deepwalker Ape that had mutated its spirit to focus entirely on physical strength.

Crusher's fur was thick and shaggy, taken from the blood of a bear dreadbeast that had inherited power from the Wandering Titan itself.

The spines that rose from his back and the claws on his long fingers came from the diamond dragon, who had been the only member of its species.

The wolf's muzzle and tall, rabbit-like ears must come from the other, more common blood samples that were mixed into the spirit for balance and tempering.

Crusher's final, hulking form stood more than twice Shoumei's height, and its strength...

As sacred artists advanced, the line between sacred artist and sacred beast became more difficult to distinguish. While humans and beasts advanced differently, there were fewer and fewer differences at each stage until the differences disappeared at the peak of Archlord. Everyone reached Sage or Herald the same way.

But as a result, it could be hard to pinpoint a sacred beast's exact strength relative to a sacred artist. You had to measure the relative weight of the madra you felt.

Crusher did not feel like an Underlord. She didn't know

how to describe his power, but he gave off the spiritual impression of overwhelming, impossible physical power.

The moment Crusher manifested, he roared.

The ground shook. The aura quivered. The light in the cave-like arena trembled.

Yerin and her Blood Shadow, both of whom had rushed forward immediately, staggered as blood aura caused the roar to affect their bodies directly. Blood streamed from Yerin's ears—madra usually preserved a sacred artist's hearing during combat, but the roar was too powerful. Yerin should have focused her spirit to protect her ears. Now it was too late.

Crusher appeared next to her.

He didn't have a spatial artifact...or any sacred arts at all, really. He *did* have incredible leg strength and dexterity.

Yerin managed to spin and get her feet beneath her, raising her sword to block. The blade began to glow with an Enforcer technique.

Crusher slapped her.

Yerin caught the blow with both hands on her sword.

And *stopped* it.

Shoumei's shock froze her thoughts. Crusher's strength was so great that it worked on a conceptual level, according to the Blood Sage. It could bend the rules of the physical world with its strength, as Heralds or Monarchs could.

Crusher couldn't do so to such a degree, of course, but no one below Herald should be able to stop his attacks. *No one.*

The ground shattered beneath Yerin's feet, and if ordinary laws still held sway, she would have been sent flying into the distance by the difference in their weight alone. But there was the clearly impossible scene of Yerin taking a blow the size of her entire body and not budging.

Until a moment later, when Crusher put more power into his hand.

Then he hurled her entire body across the arena, and Shoumei could breathe again.

A rippling crescent of sword and blood madra came at her like a wave, and she Forged a Red Crystal to protect herself.

Shoumei didn't practice a Path, exactly, but a collection of blood techniques intended to synergize well with a Shadow. This one created a multifaceted diamond of red madra around her, protecting her as Crusher did the fighting.

The Striker technique from Yerin's Blood Shadow hit the Crystal, shattered it, and crashed into Shoumei's unguarded body.

If she had met Yerin in an earlier round, this might have been the end. But she had made it to the top four, so she had earned her own gifts.

The technique hit Yan Shoumei and launched her backwards without penetrating her skin. It stung, but not a drop of blood was drawn.

The Silverscale Iron body was common for fishermen. Many sea creatures developed madra attacks when they grew old enough, so fishermen needed to be able to endure those techniques with their bodies. It fortified her spirit's natural control inside her own body, creating resistance to spiritual attacks.

But even that wouldn't have been enough against a Striker technique from Yerin, so the Dragon King had chosen his prize for Yan Shoumei carefully. He left her the Ancient Scale, a Divine Treasure that added further protection.

Together, that combination meant that she could wade through Striker techniques from a crowd of Underlords without a scratch, and as she advanced, it would show even more dramatic effects.

Her enemies would have to use Ruler techniques against her, or they would have to get in close.

Which was where Crusher came in.

Yerin's copy didn't hesitate as Yan Shoumei weathered its technique. It had already covered the gap between them, sword aura gathering around its blade as it prepared the Endless Sword.

Crusher leaped on the Shadow.

Yerin's Shadow twisted and swung its blade with both hands, slamming against the monster's plunging body. The air twisted with an explosive crack, wind blasting away from the blow, and Crusher was sent flying.

But the other Blood Shadow's head exploded too. Crusher had managed to release a kick as he was knocked away, and it popped the Shadow's skull like a grape.

Its body collapsed as blood madra sprayed all over the arena. The Shadow's head began to writhe and re-form immediately, but Yan Shoumei stood over it.

A rain of bloody needles fell from her hand, shredding Yerin's clone.

As she stood there and waited for Yerin's Blood Shadow to lose its form completely, she casually turned to regard the blinding silver light gathering in one corner of the arena.

Yerin was gathering up madra and aura into her sword, growing in power and density as it threw off waves of silver-white energy. The technique was radiant to Shoumei's eyes, and her spiritual sense cried a warning.

Shoumei didn't move.

Crusher charged into Yerin like a bull. She released her technique into him from close range, a deadly sword of madra that lanced all the way across the arena, carving up the ground and shattering the red blades that filled the battleground. The point of the technique shattered a crater in the wall, revealing the humming purple wall of the barrier beyond.

Half of Crusher's ribs had been carved out by the Forger technique, but he had accepted that hit.

His claws raked at Yerin.

Her sword chimed, and invisible sword aura deflected Crusher's claws. Shoumei was surprised that Yerin was able to use another technique so quickly after such a massive blast, but mild surprise was all it was.

While his slash was deflected, Crusher punched Yerin with the other hand.

This time, Yerin went flying.

Crusher was on her in an instant, and while she struggled for another few seconds, Yan Shoumei returned her attention to the Blood Shadow at her feet.

The body no longer resembled Yerin, but rather a mass of wriggling madra. As Shoumei continued pouring needles from her hand, the Blood Shadow could finally hold on no longer. It flowed back in Yerin's direction.

Until the arena rang with another blow from Crusher, and the Ninecloud Soul's voice echoed through their cave: "Victory! Yan Shoumei, chosen of Reigan Shen, has defeated Yerin Arelius!"

Shoumei waited to be transported away.

She had won easily, but that was how she always won these days. If she was ever forced to really exert herself, that would mean Crusher had been defeated.

Most importantly, she had won without revealing the Archlord weapon in her soulspace. After she'd been forced to reveal Crusher to get into the Uncrowned, that weapon was now her one remaining hidden card.

In the finals, it would give Sophara a surprise.

Back in the waiting room, Yerin's Blood Shadow shouted at her.

"*That's* the power we could have, that's the power we *should* have, if your spine didn't shake when you looked at me!" The Shadow's voice grew more hoarse and harsh by the word.

"Then stay on your *leash*," Yerin spat. "*Her* dog doesn't bite back."

Yerin's anger was more than a match for the Shadow's, because hers was born from the fear that filled every inch of her spirit. One more loss. That was what stood between her and the death of everyone she cared about. One more mistake.

They had prepared against Yan Shoumei, based on the records of the previous rounds, but information on her

Blood Shadow was sketchy at best. They had trained against Shoumei's techniques, taken her Iron body into account, and speculated on the sorts of prizes she might have gotten in the last round.

Those prizes would be publicly announced...eventually. After the round was over.

Something to strengthen Shoumei's Iron body wasn't out of their expectations, but Crusher's power was *wildly* beyond their highest estimates.

Then again, they knew almost nothing about Shoumei's Blood Shadow. They had only discovered its name thanks to Charity's investigation.

The Winter Sage had trained against Yerin and her Blood Shadow, adjusting her strength to the greatest level they estimated Shoumei's Shadow could reach. By pouring madra into her Steelborn Iron body, Yerin could keep up.

Then, in the actual battle, she had only blocked one attack with the full strength she could muster. Just one.

Yerin had no idea how Shoumei was keeping such a beast from hollowing her out, but she had to assume the Blood Sage was involved.

Charity cut off their argument by speaking from the shadows of the waiting room. "We don't have time for unproductive discussions. You will coordinate to kill Yan Shoumei before her Shadow kills you both, or you will lose."

Killing Yan Shoumei quickly was easier said than done. All her techniques and abilities were designed to make that impossible.

And even with everything at stake, Yerin still couldn't bring herself to back down before her Blood Shadow. She glared into a red-eyed mirror and neither retreated.

"I have a suggestion," the Winter Sage said. "Burn it."

Yerin and her clone both turned to her.

"We had discussed it for an emergency," she said coolly. "This is an emergency. Burn the Shadow."

There was a technique that Redmoon Hall could use that involved breaking down the Blood Shadow for power. It was more difficult the more complete the Shadow, as you had to overwhelm the Shadow's will with your own, so it was most often done by those who kept their Blood Shadow in the form of a weapon.

But, using the dream tablets that Eithan had given her long ago, Yerin had pieced together how to do it. If she beat her Shadow in a head-to-head clash of wills, she could add its power to her own.

That would win them this fight, almost certainly.

But it would permanently weaken the Shadow. They would be giving up a weapon against Sophara in the finals.

Her Blood Shadow stalked closer to Min Shuei. "You have had your—"

"Silence," the Winter Sage commanded.

The Shadow's voice seized up, and she even stumbled in its step.

"I don't need advice from parasites. Yerin, it's win or die. And with the Shadow's influence in your soul weakened, you will find it even easier to sense the Sword Icon."

Yerin couldn't rid herself of the Blood Shadow entirely this way, at least not without injuring herself. It could only be drained so far.

But she could weaken it. Change the power dynamic between them forever, so that Yerin was always the one in charge.

And it would win them this fight.

She walked up to the Shadow until they were almost nose-to-nose. She remembered all the times that it had tried to swallow her up. She still remembered the sticky, wet noise of her parents' blood hitting the walls.

But it had been a long time since then.

She also remembered the spirit blindfolding itself and straining to reach the Sword Icon. Emerging from her spirit to save her from Meira's scythe. Fighting by her side to save Lindon. Drawing power from Yerin's life and spirit...only to leave her alive when it could have killed her. Slipping out of her spirit in the middle of the night to change a wounded animal's bandages.

When was the last time the Shadow had really tried to take over?

"Let her go," Yerin said quietly.

An imperceptible force disappeared from around the Shadow's throat, but the spirit still didn't speak, watching Yerin in silence.

Yerin looked into red eyes. "You need a name."

The Winter Sage protested, but Charity held her back. "Coordination would be easier if they worked together."

Min Shuei glowered but didn't object any further.

"Can't name myself," the Shadow responded, but Yerin felt a wary hope from her.

"Hourglass is running down," Yerin warned. The first named spirit she thought of was Little Blue, so she threw out a suggestion. "Big Red."

The Shadow flinched back.

Yerin didn't appreciate the reaction. "Not your mother, am I? How about just plain 'Red'?"

"Scarlet," Charity suggested.

"Blood Yerin," the Winter Sage put in. "You could call her 'Blerin.'"

Everyone stared at her.

"You think I care what you name it?" She muttered. "Nobody names their tapeworm."

Yerin couldn't stand to waste another second. "We could list out red things all day. Let's pick something and be done."

"Ruby," Charity said.

The Shadow nodded slowly. "Ruby. Yes."

"*That's* the one you like?" Yerin had just sworn not to spend any more time on the Shadow's name, but she couldn't believe it. It sounded too...frilly, like it was the name for some little girl's doll.

"Rubies are worth a pile of gold, and people can't get enough of them, and they're nice to look at. I like Ruby."

"I can't believe this is how we're spending our time," Min Shuei muttered.

"Names are important," Charity said. "But we need a new

strategy. Yerin, the binding of your sword should trap even a Blood Shadow as developed as Crusher."

"It will," the Winter Sage confirmed. "If the Shadow can cover you while you activate the field."

"Ruby," the Blood Shadow corrected.

"Can you?" Yerin demanded.

Ruby gave her a disturbingly familiar grin. "We can take turns."

第二十一章
CHAPTER TWENTY-ONE

As they'd learned in the last fight, Yerin could stop the first of Crusher's strikes.

During their training inside Northstrider's pocket world, Ruby had absorbed enough blood aura from the Heart's Gem and enough essence from Yerin that it had developed a copy of her Steelborn Iron body.

It wasn't as perfect as Yerin's, because the Blood Shadow hadn't evolved enough to have earned a true human body, but it was more than good enough for their purpose.

So even before the fight began, Yerin started channeling madra to her sword. It struck her how ridiculous it was that she was betting not just her own success, but Lindon's and Mercy's lives, on her Blood Shadow.

But she continued when the wall dropped and the hideous beast leaped at her. Her decision had been made, and there was no time to question it.

Ruby's dark blade crashed into Crusher's claws, and the air exploded again. Yan Shoumei fired a huge red needle—a Striker technique—and Crusher landed to swing at Ruby one more time.

But the Shadow had done her job. Yerin had needed only moments.

Frozen Blade madra and icy aura erupted from her sword.

White blades hung in the air like snowflakes as restrictive force enveloped them all. Yerin had an easier time controlling the madra than she had before, but it was still like wrapping her arms around the neck of a mad bull and trying to steer.

Ruby dashed through the aura as Yerin forcibly kept the technique away from her. She still had to dodge the madra crystals in the air, but that wasn't too difficult.

Yan Shoumei had pushed the technique away, surrounding herself with that gem-like barrier of blood madra, but Ruby crashed through it. Her dark blade swung for Shoumei's throat when the Redmoon artist's hand came up in a claw.

Blood aura seized Ruby, and she froze.

Yerin gritted her teeth at the effort of maintaining the Winter Sage's technique, and her core drained quickly. The Madra Engine would restore her when she had a moment to breathe, but it hadn't done anything for her total capacity. She wasn't Lindon.

Meanwhile, Crusher's arms were starting to move. The monster growled and snarled as it shoved against the restriction of the technique with brute force. When its fur came in contact with the floating razors of ice, blood sprayed, but the creature kept pushing.

Yerin didn't know if Crusher would break the technique or shred itself to pieces first, but she didn't intend to maintain the stalemate. Shoumei was preparing another technique against the frozen Ruby.

Yerin prepared to drop the boundary field...and then a surge of madra from Ruby caught her attention. The Blood Shadow was speeding up their plan.

After the second round, Yerin had chosen the black sword from the Archlord vaults on Charity's advice.

Honestly, she hadn't been happy about it.

There had been swords of every description, and Yerin could have wandered through the vaults for hours in awe, but Charity had restricted her to the most boring option. A sword that could fit in her soulspace and could be used by her Blood Shadow.

It was like showing her a beautiful steak and then feeding it to a hungry dog right in front of her.

The black sword was called Netherclaw, named for the beast that guarded the Netherworld in the mythology of some culture Yerin didn't care about.

It was used by a slaughter artist centuries ago, an Archlord on a Path of blood and sword madra that had murdered anyone he came across to harvest their aura. He had eventually been stopped by a Sage...the Sage of Red Faith, in fact, though Yerin had a hard time imagining him saving anyone's life, even by accident.

Its binding was an advanced Forger technique, filled with the will of the murderer who had left it behind. Yerin had tried to activate it herself, but her compatibility with the sword was pitiful. The only reason she was able to use her master's sword was her long history with it, and her familiarity with its power.

Ruby could use the technique just fine, but she couldn't survive doing it.

Until now.

Her copy of Yerin's Diamond Veins had finally progressed far enough, her body was solid, and the spirit well had strengthened her madra.

Scarlet madra Forged in lines over Ruby's sword, weaving itself strand by strand, growing in power and intensity.

A Striker technique from Yan Shoumei pierced Ruby's chest, but she didn't falter.

Yerin, however, was starting to shake. As Crusher pushed against the technique in her sword, it put more and more pressure on her spirit. Any second, she would lose control of the field.

Ruby's technique finished Forging.

The lines snapped into the shape of a clawed hand bigger than Yan Shoumei's entire body, and the claw swept down with an Archlord's power.

As with all the bindings in these weapons, Netherclaw's technique would be more powerful when Yerin was an actual Archlady, but it was still a devastating blow. The claw hit Yan Shoumei like one of Crusher's own strikes, crashing through her diamond-shaped madra shield and landing on her skin.

Her resistance to madra was enough to prevent the strike from shredding her to ribbons.

But blood still sprayed from her body in three lines as the claws sliced through her skin. Her body tumbled back, and her Ruler technique broke.

Ruby dashed after her in an instant, and though Shoumei reacted quickly, she was pinned to the ground with Netherclaw.

Before her Remnant could rise, she dissolved into white light and vanished.

Just as Yerin gave out. She released the Frozen Blade technique, heaving for breath, holding her sword out in case Crusher could still resist.

But to her relief, the monstrous Blood Shadow disappeared at the same instant.

The Sages had speculated that the match would be over when the sacred artist was defeated, but ultimately it was up to Northstrider to determine what counted as defeat. Yerin sagged with relief as the Ninecloud Soul declared her victory.

That made one fight each. One to go.

Yerin knew better than to rely on the same opening tactic again, but now that they were certain Ruby wouldn't be able to keep fighting after Yerin's defeat, the Blood Shadow had to take on the riskier role.

They started in similar positions, with Ruby in front and Yerin behind, but this time Ruby attacked.

As expected, Crusher defended.

They didn't know what Yan Shoumei's Archlord weapon was, nor all her prizes from the previous round, but they knew she had more in store. She had played carefully the entire tournament, keeping her cards secret, but now she had no choice.

So no one was surprised when she took a weapon from her soulspace, but Yerin was somewhat surprised to see it was a bow.

Archers weren't exactly rare, but they weren't common either. You could use a Striker technique with any weapon, and a sword was still useful up close.

But Yerin knew better than to underestimate any Archlord weapon, especially when sword and blood aura began flowing to the bow from all over in the arena, condensing into a red-white light.

It was more complex than a simple arrow, reminding Yerin of Mercy's bow when she layered many techniques into one, but Yerin didn't care to find out what it did.

Ruby had already clashed with Crusher, but instead of using the time to activate her own Archlord binding, Yerin took the opening to dash right by.

Crusher tossed Ruby aside, but not quickly enough to stop Yerin from closing the gap with Yan Shoumei.

Her sword rang.

The Endless Sword technique rippled through the dense sword aura, which Shoumei had already begun gathering to herself.

Since it was under the control of her Ruler technique, the Endless Sword didn't have as much impact as Yerin had hoped. She'd *hoped* it would cause the mass of aura to explode and tear Shoumei in half.

But it still opened up bleeding wounds all over Shoumei's body, and her spirit trembled. Yerin would have finished her off, but her spirit warned her in time to spin her around and send as much madra as possible into her Steelborn Iron body.

Crusher's fist slammed down onto her upraised sword.

Yan Shoumei had named her Blood Shadow well.

Yerin was *crushed* down, cracking the ground beneath her feet, and her entire body screamed under the impact.

But she only had to endure it for a moment as Ruby dashed back into the fray, red hair streaming behind her.

Her own sword rang.

Dozens of wounds cut Shoumei all over her body, cutting her more deeply this time. She cried out in pain, and the Archlord technique pulsed, ready to escape her control.

Crusher swiped back at Ruby, but with its other hand it struck Yerin's sword again.

It felt like her bones would break under the impact, and it was all she could do to endure.

Then Yan Shoumei released her bowstring.

A lance of dense silver-and-red aura lanced out straight for Yerin, and there was nothing she could do. She still hadn't recovered from Crusher's last blow, and he loomed over her, prepared to land another.

Until something hit him from the side.

Ruby tackled Crusher, staggering him just enough to knock him into the path of Yan Shoumei's Ruler technique.

A full Archlord using the weapon would have launched the technique faster and with more focus, but Yan Shoumei had enough trouble controlling its power at all.

Both Blood Shadows fell in front of the technique.

Needles erupted from their bodies, shredding them from the inside out.

The aura controlled the blood inside them, sharpening it and bursting through their skin. Ruby was annihilated in an instant, and Yerin felt her scraps return; without Northstrider's restoration after the battle, it would take her weeks and specialized resources to recover.

But Yerin was untouched. Ruby had succeeded.

Mostly.

Clumps of Crusher oozed together, forming into a massive lump. She could already see hair growing on what looked like a limb.

But Crusher wasn't her target.

Yerin looked to Yan Shoumei, who had dropped the bow and raised both her hands into claws. She was covered in wounds, her face was torn beyond recognizing, and she shook as though she could barely stand. From head to toe, she was soaked in blood.

Pain erupted all over Yerin's body as her own flesh turned against her, seized by Yan Shoumei's own Ruler technique. She'd burned soulfire for this, as it affected Yerin quickly, making her muscles twitch and her heart convulse.

But Yerin didn't need to move her body.

Aura echoed from the black sword that had fallen at Yan Shoumei's feet. The Endless Sword rang out, opening the Redmoon artist's throat.

From his viewing platform, Reigan Shen let out a disappointed *tsk*.

It seemed that everyone who owned a powerful weapon fell to the same mistake: relying on it. Yan Shoumei had so many other options, but she was blinded by the power of her Blood Shadow and of her bow.

Then again, Yerin was perhaps her natural enemy.

Yerin could match up to Crusher's strength, however briefly, and her own Blood Shadow copied a large measure of that same power. That alone mitigated Shoumei's biggest advantage.

In virtually every other category, Shoumei was outmatched. Yerin had more powerful techniques, more combat experience, and a powerful will for her level.

He had hoped for a win, and even coached Yan Shoumei personally for a few days, but ultimately it affected little.

He had always been playing for second place.

He sent Seshethkunaaz a message through vital aura.

"Are you going to buy her out?"

The reply was quick in coming. *"I have no interest in bribery. Whoever wins the contest is most worthy of possessing the prize."*

Reigan Shen chuckled. That was an easy stance to take when you were almost guaranteed to win.

"I think I'll try my hand, then," he sent.

"Do as you wish."

Malice would never allow her final representative to give in to temptation, but it couldn't hurt to try. A victory that was *almost* guaranteed still left too much room for error.

Instead of reappearing in her waiting room, Yerin re-formed in a room she'd never seen before.

Instantly, she drew her sword.

It was a small sitting-room filled with blankets and plush furniture, and everything was some shade of purple, black, or silver. From silver lamps covered in purple shades to purple tapestries hanging on the walls sewn with images in black.

A moment later, a woman emerged from a door in the corner, wearing a simple purple dress.

Yerin had never seen Akura Malice up close with her own eyes before, only from a distance or in the blurry memories of others.

This was clearly her.

She looked like Mercy's older sister, with the addition of black lips, amethyst nails, and hair flowing behind her like shadows. She looked Yerin up and down with eyes an even brighter purple than her children's.

"Don't be startled," she said. "Shen was trying to contact you, so I decided to keep you close."

Yerin slid her sword back into its sheath, but she shivered at the thought of Reigan Shen's contact. If a Monarch wanted revenge for the defeat of his champion, she was in for a rough life. And probably a short one.

"Thanks for cutting that off," Yerin said. She collapsed back onto a purple-cushioned couch.

Though her body and spirit had been restored by Northstrider, she was still mentally tired. It had been a long day.

Malice looked surprised for a moment. Maybe Yerin hadn't been supposed to sit, but she felt like she should have some privileges as Malice's only remaining fighter, so she sank even deeper into the cushions.

It was the most comfortable seat she'd ever experienced. She tried not to sigh in relief.

"I'll have to hold you here for a moment so Shen gets the message, and it's about time that you and I got to know each other anyway. Which means you now have a Monarch at your disposal."

Malice sat in a throne-like cushioned chair, crossed one leg over the other, and leaned one elbow on the armrest. "How can I help you win this tournament?"

"Expect you'd know better than I would."

Malice's smile was slow and showed no teeth. Yerin didn't trust it.

Or anything else about this woman, really.

"Charity and Min Shuei can teach you almost anything I could. Though I have more skill and experience than they do, imparting it to you is another matter. You must advance to have the tools to win, and if you somehow fully manifest the Sword Icon, you will of course win handily."

Malice gave a frustrated huff. "But no one develops such stable authority before Archlord nowadays, sadly. It used to be more common, but then Paths had a much lower survival rate."

A question occurred to Yerin, but she wondered if she had enough spine to ask it.

Then she remembered that this Monarch's life was currently in Yerin's hands. If she didn't take advantage of it now, when would she?

"Found a question for you," Yerin said casually. "Why do you treat your daughter like your second-favorite dog?"

Malice's smile didn't slip, or even flicker. "Should I have rewarded her for failure? The world is not so kind. She had every advantage, just as Sophara did, and yet she came up lacking. Should I have soothed her feelings by pretending there are no consequences when she put our family in danger?"

"*She's* your family."

Malice's easy, casual acceptance was only making Yerin angrier. Charity came across as cool and distant, but genuine. Like she was really that detached from everyone else.

This Monarch struck Yerin as an experienced liar.

"She is *a member of* my family," Malice corrected. "A valuable member, and one who I'm very fond of and in whom I have invested time and attention. I would be devastated to lose her, but if I did, the family would continue. The Akura name is greater than any one member. Even me."

Bold as she was being, even Yerin wasn't so cracked in the head as to call a Monarch a liar to her face.

But she came close.

"Say I lose, and Sophara gets Penance. She kills you. Heralds crash on Fury, kill him, kill Mercy. You're telling me the Akura clan doesn't slide right down after House Arelius?"

Malice waved a hand lazily, still unshaken. "Of course the family still needs a Monarch. It's the position that's important, not who fills it. You also must know that I wouldn't allow myself to bet everything on one turn of the cards. I have plans to account for your loss."

That let off some tension Yerin didn't realize she was holding.

"But those are a *last* resort. If you lose, then your failure still puts my family in danger." There was no extra spiritual pressure and Malice's face didn't change, but her words carried an extra edge. "If I *had* to give up Fury and Pride and Mercy for the good of the family, it would tear my heart out, but I would do it. So I suggest you fight as though your life is on the line, because if you don't, you can imagine my...disappointment."

Maybe Yerin's survival instinct had been knocked askew by her fight today, because she felt no fear at the threat, only anger and disgust.

"You can bet I'll bring everything I have," Yerin said, "because it's not *my* life that's on the line."

Whatever plans Malice had, it was clear that Lindon, Eithan, and Mercy would be safer if Yerin won. So she would win even if it killed her.

"Wonderful," Malice said pleasantly. "I'm glad we understand each other."

Yerin was certain they didn't.

"Now, as I said, Charity has been doing a fine job putting you in a position to advance, but I could give you my perspective."

"...please," Yerin said grudgingly.

She didn't like this woman, but she wasn't so upset that she couldn't recognize an opportunity.

"An Icon, as I'm sure you've picked up, is a symbol of a powerful concept. The more you represent that concept, the better. In your case, you yourself must become a symbol of swordsmanship. Not in the eyes of mankind, but by the measure of something deeper."

"Heard that one," Yerin said.

Malice's smile widened. "*You* have to. Imitating another symbol isn't good enough."

"True enough." That was why Sages didn't take apprentices. Anyone they trained would just be a weak copy of themselves.

It was the whole mountain Yerin had to overcome.

"You know this, but have you become a symbol of swordsmanship? Or a copy of your master? What is *your* signature?"

Bleed me if I know, Yerin thought.

The Sages had taught her that it was easier to manifest an Icon the more advanced she was, and since she was already sensing it distantly, she was probably straight on the path to becoming the next Sword Sage as soon as she reached Archlord.

Anything she gained earlier than that was a bonus.

Malice leaned back in her chair. "You'll have to meditate on it. I can't give you more time, as Northstrider did. Becoming a Sage takes mostly individual insight and accomplishment, so there's only so much that can be taught or trained."

If not for the rest of their conversation, Yerin would say the Monarch was looking on her fondly. "You've already done the Akura name proud. Under other circumstances, I would reward you handsomely, win or lose. In this case, I will treat you like Mercy's sister if you win.

"You can marry into the head family. Take Pride, if you want. Take any of the Akura men who catch your eye, and your children will be considered full-blooded members of the clan. I will grant your every wish.

"Don't fail."

She sounded pleasant, not as threatening as she had before, but Yerin still didn't back down.

"Might be I'll take you up on that," she said. "But I can't be sure. I've seen what you think of your daughters."

第二十二章

CHAPTER TWENTY-TWO

As Yerin and everyone else in the world expected, Sophara obliterated Brother Aekin.

She didn't use any techniques other than her Enforcer technique and her dragon's breath, so Yerin learned nothing from the fights. Both of them together took about twenty total seconds.

That evening, she found herself once again floating on a column of rainbow light in the center of the arena, being celebrated for her accomplishments in having made it to the top two.

She was deliberately placed so that she faced away from Sophara, which was good, because her eyes would ache if she spent the whole ceremony glaring.

There was much greater fanfare for top two than there had been for the top four, meaning it took over an hour for the Ninecloud Soul to get to the point.

"And now the time has come," the Soul announced, "to award the prizes!"

Yerin's attention stopped drifting.

"The Divine Treasures, which will be awarded to our fighters, have been crafted by the finest artisans of the eight factions with these individuals in mind. They are custom pieces, unique, never to be seen again!"

Though the crowd was much smaller than it had been before, their roar was still impressive.

"These are guaranteed to improve combat ability, so they are being revealed publicly now, to avoid imbalance in the final round of the Uncrowned King tournament!"

You're fine with imbalance in the other rounds? Yerin thought.

"First, for Yerin Arelius!"

Yerin perked up and looked to the cloud of multi-colored light hovering over the stage. She had expected to be awarded second.

A shimmering ball of pale white madra streaked down from above, leaving a trail like a comet. She couldn't quite pin down what kind of madra it was, but it *looked* like a misty star.

"The Moonlight Bridge!" the Soul announced, and for some reason everyone cheered at the construct's name. "This Divine Treasure allows near-instant transportation anywhere in the world! Special credit is given to Reigan Shen, whose personal attention was crucial to the..."

Yerin's ears blanked out as her mind went still.

Instant transportation?

Anywhere?

Her own master had admitted that his skills in spatial transport were pretty poor, which meant they walked or flew most places instead of taking portals, but she knew Sages had limits on how much they could walk through space.

This sounded like a power of a Monarch. Or even the heavens.

With this, she could save Lindon. And Eithan and Mercy.

How was this possible?

"There are some restrictions, of course, on such a miraculous power!" the Ninecloud Soul went on, and Yerin quenched her expectations. "Yerin cannot bring anyone along for the ride, and the Treasure cannot be used in quick succession. If she moves all the way around the world, the Moonlight Bridge can take up to three days to recover. But traveling within sight? That, she can do as much as she likes. Imagine the possibilities!"

The Ninecloud Soul went on listing those possibilities, but Yerin's racing heart returned to normal.

This was still a prize worth calling a real Divine Treasure, but it didn't solve Yerin's current situation. She could go visit Lindon, but what good would that do if the Bridge couldn't take him back with her? She would risk getting trapped by Heralds with no chance of bringing him away.

"Which brings us to Sopharanatoth!"

Yerin and Sophara had been turned to face the same direction, so Yerin looked to her left to see the prize drifting down from the sky.

It was a small statue of a boy with broad dragon's wings. Made of gold, of course. Yerin wondered if Sophara knew there were other colors.

"The Totem of the Dragon King releases a projection of the Dragon King that carries a measure of his spirit and his authority!"

An illusion gave a demonstration, as a majestic serpentine gold dragon roared over the crowd. This one didn't come with any spiritual weight, but Yerin was still shocked.

She had been so excited about the ability to move anywhere just a moment ago, but the fight wasn't held *"anywhere."* It was in a small bowl that she couldn't leave. And she was going to be locked in there with someone who could carry a toy Monarch in her pocket?

Yerin would have appealed the injustice of the situation if there was anyone who would listen.

"The limitations of this Treasure are simple: it exerts only as much power as Sophara can control. The more powerful she is, the more powerful the Totem grows!"

Sophara cradled the construct in her hands, looking at it in awe, and Yerin looked back to her own glowing ball.

She supposed there was no reason to wait, so she began absorbing the Moonlight Bridge into her spirit. To her surprise, it slid in easily, clicking into place as though it was made to fit her.

Then again, she supposed it was.

When the ceremony finally ended, the Ninecloud Soul moved Yerin directly back to her room. She started rummaging around for food immediately; she needed to fill her stomach before the Sages arrived and took her for training.

Since the Moonlight Bridge had settled into her spirit so easily, she was eager to practice with it. The Soul had said she could use it "whenever she wanted" in short range. How short? How long did the ability take to return after she used it? How quick was the actual transportation?

Come to think of it, how did she target it? She could look at a place and will herself there, she guessed, but then how would you travel all the way across the world?

She was tempted to try it out herself in her room, but reason prevailed. It would be much smarter to try out spatial transportation with two Sages around to supervise.

Her Blood Shadow rolled inside her, and rather than resisting, Yerin let her out.

She was trying to work *with* Ruby, so that meant giving her some time to walk around.

The red-haired Yerin appeared in a state of obvious excitement. "This is a gem and a half! Why are we waiting around?"

Yerin found a platter of fruits that had been delivered fresh that afternoon. She wasn't really in the mood for fruit, but it was there, so she picked one up and took a bite. "You want to move straight into the side of a mountain?"

Ruby's brow furrowed. "Doesn't work like that."

"And you're an expert?"

"Open up and sense it yourself. You don't have to steer it, you just tell it where you want to go."

Yerin was tempted, but she was still waiting on the Sages. Especially over the word of her Blood Shadow.

Ruby shifted from foot to foot impatiently. "Come on, let's go to Lindon!"

Yerin stopped chewing.

She had been wary of the way the Shadow looked at Lindon for a long while now. Was that something Ruby developed on her own, or was it some embarrassing reflection of Yerin herself?

Definitely on her own, she decided.

"We can't bring him back," Yerin said firmly.

"You think I give one burnt hair about that?"

Yerin did not like arguing with herself at all.

"The Soul said three days, and cheers for us, three days is what we have," Ruby continued. "We can train with him!"

Now that Yerin thought about it, she could imagine how the Blood Shadow must see Lindon. Not only had the spirit's mind developed by copying Yerin's own thoughts and feelings, but Lindon had been the one to pull the Shadow out of Yerin's spirit and manifest it in the first place.

And wherever Yerin had gone, Lindon had been there too.

Other than enemies and Yerin herself, Lindon might be the only person that Ruby felt any connection to.

Even with all that, and even if the Moonlight Bridge worked, it didn't make any sense to go. They could do their best work here.

Yerin sympathized, and though she knew she wasn't the most compassionate person, she tried to inject some understanding into her tone. "That would be all flowers and rainbows if that were possible," she said with a sigh. "But it's not. We have to train with the Bridge, we can't have it down for all three days. And I still need to try to touch the Icon."

Ruby gave her a flat stare. "You don't need me for that."

And, so suddenly that Yerin was caught off-guard, the Moonlight Bridge in Yerin's spirit activated.

She tried to wrestle control back, but in a flash of sparkling white light, Ruby was gone. Yerin felt emptier, as though a big chunk of her spirit had vanished.

And left her alone, in her room, holding a half-eaten pear.

The black dragon slammed into the rocky ground. Lindon rode on top of it as it crashed, his hunger arm latched onto black scales.

The Heart of Twin Stars churned away inside of him, sending black dragon madra to his Blackflame core. He was assaulted by memories, but only flashes, a confusing jumble that he left to Dross to sort out.

The one impression that seeped through clearly, too strong for Dross to suppress, was an overwhelming fear. The black dragon panicked as it tried to escape from the hungry thing on its back, all the way to the end.

Life and blood essence flooded into him, but they did little good. This dragon had only been an Underlord.

He walked away from the corpse, still cycling, as another presence tried to seize control of his spirit. His fingers twitched and his body shuddered, but the will of the black dragon was easily overcome.

Lindon had been practicing.

The dragon's chest rose and fell as it lay in the dirt. Whatever uneasy truce kept the other Heralds and their factions from collapsing on Fury, Lindon didn't want to push it too far.

Then again, he wasn't so concerned that he intended to stop.

[Oh, here's an interesting tidbit!] Dross said excitedly. [This dragon is a regular critic of the gold dragons' rule, he had no desire to be here, and he adopted several human children. Isn't that amazing?]

"He'll recover," Lindon said defensively. "And it's not like I can pick my targets."

He needed a black dragon's madra for the current step in his advancement.

Not to add to his core, exactly; his Blackflame core had reached its limit just as his pure core had. As far as he could determine, he had reached the very peak of what an Underlord could reach.

The Consume technique in his arm made his advancement so quick that it sometimes brought tears to his eyes. It was addictive, draining power from others and making it his own.

Which still left the bottleneck to Overlord.

He sat cross-legged and meditated, tracking down the intentions embedded in his madra.

More than just their aspects, madra carried deeper impressions. His Blackflame madra felt angry, aggressive, and his pure madra—since his bond with Little Blue—felt like a cleansing tide.

There was a connection there, and he was sure that diving into it would provide his Overlord revelation.

[You already know what the link is,] Dross insisted. [I'm telling you, your Overlord revelation is that you are my host body, born to carry me around.]

Lindon stretched out his spiritual perception, reaching not further, but deeper. The Path of Black Flame burned away the physical form, and Twin Stars now wiped away the spirit. Those had clear similarities: he could see them as direct opposites, one destroying the body and the other the spirit.

Pure madra even had parallels to water madra, which he'd known since he was a little boy begging a bowl of madra to freeze. *Seven Principles* called it the Principle of Fluidity, but he found it made a nice balancing contrast to Blackflame.

Which would have been perfect, if those were his only two sources of madra.

But his hunger arm was in the mix too, a ravenous presence at the end of his elbow. Northstrider had even emphasized discovering the common ground between his *three* madra types.

Maybe Blackflame devoured the material, pure madra devoured the spiritual, and hunger madra devoured everything?

That sounded like it *could* work, but Lindon found himself pushing for some confirmation. He sensed no trembling in the aura around him, as he had when he'd discovered his Underlord revelation, but he did feel *something*.

There was a deeper principle, a concept tickling his mind like a whisper just out of hearing.

He concentrated harder on his spiritual sense, pushing harder, trying to break through a barrier he didn't understand. He strained to focus on all three types of his madra at once, drilling down, forcing a connection...

A crackling noise and a bright light filled the dusty clearing.

Lindon rolled to his feet, Blackflame running through him and dragon's breath kindling in his left hand. He hadn't felt anyone nearby, but he'd left himself open for an ambush by focusing his perception inward.

Stupid, he berated himself. He had wanted to chase down a moment of inspiration as soon as possible, but he should have at least gone back to shelter.

Yerin stumbled out of the light.

She *felt* exactly like Yerin did when she had her Blood Shadow out, a mix of sword and blood madra, but her hair and her six extended sword-arms were all bright red. His eyes and perception clashed for a long moment, as he tried to reconcile the strange details with the sense of familiarity.

When she saw him, red eyes widened.

"Lindon!" she shouted. He managed to stand up and cancel his dragon's breath as she flew into him, wrapping arms and legs around him. "I missed you!"

Dross cleared his throat. [Ah, Lindon, I don't want to bear bad news, but this isn't—]

I know.

A sick feeling started to grow in his gut. "Apologies, you're..."

She looked up at him with Yerin's face and spoke in a satisfied tone. "Ruby!"

The sickness grew.

This was what Yerin might look like if she'd been taken over.

He tried to stay calm—he didn't know anything yet— but Blackflame was still in him. His eyes heated up as they turned black, and what he had planned as a cautious question came out as a demand. "What did you do to Yerin?"

Her bright expression died. She pulled away from him, taking several steps back and holding her Goldsigns at the ready as though she thought she might have to defend herself. "Not one thing. Bet my soul against a dead leaf that you haven't heard the report from today's tournament."

"I wasn't expecting a report until at least this afternoon." It was early in the morning, and not only was there a gap in time between Sky's Edge and Ninecloud City, but it took time for news to travel.

Now anxious uncertainty joined his sick premonition. What had happened to Yerin? She was supposed to fight Yan Shoumei; had the Blood Sage done something to her?

"We won," Ruby said flatly. "Yerin stayed back to train. You'll see what's true when you get the news."

[That's not Yerin's body,] Dross confirmed. [Well, I mean, it *is*. It's an exact copy. But if she had taken Yerin, she'd be a lot more solid.]

That was a relief, but to the naked eye, it was hard to see how her human form could possibly be more complete.

She stood with her arms crossed and Goldsigns at the ready, not meeting his eyes. It looked like she was shivering.

In spite of himself, he felt bad for her.

And *unbelievably* curious.

Cautiously, he asked, "You're really just her Blood Shadow?"

"Ruby," she muttered.

"That's...*incredible!*" He swept his perception over her in awe. "You have a madra system! I never imagined that a spirit could be this complete before Herald. And your voice... you sound just like Yerin!"

The Shadow's Goldsigns eased up a little, and she slipped a step closer. "We can talk now."

"Yes, we can!"

It was crashing over him what kind of an opportunity this was. Not only was this the chance to study a fully manifested spirit in preparation for eventually advancing to Herald, but he could ask her about her unique perspective as a spiritual parasite, about her memories, about the Bleeding Phoenix. Even about Yerin.

"I have so many questions, it's hard to narrow them down."

But it wasn't. After only a moment of thought, he realized that Ruby could help him with his current project.

As much as he thought of her as being made entirely from blood madra, blood wasn't her only aspect. The Bleeding Phoenix was a Dreadgod, and like any dreadbeast, its madra had a hunger component.

The Blood Shadow's original purpose was to drain power and bring it back to the Phoenix. At its core, it was a hunger spirit.

He dipped his head to her. "Pardon, Ruby, but I'm trying to determine the...meaning...behind hunger madra, if that makes sense. The deeper aspects. The intention. Thus far, all I can determine is that it's hungry, but there should be more to it."

She nodded eagerly, moving still closer as she did so. "It's like a hungry stomach, isn't it? Always greedy for more. Can't be filled up, or it isn't hunger anymore."

He lost himself in thought.

That did fill in some of the connection he'd sensed. Blackflame was a ravenous fire that left nothing behind, and his pure madra now emptied foreign madra. Maybe you could see it as emptiness waiting to be filled.

But how did he actually connect the three?

"You're asking me, but there's somebody bigger you could ask."

He shook himself out of his trance to realize that Ruby was standing right up against him, looking up. Her chin touched his chest.

He took a polite step back. "Who?"

"The Titan. I feel him napping the day away over there." She slid after him, this time grabbing fistfuls of both his sleeves.

How do I ask the Titan anything? he thought.

[There's a clear answer, but I'm afraid to give it to you.]

As soon as the question occurred to him, an answer suggested itself, but it was stupid and maybe suicidal.

[And that's why I didn't want you to have it.]

He would have to think it through. He needed more information, not to mention permission.

Though there was a more immediate issue to deal with first.

"Pardon, Ruby, but you're...very close."

"True." She nodded. "Most times, I don't get to see or feel anything myself. Just bits and pieces from Yerin, while I sit there in the dark."

She gave him one of the broadest smiles he'd ever seen on Yerin's face. "I'm not stuck in the dark anymore."

Fury yawned. "Busy? I've never been more bored in my life. What's up?"

Lindon had needed no help finding the Herald. Everyone in the camp knew he was napping on the roof of the highest point in the fortress, but everyone who came up here with work was tossed back down. The Archlords complained about it day and night.

Considering the Dreadgod sleeping on the other end of the city and the cults floating in their headquarters overhead, Lindon would have expected Fury to be on his guard every hour.

Still, he'd judged this worth getting the Herald's permission for, and he hadn't wanted to be thrown off the roof. So he had first gone to find Mercy.

"Lindon has a request," Mercy said, "and it's pretty crazy, so I thought you might like it."

"Crazy?" Red eyes lit up. "Let me hear it! I was about to go beat on Xorrus some more, but not being able to kill her takes all the fun out of it."

More than just Mercy and Lindon had made it up to see Fury. When Pride saw his sister headed somewhere with Lindon, he had invited himself along, and was now a disapproving presence brooding on the edge of the roof.

Ruby had come too, sticking to Lindon's side. Often literally.

"Gratitude. I apologize for bothering you, but I was wondering if I might have permission to drain madra from the Wandering Titan."

Pride made a choking sound, but Fury gave a thoughtful "Hmmm..."

Mercy shrugged. "I thought you might enjoy it, but I didn't think it would work either."

Dross and Lindon had spent most of the day running through their reasoning, and Lindon thought they had a solid case.

"It's more plausible than it sounds. First, the area immediately around the hand is clear." Nobody wanted to be camped next to the Wandering Titan when it woke, not even Abyssal Palace. "Second, Northstrider regularly Consumes madra from the Dreadgods to help determine when they'll wake up."

That had been Dross' contribution; another fact he'd learned from Northstrider's collection of memories.

"That's *Northstrider*," Pride said.

"I'm not saying I can perform as well as he can, but it does show that I won't wake up the Titan." That had been one of Lindon's primary concerns. "I'll be like a flea, and I will be taking only the *smallest* possible amount, even for me."

"I don't know," Mercy said doubtfully. "I don't see why you'd take the risk."

Ruby spoke up from her position clinging to Lindon's left arm. "What's life without an edge of risk?"

Mercy shook her head. "Ruby, that is just *uncanny*. You sound too much like Yerin, it's twisting my brain."

"I want to take the risk because I think it will benefit my sacred arts," Lindon said, steering the conversation back on track. "But we could all benefit. I can read my target's strongest emotions and memories, so we should be able to get a sense of the Wandering Titan's goals."

That was why Northstrider did it, after all. Dream oracles could suggest when and where the Dreadgods would attack, but they were always vague and subject to change.

The Monarch of the Hungry Deep preferred more specific, immediate information.

"Hmmm....nope," Fury said at last.

He flopped back onto the warm tiles, crossing his arms behind his head like a pillow.

Ruby's Goldsigns slipped out, stabbing Lindon in the side. "You mind giving us a *notch* more than that?"

"Uncanny," Mercy muttered.

"Sure! Lindon doesn't understand where the real danger is. Yeah, the enemies probably won't stop a single Underlord from walking right up to the Dreadgod. Their own Underlords were doing it now and then. I let it happen because even if they attacked full-force, there's nothing they could do to make the Titan notice.

"So Xorrus won't murder you, and the Dreadgod probably won't crush you in its sleep, and even if you drink so much of its madra that it would pop you from the inside, your arm would break before you were hurt too badly."

Fury had already shut his eyes, but he cracked one open to look at Lindon. "You have to wrestle with the wills of the people you drain, don't you?"

"It's never been a problem. The less I take from them, the less I have to fight them for control."

"Yeah, you're underestimating the will of a Dreadgod." Fury's eyes closed again, and he settled back against the tiles. "Even the smallest, tiniest, little grain of it will leave you drooling on the floor. Trust me and drop it."

Lindon supposed a Herald would know best, but he hated to give up just like that. This could be the key to his revelation. And how many more opportunities would he get to learn directly from a Dreadgod?

"There should be a solution. I believe I could prepare myself, or create some kind of filter—"

Fury cut him off. "Okay then. Why don't we see how you do, huh?"

Spiritual pressure pushed down on Lindon. The phenomenon was nothing more than the spirit recognizing superior power, but he'd seen some people—like Eithan—use pressure as a focused weapon.

Though Fury still lay with his arms crossed behind his head, his attention pushed in on Lindon from every direction. Ruby was shoved away, and even his madra moved sluggishly in his channels.

"It's harder than people think," Fury went on. "Everybody thinks they can..." One eye opened. Then the other eye.

Then he was standing opposite Lindon. "Hey now, you're pretty good."

Lindon knew this was just a test, but he still felt like the Herald was underestimating him too much. This was nothing like the weight he'd felt from Northstrider.

Fury rolled back his sleeves. "I'm going to go a little harder, so don't blame me if you forget how to breathe."

The pressure redoubled, and this time Lindon had to grit his teeth and push against it. It felt like forcing the Heaven and Earth Purification Wheel, or like when he'd tried to keep Dross away from Northstrider.

"Mercy, you were right!" Fury shouted. His eyes were shining, his hair dancing in the wind. "This *is* fun!"

"Uncle Fury, no!" she shouted.

Even Pride yelled at him to stop, and Ruby dove at him, pulling a black sword from her soulspace.

They were all shoved back, and the burden on Lindon increased once again.

He was being squeezed in the fist of a giant, and he strained for every ounce of power and concentration to push the closing walls away from him. Dross was yelling at him, but Lindon's consciousness was a blur, his entire being narrowing down to his struggle to *push*.

Then it was over, and he took in a long, shuddering gasp.

He was on his knees, sweat running down his face onto the tiles. The setting sun hadn't moved, so at least he hadn't lost much time.

[Only a few seconds, but...are you...I mean, *I* couldn't even move.]

"Well, when you're wrong, you're wrong!" Fury said cheerfully. "Let's give you the night to recover and then you can head out in the morning, what do you think?"

Ruby leaped at Fury, but he shoved her down with one hand.

"Gratitude," Lindon forced out.

He couldn't wait to go lie down.

Fury started fumbling in his pockets. "Oh, right, I just remembered. You guys must have heard by now that Yerin won again, right?"

Mercy cheered, though she'd heard from Ruby already, and the last knot of worry in Lindon's chest loosened.

"Aha! Got it. Here, you should look over these." He tossed a pair of dream tablets to Lindon. "Records of the round. Make sure you share! And then hand them over to Justice when you're done, he was looking for them earlier."

Dross, Lindon thought, and the spirit connected to the tablets eagerly.

[Mmmm...delicious memories.]

Dross memorized both tablets in seconds, and though Lindon wanted to view them himself, he would have to do it when he wasn't about to collapse. Dross could bring the experience up for him anytime, so he handed the tablets to Mercy after only a few seconds.

When he got back to his tiny, cramped room tucked away in the back of the fortress, he was surprised to find that Ruby immediately followed him inside.

[No, go away!] Dross shouted. [Shoo! Don't eat Lindon!]

Lindon very much doubted that was her intention. For one thing, she was munching on a haunch of roasted meat that she must have snatched on her way down.

But she also didn't act like she had any hostile intentions

toward him. He might say it was the opposite.

She finished the meat, tossed the bone aside, and sat on the edge of the bed. The cot was barely big enough for Lindon, and the room contained nothing else aside from a rug and a small shelf.

He was afraid of where the conversation would take him if he spoke to her, so instead he turned and opened his void key.

Little Blue, who still sometimes surprised him with how tall and bright she was, stared at Ruby from within.

Blue ran out of the storage space, chimes ringing in a warning.

Ruby scooted up on the bed, farther from the Riverseed, pushing her back against the wall. Lindon couldn't tell if she was afraid of Little Blue or trying not to hurt her, but he scooped Blue up anyway.

The cheeps, chimes, and whistles from Little Blue came in a constant stream, telling him not to trust the Blood Shadow, that it was evil and vicious, and reminding him of what it had tried to do to Yerin.

Meanwhile, Lindon ran his eyes over the belongings in his void key.

It took him a minute to find what he was looking for, as it was perfectly ordinary and felt like nothing to his spiritual perception, but he finally reached out with a gentle grip of wind aura and pulled a roll of blankets from beneath a pile of boxes and packages.

"Why don't you take the bed, Ruby?" Lindon suggested. "I don't mind staying on the floor. If you need to sleep, I mean."

Lindon himself intended to only rest for an hour or two and then head out to work on Soulsmithing. He knew Little Blue slept, and even Dross rested when Lindon did, but he had never considered what a Blood Shadow needed.

Ruby was still warily eyeing Little Blue, who stood like a guard dog between him and the Blood Shadow.

"I sleep," she said. "Mostly that's all I do. And I never guessed how having my own body would tire me out."

She looked up to Lindon. "Don't leave, you hear me?"

"I'm going to take a nap myself," he said, rolling out the blankets. "Right here. On the floor."

He didn't want there to be any confusion.

Ruby curled up into a ball over the blankets. "If it looks like I'm going to slip back to her spirit, you'd stop me, true?"

Lindon hesitated. "You'll have to go back eventually."

"Two days," she sighed. "Still got two whole days."

第二十三章

CHAPTER TWENTY-THREE

In one of the broad, open training rooms provided by the Ninecloud Court, Yerin sat in a circle of natural treasures and tried to advance.

"It's not always about making guesses until one feels right," Charity said. "Sometimes you can look at yourself from a new lens and the answer will suggest itself."

Charity had given Yerin access to the records of the Uncrowned King tournament, showing her how the crowds thought of her. She'd shown Yerin memories from her own viewpoint and from Charity's.

Both Sages had even shared with Yerin the memories of their own advancements to Overlord, though those were hard to store in a dream tablet. There was so much context missing, and the memories relied so much on personal viewpoint and interpretation, that Yerin was sure she didn't get the full meaning out of either event.

But Yerin tried her best. Meditation and training helped her forget that Ruby had used the Moonlight Bridge to run off, and stopped her from imagining what she could do to the Blood Shadow when Ruby returned.

Or where she might be at that moment.

"Not every revelation is verbal either," Charity continued.

"They often are, but many Lords and Ladies advance without knowing exactly what their revelation was."

"Don't know that I can boil myself down to a handful of words," Yerin said.

They'd had this conversation already, but the Heart Sage responded patiently. "The Overlord revelation does not sum up your entire self. How can one statement do so much? Instead, it gives you a new insight into how you relate to the world."

I will stab anything in my way, Yerin thought.

No reaction from the aura.

Shame. That one had felt right.

Min Shuei walked up carrying two identical swords and tapped Charity on the shoulder. "How about we tag out? I'm sure the Akura clan is falling apart right about now."

Charity gave her a cool look. "The Akura clan is perfectly capable of operating on its own in times of crisis. While we give the clan insight and guidance, we are hardly—"

"Yes, sorry, I'm sorry, but nonetheless I'm sure you're very busy." The Winter Sage tossed Yerin her master's sword. "Why don't you go get some work done, and I'll hold it down here?"

"We have less than thirty-six hours left," Charity said. "I'll be back in one."

She looked over the both of them as though expecting an objection, then swept from the room.

Yerin let out a breath. "I owe you. Don't know what else I can shake loose on my own."

"Oh, this isn't a break. Just a change of pace."

The Winter Sage came at Yerin—no Enforcer technique, but she had the strength of an Archlady. Yerin had to fuel her Steelborn Iron body just to turn her first blow aside.

"Did you know how Adama advanced to Overlord?" the Winter Sage asked casually, as she swept Yerin's counterattack aside.

Yerin groaned inwardly. She did know the story.

Not from her master, who didn't like sharing stories about himself, but from the Winter Sage. She seemed to think she could hammer Yerin into his mold by sheer repetition.

"He dueled every sword artist he could reach." It was impressive seeing Min Shuei keep up a chat while landing a blow that launched Yerin to the ceiling. "Overlords, Underlords, even Lowgolds."

Yerin herself found it hard to listen when she was desperately trying to defend herself. She focused on the fight, letting the words flow past her.

"After every duel, he would ask the other person what they thought of his style."

Yerin tried to be clever by catching one strike on her Goldsigns, but the Winter Sage retaliated by reaching out with one of her own: a four-foot-long claw of ice extending from her forearm.

"He wasn't as powerful as you are, you know," she went on. "He was disciplined. He was renowned."

Yerin leaped back, creating space. "Thought my Overlord revelation was supposed to be about *me*."

"You think you know better than I do?" Min Shuei snapped. There were no Striker techniques allowed, but it looked like she was about to throw one. "Who better to give you inspiration? You have his Path, his sword, his Remnant, his clothes."

"I hear you," Yerin muttered. She moved in for a half-hearted strike, trying to start the fight up again, but the Winter Sage slapped her blade aside.

"*He* is the reason why you are alive, not to mention why you have any connection to sword authority at all. Do you think you have nothing to learn from him? Do you think that because you have more power than he did at your age, that means you have more wisdom?"

"I get it!" Yerin shouted, using more power into her strike than she meant to.

The two blades clashed like thunder, but this time the Sage had put more than just physical strength into her block. She didn't move an inch, though her white hair rippled in the shockwave, and she looked furious.

"You don't want to hear about him, you don't want to talk

about him, but you want to succeed him. Well, if you want to be the next Sage of the Endless Sword, you should know *everything* about him! You should remember him!"

Yerin hurled her sword.

It wasn't an attack—the blade tumbled over the Sage's shoulder and stuck in the wall.

She'd just had enough.

"I'm not him!" Something flickered in her spirit, but she kept going. "Not trying to be *him,* am I? He would have wanted me here, so I'm here. All he wanted was to pass on his Path, and I'm going to do it if I bleed for it! But I'm *not him!*"

Her spirit trembled again, and this time she noticed.

The blood had drained from the Winter Sage's face.

"Cycling position," she ordered. "Quickly."

Though she felt numb, Yerin followed instructions. She sat down in the center of natural treasures she'd felt earlier, sensing the unity of aura around her, creating a bridge between the soulfire inside her and the artifacts all around her.

They crumbled away, turning to gray fire and sweeping through her.

Advancing to Overlord wasn't as dramatic as the transition to Underlord, but Yerin couldn't feel it either way.

Her own thoughts sat there like a limp corpse.

I'm not him. That was her revelation. *I'm not the Sage of the Endless Sword.*

Why was that it?

She'd known that.

She had never tried to be a little copy of her master, even when he was alive. She respected him, she loved him, she admired him. He had cared for her like a daughter.

This was the truth that was supposed to advance her and connect her to the rest of the world?

It wasn't even about her.

"Congratulations," the Winter Sage whispered.

Even she didn't seem to feel it.

"The most important thing about me is that I'm *not* somebody else," Yerin said dully.

"What? No! That's not what the Overlord revelation is. It's a way to recognize and refocus who you are, it's not the most important fact about you."

Still sitting in a cycling position, Yerin looked up to the Sage. "Not two seconds ago, you were saying how I'd taken everything I have from him."

"That's...I was only saying you should learn from his example, that's all I meant."

Yerin pushed herself to her feet, limbering up. "Well, I'm an Overlady now. We should work on settling my spirit now, true? Not much time left."

The Sage nodded, but she was clearly shaken. Maybe by what she'd said, maybe by Yerin's reaction, or maybe by the revelation itself.

Yerin shoved it all to the back of her mind. She'd have plenty of time to search her soul once the fight was over. Now, she had enough weapons to win.

But she'd expected that to bring her some satisfaction.

She only felt numb.

Lindon didn't end up Soulsmithing anything, and he rested for more than the hour he'd planned. Not entirely out of his own choice.

Ruby woke up struggling only minutes after she'd gone to sleep, shredding a blanket with her Goldsigns.

Sleep had reminded her of being back in the dark, she said. She'd thought she was alone again.

Lindon tried not to feel bad for her, but he didn't quite make it. It was hard to convince himself that she was just a Blood Shadow, especially when she looked so much like Yerin. He held her hand as she fell asleep again, just so she could remember someone was there.

Little Blue did her best to tug their hands apart.

It was almost dawn when Ruby woke again, and this time she sat bolt upright. Lindon had already sensed a change in her spirit, but he'd assumed it was another dream.

"Yerin's an Overlady," she said.

"Already?" Lindon had the advantage of Northstrider's hunger madra technique, so he couldn't imagine anyone gathering power faster than he had, and *still* Yerin had beaten him.

The Akura family would pump all their resources into her now that their family prosperity was directly in her hands, but even so, elixirs and spirit-fruits could only do so much.

"What about you?" he asked curiously. The Blood Shadow had shared Yerin's advancement, but that had been before Ruby was...herself.

"Not yet. Not until I go back." She hopped out of the bed and tugged on his shoulder to pull him to his feet. "It's morning, true? Let's get on the road."

Little Blue objected loudly.

There were a number of preparations to make before they could leave. Lindon washed up, checked the contents of his void key just in case, and gathered up the team that would be going with him to the Dreadgod.

Since his return, the actions of teams had been limited. There weren't many assignments when they were all locked up in the same fortress most of the time. He still saw his former team members often, especially Grace and Naru Saeya, but he spent most of his time operating on his own.

This time too, though he needed people to back him up, he tried to limit the number of people attending.

Fury had to watch over them, to prevent another Herald's interference, though of course he wouldn't be following them down to the beach personally. He'd seen enough Dreadgods, he said, and they were far more fun when they were awake.

Lindon was glad to have Mercy at his side, and he doubted he could prevent Ruby from coming. With the two of them together and Fury watching for Heralds, he felt much safer.

And it was to no surprise whatsoever that he walked up to the gate leading out of the fort and saw Eithan waiting for them.

The Arelius Overlord swept his long blond hair away from his face and affected an offended expression. "I'm afraid your invitation never reached me. Your many messengers must have betrayed you, or been waylaid by enemies."

Lindon pressed his fists together and bowed. "What need is there for an invitation between brothers? I know that wherever I go, you go as well."

Over the years, Lindon had learned how to handle Eithan.

Eithan laughed loudly and threw his arm around Lindon. "Well said! Now, I understand there isn't supposed to be danger to anyone but you on this mission, but when I look at your three companions, I have to assume you're preparing for combat."

Three companions? Was Eithan counting himself?

No, Lindon realized with a sigh, *he's warning me. Dross, why didn't you tell me someone was following me?*

[It's because I thought you'd enjoy a surprise, and *not* because I wasn't paying attention.]

Now knowing that he'd been spotted, Pride strode from the shadow of a nearby building, straining for every inch of height. "I heard the entire story; I don't know why you bothered trying to leave me behind."

Lindon considered a number of responses to that, but none were constructive, so he said nothing.

Ruby didn't feel the same. "You want to follow at our heels, I can find you a leash."

"Delightful," Eithan said with a sigh. "She really is like having a second Yerin. Not that you aren't wonderful in your own right, Ruby."

Ruby narrowed her eyes. "I don't remember caring much for you."

Eithan clapped a hand to his chest and staggered as though suffering a wound.

"She's just kidding, Pride," Mercy said. "Of course you can come along!"

"I *am* coming, whether she's kidding or not."

"You tell me what part sounded like a joke, and I'll change it," Ruby said.

The section of wall that served as a gate melted away, and they passed through the new opening.

It was a good thing the plan called for them to openly walk down a street with no attempt to hide, because this was perhaps the farthest thing from stealth that Lindon could imagine.

"Ha, yes, by all means let's continue to make jokes at Pride's expense," Eithan said, "but is that how *you* think of me, Ruby, or how Yerin does?"

"Take three guesses, then pick the answer you like best."

"I'm the son of a Monarch," Pride reminded them.

Mercy patted him on the arm. "I know you are!"

The stone hand was visible above the ruined homes of Sky's Edge, and there was a completely straight road from the fortress straight to the tip of the middle finger. Cracks running through the street made their footing uneven, but Lindon was less concerned about their route and more about the skies around them.

The headquarters of Abyssal Palace, Redmoon Hall, the Stormcallers, and the Silent Servants surrounded the valley, and dragons flitted across the sky. Every time Lindon's spirit shivered, indicating that someone had swept him with their perception, he tensed and readied himself for battle.

But no one attacked, so he took the opportunity to ask some questions.

"Pardon if this is too personal, Ruby, but do *you* remember Eithan? Or does that come from Yerin?"

"Hard to separate one from the other," she said immediately. "By and large, it's the same thing. Not even fair to say we're completely different people, so much is the same. Only a little is totally mine or totally hers."

"That is almost *exactly* the question I asked," Eithan pointed out.

Ruby linked an arm around Lindon's elbow.

"I have a question!" Mercy said, with her hand in the air. "Do you like being on your own?"

Ruby nodded. "It's *me* and *her* now, not all *us.*" She squeezed Lindon's arm, and he sensed more fear in the gesture than anything else. "Now I have something for me."

Mercy melted. "Awww!"

A dreadbeast hurtled out of the darkness, but a casual black arrow pinned it against a nearby wall.

"What do you think your odds are in the finals tomorrow?" Pride asked, immediately throwing cold water over the conversation.

[I can answer that!] Dross spun out onto Lindon's shoulder and made a show of coughing into the end of one of his tentacles. [And I will, because you've been speaking without me for too long. Based on Sophara's match against Mercy, Yerin's advancement, and Ruby's...entire existence...we have a good forty or fifty percent chance of victory!]

He said it so proudly, but those numbers weighed heavily on Lindon.

Fifty percent chance. Who wanted to bet their lives on the flip of a coin?

"That's not too bad!" Mercy said.

[Now, that *is* assuming Sophara will make no further improvements. I can't account for those. Don't blame me for anything I couldn't know about!]

"Wonderful!" Eithan agreed. "If only there were something one of us could do to influence that outcome in our favor."

Ruby stabbed at him with one of her Goldsigns.

"Uncanny," Mercy whispered again.

Dross, Lindon asked, *can you give Ruby a simulation against Sophara?*

[Not as well as I can you,] Dross warned, [and not for long. But yes, I could do that, theoretically speaking. I mean, absolutely yes! I'm almost certain.]

When we get back.

He wasn't sure Ruby would want to spend her one and

only holiday training for this fight, but they needed to give Yerin any edge they could.

A number of Abyssal Palace collection towers had been erected over the homes of Sky's Edge, identical to the other towers that Lindon had destroyed. Like the others, these were scripted to prevent spiritual detection, but Eithan assured them they were empty.

These towers closest to the Dreadgod would be operated remotely, once the Titan awakened. They would be destroyed in seconds, at most, but those were seconds in which they could collect Dreadgod madra for their sect.

Only when Lindon stood against the Wandering Titan's finger, which loomed over him like a black stone wall, did his situation become fully real to him.

Ruby patted him on the shoulder and released him, taking a step away.

The moment had come so much more quickly than he'd expected. For some reason, despite knowing the plan, he had thought they would have to fight their way through guards or...something. He had expected something to go wrong.

Gingerly, he extended his right hand, stretching fingers of white madra. The arm wanted to shoot forward and feast, but he had such control that the limb didn't even tremble.

Ruby and Mercy called encouragement, while Pride stayed icily silent.

"Soothe yourself," Eithan said. "Relax. Pretend that you're not doing something monumentally dangerous."

[Oh, that's good advice! Try that.]

Lindon shut them out and placed his Remnant hand against the Dreadgod's.

With as little madra as he could use, he activated the binding in his right arm. A tiny spark of power trickled into him.

His consciousness disappeared.

Sleep had held him for too long, but he had almost shaken free of it. Soon, he would walk again. And this time he was hungry for more than just the delicious powers he could feel within the earth.

He smelled the one thing that could fill the endless hunger inside of him. He pictured himself wading through mountains like tall grass, tossing them aside, and finally finding the one meal that would put an end to his eons of starvation.

Home.

He would find what he needed at home, in the tunnels where he had been born.

Home.

He was going home, to his brother tucked away between four peaks.

Home.

Lindon fought his way back to awareness as though struggling to the surface amid storm-tossed waves.

He was lying on his back. He tasted blood. Dross was screaming at him, and Ruby stood over him with teeth bared and Goldsigns extended, a fence of blood and sword aura shredding anything that came close.

All around, dreadbeasts threw themselves at him like they'd gone insane.

Lindon tried to push his way up to fight, but his body wouldn't listen. He was still swallowed in the vision, in the overwhelming desire to get *home.*

He was starting to separate his own memories from the Dreadgod's now, but that only made his fear sharper. More real.

The Dreadgod's home *was* his home.

When it woke, it would head straight for Sacred Valley.

Before he could speak, he passed out.

第二十四章

CHAPTER TWENTY-FOUR

When Lindon woke again, it was to find nine eyes staring at him.

He was lying in a bed in some kind of makeshift medical center, with Ruby, Mercy, and Eithan all leaning over his bed. Little Blue stood on his chest, and Dross hovered over his face.

The second he woke, they all made some kind of noise.

It was almost enough to knock him out again.

"*Knew* that wouldn't bury you," Ruby said, squeezing his hand.

Little Blue chimed her relief and threw her arms around his neck in a hug.

"How are you feeling?" Mercy asked. "Are you thirsty?"

[Physically, you were totally unhurt. Mentally, it was like you were...well, how afraid are you of death?]

Eithan beamed. "Pride owes me ten scales."

Lindon sat up, careful not to dislodge Little Blue, who refused to let go and ended up dangling from his neck. "The Titan is heading east. It's not going to get distracted, and it could wake up within the week."

Home. It echoed through his spirit.

And once again, he saw himself as the Dreadgod, wading through mountains.

The vision overlapped with his memory of Suriel's vision of the future. Something incomprehensibly gigantic tramping Sacred Valley.

He turned to the side of the bed, and Eithan pulled Ruby out of the way.

Lindon vomited all over the floor.

When he could speak again, Eithan handed him a handkerchief and a mint leaf. He took them both.

"Gratitude." Given that he owed them some kind of explanation, he spoke. "The Dreadgod is heading home...for *my* home. The valley where I was born."

"As expected!" Eithan said brightly. "Still, it's good to have confirmation."

Lindon couldn't put his feelings into words. It was one thing to slowly, intellectually realize that Sacred Valley had a connection to the Dreadgods, and that his vision of the future was one of them devastating his home one day in the distant future.

It was entirely something else to *feel* it happen. To know that it could be only days away.

He wiped his mouth clean, popped in the leaf, and slid out of his bed. Little Blue climbed to his shoulder, and Ruby moved as though to support him.

"Apologies, but I have to go. If I warn them in time, they can still leave."

Mercy put her hands out to stop him. "We'll help you. We won't leave anyone in the Dreadgod's path if we can help it. But...you know you can't leave."

On some level, he did. The Archlords and Heralds might not interfere with one Underlord running around while he was still in their grip, but they would stop anyone trying to escape. There was no point encircling the Akura encampment if anyone could just slip away whenever they wanted.

"There has to be a way out," Lindon said firmly. "I can sneak away."

"You won't need to!" Mercy assured him. "We're evacuating everyone in the Dreadgod's path."

That was *some* relief, but in the future Suriel had shown him, Sacred Valley hadn't been evacuated.

Dross waved a tendril. [Ah, about that. Actually, Lindon's home is designated a special danger zone, so in fact it is *illegal* to enter that area for evacuation purposes. Interesting how the law works, isn't it?]

Lindon straightened and readied himself to leave. Ruby turned as though to follow him.

Eithan raised a finger. "Ah, but there is a way! Once the tournament is over."

"My mother *did* give us a way out," Mercy said hurriedly. "Uncle Fury told us. We're just staying here to keep the enemy Heralds here. Once the tournament ends, no matter how it...turns out...we have a way to evacuate anyone who needs to leave."

Lindon made himself breathe, concentrating on his cycling.

"If I stay here, can you guarantee me that we will make it to Sacred Valley before the Dreadgod does?"

"Lindon..." Mercy began, but stopped herself.

[I don't think anybody can tell you that,] Dross said. [Except maybe the Dreadgod. You didn't ask him, did you?]

Eithan met his eyes, and with complete confidence, answered "Yes."

Lindon watched him for a long moment before deciding to trust Eithan.

"All right. I still need to advance." And he'd have to cash in his points with Fury. Assuming they were still split among his team, he'd have to find out exactly how many points they had.

Ruby looked to her feet. "I've got to run back. The Bridge is up again, and my three days is almost burned up."

Lindon looked into Ruby's red eyes, and he remembered his worry for Yerin. At some point in the next few hours, she was going into battle against Sophara.

Saying good-bye to her felt too much like saying good-bye to Yerin.

"Don't worry about us," he assured Ruby. "You two will bury her."

Ruby gave him a familiar smile. "I look worried to you?"

Then she leaned in close, and Lindon had an uncomfortable premonition.

Sure enough, she went on tiptoes to kiss him.

With a hand on her shoulder, he held her back, conscious of all the eyes on them both. "Ah...apologies, but..."

She looked hurt and confused, but he had to go on.

"You're...not Yerin."

Ruby dropped back down. For a second, she shifted her weight from one foot to the other, and then she nodded. "No, I'm not...I'm not. I'm me."

She forced a smile that was painfully different from the last. "Bye, Lindon."

Then, in a flash of moonlight, she vanished.

Leaving Lindon standing in a circle of onlookers.

[Oh, that was cruel. Just shattering a spirit's heart right before the biggest fight of her life. You're not going to do that to me, are you?]

"Don't try to kiss me," Lindon muttered.

Little Blue chimed in her encouragement. He was right to turn her away.

"You did the right thing," Mercy agreed. "But poor Ruby! But you had to let her down. But that must have hurt so much!"

That didn't help Lindon feel any better.

Eithan waved a hand vaguely in the air. "It makes me wonder about the ethics of the whole situation. Is a copy of Yerin still Yerin? From a certain point of view, the heart you broke may have been *Yerin's*. Do you think she feels a sense of absolute, crushing rejection right now without even knowing where it came from?"

Lindon walked away.

⬡

Calan Archer had seen Reigan Shen before, but he'd never met the Monarch in person.

The Monarch transported him to an opulent, gold-paneled display hall where weapons and constructs of every description were sealed in transparent cases or hanging from the wall.

Under other circumstances, he would have enjoyed looking at each one, but it seemed he was last to arrive.

Aekin stood nearby, still totally covered with one eye of his stone mask glowing yellow. Shoumei was next to him, and she glanced up at Calan through her long black hair. The Blood Sage crouched on his heels at the feet of the Monarch.

Reigan Shen looked over them all, his hands clasped behind his back. He nodded his white-maned head to Calan, so Calan immediately bowed and saluted.

"Now that you've all arrived, I'll get right to it. You have each done me and your masters proud. No matter who ultimately wins, the world will know that three of the eight Uncrowned belonged to me."

Calan didn't feel like he'd been given any support from Reigan Shen at all, but he knew that even the thought was dangerous.

There was no contradicting a Monarch. If he claimed responsibility for Calan's success, then he was responsible.

"I have one final assignment for you. I will provide you with a gatekey that I created long ago. When the tournament concludes, you will travel through it." He held up the key. "And you will kill Malice's youngest children."

Calan's mind immediately flashed to Mercy's fight against Sophara.

There was no way he could keep up with that.

If Shen had some way to prevent Mercy from getting any backup, then the three of them combined could probably kill her. Maybe.

He had to speak up.

"I apologize, Monarch, but I'm not sure we're capable."

Shen turned to him, and to Calan's relief the Monarch

didn't seem angry. "I have agents in place. One of them will summon you when Mercy and Pride are as isolated as possible, and you will be accompanied by Overlords who will deal with any interference. The Sage of Red Faith will lead your expedition, and he will prevent higher-level intrusion while I hold Malice here."

Calan tried to rearrange his thoughts, to ask for clarification without looking like he was questioning the Monarch, but Reigan Shen waved a hand covered in jeweled rings.

"Malice crossed me," he said simply. "She interfered with a message I meant to send, so now my Uncrowned will kill hers. This has nothing to do with Penance, so the heavens will not stop me. And if anything goes wrong...well, that's why Red Faith is there. Not to mention the other sects."

Calan felt like a worm while the fisherman explained why he was being placed on a hook. Whatever justification Shen had, Calan was going to be personally responsible for the death of a Monarch's daughter.

"Please forgive one more question, but if you're sending a Sage, why do you need us at all?"

"As I said, I don't *need* you. I have chosen you because the parallels are pleasing to me."

He supposed that was as much answer as he would get.

"And when you return," Shen went on, "I will give you anything you desire."

Calan's breath stopped.

"Shoumei, you can have Anagi's head on a plate. Calan, you grew up in my city of Rak Jagga. You can have it. The whole city. Brother Aekin, your master recently suffered a crippling injury? It's healed.

"Do any of you fear reprisal from Malice? It is likely she will be dead before moonrise tonight, but even if she lives, you are mine now. I do not give up what is mine."

Like the others, Calan Archer fell to one knee.

Sophara could feel her spirit unraveling piece by piece.

When she cycled, she could see the cracks in her madra channels shine brightly. They were still hair-thin, but they would widen with time.

They didn't weaken her. If anything, the leaks made her stronger as she burned through more and more of her power.

While she wouldn't last for long, her performance in this next fight would be extraordinary. Her battle was imminent. Not just her battle; her *victory*.

The King's eyes glowed as he looked down on her. "When you win, we will make your body and spirit anew. You will become the next Monarch from my bloodline. There is no failure in you."

Sophara's breathing was even, her madra calm and her heart full of joy. The Totem inside her carried an echo of the same power that now stood in front of her.

"What do numbers mean to you?" Seshethkunaaz whispered. "What is strategy? You are the hunter. She is the prey. And now, the hunt is here."

Sophara was ready.

Yerin and Ruby marched down the tunnels to the waiting room side-by-side.

"We're hitched to the same wagon," Yerin said. "Couldn't say why you wanted to stab yourself in the back."

"There's a chance you wouldn't have advanced with me around," Ruby responded. "Couldn't say why you blame me for leaving."

"You're the reason we can't practice moving with the Bridge!"

"Didn't need practice to use it myself, did I?"

Yerin still hated arguing with a copy of herself.

The Sages had consulted with Northstrider and confirmed that he would restore the Moonlight Bridge so Yerin could use it during the fight. Ruby claimed to have expected that all along, but she was a liar.

Charity had been forced to restrain Min Shuei so she didn't beat Ruby to death for endangering all their chances, but Ruby hadn't come anywhere close to apologizing.

And she wouldn't give Yerin a hint of what had happened in the three days while she was gone, except saying that she was with Lindon.

Which drove Yerin to pulling out her own hair.

"Shape up," the Winter Sage snapped as they approached the waiting room. "Time for you *both* to show what you can do."

When they arrived in the waiting room, Charity sat them down. Since Ruby had returned the night before, they'd spent every moment catching her up to Yerin's status as an Overlady.

Since Yerin could use the Blood Sage's technique to send power straight to her Blood Shadow, it hadn't been much of an issue, but that didn't make Yerin any happier about having to do it. If Ruby had just stayed, she would have advanced the moment Yerin did.

There was nothing left to discuss, but Charity ran them through the plan again. She even placed her hands on their foreheads, soothing their anxiety.

Ruby claimed that Dross had given her his analysis of Sophara's fighting style, but she'd been unable to teach Yerin, and their general strategy remained in place.

The Heart Sage lectured them, but Yerin had already honed herself to a sharp edge.

She'd done everything she could do.

The arena was sealed off again, and it looked so different that Yerin could imagine it was a separate world. Shining, burning waterfalls cascaded down from a ceiling that was out of view, crashing like pillars into pools in the ground. They lit the whole place brighter than noon.

Sharp blades drifted through the air, high overhead, like razor-winged birds. They made the place rich in sword aura, but they weren't so close that Yerin could dice Sophara to pieces from the start.

This time, Yerin and Sophara walked out at the same time.

The dragon wore a sacred artist's robe instead of her usual jewels and silk. Gold, of course, matching her shimmering hair and the thin tail that lashed behind her.

The scripted golden disc floated above her, and Quickriver—her liquid metal whip—was already in her hand.

She met Yerin's gaze not with fury, as Yerin had expected, but with smug confidence.

Yerin felt her own feelings echoed in Ruby.

They *both* wanted to knock that look off Sophara's face.

For the finals, even Northstrider had changed his normal appearance. He must have shaved at some point, because his scruffy beard was trimmed, his hair controlled. He wore black pants that looked as though they'd been made that morning, tied with a red cloth belt, and a spotless white shirt.

The clothes were largely ordinary, but they made a huge contrast to the Monarch's usual appearance. The man wearing them hadn't changed. He speared Yerin with a dragon's glare.

"Renew," he commanded, and Yerin could feel the Moonlight Bridge in her spirit glow bright again. Everything about her felt fresh-made, from her spirit to her mind, so it was like she'd just woken from a restful sleep.

Northstrider didn't do anything for Sophara, but Yerin didn't sense any problem with the dragon Overlady's spirit. Either she was in top condition already, or her own Monarch had restored her.

Yerin's perception pierced that space so easily that Yerin realized Northstrider hadn't put up a barrier. There was nothing separating her from Sophara.

Not that they could just begin brawling with a Monarch between them anyway.

Yerin didn't hear the Ninecloud Soul at all, and for the first time, Northstrider was the one reminding them of the rules.

"The finals are the first to three victories out of five. As before, you have half an hour in between each fight to develop your strategies."

He looked to them both. "This is traditionally the first time I would reveal to you the nature of the grand prize, but this year few traditions were respected. The winner of the tournament will come before the collected Monarchs and be granted one request."

Yerin had known for some time that the winner would earn an audience with the Monarchs, but she hadn't been sure what that entailed.

She felt Ruby's amazement...and her sudden desire.

Yerin couldn't read Ruby's mind, but she knew what *she* would want in Ruby's position, so it was probably what Ruby wished for.

Complete separation from Yerin.

Come to think of it, that wouldn't be a bad wish for Yerin.

"You cannot make a request that harms another Monarch, and there are wishes that even we cannot or will not grant. Victors often desire unparalleled weapons, secret knowledge, rank and territory, or protection."

He tilted his head up. "This year, there is an additional grand prize, but that is not in my power to assign. Whichever of you defeats the other will receive both prizes. Now... with the eyes of heaven and the world upon you, prepare for battle."

Yerin, Ruby, and Sophara all began cycling madra for their techniques. Aura swirled and gathered from all over the arena, thickening around them.

"Begin."

He vanished, and so did Yerin.

Liquid golden fire thundered out from Sophara, but Yerin used the Moonlight Bridge.

Ruby was right; it *was* easy to use.

Sophara's back was in front of her. Her blade already

shone with the Flowing Sword Enforcer technique, and she stabbed at Sophara from behind.

A golden tail slapped her away, but then Ruby fell from the sky with her *own* Flowing Sword, having leaped over the dragon's breath.

The three clashed at once.

Sophara's movements were so fast and fluid it was like she could see the future, so Yerin knew she was burning ghostwater. Without the mental enhancement the Eight-Man Empire had given Yerin, she wouldn't have been able to keep up.

Alone, she would have been overwhelmed as well.

But she wasn't alone.

Their blows thundered, sending shockwaves through the air. When Ruby was knocked away, she used the Moonlight Bridge to return in a flash, driving her black blade down on Sophara.

Every blow Yerin took would crack her bones if she didn't keep her Steelborn Iron body fueled, and even so it wasn't designed with protection in mind. She was taking a beating, and her madra drained dangerously fast.

But she could keep up.

Yerin slammed her blade into Sophara's, and this time Sophara couldn't hold her ground. She was sent flying, her body blasting through a burning waterfall, but Ruby used the Moonlight Bridge to disappear in a blink and reappear above her, kicking her into the ground and sending a Rippling Sword after her.

When the Bridge refreshed a moment later, Yerin followed, her own blade ringing and sending a wind of furious sword aura after the dragon.

Sparks flew up from Sophara's *skin* as though she was covered in scales, but her own spirit dipped. She was spending madra freely herself. At this rate, Yerin would outlast her.

Ruby had already begun activating her sword, but Sophara had been building a technique of her own.

A blue moon rose from her hand, a sphere of sapphire madra and aura that hung in the air behind her.

Her Azure Moon Reigns technique looked different than

it had when she used it against Mercy. It was smaller, denser, and Yerin felt its power cover the arena.

While it had been an inconvenience to Mercy, Yerin felt real danger from it this time. Water aura pressed down on her like a wet blanket over her entire body.

And a nearby burning pool leaped up as though to grab her.

Yerin didn't know what would happen to her if it landed, but she was sure it was more than damp hair. She used the Bridge to move away and closer to Sophara, driving her Flowing Sword into Sophara's chest.

At the same time, Ruby finished unleashing Netherclaw.

The second the huge red claw Forged, it slashed down at Sophara.

And slammed right into her Imperial Aegis.

Sophara still dashed away before her shield could be torn down, so Yerin's sword only gave her a shallow cut.

It drew blood.

Yerin didn't chase. Ruby had her pinned down, so it was time to take advantage of the opening.

She poured madra and aura into a Final Sword.

As Sophara fought the huge clawed hand that Ruby struggled to control, Yerin's sword glowed brighter and brighter silver.

A jet of water madra blasted out from the Azure Moon, but Yerin sensed it easily. She slipped out of the way.

And as soon as her technique stabilized, she vanished.

She appeared beneath Sophara.

The dragon had managed to complete her Crimson Sun Rises, which now hung in the center of the arena as a blazing sphere. She had leaped into the air, slashing Quickriver at Ruby.

From twenty feet down, Yerin released her Final Sword.

Her power formed a rising sword of silver madra so dense it appeared white.

Sophara's Imperial Aegis was blasted away, and she took the technique on her own body.

Something knocked Yerin off her feet.

Finally, a wave of water had caught her off-guard. Heat from the sun pressed down on her, and fire spurted from the surface of the Crimson Sun, forcing her to use the Bridge to travel away.

Ruby had begun using her own Final Sword while Sophara used wind aura to soar through the air. The dragon trailed blood, her skin torn and her body battered.

She wasn't ripped in half, as Yerin had hoped.

But this wasn't time to let up.

Yerin focused on her master's blade, activating the technique. Frozen Blade madra locked down the center of the arena.

Sophara didn't stop moving.

Her control of soulfire was a level beyond Yerin's. She pushed the Ruler technique aside and continued soaring down; even the blades of madra hanging in the air parted before her.

That had to take up an extraordinary amount of soulfire and madra, but so did maintaining the technique. When Sophara raised her hand for a dragon's breath, Yerin had to release the Ruler binding.

If she kept it up, it would get her killed.

She and Ruby used the Moonlight Bridge to appear and disappear, keeping the pressure on Sophara. Her ghostwater was gone, but her Moon and Sun techniques remained in the air. Even when Yerin sent a Rippling Sword at one, the Imperial Aegis defended it and Sophara took the opening to swing at Ruby.

The Madra Engine proved its value, recovering Yerin's madra and allowing her to keep fighting, and Ruby finally managed to complete a Final Sword of her own.

She traveled the Moonlight Bridge over Sophara's head, blasting down.

Instead of waiting for the result, Yerin reached out.

Though she and Ruby were hardly in prime shape, Sophara had taken a real beating. Yerin had to close out the battle.

She couldn't drop her soulfire control over the surrounding aura, or the Moon and Sun would batter her on their own, but she still closed her eyes and stretched her perception out through the sword aura.

She was almost there. So *close.*

The feeling of the Sword Icon settled around her like familiar music, and she moved accordingly.

Sophara pushed through Ruby's Final Sword, landing a heavy slash on the Shadow that sent blood spraying up and her body crashing into the wall.

But as Sophara tried to follow up with dragon's breath, Yerin appeared to her side.

Quickriver clashed with the Sword Sage's nameless blade, and Sophara was left with a cut on the arm.

Yerin knew exactly how to move, and it all felt *right.*

Even when she took a hit from Sophara's tail on her shin, she was able to stab the dragon's shoulder.

When her left hand was burned by Flowing Flame madra, she didn't feel it. She took out Sophara's eye.

Quickriver gave her a shallow cut across the ribs, but she scored a deeper one.

They traded slashes and Striker techniques, swinging faster and stronger than Yerin had ever imagined back when she was only Underlord. She relied on the Moonlight Bridge to dodge when she needed to, but she often didn't, moving as little as possible.

Ruby had recovered and was preparing a technique of her own.

Yerin had Sophara on the verge of defeat.

Then Yerin's consciousness fuzzed.

The state of perfect concentration fled, and pain came *screaming* into its place.

Yerin hadn't realized how much she'd been sliced to ribbons. She looked bloodier than Ruby ever had.

While Yerin was still shocked, Sophara's Archlord weapon ignited.

When Yerin's head came off, the last thing she saw was that same smug look on Sophara's face.

第二十五章

CHAPTER TWENTY-FIVE

"You're chipped in the head if you think I should keep leaning on a technique I can't control," Yerin insisted.

The Winter Sage gripped her hands together, taking deep breaths. "It is *not* a technique. It is a connection to greater power, and a state of mind. Most Sages do not have this... long intermediary period, you know. They gradually touch their Icon, but they manifest it quickly."

"Most Overladies cannot consistently tap into an Icon either," Charity pointed out. "Even those who become Sages. What you've done is extraordinary, Yerin, but it is incomplete. You need to either discard it or push it to completion, right now."

"Oh, that's stone simple then. I'll just finish it up."

"I *know* that is not a fair request of someone below Archlord," Min Shuei said. "But it is your best chance of victory."

Yerin felt like the walls were closing in. Half an hour had never felt so short.

She had given Sophara everything she had, and it still hadn't been enough. The worst of it was, Sophara *hadn't* given it everything. The Dragon King's Totem, her prize from the last round, still hadn't made an appearance.

So, reluctantly, Yerin dropped to a cycling position and stretched her master's sword across her lap.

She searched for the Sword Icon, but it was hard when she heard her own voice coming from Ruby's mouth.

"I'd contend I should give it a try too," the Blood Shadow said. "Can't bleed worse than we did already."

The Winter Sage huffed. "There's no point. Just cycle."

"Your madra is not a reflection of the Sword Icon," Charity explained, though she had taught this concept many times before. "You are hunger and blood as well as swords. Besides, spirits cannot touch Icons, only living humans can. It's hard enough for Heralds, who are only half spirits."

Yerin sensed frustration in Ruby's silence.

"Your job is to sacrifice yourself to buy time," the Winter Sage said.

Then Yerin shut them all out.

Memories of her own movements, the feel of the Sword Icon, and the Winter Sage's training wove in her mind with the image of her master moving. The sword codex, given to her by Emriss, flowed through her.

She let go of her fear, her anxiety, her attachment to victory.

Yerin left it all behind and pursued the heart of a Sage.

When she walked out again for the second fight, her every footstep was to the rhythm of sword authority. The aura sang as it whispered around her, and rang in a constant chorus. Everything was within reach of her sword.

Rather than hearing Northstrider's announcement to start the fight, she felt it.

Ruby winked out of existence and appeared in front of Sophara, their battle crashing over the landscape, and Yerin could feel where it was going.

She stepped in easily, cutting Sophara across the elbow.

It was supposed to sever her arm, but the dragon's arm stayed where it was. Blood sprayed. The unexpected couldn't sway Yerin; she was deep in the music, and she could sense her next move.

She knocked aside Sophara's tail and her blade, with soulfire empowering her Flowing Sword. The tip of the tail flew off.

Ruby's Endless Sword opened cuts all over Sophara's body.

Quickriver pierced Ruby's chest.

Yerin drove her own sword through the dragon's back, but the dragon tore Ruby to bloody pieces as she did.

Then spiritual and physical power clamped down on Yerin's blade, locking it inside Sophara's body.

The Sword Icon told her to run power through her sword and pull it free, so she tried, but she was too weak. It took her an instant too long, and Sophara was too strong. Yerin missed the beat of the music by a hair.

Burning madra the color of a sunset swallowed her body whole.

Charity was pacing up and down the waiting room when Yerin returned. "Forget the Sword Icon," she insisted. "It's doing nothing but making us more vulnerable. Until you can manifest it fully, it's giving you the wrong advice."

"That was so *close!*" Min Shuei insisted. She was arguing with Charity, not with Yerin. As though Yerin's opinion didn't matter.

"If my memory's true, it took even less time for her to bury me the second time," Yerin said.

"But you almost killed *her.* Sword artists evolve through combat; this is your time!"

The Winter Sage's voice was earnest, her expression sincere.

Ruby hunched over in the corner, silent.

She carried the Heart's Gem from the Blood Sage around, cycling its blood aura. It couldn't improve her much in this short time, but every little bit could help.

Her despair weighed down Yerin's own spirit.

They were going to lose.

Whatever Malice's plans were to save Fury, would they extend to Lindon and Eithan? Would they even extend to Mercy?

And what would happen if Penance was used on Malice instantly?

Everything had come down to Yerin, and Yerin was about to break.

"Could you leave us to talk?" Yerin asked.

The Sages turned to her in astonishment.

"There's no time!" the Winter Sage insisted. "We can guide you through this."

"Please," Yerin said. She knew that Min Shuei would listen if there were tears in her eyes, so she tried to bring them up. It was easier than she'd thought.

"*Please,*" she repeated.

"We'll be back in five minutes," Charity said.

But they both left.

Ruby was looking toward her, her red hair and eyes bright in the dark, and Yerin wondered if she knew what was going through Yerin's head.

If she did, she should have looked happier.

Yerin stilled the trembling in her own hands. She pushed years of nightmares to the back of her head.

"If you swallow my spirit and take my body," Yerin said, "can you win?"

Ruby watched her quietly for a moment.

"You thinking Northstrider can split us up again after?"

Yerin held on to that hope, but it still wasn't a risk she wanted to take. What if he couldn't? What if he could, but he didn't? Even if he could, what could Ruby do while she had control of Yerin's body?

The idea had haunted her since she was a little girl.

Yerin kept the shaking from her voice. "Can't bet my soul on it. But that's what I'll be doing."

Ruby paced over to her. She looked Yerin up and down, and Yerin could feel the hunger in her spirit.

"Nah," Ruby said. "No hope of that."

She sat down on a bench, turning back to the Heart's Gem.

Yerin didn't trust her ears. "You acting like we're lifetime friends now?"

Ruby shrugged one shoulder. "Lindon would hate me."

For some reason, that answer enraged Yerin more than any other.

She stalked over and seized Ruby by the collar of her robe. "Bleed and bury what Lindon wants!" Yerin shouted. "What do *you* want?"

Ruby stood and met her face-to-face. "*I'm* aiming for us all to live! You hearing me? *Everybody!*"

Every passing second was another second closer to Yerin's third loss. The pressure squeezed her heart until she thought it would pop.

She'd spent months trying to tap into the Sword Icon. It was ordinarily something Archlords spent lifetimes pursuing; she had made it so far only because she'd had Sages to teach her. Not just now, but all her life.

How could she force that now? How could she count on it? *I am not the Sage of the Endless Sword.*

What did that mean for her? Should she be chasing down some other Icon?

Malice had asked her: "*What is* your *signature?*"

Bleed me if I know.

Yerin's trembling stopped. Her eyes fell on the Heart's Gem that sat in the corner, the scarlet chunk of petrified blood drifting in its scripted glass tank.

Thinking too deeply didn't suit her.

Why was she trying to be a Sage again?

She gripped Ruby's robe with renewed intensity. "We should combine."

Ruby narrowed one eye. "You cracked in the head?"

"Like Heralds do with their Remnants!" Yerin insisted. "The Blood Sage was all lit up about us doing it at Archlord."

"You don't look like an Archlady to me," Ruby said.

"Supposed to wait for Archlord to be a Sage too, aren't we? If we're jumping the fence, let's do it *all the way.*" Yerin released Ruby's robes and grabbed her shoulders. "It fails when the Remnant and the artist fight each other, so they end up destroying the other, but we're nine parts the same. We going to fight each other?"

In eyes that were a red reflection of her own, Yerin watched doubt ignite into baseless, reckless confidence.

"Bleed and bury me," Ruby said, "I'm in."

There was a trembling to her spirit, a deep underlying terror. She was easily as afraid as Yerin was.

But they were both more afraid of losing.

They clasped identical hands.

Yerin opened her spirit and focused her will, pulling the Blood Shadow back into her spirit. Where she belonged.

Ruby didn't melt and flow back into Yerin's spirit, but while Yerin was pulling, Ruby started to *push*. Her own will flowed into Yerin, trying to take over Yerin's body as Yerin fought to take her spirit.

It was so much harder than Yerin had expected.

Her every instinct was to reject intrusion from an outside power. Even without her consciously directing it, her spirit fought against Ruby, trying to push out the Blood Shadow.

Ruby was the same; her madra fought against Yerin's command even when Ruby wasn't controlling it.

It was only then that Yerin appreciated what Charity had meant when she'd said that there was no better willpower training than fighting a Blood Shadow.

Every time the Shadow tried to take over Yerin and Yerin resisted, it was a direct clash of wills. Yerin grew stronger as she resisted.

But the opposite was true too.

Their years of fights had sharpened Yerin's will, but they had also sharpened the spirit that would become Ruby.

And all that sharpening against one another had perfectly prepared them to work together.

After a few endless seconds of intense struggle, their wills snapped into place. They wanted the same thing, after all, they were just coming at it from different angles.

Red madra began to flow through Yerin's channels in reverse.

And her silver madra let it happen.

At that moment, the door burst open. The Winter Sage marched in, fury and terror whipping the air around her.

"Stop!" she shouted, and reality responded to her authority.

Yerin and Ruby froze.

Their spirits froze.

Even the air froze.

Together, they recognized what would happen if this continued. The Winter Sage would separate them, afraid of what they would become, and then they would go into the third fight no better prepared than in the second.

They focused on her working, and together they pushed against it.

An unseen force snapped, and their madra flowed freely again.

The Winter Sage gasped, then set herself to try again. Yerin clenched her jaw, and Ruby made the same motion. If they had to keep resisting a Sage, they would lose control of their fusion.

Charity threw out a hand. "Stop! Don't take away what chance they have!"

Reluctantly, painfully, the Winter Sage backed down.

Yerin returned, looking back to Ruby. New memories flowed into her now—records of Sophara that Dross had given her, wielding the Endless Sword to protect an unconscious Lindon from a sea of dreadbeasts, Lindon holding her hand as she tried to fall asleep.

There was no resistance, but Yerin felt grief and regret flow from Ruby along with her madra. Her time had been too short.

Then it was *her* grief. *Her* regret.

And what was she sad about, anyway? She wasn't going anywhere.

Madra soaked into Yerin's channels, her spirit, and stained the bright silver a vivid crimson.

Her body tore itself apart, but there was no pain. She dissolved into silver-red light...and she felt a chance.

She had to Forge herself back together.

But her old body wasn't quite...right. It didn't represent who she was anymore. She had some choices to make.

She hadn't liked bright red hair, but it had become part of her. Maybe one lock. Her eyes...she didn't really want eyes so similar to Fury's. Then again, when she tried to change them to Yerin's black, she found it easier to keep them as Ruby's red.

She didn't mind what color her eyes were anyway.

She could make more dramatic changes to her body, but she didn't need them. She liked the way she looked. It was *her*, and now there were enough changes to represent the new her.

One change, though, she didn't have any control over.

When her body returned, condensing into reality, she extended all six of her Goldsigns. They still had a metallic gleam, but now they were a bright, vivid scarlet.

Two spiritual perceptions swept through her as the Sages checked her.

"Heavens above," Charity breathed.

The Winter Sage's eyes filled with tears.

Then other spirits scanned Yerin. Though most weren't close by, she recognized them.

The Monarchs.

At some point, the door had opened completely, but Northstrider hadn't moved her outside. Instead, he stood in the center of the arena with his arms crossed.

Experimentally, Yerin examined herself. She didn't feel so different. She remembered being Ruby, but it didn't feel like being a different person. Just...herself in a different mood. Or in a different light, maybe.

Her techniques would need refining now, with the introduction of blood madra. She supposed she wasn't really on the Path of the Endless Sword anymore, which sent a pang of regret through her.

She tried to sense the Sword Icon, and she heard not a whisper.

But her madra felt...boundless.

Her channels were more real in her mind's eye than ever, and she could feel them in her actual body. Her core sat below her stomach, and power filled every inch of her.

It wasn't exactly like advancement; her madra hadn't gone

up a level in quality. It was more like all the restrictions of Overlord had been removed. Yerin didn't understand it fully.

So she needed to test it.

Instead of using the Moonlight Bridge, she decided to run to Northstrider's side.

It took her one leap.

The air tore as she passed through it, and she came to a stumbling halt next to him in a storm of wind.

"That one's on my account," she said. "Not used to my new legs."

Sophara looked like she'd just seen her children murdered in front of her.

"We have a problem," the Monarch said, and Yerin's heart leaped into her throat. "The Uncrowned King tournament has a rule against advancing past Overlord. Archlords cannot compete. Neither can Heralds."

Yerin's stomach froze.

"But you have not advanced," he went on. "We have no rule for this."

"What does that mean?" Sophara demanded. "Let me fight her!"

Northstrider didn't look to her. "You have no input here. We are about to either disqualify Yerin or declare her the winner."

Yerin's heart was getting whiplash. "Run that back for me."

"There is no such thing as an Overlord Herald," Northstrider said. His stony face quirked into a small smile. "Until now."

She had never seen anything like a smile on him before.

It was unnerving.

He looked from one Monarch tower to the other, presumably tallying votes. "It seems we have a tie. As the arbiter of this contest, I should not break it." He looked up. "Kiuran of the Hounds, we could use the judgment of the heavens in this matter."

There came a halfhearted blue flash, and then an irritated-looking heavenly messenger appeared in the center of the arena. "Can you not settle something this simple on your own? Let them fight it out."

Sophara's tail lashed. "Yes. I have not shown everything I can do."

Northstrider turned to her. "Let the will of Heaven be done. Sopharanatoth of the gold dragons, are you ready?"

Sophara's shield drifted above her, and she snapped Quickriver into the form of a short, broad sword.

Yerin started cycling madra into her Flowing Sword, and she was shocked at how quickly and easily the madra flooded into her weapon. It glowed red-and-white almost immediately, blazing with power.

Northstrider shook his head. "Release your technique, Yerin."

Suspicious, Yerin did so.

"Still your madra."

Yerin wanted to protest, but she did as instructed. She hadn't been forced to do this on any other rounds.

"If you start at the same time as she does," Northstrider explained, "the fight will be too short."

Yerin didn't know what to say to that.

The Monarch stepped back. "Now...begin."

Dragon's breath shot toward Yerin in a wave, and she used the Moonlight Bridge to appear behind Sophara. She put madra into her Steelborn Iron body and swung.

With ghostwater speeding her reflexes, Sophara turned and caught Yerin's blow on her own sword.

She went flying into the distant ceiling.

Yerin had already started her follow-up swing, so finding no opponent was a shock. A moment later, she shook herself out of it, using the Moonlight Bridge to follow.

As she fell, Sophara began to gather gold light into the image of a dragon over her head. Yerin felt dangerous power in that, so she sent a Rippling Sword at Sophara.

It crashed into Sophara's Imperial Aegis and knocked the shield aside.

The second one cut Sophara in half.

Yerin found herself falling to the sand as Sophara turned to white light and dispersed.

Yerin blinked.

Northstrider reappeared before her. "A Herald's spirit and body are one. You can use your power freely, and your own body can shift to spiritual or physical form. Like sacred instruments that can be stored in a soulspace."

A black orb appeared on his shoulder, and her spirit shivered. She got the impression that *it* was scanning her.

"You will not be a true Herald until you advance to the peak of Archlord the traditional way, but you can think of yourself as being...*more* than any other Overlord." He looked into the black orb as though checking something. "It's fascinating. The Blood Sage will do anything to examine you. I would advise you not to let him."

That was advice Yerin didn't need.

But the fight wasn't over. She gestured vaguely to the waiting room on the far side. "So they're just going to let me beat on her two more times?"

"The Dragon King, as you can imagine, is less than satisfied by this turn of events. I have been hiding his anger from you."

Yerin felt a wave of something pass from Northstrider, as though he tore down an invisible curtain, and then an overwhelming anger crashed like a wave around her. Anger... and helplessness.

"There is nothing he can do with the Abidan and six other Monarchs here." Northstrider murmured. "Nothing to do with all his power, all his wealth."

His smile was like the cracking of stone. "Poor little dragon."

Tension held the atmosphere in stasis as enemies filled the air over the Sky's Edge fortress.

Lindon had to withdraw his spiritual sense, as the pressure of so many hostile spirits was grating on him. His own nerves were bad enough.

[There's no point in worrying,] Dross said. [How can worry help? Look at me! I'm not worried.]

Lindon didn't respond.

Five seconds later, Dross continued. [It's a strange human thing, worrying. There's no point to it, like I said. What will happen if Yerin loses, anyway? I have so many scenarios. Some of them aren't too bad!]

More than just dragons flew through the air. The sacred artists from the Dreadgod cults hovered above them too, ready to attack at news of Sophara's victory.

Even Fury drifted over the fortress, hands tucked into his pockets. He didn't look as lazy or as unconcerned as he had before, looking to each of the four Herald spirits around him as though he couldn't wait to fight.

Four.

Lindon focused on his breathing, and he had to focus twice as hard when he saw a flickering violet star appear in front of Fury.

A messenger construct.

What did it say? Lindon asked Dross desperately, but Dross had already begun a dull response.

[Sophara's won twice, and there's a delay in the third fight.]

Lindon's heart crashed.

[Maybe a delay is a good thing! Maybe she's...advancing.]

A rousing cheer went up from every direction outside their forces. The enemy was spreading the news far and wide.

A few stray Striker techniques crashed here and there around the fortress, though the only ones likely to do any harm were annihilated by a casual flick of Fury's hand.

But he didn't retaliate.

Beneath him, under the roof of the fortress, Archlords had started to gather up the Golds in front of a tall, scripted stone.

This was their emergency escape: an evacuation portal. It connected to a network of permanent gates, but even so it was a huge expense to activate. Especially since it was meant to escape four hostile Heralds.

Mercy and Pride stood whispering frantically to one another near the portal, and Lindon could imagine from their gestures what they were arguing about.

Either Pride wanted them both to leave and Mercy wanted to stay until the others were evacuated, or they each wanted the other to leave.

He wanted to go weigh in his opinion—Mercy and Pride should both leave, given their relative importance to the Akura clan—but the Seishen Underlords were nearby. Meira stood in full armor, looking up the stairs, while Daji glared holes through Mercy and Pride.

At least he wasn't angry at Lindon.

Lindon exchanged nods with Akura Grace as he walked further away. Talking with the Seishen Kingdom around would be too uncomfortable.

And he wanted to be close to Fury so he could get the battle report that little bit sooner.

When the violet spark appeared only a moment later, his throat clenched shut. The only reason for the fight to be so short was Sophara annihilating Yerin.

[Yerin won,] Dross repeated. [Yerin won! She...wow, we owe Yerin some congratulations.]

Overhead, Fury began to laugh.

Yerin started the second fight once again with no technique forming and her madra still.

Gold light began to condense over Sophara's head.

She didn't play around with Ruler techniques this time.

She didn't even start out with dragon's breath.

The Dragon King's Totem condensed into a crown of power over her head. A majestic golden serpent drifted over her, crafted from powerful madra, whipping up a sandstorm of Forged madra. The spirit of the Totem glared down on Yerin with majesty that pressed against her spirit...and given that her spirit was now interwoven with her flesh, it felt like it was pushing down on her body.

"Begin," Northstrider said.

Yerin used the Final Sword.

Her sword shone mostly silver, but even this was tinged with red. A greater will battered at hers, trying to stop her technique, and sand tore her skin.

Yerin unleashed her technique, and red-white light blasted through the image of the golden dragon overhead.

It detonated, blasting out a hurricane of wind. The burning waterfalls from the ceiling sprayed outwards, and sparks of golden essence filled the sky like fireworks.

Sophara staggered back as her technique was broken, and Yerin appeared at her throat with the Moonlight Bridge.

A white blade lopped off the dragon's head.

Reigan Shen turned to the Blood Sage.

"Ready yourself," he said. "This tournament is over."

Over the Sky's Edge fortress, Akura Fury drifted higher into the air.

His voice boomed out over the valley, echoing across every inch between the giant white blade stabbed into the earth and the black stone hand clutching the bay. "What's wrong, everybody? You don't want to play anymore?"

Inside the fortress, a doorway ignited. Blue light swirled, and the Archlords started loading Golds into it.

A massive gold dragon slithered out of the clouds on the back of a sandstorm. "Don't get excited, Fury," she said. "We're not letting you leave because we're afraid of *you.*"

Fury laughed heartily.

"You're letting *me* leave, you say?"

In the fifth and final fight of the last round of the Uncrowned King tournament, Sophara launched herself at Yerin, screaming.

Northstrider hadn't even called the beginning of the fight yet, but he didn't stop her. Quickriver was covered in orange flame, the Archlord Enforcer binding, and Sophara launched dragon's breath from her left hand.

Yerin's spirit gave her no sense of danger, so she decided to experiment.

The Moonlight Bridge carried her behind Sophara, and she realized that there was still something in her soulspace.

She summoned the black-bladed sword, Netherclaw, and activated the technique.

Sophara whirled and tried to engage Yerin blade-to-blade, but Yerin moved away in an instant flash of moonlight.

The clawed hand appeared faster than it ever had before, and more solid than she'd ever seen it. It filled the arena with so much power that it almost felt like a real Archlord technique.

Yerin poured not only soulfire into it, but put all her will behind it. She *urged* the claw to become stronger.

Sophara put both hands behind a river of dragon's breath, still screaming.

The Netherclaw crashed into the ground.

It crushed Sophara.

It shattered the ground.

It split the arena in two, revealing a shimmering barrier of purple light separating the arena from the outside world.

And then even that barrier cracked.

The Ninecloud Soul's voice leaked in from outside. "...witnessing history here today! Sacred artists one and all, bear witness to the eighteenth Uncrowned King!"

Sophara's dragon's breath faded to white.

Lindon wondered if Fury was going to get them all killed.

Why was he taunting the enemy at a four-to-one disadvantage? It was insanity.

Xorrus the gold dragon Herald gave a sigh that rang over Sky's Edge. "We're letting you out of the trap, humans. Go home."

Inwardly, Lindon urged Fury to take the deal.

But the Akura Herald was still laughing. "Yeah, but see, we're not the ones trapped here."

Lindon didn't see the punch, but he saw the aftermath. Fury disappeared and reappeared beneath Xorrus, driving his fist up and into the dragon's stomach. Lindon saw no flash of darkness; as far as he could tell, that was just a punch.

In the sky, clouds split apart.

And Fury shouted in a command that shook reality itself: **"Break."**

It was the authority of a Sage.

The dragon split into fragments, each piece dissolving into shining golden sand.

Xorrus started re-forming herself, but a new image had appeared across the entire sky: a fist, facing down as though about to plunge and annihilate the earth beneath them.

The image shook Lindon's spirit with the impression of absolute strength before it vanished a moment later.

What was that? he asked, shaken.

[Uh, well, I've never seen it before, but it's pretty...distinct. That's called the Strength Icon, or the Fist Icon, or the Symbol of Bodily Power, depending on where you're from.]

An Icon. Fury had broken through.

He was ascending to Monarch.

Only then did Lindon feel the madra, overwhelming and impossibly powerful, as the entire valley was covered in shadow.

Xorrus choked out a voice tinged with fear and anger, "Why? If you could advance, why did you wait?"

A Forged hand of shadow grabbed her by the scaled throat, and Fury pulled her close. He was only the size of one of her eyes. *"To see this look on your face."*

Then three other Heralds unveiled their power, and the true battle began.

CHAPTER TWENTY-SIX

INFORMATION REQUESTED: AKURA MALICE, QUEEN OF SHADOWS AND RULER OF THE WESTERN ASHWIND CONTINENT.

BEGINNING REPORT...

Path: Eternal Night. Though she is famous for the creation of the Path of Seven Pages, Malice herself has no Book. She is the practitioner of a pure shadow Path with an emphasis on Forger and Ruler techniques, and she sees her madra as a perfect blend of power and utility. However, her dissatisfaction with her own Path led her to create an idealized version: her Book of Eternal Night.

Everyone in the Akura family is named after a virtue. Even Malice.

When Malice was born, the Akura family was a tiny band of humans in a vicious wilderness. They were destroyed by a rival when she was only days old, their members dispersed.

She was named for the quality of ruthlessness, spite, focused hatred that her parents hoped would guide her to avenge them.

Malice grew up among exiles working with vengeance as her only goal, but she slowly realized how hollow revenge really was.

To her, the only thing that matters is the good of the family.

She had a firm sense of justice, defending the weak and fighting the strong, but she learned that the world of vicious competition was unfair to those born human. The best way to protect the weak was to gather them under one banner.

And to remove all threats at the roots.

The family is safest when its rivals are dead.

SUGGESTED TOPIC: THE BIRTH OF AKURA FURY.

DENIED, REPORT COMPLETE.

The four Monarchs bound to Ninecloud City had come together in the Court's royal audience hall, allegedly to discuss the end of the tournament in peace.

Northstrider knew what was really going to happen. He was ready.

"I accept the results," Seshethkunaaz said coldly. "Freak twists of fate are part of strength as well. If I must ascend, so be it."

Reigan Shen idly toyed with one of his rings. "I would imagine she will exterminate the Bleeding Phoenix, as some portion of her link to it no doubt remains. But if I am forced to ascend, I suppose I will see you all sooner or later."

They were not as fatalistic as they pretended, Northstrider knew. The dragon, at least, was seething inside. He wasn't even doing a good job of hiding it.

But he was more interested in someone else's act.

Malice's smirk widened into a smile. "Sometimes I wonder if you know me at all, Sesh. Your people destroyed the Rising Earth sect and tried to destroy two more of my teams."

Northstrider sensed something in the great distance.

The dragon and the lion looked up at the same time.

"Did you think that I would let that go?" Malice continued. "Did you think I couldn't reach you?" Her smile widened further into a fierce, maniacal grin. "Did you forget my *name*?"

As the power in the distance grew, Malice's laughter and her shadows boiled up to fill the hall.

Fury was advancing to Monarch.

At last.

Seshethkunaaz rose up on a cloud of golden sand. "You cannot stop me from interfering." His power exploded, tearing off the entire roof of the tower and dissolving it to sand in an instant. "Use the arrow! I will take your son with me to the *grave*."

With the tournament over, and all four Monarchs ready to leave, the barrier trapping them in Ninecloud City fell apart.

A gust of sand in the shape of a snarling serpent, containing the full willpower of the Dragon King, struck at Malice.

She held up one hand to stop it.

An amethyst gauntlet bigger than the entire top of the tower formed in front of her, and the sand crashed into it like water into a boulder.

Malice's eyes blazed, and she rose into the air. An instant later, she and the dragon were miles away, slowly ramping up to their full power.

All over Ninecloud City, alarms blared. Sha Miara's power covered them, rainbow light moving citizens to shelter or blocking stray bursts of power.

Northstrider kept his eyes on Reigan Shen.

The lion twisted his rings, looking disturbed. "This really isn't necessary. We could have worked together to mutual benefit."

Northstrider stayed quiet. Those were words that Tiberian Arelius had used on Shen.

They hadn't worked then, and they certainly wouldn't work now.

"Well, Penance is beyond our reach," the lion continued.

He glanced up, and Northstrider knew he was looking at the blue bubble of the Way that contained Kiuran the Hound and Yerin Arelius, victor of the Uncrowned King tournament.

"...and I think we've already settled the hierarchy between us to our satisfaction."

In fact, Reigan Shen hadn't beaten Northstrider. The Weeping Dragon had. But Shen was no easy opponent himself, and his mastery over spatial travel meant he could escape anything.

"So let's just go about our business, shall we?"

Space tore open behind Shen, revealing the blue of the Way.

"Stop," Northstrider commanded.

The portal sealed itself.

Reigan Shen turned, and his own authority matched or even exceeded Northstrider's. "Do not play games with me, human. If you want a battle, I will give you one."

Blood madra began to rise from Northstrider.

He reached into his soulspace and tapped into his black orb. His oracle codex.

His experimental Presence.

INFORMATION REQUESTED: COMBAT REPORT ON REIGAN SHEN.

The report began, but Northstrider pushed it to his subconscious.

Northstrider had clashed with Reigan Shen many times. He had gathered more information on the Emperor of Lions than anyone else alive, and his construct had analyzed the Path of the King's Key a million different ways.

But it had taken Dross to bring all that together.

Now, his weapon was complete.

King's Key madra tore open space to Shen's left and right, but Northstrider knew what weapons were about to come out.

He Forged a crimson dragon from blood madra, filling it with the authority of the Dragon Icon. The serpent roared as it rushed at Shen, blocking the line of fire from both launchers that the lion had just summoned.

Shen was already traveling away, but Northstrider could see where.

He moved at the same time Reigan Shen did.

The Dragon was not the only Icon that Northstrider had manifested. He launched a punch, and the authority of the Strength Icon empowered him.

Reigan Shen appeared out of the Way, and Northstrider's black-scaled knuckles caught him in the white-gold mane.

The shockwave cracked the tower beneath them, and Shen was sent flying out of Ninecloud City.

With a brief effort of will, Northstrider followed.

Sophara trembled more violently than the city cracking around her.

She'd failed...and it wasn't even her *fault*.

As the ceiling crumbled around her, she knelt on the floor and desperately tried to figure out how to salvage this situation.

The reality crashed in on her: her spirit was finished. Her future as a sacred artist was gone.

She'd borrowed too much from her future, and it hadn't even paid off. Even if her king was willing to invest more resources in her, he wouldn't survive the night.

Penance. The arrow was going to kill her great-grandfather.

How could it go anywhere else?

What could she do? There *had* to be something. There was always something.

A pale human with bloody streaks down his face appeared in front of her.

She swept her sword at him, but he stopped it with one hand. "Don't forget who you are. We're going to kill Akura Mercy and her brother, Pride. Come with us, and Reigan Shen can extend your life."

She recognized the Sage of Red Faith, as well as the half-dozen people behind him. Calan Archer, Yan Shoumei, and Brother Aekin had competed against her, and the other three were Overlords from Redmoon Hall that she didn't know.

For one reckless instant, she considered trying to kill them all.

If the Dragon King's Totem could stall the Sage, she could kill the rest, she was sure. Yerin might see it and appreciate that she'd saved Akura Mercy. Then she would use Penance on Reigan Shen instead.

Despair stopped her. She had no reason to think that Yerin would see any of this. Even if she did, she might not even care.

Sophara's head drooped. The best she could do was cling to this thin thread of hope.

And take out her pain on her enemies.

She drew herself to her feet. "I can handle Mercy," she said.

The Blood Sage chewed on his thumb. "Then we await our summons."

When Fury advanced to Monarch, Lindon expected him to instantly wipe out all the enemies.

Instead, a battle had begun that tore the sky and annihilated the city below. Chunks of the surrounding mountains hurled themselves at Fury, courtesy of the Abyssal Palace Herald. The Herald of Redmoon Hall struck with waves of bloody needles like crimson cloud banks, while the Herald of the Silent Servants cut at Fury with endless slashes of a white sword that lit up the sky.

The Stormcallers had no Herald, but one Sage. It was hard for Lindon to follow the exact details of the fight, but the Sage of Calling Storms seemed to be wrestling against Fury's authority, opposing whenever Fury made one of his echoing commands.

Lindon could feel the will pressing down on Fury, constraining him.

The newborn Monarch kept fighting.

Palms of shadow struck at the side of the Abyssal Palace fortress, sending it careening to the side. A blazing ball of inky shadow crashed into the swordswoman Herald of the Silent Servants, and she had to focus all her power on keeping it from annihilating her.

Throughout the battle, Fury's laughter echoed.

The remainder of the Akura faction had a war of their own to handle. Most of the enemies had retreated in the chaos, but not all, and it fell to the most advanced among them to stop the barrage of techniques from killing Golds as they tried to retreat.

Lindon himself struck down a cloud with dragon's breath, used the Hollow Domain for an instant to wipe out a barrage of weaker Striker techniques, and leaped to drive his Empty Palm into an enemy Underlord's core.

There were relatively few Archlords on the battlefield, and most were trying to help suppress Fury, but four focused on the fortress.

There were only three Archlords among the Akura, and those seven formed the loudest and most intense battle in Lindon's immediate vicinity. Akura Justice, the old man with the long beard who had examined Lindon's spirit in Moongrave, used his shadow madra to try and drag their fight away.

It had taken all of Lindon's power just to deflect some stray madra from that fight, so he was relieved when that flashing cage of madra moved away from them.

He glanced down the stairs to see that most of the Golds were gone. It would be the Underlords' turn to evacuate next, and Lindon would be happy to leave as long as Mercy and Pride left first.

Though he did briefly wonder who would redeem his points if Fury didn't make it back.

At the thought of Mercy and Pride, Lindon looked across the roof of the fortress to see them engaging in battle. Pride was covered in crystalline armor, beating senseless an Abyssal Palace priest, and Mercy was keeping up a barrage of dark arrows.

They fought side-by-side with the Seishen Kingdom Underlords, but Malice's children were doing more than their share of the work.

Grace wove through the few enemies that landed, her sword tracing a black line as she danced. Her cousins Douji and Courage watched over her, covering her with lightning and flying swords as she fought, and Naru Saeya was a green blur in the air overhead.

[Well, it would be rude not to join the gang,] Dross pointed out.

Lindon moved to join them.

Then he saw Seishen Daji pull something out of a pocket and toss it at Mercy's feet.

It looked like a spike the size of his arm, covered in rings of script.

An instant later, a group of people appeared out of nowhere standing over the spike. A pale, lanky man with long, white hair and bare feet loomed over Mercy, and behind him...

Lindon's heart stopped.

Behind him, all four enemy Uncrowned.

The Soul Cloak rose up in Lindon, Dross shouted a warning, and Lindon ran as fast as he could.

He didn't react as quickly as Eithan.

The Arelius Overlord dove and rolled close to the group.

An instant before they all disappeared.

Eithan rolled to his feet and launched a Hollow King's Spear.

Not the imitation Striker technique he'd been forced to use when he was only an Underlord. A real one.

It resembled an actual spear of blue-white madra, lancing into the group of enemies surrounding Mercy and Pride. It was effectively the same technique as it had been, just a lance of pure madra, but in this form it conducted willpower much better.

The spear drove through the spirit of one of the Redmoon Overlords, instantly destroying his soul.

The Underlords ran out of the way, but they wouldn't have made it if the Sage hadn't interfered.

Red Faith slapped the spearhead, blowing it into a cloud of pure madra essence.

Then he stopped to examine Eithan and chew on a knuckle.

Only then did Eithan pay attention to where they'd been taken.

He knew it couldn't have been *too* far, because the Blood Sage had carried too many people. The gatekey that had taken them here would work only in one direction, and that device had already done its job.

They stood in a wide-open room filled with dusty furniture. Stone walls, stone floor; it was the base of a tower that you could find almost anywhere. They were far enough away that the battle between Heralds—well, one Monarch and four Heralds—didn't loom over them, but not so far that they couldn't hear the thunder or feel the ground shaking.

Most importantly, Eithan's Spear had forced the group of enemies away from Mercy and Pride.

There were more people all throughout the tower, innocent bystanders caught up in the Blood Sage's reckless teleportation.

And seven enemies left.

There was a staircase at Mercy's back, and in the moment of uncertainty after the transportation, Eithan was the first to speak.

"Up the stairs!" he shouted.

Akura Douji and Courage shot up, but Pride and Mercy waited for Grace and Naru Saeya.

Saeya stopped at the bottom stair for an instant as though thinking she could help, but after a moment of agony she flew upwards.

Eithan sighed in relief as he strolled over to stand at the bottom stair. The enemies had fanned out instead of following, which was considerate of them. They focused on him.

Calan Archer conjured a lightning dragon. Yan Shoumei gathered blood madra in her palms, but didn't summon Crusher. Brother Aekin covered himself in his Enforcer technique, taking on the vague aspect of the Wandering Titan.

The two remaining Redmoon Overlords summoned their Blood Shadows around their weapons: a spear and an axe. The one he'd downed had carried a sword.

Nice of them to have such a variety; it made them easy to tell apart.

Eithan pulled out his scissors. "Well," he said, "isn't this an *interesting* situation in which I find myself."

Sophara glowered at him. An Enforcer technique hummed through her, her shield drifted over her head, and her liquid whip pooled at her side.

None of them attacked him, which showed unusually keen instincts on their side. They couldn't have pierced his veil, but they still knew something was off.

The Sage of Red Faith took a bloody finger from his mouth. "How did you advance so quickly? Even with our Monarch providing you with resources, it should have taken you much longer."

"Well, I wasn't competing, so I didn't have to adhere to tournament rules anymore," Eithan said. And then, since the proverbial cat was out of the bag, he released his veil.

His Archlord power covered the entire tower.

As the Sage of a Thousand Eyes had said, reaching Archlord had never been a problem for him. It had only been a question of resources.

And Reigan Shen was a cat of his word. He'd promised to sponsor Eithan's advancement, and his deliveries had been prompt. Though no doubt he'd expected his first shipment to last Eithan for years.

Well, Eithan hoped to surprise him many more times in the future.

Of course, that would require him to survive.

Archlord had been trivial, since he'd started with the requisite insight, but Sage was still a different matter entirely.

"I didn't ask you *why*," the Blood Sage said irritably, "I asked you *how*. Children, go upstairs. Arelius, you **move**."

A great pressure squeezed Eithan from every direction as space itself tried to move him.

But he pushed back.

It was a harder task than he would have preferred.

"I...don't think...I will."

The Blood Sage's working peaked, then collapsed.

Eithan's outer robe fluttered before it fell back down. He remained right where he was.

The Blood Sage chewed on his knuckle for a moment, then spoke another command. **"Die."**

This time, the working of will was accompanied by a Ruler technique. The blood aura in Eithan's body twisted up, seizing his heart.

Eithan crumpled, pushing with his soulfire and his madra, fighting the aura with every ounce of the willpower he'd trained every day for as long as he could remember.

By the time the fit passed, he and the Blood Sage were alone, and battle was beginning upstairs.

"They probably could have gotten me," Eithan said, his breath still coming heavily. "Thank you for holding them back."

The Blood Sage's head tilted all the way to one shoulder, then to the other. "I'm going to study you."

"I'll sign a portrait for you," Eithan said pleasantly.

Then their spirits clashed.

Lindon stood, shaking, on the empty half of the roof.

People shouted urgent questions, but Lindon stood and scooped up the scripted stone spike. It was just a teleportation anchor. It had guided them here; it hadn't taken them anywhere else.

The Blood Sage had done that.

[Couldn't have been far!] Dross said desperately. [We can find them!]

Not with the chaos all around them. Lindon couldn't stretch his spiritual perception far enough to sense anything clearly.

"Tell Fury," Lindon instructed.

[You, uh, you really want to distract him right now?]

"Do it!"

Dross sent him a message, but they didn't hear anything back. With nothing else to do, Lindon swept the empty space with his perception. Maybe the Blood Sage had left a trail.

He didn't expect to find anything, so he was filled with surprise when he actually did.

Not a trail, but a...bump...in the middle of the air.

It reminded him of the spatial cracks that had begun to appear when Ghostwater crumbled, but those had been visible to the naked eye. This one he could barely sense, even with his perception right on it.

Desperately, he pushed against it. Just as he had when trying to resist Fury, or when he'd held on to Dross.

Something shifted, but he couldn't tell what. He pushed harder.

The invisible bump in the air collapsed, stretching into a crack. If he released the pressure, the crack disappeared, and the bump returned.

Someone grabbed him by the shoulder, but he shook them off, cycling pure madra and pushing with everything he had.

Pride was there, and the rest of his team. Eithan and Mercy were there.

He was going there too.

It felt like his spirit was going to tear in half, but finally the crack deepened. It widened into a rift the length of his hand, and the edges shone blue.

But with all his concentration, that was as far as he could get.

Eithan's Hollow Armor formed an actual suit of armor. An observer could see a faint, transparent helmet over his head and plates covering his body.

The formless version, the layer of madra that covered his skin, wasn't even comparable to the performance of this complete technique.

And even so, the Blood Sage slashed through it with a Forged claw.

Eithan deflected a flying hawk of blood with his Hollow King's Mantle, which now resembled a sweeping cloak the size of the room. It swept up the Striker technique, hurling it back.

Though the hawk crashed into the Sage and did very little.

A follow-up slash from Red Faith's claws breached the gap in Eithan's armor and split open the skin of his chest. Only Eithan's reflexes kept that from including his rib cage.

He Forged his armor again and continued adding another star to the crown over his head. When the Hollow King's Crown was complete, he would have a further weapon against the Sage.

But he was exhausted and bleeding, while the Sage looked fresh as a...well, the Sage always somewhat resembled a skeleton with skin, but he was uninjured.

Despite the best efforts of Eithan's scissors.

"You know I'm not going to kill the children myself," the Blood Sage said. "You will have worked that out because I transported them here instead of killing them on the rooftop."

"Unless *my* children beat yours," Eithan pointed out. "You're here in case something goes wrong."

"That isn't what's happening."

That was true.

Other than the Overlord Eithan had ruined with so much spiritual damage that even his Remnant had been destroyed, there were no deaths on the Blood Sage's team.

All the blood drawn had been on Eithan's side.

Then Eithan saw something behind him. A flare of blue. The Blood Sage sensed it at the same time he did, but Eithan was closer.

Someone was trying to drill through.

And Eithan knew who.

As the Blood Sage tried to force the rift shut, Eithan joined his will to Lindon's.

The hole in space tore open.

From the roof of the Sky's Edge fortress, Lindon suddenly stumbled into a wide, dusty basement.

It was filled with chaotic clashes of spirit, and Lindon didn't feel like he had gone through a portal. It felt like he alone had been drawn through.

Sure enough, there was no portal behind him. No exit.

And the Blood Sage was standing opposite a bleeding, grinning Eithan. Who was an *Archlord*.

Somehow, that was the least surprising part of all this.

Lindon cycled his madra to its limit and focused on the Blood Sage, but when he leaped, Eithan struck at him with his scissors.

The scissors inflated to ten times their size, trailing gray mist that felt almost like destruction aura.

The Sage flipped to avoid the attack, launching a Striker technique as he did, but Eithan swept it aside with the Hollow King's Mantle.

"Stop," the Blood Sage commanded, and Lindon froze.

For a moment. Then Eithan threw a Hollow Spear at the Sage, who took a glancing blow. His concentration had been shaken enough that Lindon could push his way free.

And up the stairs.

He could tell what was going on, and Eithan could take care of himself.

"Good work!" Eithan called. "I'll just—"

His voice was cut off by an explosion of madra, but Lindon was already dashing upstairs.

There was a body on the stairs. Akura Courage, his swords spilled around him and mouth open in surprise.

A black-and-silver Remnant lurked on the next stair, staring at Lindon with wide, accusing eyes, but Lindon didn't stop for it.

Lindon dashed past the spirit and into the wide, open room at the top of the staircase. There was more abandoned furniture here, covered in dust and many hidden behind sheets. The air was thick with dust, and most of the furniture had been crushed.

A Seishen Kingdom Underlord that Lindon had never seen before lay in several pieces on the floor, blood soaking the floor. His face was twisted around to face upward. A dead gray Remnant slowly dissolved around him.

Naru Saeya landed on the corpse, rolling over it, and she was so covered in injuries that Lindon couldn't tell how much of the blood was hers and how much came from the corpse.

He ran over to her, sweeping his spiritual perception through her. She choked out a word, but he couldn't tell what it was.

[She'll live,] Dross said. [At least, I think she will. But we have a slightly bigger problem.]

Lindon knew what he was referring to.

The man who had beaten everyone on this floor was there with one eye in his mask glowing, pulling together shards of stone with earth madra into a destructive ball between his palms. He was preparing his technique to finish off Naru Saeya, and he wouldn't mind if Lindon was caught up in it.

Brother Aekin, Uncrowned of Abyssal Palace, launched his Striker technique.

[Yes sir, our slightly bigger problem is waiting upstairs.]

Lindon had trained against Brother Aekin's projection seventy-five times.

INFORMATION REQUESTED: DESTROYING BROTHER AEKIN IN AS LITTLE TIME AS POSSIBLE.

BEGINNING REPORT...

In the blue light of the Hollow Domain, Brother Aekin's technique falls apart. The Ruler component continues for a moment, spraying Lindon with pebbles.

Lindon dashes up with the Soul Cloak, carrying the Hollow Domain in an orb around him. When he gets close enough, even Aekin's Enforcer technique falters.

They clash hand-to-hand for a moment, but Aekin is no match for Lindon.

Lindon drops his Hollow Domain and drives dragon's breath through the cultist's chest, continuing up the stairs at a sprint.

REPORT COMPLETE.

As Lindon saw the report, he acted.

Aekin was dead in seconds.

It was strangely easy to switch from pure madra to Blackflame and back. Easier than it ever had been before, as though he no longer had to cycle differently. As though the madra obeyed him directly.

That was a thought for later.

He intended to turn around and annihilate the Remnant with another Striker technique, but he saw something around the bear-like yellow monster that rose from Aekin's body: a white ring.

Lindon stopped and ran back, grabbing the ring with his Remnant arm. It was hard to separate, but with a little touch of the Consume technique, he sucked away a measure of the Remnant's strength.

The ring came off, and Lindon casually annihilated the spirit before examining the ring.

It unfolded into a white crown.

Lindon would love to examine the Broken Crown construct closer, but Overlords were clashing upstairs, so he opened his void key and tossed the Divine Treasure inside, summoning his flying sword as he did so.

Then he ran upwards.

He felt the situation before he saw it. Calan Archer's dragon was feeding on a crackling purple lightning spirit. Akura Douji's Remnant.

Another dead member of Lindon's team.

The dragon was growing fat, but Calan had sensed Lindon coming. His seven Jadeclaw Rings were arranged in the sky above him, and the muscular blond man waited for Lindon with a stony expression. As soon as Lindon appeared at the top of the stairs, blue-gold light rained down, the storm dragon turned on him, and Calan Archer's rings swarmed him.

Lindon had trained against Calan Archer's projection thirty-eight times.

With a generous portion of soulfire, the Hollow Domain wiped everything out.

Wavedancer soared out from behind Lindon. Before Calan Archer recovered from his astonishment, the flying sword had pierced him all the way through.

He looked down at himself, eyes wide in surprise, but Lindon didn't have time to waste waiting on a Remnant.

He seized the top of Calan's head in his right hand, Consuming his power.

Energy flooded into Lindon, and he sorted it with the Heart of Twin Stars. Most he vented, some he added back to his pure core, and the rest went into his body. It wasn't much to him now, but every bit helped. This was like receiving a little jolt of energy that fought his exhaustion.

Dross held onto any memories, but Lindon wrestled down Calan's remaining willpower. He received one brief impression of Calan's last moments.

He'd sensed the Hollow Domain. To him, it had felt like absolute emptiness. Like the death of the spirit.

In his case, he was correct.

Lindon stopped when there wasn't enough structure to Calan's madra left to form a Remnant, vented the rest of the storm madra, and hurried up.

He could feel Mercy.

Someone had come down from two floors above to stop him on the next floor, and he could already tell who it was: the Uncrowned of Redmoon Hall, Yan Shoumei.

When she summoned her Blood Shadow, Crusher, the entire tower shook.

Dross gasped in excitement.

It wasn't the time, and Lindon knew that, but he couldn't help a little excitement himself.

He activated the binding in his hunger arm, opening and closing his fingers as he emerged from the stairs and saw Crusher. The snarling monster of blood loomed over him, raising a claw.

It looked down to his white hand and hesitated.

Lindon had hoped to run into Crusher ever since he had realized what it was. Shoumei's Shadow was essentially a mass of blood essence so ripe with physical power that it could still strengthen Lindon's body.

Underlord blood essence didn't do anything for him anymore, but Crusher was a different story.

The moment stretched between them as Crusher looked down on them. Dross and Lindon prepared to feed.

The Blood Shadow turned and ran.

Yan Shoumei looked more shocked than Lindon felt. He

could only see his meal running away. He ignited the Burning Cloak, fired a burst of dragon's breath at the Redmoon girl, and leaped after Crusher.

He landed on the monster's back and began to Consume.

Rather than memories, Crusher had only bestial impressions. One of those was the instinct of a wild animal. In Lindon's arm, the spirit felt a predator.

He funneled everything from the Blood Shadow into his body, and when it tried to swipe back at him, he dodged and kept feasting.

In seconds, Crusher collapsed into a red stream and flowed back to Yan Shoumei, who was somewhere behind a collapsed wall.

Dross made a disappointed noise. [Quitter.]

Lindon intended to move back and finish off Yan Shoumei, but now he heard Mercy's scream. One last time, he dashed up the stairs. To the top of the tower.

The first sight that greeted him was Akura Grace's body.

She had been pinned to the wall by a Forged spear, her eyes glassed over and her hair hanging loose. Her Remnant, a glossy black and silver, slowly dissolved in pieces nearby.

Her hand still clutched her sword.

This one stopped Lindon in his tracks. Courage and Douji's lives weighed on him more than he expected, and he hadn't even *liked* them.

Now Grace was dead because he had been standing too far away.

Beyond her Remnant, Pride was in little better shape.

He swayed on his feet, covered in blood. His left arm was...not gone, but mangled. Wrung out like a dishrag.

He faced two Overlords from Redmoon Hall. One turned to Lindon, forming a ball of fire, and the other struck Pride with an axe.

Somehow, Pride formed crystal armor on his shoulder that caught the blow. He was still knocked into the corner of the room, his armor broken.

But he climbed to his feet again and raised his fists.

Weak words passed his lips. Lindon thought they were, "I'm still here."

In Lindon's spiritual sense, Pride felt even worse than he looked.

"Dross!" Lindon shouted.

And Dross showed both Overlords a vision.

It was difficult to project something into someone else's mind unless they allowed you to. Your own madra reigned supreme inside your body. These Overlords would shake off Dross' illusion.

But not soon enough.

A ball of fire flew over Lindon's shoulder, blowing a hole in the wall, but it was thrown wide as Dross disrupted his concentration.

The Hollow Domain expanded between the two enemies, wiping out the rest of their madra. Wavedancer drove through one, but stuck on the second man as he used his Blood Shadow to Enforce himself.

Lindon dropped the Domain and drove dragon's breath through him.

He finished off the second man with another dragon's breath, then dashed over to Pride. He was still on his feet, but Lindon didn't need a thorough examination to know that he was in far worse shape than Naru Saeya had been.

Lindon's void key slid open.

Little Blue hurried out, exclaiming in worry, and Lindon sorted through his boxes. "Do what you can for him," he instructed. He pulled out a pill and tossed it to the spirit; Little Blue caught it easily. "Give him this."

Considering how many times a day he fought, he would be a fool *not* to carry medical elixirs with him.

Little Blue cheeped her agreement, and Lindon finally turned to the east wall. Or what was left of it.

It had been blown out, wind whistling from outside, where Sophara and Mercy clashed on a narrow ridge of stone.

The Dragon King's Totem filled the sky, pushing down on a fully armored Mercy, who released a volley of violet arrows from her Archlord bow.

Sophara screamed as she annihilated them with dragon's breath.

Lindon barreled into her.

Her tail intercepted him as her Imperial Aegis blocked an arrow from Mercy, but Lindon spun into a kick that knocked the dragon off the tower.

[She'll be back up in about two seconds,] Dross warned, which didn't surprise Lindon at all.

He looked to Mercy. "Go see about Pride."

"Finish her!" Mercy cried, pulling back on her bow.

Lindon met her eyes. They were wild and panicked, filled with grief, and she was covered in wounds. Her spirit was exhausted.

Lindon gave her a weary smile. "I'm here to punch a hole in the sky."

It was another second before she nodded and hurried back to her brother.

Sophara leaped up to the ledge and stalked after him, golden eyes blazing. "Thank you," she whispered. "I'm so glad you're here."

How are we doing, Dross? Lindon asked.

[No problems,] Dross assured him. [She can't concentrate enough to hold the Totem.]

Sure enough, the Dragon King's Totem had begun to dissolve in the sky overhead.

Good, Lindon said, stretching his Remnant hand again.

He would hate to die here because he was overconfident, but he didn't expect that. He had already lost this fight. Over and over and over again.

Until eventually, so gradually he almost didn't notice, he'd started to win more than he lost. Then she would gain some new power, and he would start the process over again.

He had trained against Sophara six hundred and forty-four times.

第二十七章

CHAPTER TWENTY-SEVEN

Yerin hovered on an invisible platform next to Kiuran, watching Malice fight the Dragon King.

It was almost impossible to comprehend. Malice stood like a Dreadgod in her full armor, her amethyst helmet in the clouds. She strode along the ground outside the city, steps crushing homes and trees, launching a technique that filled half the world with flying skulls of shadow.

Yerin couldn't even see what Sesh was doing inside his monumental sandstorm, but she felt his power and made out flashes of golden light.

The entire countryside was being ravaged. She could see rainbow light as Sha Miara contained what she could, but even if she saved everyone in the city, people outside were dying.

"You're not aiming to keep civilians out of it?" Yerin asked her companion.

Kiuran the Hound chuckled, looking over the world beneath him like a rat-faced king. "You'll learn, when you leave this place. Whatever happens to the people down there, it won't affect anything *real.*"

Yerin wished she could have met Lindon's heavenly messenger instead. She wanted to put a sword through this one.

Casually, the Abidan handed her Penance.

Just like that, the silver-edged black arrowhead fell into her hands. It was heavier than she expected, and in more ways than just the physical. It *felt* like death. Finality. The end.

"There would normally be a ceremony," Kiuran said, "but circumstances as they are, your decision is before you now. So! Who's it going to be?"

He seemed perversely excited.

"The dragon is the obvious target, but then Reigan Shen is the one binding the Dreadgod factions together. Or you could be rid of the Bleeding Phoenix, which would free you from any influence it might have over you. And, of course, the Wandering Titan is about to awaken."

Malice drew a bow the size of a tower that shone deep blue, purple, and green, like sunlight through a glacier. She launched an arrow that blasted the sandstorm apart.

In the distance, a mountain was reduced to a spray of rubble.

"Or you could use it on the other Monarchs, if you like," Kiuran suggested. "I do have a personal request. If you would like to execute Northstrider, please give him a chance to ascend first. He would hate that more than death. If you do, I can offer you a weapon from my personal collection to sweeten the deal."

She was starting to wonder if she could use it on *him*.

"Oh, and if you'd rather kill the Eight-Man Empire, that's fine too. I don't like how they assumed it couldn't be used against them. You remove one, and I'll take care of the rest. What do you think?"

"I'm thinking I'd rather sit on it," she said. "The threat seems sharper than the arrow."

"Good judgment! You're correct, but I'm afraid I can't allow it. Sorry. Letting it sit in Cradle is too much of a disruption of the balance."

Yerin was sure he'd withheld that particular rule on purpose. *Everyone* had assumed they could hold on to the arrow and use it when they wished.

Maybe he'd changed his mind just to mess with her.

Their protective bubble seemed to move itself, and then they were hovering over the Monarch battle.

The sandstorm was shredding Malice's armor now, tearing it apart in streaming sparks.

She was so much bigger, Sesh only a tiny speck of sand inside the storm, but he *felt* stronger.

It was obvious to use it on him, and there was nothing wrong with doing the obvious thing.

"Can you show me Sophara?"

He smiled. "Easily."

They moved again.

Sophara tried to end the battle quickly, but the nightmare only continued.

A blue dome of pure madra surrounded Lindon, catching her, and her dragon's breath came out in a pathetic stream. As though something devoured her madra as it tried to leave her body.

While he maintained the field, his eyes looked like deep blue gems.

She swung her sword at him, but he ducked as though he could see it coming. She didn't have any drops of ghostwater left, but he was still an Underlord. He couldn't do anything to her, especially with this pure madra dome up, so he couldn't use dragon's breath of his own.

His white hand brushed her, and he consumed a sip of her power.

She jerked back, slapping at him with her tail, but a flying sword deflected her tail.

"Devoured," he muttered. "Pure madra devouring..."

She tried to escape his field, but his Enforcer technique worked better than hers, and even without it he was stronger than an Underlord had any right to be. His body gave her the faint impression of more-than-physical strength, like Yan Shoumei's Blood Shadow.

Which was a horrifying prospect.

He knocked her down before she could leave the roof, and though she came within a hair of slitting his throat, he slipped aside again.

And he drew more of her power into himself. He was like a whirlpool she couldn't escape.

"Whirlpool. I am...a whirlpool."

Was he trying to advance to Overlord?

She raised Quickriver, pouring her madra into the binding. Whatever he was doing, he wasn't an Archlord, so she could cut him in two.

Something intruded into her mind, and her senses blanked out.

She saw, heard, and felt only whiteness and silence.

Sophara pushed the dream aura out of herself, but she saw Lindon beneath her, slamming a palm technique into her stomach. A Forged palm of pure madra overlaid his own, wiping out her spirit.

The Archlord technique around her weapon flickered and died.

She looked into his eyes, which had transformed into blue crystal. He was the end of her every technique, and as she stared into that merciless gaze, she realized he was *her* end.

White fingers brushed across her, and the blue crystal faded to ordinary human black.

He jumped back, suddenly looking brighter. "That's it! A bottomless pit, emptiness, endless...that's it."

He pressed his fists together to her. "Gratitude."

She snarled and ran at him.

"I am the end," Lindon said.

Something trembled around her. Not the aura.

He'd triggered something, but it wasn't Overlord.

Northstrider unleashed a shield of his own, and its binding covered a square mile.

A barrage of deadly rain fell from one of Shen's city-destroying weapons. As Northstrider searched his projection for the prediction of where Shen would end up next, he sensed something in the distance.

A few miles away from Sky's Edge, someone had manifested another Icon.

Fury? Had Fury really been sitting on not one, but *two* different sources of authority?

No, he realized in a moment. *Not Fury.*

The Blood Sage looked up. "This isn't you. Who is this?"

Eithan dragged himself to his feet and gave him a bloody smile. "My apprentice."

Yerin turned to Kiuran.

"I'm burying that dragon," she said.

Sophara must have gone straight from the arena to an assassination attempt on Mercy and Lindon. Yerin could show her what that cost.

And the sooner she used Penance, the sooner she could take the Moonlight Bridge and join the fight herself.

Not that Lindon seemed to need help.

The Hound sighed. "I suppose the Dragon King doesn't intend to advance. There was a chance he would, given the threat. Give me a moment."

His eyes spun with violet script. Lindon would try to remember each of the runes, she was sure.

"Oh...oh, I see. No, this is even better."

Yerin didn't know what he was seeing, but she tapped her foot impatiently, hoping he would notice.

"Yes, you can go ahead. This will work quite nicely. A whole batch of recruits."

"How do I use it?" Yerin demanded.

"*How?*" He chuckled. "You'll learn that 'how' is a useless question. Just use it."

For a second time, she wondered if she could use it on him.

Their bubble shifted back to the battle between Malice and the Dragon King, and Yerin pointed the arrowhead at the dragon.

"Kill him," she said aloud.

The arrow vanished.

At the same instant, the power behind the sandstorm disappeared. A single, small body fell through the cloud of sand.

Just like that, a Monarch was dead.

Yerin had seen a lot of unceremonious deaths in her life, but this was maybe the most boring. One second, he was alive. The next, he was dead. No battle, no Remnant, not even a flash of light.

It scared her.

"Well, I look forward to meeting you on the other side," the Abidan said. "No doubt you'll be a Wolf yourself someday. And tell Judge Suriel's favorite I hope to see him too."

So it *was* common knowledge up there that this Suriel had come down to see Lindon. Yerin had wondered.

"If my memory's true, I'm supposed to get another grand prize," Yerin said.

He spread his hands. "The Monarchs are bound by oath to give it to you, so they will, but that isn't my role. Good luck.

When things settle, you'll get it."

He vanished, and Yerin reappeared in the center of the arena.

Or the rubble where the arena had been. The audience towers and most of the surrounding towers were nothing but debris now.

"Could have put me down somewhere better," she muttered.

Then again, she could be wherever she wanted.

She focused on Lindon, and the Moonlight Bridge flashed.

From a hundred miles away, Northstrider felt Seshethkunaaz die.

They had a long history, spanning centuries, complete with blood spilled and reluctant alliances aplenty. Northstrider had planned the dragon's death dozens of times.

He had expected a simple death to be too good for someone like Sesh.

He was wrong. This was very satisfying.

Reigan Shen, from the heart of the mountain where he was planning an ambush, began to tear open a portal.

"Stay," Northstrider commanded, and his will opposed the opening of the portal.

Shen wrestled it open, and combined with his mastery of space, he would surely win the contest.

An ice-blue arrow the size of a lighthouse crashed through the mountain and crushed the King of Lions.

Malice's attack would be little more than an inconvenience for Reigan Shen, but it would slow him down. Northstrider had a chance.

But rather than pursuing the lion, Northstrider flew over to collect Seshethkunaaz's body. The dragon hadn't become a Remnant thanks to Penance, and the corpse of a Monarch was a valuable material. Especially to him.

With the dragon's body tucked away, Northstrider was prepared to chase after Reigan Shen. The cat could run, but the more he depleted his arsenal now, the better.

But his Presence sounded an alert, and Northstrider stopped.

Finally, the battle around the Dreadgod had become too much. The Wandering Titan was waking early.

Northstrider felt Reigan Shen escape and allowed it. There was more important work to do.

He stepped into the Way, leaving Malice's triumphant laughter to ring out over the countryside.

[Lindon...] Dross said. [You're not an Overlord.]

A black hole swallowed the sky. Directly over Lindon's head.

The void wasn't dangerous. It was a reflection of Lindon, linked to him somehow. Or he was linked to it.

Lindon wasn't exactly sure what he'd done. But he had his guess. Some things that were hidden before felt clearer now, as though his spiritual sense had evolved to another level.

He stood over a hopeless Sophara. In simulations, he had mostly beaten her by finding a chance to use The Dragon Descends, but now he didn't want to obliterate her body. He was here to Consume her power...and besides, if he incinerated her void key, he couldn't take it himself.

Sophara lifted her chin proudly and clutched her sword.

"Kill me," she challenged, "like you killed my—"

Lindon blasted dragon's breath through her chest, exactly like he'd killed Ekeri.

She sagged, but he was there to catch her...and to drain the remaining power from her body. The last thing he wanted was to fight her Remnant.

Sophara was even stronger than he'd expected. The madra

he vented from the purification process melted the tiles and stones of the crumbling roof.

When her Remnant was in no danger of rising, Lindon plucked the void key from around her neck and slipped it into his pocket. Then he moved to the edge of the roof and jumped down.

He landed on half of another crumbled wall, then hopped inside.

Eithan lay on the floor, bleeding with his breathing ragged. "I'm fine," he said as soon as Lindon showed himself. "No tears for me, please. I'll be..." He coughed loudly. "...as good as new any sec..."

The word trailed off. He gave a clear death rattle.

Lindon stood over him. "What did I do?"

Eithan opened one eye. "You have to have some guess."

"I want you to tell me."

Eithan groaned as he sat up. The Blood Sage had obviously run off; Lindon felt a slowly healing tear in space nearby.

"I did tell you that our cycling technique had a long and fascinating history," Eithan said pointedly.

Lindon gave a hollow laugh. "I thought you were trying not to keep secrets."

"Honestly, I thought of this one as more of a surprise."

A white glow filled the space, and then Yerin appeared. She looked over them both, and for a moment Lindon was as alarmed as he'd been before.

Her Goldsigns, her eyes, and a lock of her hair had turned crimson. Dross had overheard the report Fury received about Yerin becoming some kind of half-Herald, but he hadn't known what to make of it. Who was this?

"Yerin or Ruby?" he asked warily.

She gave him a grin. "Take a guess."

He let out a sigh of relief. "Glad to see you."

"Same to you." She looked up the stairs. "We need to get them to a healer two days ago. Eithan, you have that cloudship?"

"Better! I have Lindon."

Lindon recognized a cue when he heard one. He focused on the older of the two spatial tears in the room, locking his spiritual perception on it and gathering his concentration.

It was just as hard as it had been earlier, and it took him an embarrassingly long amount of time. He was afraid sweat was starting to bead on his head before he finally managed to say, **"Open."**

The portal opened.

Pride and Naru Saeya survived.

Barely.

Lindon and the others reappeared on the fortress, where Akura Justice defended the portal alone. They dove through together, emerging back in Ninecloud City.

Which didn't look much better than the battlefield they'd just left, but at least it wasn't an active warzone.

The entire Akura faction was a buzzing mess of people, but they found healers quickly. When Mercy really demanded something in the Akura clan, it got done.

Saeya and Pride received medical attention, but Pride would have died if not for the immediate treatment Lindon had given him. The healers were skeptical that either would ever recover completely.

So, in a way, his entire team was gone.

That wasn't strictly true. The Maten sisters had avoided capture and were perfectly safe. When the Akura clan settled down, Lindon intended to find out how many contribution points the team had earned. Assuming the clan was still honoring points at all.

They wouldn't go to him. The thought almost surprised him, but he felt the others needed more support than he did. The Maten twins and Naru Saeya, at the very least, could use all the help they could get.

Now Mercy was glued to her brother's side, and Yerin was pinned in place by the Heart and Winter Sages.

While he had a moment to himself, Lindon managed to corner Eithan.

The Arelius Archlord had accepted quick bandaging and some elixirs before sneaking out to the docks, where crewmen were loading crates onto cloudships to head back to Akura territory.

Most of the crates contained what they'd taken from Sky's Edge, either from the mine or from their enemies.

Eithan's entire body was wrapped in bloody bandages, but he seemed content as he watched the packing process. He leaned back, elbows propped against the railing, as people passed him by.

Lindon joined him. "I'm glad you survived."

"It was closer than you might think. I might remind you that I am *not* a Sage."

"Am I?" Lindon asked. It was the question he had been afraid to ask Dross.

No matter how many times Dross had slipped in his own opinion.

"That is a matter for scholarly debate," Eithan answered. "In the past, the concept of a Sage was much more...fluid... than it is today. When manifesting an Icon, it is very important to understand the significance of your madra and to sense it deeply. Equally important is some kind of technique to regularly train your willpower. For years. An exercise that pushes your focus and concentration ever further, and that most people would give up or abandon for easier trails."

The Heaven and Earth Purification Wheel.

Eithan's head was sweeping back and forth, though Lindon was certain he didn't need to watch anything with his eyes, and Lindon followed Eithan's bloodline power with his own spiritual sense. He was searching inside the chests that flowed by in the crowd.

"Now, the specific Icon you manifest depends not only on the nature of your madra currently, but on a concept that has always been core to your identity. Even in childhood. Ah, here we are."

Eithan slipped into the crowd, had a quick exchange with a startled-looking woman who had a bird nesting on her shoulder, and then came back to Lindon with a box a little bigger than his hand.

Lindon was uncertain whether he had asked the woman for this box or distracted her and then stolen it.

The chest cracked and revealed that it was filled with a smooth, white, lumpy rock.

Wintersteel ore.

It flew into Eithan's palm and began slowly melting.

"Some ancient cultures, as you are aware, had a custom of wearing badges with symbols carved into them. Originally, those symbols represented the Icon that the wearer aimed to embody."

Lindon's real fingers ran across the halfsilver hammer badge on his chest, his fingertips tingling at the touch of the madra-disrupting metal.

"In those days," Eithan went on, "Sage was not considered its own rank, but rather a separate mark of distinction that some Lords and Ladies achieved. Different materials were used for different cultures, but often Heralds wore badges of red and Monarchs of blue."

Lindon thought back to his collection of badges. At least that was one minor mystery solved.

"Later, when the concept of a Sage became popularized as a stage of advancement in its own right, they began to make badges from a material that could only be worked by will."

He held up the ore, which he had finished molding.

It was now a round, palm-sized wintersteel badge. A duplicate of the one on Lindon's chest, only with no hammer.

Lindon took the badge. "I manifested the Void Icon."

Eithan nodded to him. "Ah, but what symbolizes nothingness? A blank badge looks the same as one with no Icon at all, so rather than a picture, the ancients chose to write one character."

At Eithan's will, lines appeared on the wintersteel badge, etching out one familiar word in the old language: Empty.

Or, as they would say in Sacred Valley: Unsouled.

With one foreleg, Orthos shoved a severed wooden beam out of his way.

A fragment of pale light madra shone on the ground, the remains of a broken Forger technique. It had mostly dissolved to essence in the hours that had passed since the battle here, but a piece no bigger than the tip of his teeth had survived.

The splinter of madra slithered toward him like a glowing white snake before it, too, melted into particles and disappeared.

Sometimes he thought that everyone here practiced a light Path. What a waste. Light was pathetic next to fire.

Only that morning, this building had been an outpost of the Wei clan. In its basement was a training ground for light and dream aura, which was why Orthos had been keeping an eye on it. It was the perfect place for Kelsa to advance.

He had been considering burning the place down himself to claim the basement, but in the end someone else had done it for him.

The outpost was reduced to a pile of kindling, leaving the basement undefended. Orthos had come as soon as he'd felt the battle, but by the time he'd arrived, the attackers had left.

He didn't know who had attacked the Wei clan or why, but he had his guess.

It was one of the invaders.

Shortly before his arrival in Sacred Valley, two other outsiders had punched through the defenses of Heaven's Glory and gone into hiding. They hid from the three clans and four schools, just as Orthos and Kelsa did, so he'd never met the invaders himself.

But he was starting to suspect he knew them.

This was the closest he'd ever come to them, and the feeling of this leftover madra stoked his suspicions. He couldn't be certain, but this felt like Stellar Spear madra.

Someone from the Jai clan was here in Sacred Valley.

Before he could continue poking around the ruined building, he felt a new surge of power from underground. Orthos grunted in satisfaction. The Path of the White Fox had a new Jade.

It was about time. He had spent months helping Kelsa attain a *real* Iron body, which would have been infinitely easier if she hadn't advanced to Iron already. Retraining was always harder than learning the right way the first time.

Compared to getting her the Skyhunter Iron body, pushing Kelsa to Jade had been easy.

The trap door to the basement slammed open, releasing a gust of dream and light aura that traced phantom images in the air.

Kelsa emerged from downstairs, wearing a fresh robe. Her black hair was soaking wet, plastered to her head and neck.

He had left her with spare clothes and several buckets of warm water. Advancing to Jade was usually a mess.

She radiated satisfaction as she reached the top of the stairs. "Apologies for the wait, Orthos. Now we can begin."

Orthos hated waiting around for no reason, but he wondered if impatience ran in this family.

"You just earned your eyes, and now you want to stare into the sun." Orthos chomped into the end of the fallen timber. It had a nice singe to it that gave it a pleasant charred flavor.

A shiver passed through his spirit as Kelsa clumsily scanned him with her newborn spiritual sense. "I'll need to practice, of course, but now I won't slow you down if it comes to a fight."

No matter how many times Orthos explained the difference in sacred arts outside the Valley, Kelsa didn't truly understand.

She couldn't, really. Not until she left and saw for herself.

"That's the first step," Orthos grumbled. "We still need help."

She looked to him with a stern expression. "I've left my mother to suffer for too long already."

She really *had* been patient all these months, training under his direction and preparing herself to reach Jade. But now that she had, he would have to sit on her to stop her from running off to rescue her mother from Heaven's Glory.

But she learned a few new techniques and advanced one stage and thought herself invincible. Orthos knew better; it would be easier to burn the Heaven's Glory school to the ground than it would be to safely free a prisoner.

They needed help.

As they left the ruined outpost, they continued bickering. Kelsa's father couldn't help, and no one else in camp met Orthos' standards. Almost no one in the Valley did.

As they walked, he kept his spiritual perception extended, hunting for the Jai clan invader. He would be nearby, most likely under a veil, but Orthos hoped to feel him slip. Kelsa did the same, though her perception was wobbly and inconsistent with her lack of experience.

If they couldn't find help, Orthos was certain Kelsa would try to slip into the Heaven's Glory school with or without him, which would end in disaster. Even if she could slip in unnoticed with her illusion techniques, it would be much harder to leave with her mother in tow. They didn't even know where Wei Shi Seisha was being kept, or what condition she was in. The best they could tell was that the Soulsmith was alive.

Kelsa would be sneaking off to her death, which frustrated Orthos to no end. He couldn't watch her all day, every day.

While he demanded that she listen to reason and she appealed to his sympathy, he felt something growing in the air.

It felt like a distant wave approaching from the west.

Then the ground started to shake, and he shouted to Kelsa. "Pull your spirit back!"

Though she didn't understand, she had trained under him for a long time now. She obeyed immediately, reeling her perception back.

Just in time for the spiritual pressure of the Dreadgod to crash over the Valley.

The impression was weakened by the same curse that limited Orthos' power, but still the air shook and the ground quaked. Earth aura brightened in golden veins beneath his feet, leaves fell from shaken trees, and startled birds took wing.

The symptoms passed quickly, but Orthos cycled his madra in panic, ready to defend Kelsa. He'd never sensed the Wandering Titan before, but it could be nothing else.

The Titan had awakened, and it was close.

Kelsa patted him on the neck. "It's just an earthquake."

Orthos didn't have the words to explain how wrong she was. "We're out of time. Anyone who can feel that is too close."

Cautiously, he extended his spiritual perception, ready to withdraw it again if the power in the air was too strong.

And he felt someone else doing the same. Someone on a sword and light Path.

Kelsa asked him another question, but a black-and-red haze had already sprung up over his body as he used his Enforcer technique.

He'd found his prey.

The invader's presence vanished as he put his veil back into place, but it was too late. Orthos had his location.

He blasted into the trees, leaving Kelsa behind. With her Skyhunter Iron body, she should be able to follow him with her eyes, but she would never catch up. His every step was a leap, and he even withdrew his head into his shell to crash through trees when he didn't feel like dodging out of the way.

In less than a minute, he arrived at the last location where he'd sensed the Stellar Spear madra.

It was an unremarkable nook near a stream, nestled between some foothills behind a thicket of trees. If he hadn't been drawn here, he would have passed it without thought.

Only when he scanned the ground thoroughly did he find the buried script-circle.

He crossed it easily, though it pressed against his spirit. It was a simple repelling script, meant to keep out weak Remnants.

"Stop hiding!" Orthos shouted. "It's beneath you."

No one responded, so Orthos slowly began cycling madra into dragon's breath. His prey would feel it and respond, he was sure.

If not, Orthos could always smoke him out.

A cold voice echoed through the trees. "You would chase us this far?"

Orthos snorted. "You think too much of yourself."

A lean man stepped into view. He wore simple brown clothes and carried a long, ornate spear with a blue haft. His head was wrapped in red, scripted bandages so that nothing was visible of his face except gleaming eyes.

"Did Underlord Arelius send you to find me?" Jai Long asked.

"He doesn't need me to do his hunting for him. I'm here for my own reasons." Orthos glanced west. "And it doesn't look like I'll be staying much longer."

"Then we should travel separate paths."

Jai Long was still holding his spear ready, his madra cycling steadily. It wasn't a threatening posture, but it wasn't quite friendly either.

Orthos let his own madra settle. He didn't feel a threat from this pup.

"I have one last thing to do before I leave. And here you are to help me."

Yerin finally pried herself away from the questions of the Sages, only to find Lindon and Eithan on the cloudship dock.

Lindon wore a wintersteel badge with his old Unsouled symbol on it. She wondered what that was about.

But that thought fled from her when she truly *saw* him. Now that they weren't in danger, the fact of his presence really sank in.

He was safe. So was she.

Everything was okay.

She remembered running up to him as Ruby, throwing her arms and legs around him, and she braced herself for embarrassment.

It never came. Why did she care what a bunch of outsiders thought?

By the time she realized where her thoughts had gone, she was standing against him, looking up, her chin on his chest.

He looked down on her, eyes clouded. "Ruby?"

"Only a little," she responded.

He thought about that, and his expression grew complicated. She understood; she didn't know how she'd feel about it either, if she were in his position.

Eithan's head slowly slid up over Lindon's shoulder.

"The Ninecloud Soul is quite busy," he said brightly, "but I know we're in a situation of some urgency, so I took the liberty of having your first-round prizes delivered...now."

He grabbed Lindon and turned him to look to the side of the dock, where a cloudship was coming to a halt.

It was the size of two homes together, and only half of it was covered in a two-story house with dark blue tiles. The cloud base was dark blue as well, which she guessed represented the Arelius family.

As that house covered the right side of the cloud, the left half was covered by a pond, a lone tree, and a miniature mountain. It spewed dark fire from the top, and within a cave she could sense dense sword aura.

Just as they'd requested after the first round of the tournament, this would be a perfect home for her.

Not just her home. *Their* home.

A comforting warmth settled into her stomach.

Then another cloudship descended from the sky.

This one was a perfect rectangle, as though it was made to fill out exactly the maximum amount of space allowed. Its cloud base was the same dark blue as theirs, and as it settled into the back, its plot of land slid exactly into place.

As though it had been designed to fit there all along.

Three-quarters of the space was covered in what looked like a garden, or maybe a section of farmland. The remaining quarter was taken up by a tiny hut.

Yerin knew who the owner was without even asking.

"It's a meager living space," Eithan said, "but I was excited to maximize the amount of land to grow crops."

Lindon glared at him. "You could have flown alongside us. You didn't have to attach yourself."

"As you can see, mine only makes up half the size of yours. We have a whole quarter of our floating island left to fill in."

Yet a third cloudship descended.

This one didn't lock into place as Eithan's had. It drifted alongside the others, and it was the exact image that came to Yerin's mind when she heard the words "cloud fortress": a blank stone fort sitting on a cloud. It looked as though its owner hadn't bothered to make any customization requests of their own.

A moment after the cloud docked, Ziel walked out of the front, his emerald horns glistening in the sun and his cloak flapping. He raised a hand.

"Did you kidnap his oldest son, or what?" Yerin asked.

"I negotiated his company for a year. At a reasonable rate."

She was still leaning against Lindon, and Eithan noticed. "You'll have plenty of time to spend together once we're on our way."

Lindon seemed to realize their situation himself. "Apologies, you're right. We need to be on our way." He gently tried to separate from Yerin.

She didn't let him go.

There were dozens of strangers around, not to mention people that actually knew them, but Yerin no longer cared.

She grabbed him by the back of the head, stood up on her tiptoes, and kissed him.

He reacted in stunned surprise for a moment, and a fear rose up from a deep part of her that he was going to push her away again.

Then he leaned in, wrapping his arms around her, and kissed her back.

When they separated and she caught her breath, Ziel was standing next to them. He didn't look like he cared *what* they did, and he would probably wear that expression if the sky collapsed.

"So," he said, "where are we going?"

Yerin was gratified to see that Lindon was red-faced and focused on his own cycling. After a moment collecting himself, he looked away from her and toward Ziel.

"Home," he said.

THE END
of Cradle: Volume Eight
Wintersteel

LINDON'S STORY CONTINUES IN

BLOODLINE

CRADLE : VOLUME NINE

下属主

AND NOW THIS...

Yerin hefted Penance. "How do I use it?" she demanded.

Kiuran chuckled. "Oh, it's quite simple. Just say the name of the person you wish to kill."

Their bubble shifted back to the battle between Malice and the Dragon King, and Yerin pointed the arrowhead at the dragon.

"Kill him," she said aloud.

Nothing happened.

"Say his name, I said. His name."

"Kill...Seshthkaz. Shethkanaz. Seshethsusheth."

The arrow vanished.

The Monarch didn't.

Yerin seized the Abidan by his armor. "What happened?"

"I believe someone named Seshethsusheth has just had a very bad afternoon."

[Lindon...] Dross said. [You're not an Overlord.]

An image had swallowed the sky, directly over Lindon's head: a collection of numbers.

[I don't quite understand it. It looks like an Icon, but I can't tell what it's supposed to be.]

"I can," Lindon responded.

Power filled him, and he could feel his newfound authority radiating out, connecting him to a concept greater than humanity. A concept he knew well.

"I am...the Points Sage."

Yerin couldn't even see what Sesh was doing inside his monumental sandstorm, but she felt his power and made out flashes of golden light. Light that pulsed to a rhythmic, regular beat.

She thought she could even hear music along with it... and then a moment later, she *could* hear music, a series of repetitive fast-paced notes that sounded like they came from otherworldly instruments.

"What do you call that song?" she shouted to Kiuran.

The Abidan looked grave. "That's the Dragon King's most feared technique. The dreaded Darude Sandstorm."

The elders of Heaven's Glory walked Adama to the doorstep, and the woman cleared her throat.

"It was an honor to serve you today, Sage of Swords."

That wasn't exactly his title, but Adama had never cared much for titles anyway.

He waved a hand. "Oh, you don't have to call me that. My full name is Timaias Adama, but that can be a mouthful. Most people prefer it shorter. There are some who call me...Tim."

Charity raised an arm, and an owl of living madra came down to perch on it. She scratched it behind the head as she asked, "What do you think of Grace?"

Lindon continued to answer safely. "I can trust her judgment more than...others."

"And what if we allowed you to marry her?"

Lindon couldn't believe his luck.

"Are you serious? Of course!"

Charity rested her hand on the owl. "I thought I would have to persuade you."

"Why? Grace is rich, she's hot, and she's good at the sacred arts. I'd be a fool to turn her down. So am I supposed to buy a ring, or what?"

One of Dross' stubby, flexible arms touched the surface of the black orb. Light rippled on Northstrider's construct, but otherwise nothing happened.

[Just a moment, this is...hmmm. This is tougher than it looks.] Dross furrowed his purple brow and pushed harder. Until, as though he'd broken through a barrier, Dross finally pushed through.

[Oooohhh, it's amazing! So much space! Now, how do I get out?]

Lindon looked to Northstrider in a panic, but the Monarch's arms were folded and his face was impassive as always.

"He'll figure it out," Northstrider said.

[While I'm in here, I might as well touch some things. Hey, what's that? AAAHHHH!]

The surface of the orb flashed purple for a moment and then went dark.

The Monarch shook the construct, then peered inside. "Never mind, I was wrong. He's dead."

Suriel felt the cool wood of the table against her forehead.

"I don't know what I did wrong," she said. "I've been around from the very beginning."

Makiel gave her a sympathetic pat on the back. "Don't worry, they all like you better than me."

"Then why am I not in the book?"

"It's a long book as it is," Makiel said. "I'm sure you would have been included if there was more space."

"I don't take up much space! It could have been a *few* pages longer. Cut some of the fights! Take out some Eithan scenes!"

"Whoa now. Let's not go crazy."

Suriel sobbed into the tabletop.

WILL WIGHT lives in Florida, among the citrus fruits and slithering sea creatures. He's the author of the Amazon best-selling *Traveler's Gate Trilogy*, *The Elder Empire* (which cleverly offers twice the fun and twice the work), and his series of mythical martial arts magic: *Cradle*.

He graduated from the University of Central Florida in 2013, earning a Master's of Fine Arts in Creative Writing and a flute of dragon's bone. He is also, apparently, invisible to cameras.

He also claims that *www.WillWight.com* is the best source for book updates, new stories, fresh coriander, and miracle cures for all your aches and pains!